SIE

SIFU

AN UNUSUAL TEACHER IN THE
TURBULENCE OF THE MALAYAN WAR

KHOO KHENG-HOR

Specially printed for

This edition specially printed for
MPH BOOKSTORES SDN. BHD.
5th Floor, 15 Jalan Tandang,
46050 Petaling Jaya, Selangor, Malaysia.
website: *www.mphonline.com*

Published by
Pelanduk Publications (M) Sdn. Bhd.
(Co. No: 113307-W)
12 Jalan SS13/3E, Subang Jaya Industrial Estate,
47500 Subang Jaya, Selangor, Malaysia.
email: *rusaone@tm.net.my*
website: *www.pelanduk.com*

Perpustakaan Negara Malaysia   Cataloguing-in-Publication Date

Khoo, Kheng-Hor, 1956-
    Sifu : an unusual teacher in the turbulence of the Malayan war /
    Khoo Kheng-Hor
    ISBN 978-967-978-967-6
    1. English fiction. 2. Malaysian fiction (English). I. Title.
    823

Printed by
Academe Art & Printing Services Sdn. Bhd.

Dedicated to the memory of
Judy Hwang Chung Mei,
my wife and greatest critic, who
encouraged me to write this
fourth novel from having had
enjoyed reading the earlier three.

My greatest regret is that she
didn't get to finish reading the
book. She passed away on
December 19, 2007 after reading
only one-third of the book.
Hence, unlike the three earlier
novels, this one doesn't carry
her calligraphy work.

Author's Message

*H*aving had written *Taikor*, *Mamasan*, and *Nanyang*, all of which were set in Malaysia and Singapore, I intend to cover Thailand as well.

After all, like most people who have visited Thailand, my wife and I, enchanted as we have been by its temples, monks in saffron robes, exotic fruits, spicy tom yam and other delicious foods, and shopping, we really know very little of the history of the land. And so, this fourth novel, *Sifu*, is now in your hands.

Be assured that my basic philosophy remains unchanged. I am first and foremost, a story-teller. Thus, once again, I echo the sentiments of Shih Nai-an, who, when asked why he wrote the Chinese classic, *The Water Margin*, had simply replied that the book was just a hotchpotch, which won't make him famous or even discredit him, and was written to fill up his spare time, and to give pleasure to himself. Indeed, I write primarily to amuse myself, and in the process, entertain my wife, friends and readers. Hence, much as I take pleasure in having my works recognized, for example, the National Library of Malaysia nominated *Taikor* for the 2006 International IMPAC Dublin Literary Award, my first consideration is my readers' enjoyment of the stories I spin.

And like my three earlier novels, although mention is made of certain well-known figures within the historical context of the period, and some of the events may resembled documented history (an example being the massacre of 24 villagers at Batang Kali on December 12, 1948), this book is nonetheless a work of fiction created out of my imagination. Hence, no reference is intended to any living person.

And while I have tried as much as possible to be accurate, certain events of historical value may have been moved forward or backward in the calendar year so as to conform to the flow of the story.

Happy reading!

Khoo Kheng-Hor

http://www.khookhenghor.com

sunzi@khookhenghor.com

Prologue

*H*as anyone asked you how many teachers have had influenced your life? If that question has been posed to you, I believe, like me, you might have difficulty trying to come up with a definite number. But, perhaps like me, regardless of the number of teachers, only one person's name would immediately spring to mind, to be followed next by a vivid image of his or her face.

Yes, in my case, I had gained much from the guidance of a few teachers but only one man comes to my thought without any hesitation. He is my *sifu,* as those of my race, the Chinese people, called their specially revered teacher, master, instructor, or mentor.

Much as I revered him and cherished the many long hours I had spent with him, I had long ago come to the startling realization that I knew him and yet, I didn't quite know him at all. Let me explain. Though he had taught me all he knew, and more, at the same time, I discovered there was so little of his life that I really knew.

As a matter of fact, one day in 1989, when I was in London to recover from my depression after learning about the death of my mother and uncle, both of whom perished in a fire that razed my uncle's shop house cum home in Padang Besar to the ground, I went to a West End theatre to watch the *Phantom of the Opera.* The sight of Colm Wilkinson playing the role of the Phantom, wearing a mask on one side of his face, fascinated me so much that I went back to the theatre not once, but many times to re-watch the play.

I went back partly to watch Wilkinson's marvelous performance and listened to his fantastic voice, and also partly because his half-mask reminded me of my *sifu* and my relationship with him. There was the side about him that I know and the side I don't. There was also the good side in him and a darker one as well. In short, he will always remain an enigma to me.

Having had from time to time heard people telling me that a pupil or disciple reflects his or her *sifu,* I suppose the following tale may perhaps throw some light on my *sifu* despite the mask he wore.

BOOK 1
THE APPRENTICE

*"A general who accepts my
advice should be employed for
he is certain to gain victory."*
Sun Tzu

One

*M*ao Dong Po was just two months short of his fourteenth birthday when he witnessed an incident which could never be erased from his memory. On some nights, it would also haunt his sleep. He would always remember November 6, 1951, which was exactly one month after the assassination of Sir Henry Lovell Goldsworthy Gurney on the road from Kuala Kubu Baru to Fraser's Hill.

On that hot afternoon, a convoy of British Army trucks came to his village, near Batang Kali, in the State of Selangor. The soldiers who jumped out of the trucks were soon knocking loudly on the doors of the villagers' homes. They noisily ordered the women and children to wait near the empty trucks, and shouted impatiently at the men to line up on the main road of the village. Those who were slow to move were unceremoniously shoved. Though a month had passed since Sir Henry's death, feelings still ran high among the British troopers.

Dong Po who looked older than his age nonchalantly joined his father, an uncle and two cousin brothers in the rapidly formed line of men. Having already lived through such "round ups" several years back when during the Japanese Occupation, the yellow dwarfs –

the name the Chinese derisively gave the Japanese invaders – had done the same as what the British soldiers were doing that day, he took the mad scramble in his stride. After the return of the British to Malaya, the insurgency by the communist terrorists often saw British soldiers coming to the village to assemble and warn the villagers against giving support to the rebels. But Dong Po was unable to foresee the British soldiers' visit that day was going to end with a totally unexpected outcome.

A stout, middle-aged British officer with a small neat moustache – the three pips he wore on the epaulette of each shoulder denoted his rank as a captain – marched pompously towards the male villagers. Through the fawning Chinese interpreter who trotted by his side, he began accusing the villagers of supplying the communist terrorists with food. His tone was harsh and stern.

As the British officer ranted on, his red face grew redder. Dong Po's observant young mind mused that it was more on account of the midday heat and perhaps his drinking habit – he had seen the faces of some men in his village turning red from being unable to hold their liquor – rather than the fieriness of his speech since the Englishman lost momentum from pausing now and then for the interpreter to do his job. Finally, fixing his pale blue eyes fiercely on the villagers, the British officer said in his deep gravelly voice: "We know you had a meeting with the communists three days ago, during which, one of you…"

After pausing to read the piece of paper in his hand and also to allow the interpreter to translate, the officer continued, "One of you, Mao Chen Lin, promised to gather food for the bandits."

Hearing his father's name being spoken aloud by the interpreter, Dong Po lifted his head with sudden interest. He knew the officer was referring to the communist terrorists who came out of the jungle just the other day.

The boy's agile mind switched swiftly back to the day when those men, clad in their khaki uniforms, had come straight to the only school in the village. Quite a number of the villagers had already gathered in the school hall. The villagers, who had earlier been informed of the meeting by members of the *Min Yuen*, the clandestine civilian supporters of the Malayan Communist Party, one of whom was Dong Po's schoolteacher, knew the serious consequence of not attending the meeting.

On the same morning, the schoolteacher had even told the students that their attendance would be required as "something important is about to take place in the school hall later in the afternoon." Thus, upon seeing the unsmiling communist guerillas trooping silently past the classroom's window, Dong Po's schoolteacher had immediately stopped the lesson and told all his young pupils to follow him.

In the hall, one of the communist terrorists, a morose-looking man with cold black eyes, announced with pride: "We have already slain the man whose resettlement policy had caused many of our people to suffer so much."

Young as he was, Dong Po, had already acquired a habit of keeping his ears opened to the daily gossips at home or when joining his father to drink tea with the other villagers in the village's only coffee shop. Thus, he knew the leader of the ragged band of guerillas was talking about Sir Henry. From his schoolteacher who was another source of information, the young boy had heard about the British High Commissioner's assassination. Even though the young boy instinctively knew that not all his schoolteacher's words could be believed, he nonetheless thought the man's information to be worth listening at times.

Hence, Dong Po knew about the insurgency of the communists whom the British had provided with arms and supplies to fight the Japanese during the war. But after the Japanese had surrendered, the communist faction in the Malayan People's Anti-Japanese Army had gone back to the jungle, this time to wage a guerilla war against the British as they wanted to seize control of the country for themselves.

He had also heard that British soldiers had been forcing many Chinese farmers living in the jungle fringes to move out of their homes into "New Villages" which were surrounded by high barbed-wire fences. This came about from their belief that the Chinese civilians were pro-communists and the resettlement would sever the supply lines between the *Min Yuen* and the communist terrorists. Although the resettlement policy was Sir Henry's idea, Dong Po had heard many people calling it the Brigg's Plan as though it was another man's initiative.

At the end of his long speech about the atrocities of the British Military Administration which was aimed at gaining the villagers' support, the gloomy communist leader suddenly pointed at Dong Po's father and said:

"Mao Chen Lin, as we know you are a man respected by your fellow villagers, you shall be responsible for gathering food and medicine for our cause. Of course, we will reward you well after this country has fallen into our hands. Besides, as your family name is Mao, that makes you to be a kinsman of our revered spiritual leader, the great Chairman Mao Tse-tung."

Surprised to be singled out by name, and disturbed that a stranger could so easily identify him, Chen Lin licked his lips nervously. Having counted ten armed communist terrorists, who had the temerity to march into the village in broad daylight, he knew better than to argue. He put on a smile and said amicably, "I'll do my best."

"We don't want your best," snapped the communist terrorist impatiently. "We want food and medicine, and we want it before the end of this week."

"Please give us more time, say, by the end of this month," pleaded Chen Lin.

And now, with the British troopers replacing the communist terrorists, the villagers shifted their feet uneasily under the mercilessly hot sun. Dong Po guessed someone had reported that incident to the authorities, which was why his father had once again been singled out, this time by the British officer. As half his mind was still dwelling on the recent visit of the communist terrorists, he hadn't caught much of what the British officer was saying. But at a sudden signal given by the officer, two soldiers stepped forward to seize Dong Po's father.

Just as the soldiers were pulling Chen Lin away, Dong Po felt his uncle's hand gripping his left forearm, restraining him. From that moment, everything seemed to be moving in slow motion. Three other villagers were also dragged away. A while later, four gun shots were heard, and then four soldiers returned, each holding a severed head in his hand. One of the heads, still dripping blood, was his father's.

"No!" screamed Dong Po. Just as his uncle tugged furiously at his arm to restrain him, the boy felt a dull blow against his head and everything went black.

He later heard from his uncle that after he went off into his hysterical act, a soldier had come up from behind them to knock his head with a rifle butt.

☆ ☆ ☆ ☆

Though Captain Neil Walker was a bit apprehensive about how his superiors would take the death of four villagers arising from that day's outing, on the whole, he felt justified and elated.

He felt justified because he had long detested the ingratitude of the locals. Ever since the British came back to free the people of Malaya from the yokes of the Japanese invaders, many were still so ungrateful as to support the communist terrorists in their insurgency against the British. After news broke out about the assassination of the British High Commissioner, Captain Walker was among those who had bayed for blood. As he vociferously put it, such a blatant act required an eye for an eye, a tooth for a tooth.

His elation came from what he assumed to be the belated respect which his men had finally begun to show him. He had seen the fearful looks they had exchanged with one another, and especially when they looked away nervously each time his eyes fell on any of them.

Last year when he was on the troopship sailing with them towards Malaya, he had already heard their grouses. Most were fresh conscripts. On hearing about the fighting in Malaya due to the communists' attempts to seize power, they felt it was their government's way of punishing them for having missed the recent war against the Germans. Even after they had settled in their barracks near Kuala Kubu Baru, he still heard their complaints. If they weren't grumbling about the ghastly weather, they would be pining for home. Or they would grouse that this wasn't their war. The end result was their growing animosity towards the officers.

Ironically, the most common source of their discontent was the boredom. As Sergeant John Gow had once told him, "We're soldiers, sir. As soldiers, we expect some action. But we aren't getting any though there's a bloody war going on."

Captain Walker knew too well the sergeant's feelings because he too had hankered for action but all these years, he had never seen any. At the time when the Allied forces were charging up the beaches in Normandy, he was stationed at Military Headquarters in London. And when the British Army fought their way towards Berlin, he was running around France from being assigned as an aide to a brigadier whose job was to ensure supplies reached the frontline troops.

Being the only son of a retired brigadier who had won numerous medals for gallantry during the First World War, he felt he ought to do better than his old man. To him, action meant opportunities for gaining promotion and bagging medals. His sense of grandiosity and a thirst for admiration had led him to volunteer for this tour of duty. But at the same time, he often suspected his men, especially those, like Sergeant Gow, who had seen action against the Germans, were laughing at him behind his back for being a desk-bound officer.

But on that day, after they had returned to their barracks, everything had changed. Now that they had their action at last, and blooded in the process, Captain Walker could see the expressions that played across their faces as they stood stiffly to attention awaiting his order for them to dismiss. He thought he saw excitement, exultation, trepidation, and satisfaction.

The only exceptions seemed to be Private Martin Sunderland and Private Peter Brown. Both looked almost sick with repulsive guilt. But then what to expect from non-combatants who were only assigned to drive trucks? Even then, when all of them looked at him that day, he could detect respect and even fear in their eyes. He thought with some satisfaction that Sergeant Gow had led his men to carry out his orders without any hint of insubordination.

The thought that the veteran sergeant had obeyed him without question, and some of his men actually feared him sent a thrill through him. Suddenly, feeling ridiculously pleased, he decided it would be more fitting to wrap up the day with a short speech before dismissing his men.

He cleared his throat, and in his gravelly voice began to speak. "By Jove, lads, we're one up against the bandits. I say, don't let the looks of those whom we had executed today fooled you. We're fighting against desperate guerillas. They neither expect nor give any quarter. And there's no doubt about those men who, in providing aid to the communist terrorists in the jungle, may be the death of us yet. It's beastly business but killing one of them is worth more than ridding ten of those in the bushes. I'm truly proud to have you all with me on this mission as you have proven yourselves to be splendid soldiers."

It was a good thing he couldn't hear Sergeant Gow muttering under his breath, "Get over it, man." As the captain was most determined to deceive himself, he failed to sense the impatience and irritation of his men who were dying to take a cold, refreshing shower before meal. Most felt dirty from that day's outing though none had thought it wise to challenge their officer. It was simply not the way of the British Army, where the rank-and-file learned very early it was better to obey even a ridiculous order than to get in the bad book of a dumb officer.

Captain Walker finally gave the order for them to dismiss. Seeing the soldiers trooping away, he thought his speech went rather well as he truly believed his men had stiffened with pride from his words.

Two

After the execution of his father and three villagers, one of whom was Mao Dong Po's schoolteacher, the grief-stricken boy and the rest of the villagers were uprooted to one of the barbed-wire villages that had sprouted up throughout the country. Their assigned "New Village" was located about 10 kilometers away from their former homes.

Each family was given half an hour to pack their essentials limited to a single piece of luggage per person. They were told that food provisions and materials to rebuild their homes would be provided at the "New Village" as the barbed-wire villages were called. On their first night, all of them put up at the community hall. It was quite late when Dong Po's aunt offered him the food she had cooked. He took some to his mother who had been weeping silently. As the thought of food initially nauseated her, she shook her head. But when she saw her son was also not eating, she abruptly changed her mind. "We'll have to eat to keep our strength. We have got to be strong."

The following day, despite the strict surveillance of the sentries from the Home Guards who manned the main gates, Dong Po and his grieving mother were allowed to leave the "New Village" since his uncle had managed to bribe a member of the Home Guards. They were however thoroughly searched to ensure they were not taking out any food from the village.

Some two hours later, they arrived at their old home. As his uncle had seen the slain villagers' bodies being buried the previous day, though without their severed heads, both mother and son searched frantically for some time until they found the discarded head of Dong Po's father. It was fortunate that the head which was dumped in a garbage heap was unnoticed by stray dogs. Miraculously, it was also not set upon by ants though many flies had swarmed it. When they first set eyes on the severed head, Dong Po's mother turned her head away and cried.

Hearing the heart-wrenching sobs coming from his mother, the boy knew it was left to him to accomplish what they had set forth to do. Willing himself to keep his mind devoid of all emotions, he stoically lifted the head, ignored the stench and took it to a spot which had caught his notice. After placing his father's head on the ground, he began digging a hole large enough for the object. He was about to cover up the hole he had dug when he stopped for a moment to blink his eyes a few times as he realized they were filled with tears.

Once the task was done, both mother and son returned to the barbed-wire village, walking all the way in silence. The bribed sentry was still on duty and he smiled at them as they walked past him. Both mother and son were however in no mood to return the man's smile. Each was filled with personal thoughts which included the realization that life had to go on. It was with this goal in mind that upon returning to the "New Village", Dong Po immediately went to work alongside his uncle and two cousin brothers to rebuild a home with the materials they had been given.

Although the "New Villages" promised a better life in the form of protection from the communist terrorists, land of their own to rebuild their homes, government subsidy, free medical care, free schooling for the children, free water, and good roads, the reality of life in the heavily-guarded barbed-wire villages was initially tough for the settlers. Since many of the British soldiers regarded almost every one of the Chinese villagers to be a communist terrorist or at least, a potential one, they had only one treatment for them: Push them around. If they show any sign of resistance, bash them up.

In addition, the villagers no longer had any freedom to move about freely. They were not permitted to go outside beyond the barbed-wire fences without authorization. Those who had to work outside, such as rubber tappers, had to assemble at the gate at 4:00 a.m. to be searched before being allowed to leave. Curfew was imposed within the village at night. A few days after moving into their new homes, the villagers were also ordered to register themselves and members of their respective family, after which each person was issued an identity card.

Though Dong Po resented such mistreatment and kept clear of the British soldiers, surprisingly he bore no hatred towards them. He instinctively knew that not every British soldier was like the officer who had ordered his father's execution based on nothing more concrete than mere suspicion. After all, he could still remember his childhood during the Japanese Occupation, where despite the numerous atrocities committed by many of the yellow dwarfs, there was one Sergeant Kimura who would now and then give him and the other children in his village bits of candy wrapped in rice paper.

Hence, the thought of running away into the jungle to join the communist terrorists and wreck vengeance against the British soldiers had never occurred to him. He was, after all, his father's son. He remembered the many times when his father had told him how he had fled Shanghai in 1937, to avoid being killed by gangsters used by Chiang Kai-shek to eliminate communists.

"I am cursed to be born a Mao, and to have come from Hunan, like Mao Tse-tung," he recalled his father telling him as a child. "Though we may possibly have been distant relatives, but we don't share the same ideology. I also don't care a damn for Chiang Kai-shek's politics. But when Chiang's thugs begun killing the communists, I knew it was time to run. To them, a Mao is a Mao, and surely a communist. As such, I had fled Shanghai to come to this country."

Like his father, he had little regard for politics and thus unaffected by the communists' propaganda. He was far more pragmatic, and being his father's only son, he knew his responsibility was to look after his mother now that his father had died. Though both mother and son were living with his uncle, Dong Po knew he had to grow up fast to assume responsibility for his mother.

Besides, there was an outstanding debt he had to collect. Though he hadn't hated the British, he was however duty-bound to kill the captain who had murdered his father. To do that, he knew he had to grow up by which, he meant developing his physique and honing his mind. Despite his youth, he was yet cunning enough to know that if he wanted to avenge his father's unjust death, he had to learn the language of the enemy and study their ways. With this aim, he enrolled for the English class in the missionary school in the village.

Not knowing what had gone through her son's mind, Dong Po's mother was pleased upon hearing about his enrolment. "That's what your father would have wanted you to do. He was the one who had given you the name, Dong Po, because Su Dong Po was a famous scholar during the Song Dynasty. Your father's spirit would be happy should you live up to his expectation in becoming a scholar."

☆ ☆ ☆ ☆

Captain Neil Walker, at thirty-five, was still a bachelor. Thus, he usually took his meals at the Officers' Mess. And he usually ate alone because his fellow officers avoided him as much as they could. They regarded him with some distaste for being a pompous gong hunter since he was given to lament on missing the action to win medals. Besides, they could not stand his snobbishness.

That night, just as he was chewing on the last bit of his dinner of roast beef, Captain David Cartwright, glass in hand, approached his table.

Captain Cartwright was a big, husky fellow. At twenty-eight, he was seven years younger than Captain Walker. With his red hair, high cheek bones and large brown eyes sunken in deep sockets, and a wide mouth, some people would consider him a rather ugly man. However, his wife, Rosemary, was regarded as the prettiest among the officers' wives in the married quarters. Moreover, Captain Cartwright was already a decorated war hero, first at Dunkirk, and then Normandy. He was also well-liked by his peers and subordinates as he, unlike Captain Walker, was not one to put on air. It also spoke volumes for his good manners to wait until Captain Walker had finished his main dinner before approaching the latter.

"I say, old boy, do you mind if I sit down here and talk to you for a moment?" asked Captain Cartwright in his usual blithe manner and in a voice that was loud and hearty.

Captain Walker looked up with a start. After regarding Captain Cartwright coolly with his pale blue eyes, he said with some reluctance: "Well, all right. What do you want to talk about?"

"I've heard you'd led a resettlement team to a village near Batang Kali yesterday," began Captain Cartwright.

"What about it?" demanded Captain Walker as his beady eyes flicked suspiciously over his colleague's face.

"Rotten luck, isn't it that you had to order the execution of four villagers?"

The stout man looked at his well-built colleague sharply. Was it his fancy that there was an odd look in Captain Cartwright's eyes?

"What are you implying?"

Captain Cartwright shrugged. "I'm not implying anything. I just want to hear from you whether it was really necessary to shoot those chaps."

"Of course, it was necessary. There was such an awful confusion. You should know it could be quite dicey to be in any of those remote villages. My men could be caught like sitting ducks if the bandits were to open fire at us. Besides, we have intelligence and we ought to make examples of those bastards who were trying to flee," said Captain Walker with some emotion.

Suddenly realizing there was no need for him to explain anything to Captain Cartwright who was, after all, his equal, he snapped, "I've already sent my report to the Old Man. There's nothing for me to add. Ask him if you want more."

"All right, all right. No offence intended," said Captain Cartwright, raising both hands in a placating gesture. "I hope the Old Man will give you a medal for it."

Captain Walker looked into his colleague's shrewd but honest eyes, and sought to make sense of his words. Was he mocking him?

As the combat-experienced officer got up to walk briskly out of the Officers' Mess, Captain Walker bristled. *What damned cheek of Captain Cartwright to waylay me like this, and to put to me that impertinent question of whether it was necessary to kill the enemy.*

Of all persons, Captain Cartwright ought to know better that they weren't taking a leisure stroll through the park but were in a state of war, or to be more precise, a state of Emergency as former High Commissioner Sir Edward Gent had put it some three years ago.

After all, even the Old Man himself had approved, thought Captain Walker, as his mind returned to the earlier part of the day when he met up with the Commanding Officer or Old Man as Colonel Alexander Campbell was called by his men behind his back.

After reading Captain Walker's report, the Old Man had summoned him to his office.

"Going by your report that those men were trying to escape, I should say they deserved to be shot," said Colonel Campbell who fleeting thought of his nephew. He was among those planters killed by the communist terrorists two years ago. "If I have my way, I would hang or shoot every one of them since it would be a waste of time to bring them to trial."

"That's what I'd thought too, sir."

"Well, make sure you tell the newspaper chaps those men were shot while attempting to escape," the Commanding Officer said non-committally as he rose from his chair.

Captain Walker's mind returned to the present as a white-jacketed Chinese waiter brought him the dessert. The recollection of his meeting with the Old Man and the sight of the ice cream helped to mollify Captain

Walker a bit over the impertinence of Captain Cartwright. And as he dug his spoon into the ice cream, he thought Captain Cartwright might turn out to be right after all. *Come to think of it, the Old Man may probably recommend me for a medal as Captain Cartwright had said,* he thought. *Yes, indeed why not?*

And the more he thought about it, the more he believed he had done the right thing. *Strike fear into the enemy. After this day, word will spread and those bandits will certainly think twice before trying to mess with us,* he thought happily. *By Jove, the top brass may perhaps even adopt my tactic.*

Three

*I*t was at the English class that Mao Dong Po came to know Reverend Brother Michael MacDuff who was the only teacher.

Brother Duffy as he was affectionately called by his pupils was an elderly missionary who had been posted to various parts of China before the outbreak of the Second World War and so had learned to speak some Mandarin and a sprinkling of Chinese dialects. Though his mission was primarily to spread the Gospel and hopefully convert the villagers to Christianity through social work to alleviate their hardship, teaching English was however his joy.

Dong Po and the other students found the Scotsman had an odd manner of speech because he often interjected Scottish brogue in his spoken English. But when he made a conscious effort, his spoken English was faultless. He apparently knew his own shortcoming because he told his pupils in no uncertain term that he would not hesitate to cane those who had the temerity to imitate the way he spoke.

This was how he had put it to them, "I'm too auld tae change. But aw ye, lads, are still young."

Initially, Dong Po was very reserved towards the tall, jovial Scotsman who cannily was able to sense the aloofness in his pupil. Somehow, Brother Duffy felt a disquieting maturity about the young Chinese lad. Hence, he was always trying to draw Dong Po into conversation.

He began by asking Dong Po, "I hear yer faither cam frae Hunan. Dae ye speak the Hunan dialect?"

"No, I only speak Chow Chou which is my mother's dialect," Dong Po said pleasantly though his face clouded visibly at the mention of his late father. Though he thereafter refused to answer any more of Brother Duffy's probing questions, Brother Duffy was however not a man who gave up easily as the boy was to discover.

One day in June 1952, after Dong Po was absent from school for two days to look after his mother who was down with high fever, the lad was surprised to find Brother Duffy at his door when he went to answer the persistent knocking.

"Are ye aw right?" asked Brother Duffy anxiously as he peered down at the boy. After all, standing well over six feet, he was a tall man, especially so in the eyes of the shorter Chinese.

"I'm fine," Dong Po said, and then remembering his manners, added politely, "Thank you, Brother Duffy, for your concern."

"Then why dae ye nae cam tae school?"

"My mother's sick."

"Good Lord, huv yer mither seen a doctor?"

"A *sinseh* had already treated her."

Brother Duffy rolled his eyes upwards though he knew better than to voice aloud his personal opinion of *sinsehs* since the Chinese had much faith in their traditional herbalists. Instead, he asked gently: "May I say hello tae yer mither?"

As he watched Brother Duffy attempting to communicate with his mother through hand gestures and a smattering of Chow Chou words that he had learned, Dong Po couldn't help feeling grateful towards the lanky Scotsman for his effort. After returning to the missionary school, the Scotsman lost no time in contacting his head office. From his labored conversation with Dong Po's mother, he suspected the middle-aged woman to be suffering from some lung infection. Through his influence, a doctor attached to the mission headquarters in Kuala Lumpur subsequently came all the way to the village to treat Dong Po's mother.

The day after the doctor came to treat his mother for her illness, Dong Po went to thank Brother Duffy. The Scotsman was standing by the window of his Spartan office. His eyes winkled when he said, "I'm nae worried aboot yer mither. It's ye I'm concerned aboot. Dae ye hae a problem, laddie?"

Dong Po looked at him, puzzled. "What do you mean, Brother Duffy?"

"I dinna mean tae pry, but I huv heard aboot yer faither's death."

Since any mention of his father's demise would bring a frown to Dong Po's face, on that day, his face clouded visibly. Seeing the change in the young boy, Brother Duffy added softly, "I dinna ken whit ma people dae most times. I only ken those in the British Military Administration to be damned gowks."

"Gowks?" That was new to the young boy.

"I mean fools."

Dong Po nodded eagerly. Noticing the slight smile on the boy's face Brother Duffy said cautiously, "After the war, when the British cam tae yer country, they found everything huv changed. The people dinna respect them as they used tae dae before the Nips cam."

"Respect has to be earned," Dong Po said fiercely.

"Aye, that's true, lad," Brother Duffy agreed. "But the British dinna ken whit tae dae in this damned war agin the commies. But they ken the damned commies got their food frae the squatter farmers. Believe me, laddie, the British huv nae choice but tae gie gaun the unpopular policy of resettling the squatter farmers tae new villages, like this wun. Their intention is tae isolate the villagers frae the commies guerillas."

Dong Po frowned. "I can accept that but the British soldiers have no right to push us around or take away our basic freedom as they have."

"Aye, I agree fully wi' ye," Brother Duffy said. "But consider the situation frae their viewpoint. They're very frustrated tae find the Chinese civilians indifferent in this war agin the commies, who incidentally are mostly yer people. Therefore, ye cud nae blame the soldiers fur becoming paranoid. As they think all Chinese are commies, they becam more guarded and less kind. They dinna ken better and sae dinna mean it"

Some time in late 1952, during a class discussion on leadership, Brother Duffy said: "When soldiers wisnae obeying orders but kill people at wull, they dae sae because there was nae leader around or the leadership wisnae capable."

Dong Po who had learned to like and trust Brother Duffy, raised his hand and said, "But can we excuse soldiers for wanton killing by blaming on the leaders alone? I think they're all the same. Being warlike by nature, soldiers are prone to kill, kill, and kill."

Brother Duffy thought for a moment before saying "Nae, I huv tae disagree wi' ye, laddie. Not aw commanders hae this urge to kill. There're those who wud impose better discipline."

Dong Po persisted. "Care to give me an example?"

"Well, the current British High Commissioner is an example. After Sir Gerald took over earlier this year, when asked whether he hae enough troops tae fight the commies, the mon replied that the answer wisnae pouring more soldiers into the jungle, but winning the hearts and minds of the Malayan people."

Though Dong Po had heard about Lieutenant-General Sir Gerald Templer, he wasn't about to abandon his stand. "Even so, Sir Gerald has a reputation for ticking off people with his sharp, caustic tongue."

Brother Duffy laughed. "Aye, Sir Gerald certainly hae a sharp and caustic tongue. At times, his chastising of the people huv humorous moments. Want tae hear aboot an incident?"

When the pupils, including Dong Po, nodded eagerly as they sensed an interesting story was in store, the Scotsman began, "He recently harangued some villagers near whaur commies huv staged an ambush. The general started off by telling them that they're a bunch of bastards, whereby the translator said, "His Excellency informs ye that he ken that none of yer mithers and faithers were married when ye were born." And when the General went on tae say the villagers cud find him a bigger bastard, the translator said, "His Excellency also admits that his faither wisnae married tae his mither when he wus born."

The class was silent for a moment but when the implication sank in, everyone roared with laughter. Dong Po laughed the loudest. It was the first time he had laughed aloud since his father's death.

The second time he laughed was during that year's Christmas party when Brother Duffy not only played his favorite *Scotland the Brave* on the gramophone but had suddenly leaped up to dance and sing, "Land of mair high endeavor, land of the shining river, land of mair heart forever, Scotland the brave."

The sight of the Scotsman in his long, white gown leaping, twirling and kicking as he did the Highland fling was too much for Dong Po. He laughed till his sides ached.

Although he had learned to understand the situation better to dislike the British less, on the whole, Dong Po was however unable to forget or forgive Captain Neil

Walker, the man who had high-handedly ordered his father's execution. He had found out the man's name after he woke up on the lorry sending him, his uncle and the other villagers to their new home behind the barbed-wire fences.

A soldier, who was guarding them, had told his comrade on the ride, "The captain should have taken the prisoners in for interrogation instead of killing them."

"You the captain or Neil Walker's the captain?" asked the other soldier.

The same question of whether to take the prisoners in for interrogation or to summarily execute them was still being debated several months after the incident.

This time the debate took place at the Spotted Dog as the rambling Tudor-style Selangor Club in Kuala Lumpur was popularly called because the wife of a member often left her Dalmatian at the entrance whenever she came to the club.

"We must never take the law into our own hands," said Colonel Robert Stewart, after taking a puff of his cigar. "If we do, we're no better than bloody Charlie Tango, and that surely won't be the way to win the hearts and minds of the people."

Amused by his colleague's usage of Charlie Tango for the communist terrorists, Colonel Leslie Neville gave him a sidelong glance. He was quite sure his colleague had definitely put on weight since they last met at Sir Gerald's welcoming party. Even then, Colonel Neville thought his colleague still cut a rather imposing figure as he was tall with curly grey hair.

Unaware that Colonel Neville was more interested in his looks than his opinion, Colonel Stewart continued: "This was why I had urged for an official enquiry into what had really happened at Batang Kali last year. I have my doubts about the official account given by that officer, a Captain Walker-Somebody-or-other."

Mention of Batang Kali and Captain Walker aroused Colonel Neville's interest. He felt he ought to say something. After all, Brigadier Peter Walker, the father of the said Captain Neil Walker, had many years ago been one of his admired instructors when he was at the Royal Military College at Sandhurst.

He cleared his throat and said: "I dare say it was beastly, the whole thing, about having to shoot four villagers but then, Bob, it wasn't like they were shot in cold blood. Remember they were trying to escape."

This time, it was Colonel Stewart's turn to appraise his colleague. *If I hadn't known you better as a vicious cold-blooded bastard, with your delicate features, especially those large, melancholy eyes, and soft, beautiful hands, I would have thought you a bloody fairy and may even desire you,* he mused. But instead he said aloud, "I doubt they were trying to run away, Les".

"What led you to say that?"

"They were unarmed and had no reason to flee."

Colonel Neville wagged a delicate forefinger. "Oh, then I would have to disagree with you, Bob. They may be unarmed but there was no way to tell at the time when they were trying to escape. Besides, Special Branch had provided ample evidence against those men which made them all the more likely to want to bolt."

"But from what I've heard about Captain Walker, I have my doubts…"

Colonel Neville interrupted his colleague. "You should know better than to listen to those who have nothing to do except wag their frightful tongues, Bob. I know Captain Walker. Nice fellow, if you ask me. He may be a bit airy but he's all right as he's one of the old gang. I dare say he's definitely out of the top drawer."

"What made you so sure, old chap?"

"Well, you should have known his old man, Brigadier Walker."

"Say, you don't mean Brigadier Peter Walker, do you?"

"The one and only," Colonel Neville said. "He's a regular tartar and proud as the devil."

"Well, in that case, I shall perish all doubts about Captain Walker," said Colonel Stewart as he reached out for his whiskey and soda. "There's nothing like heredity, Les. It's a fellow's pedigree and breeding that counts."

Having reached an agreement, the two gentlemen ordered another round of whiskey and soda.

Four

*M*ao Dong Po turned fifteen on January 6, 1953.

Although Dong Po had never before celebrated any birthday since his father was a firm believer that only deities would be privileged to celebrate birthdays, Brother Duffy had insisted in taking him to Kuala Lumpur to watch the western movie, *Shane*. Thus, he was initially hesitant but after some persuasion, Dong Po took leave from the Chinese medical hall where he worked part-time as an assistant to the *sinseh*.

Although it was the western medicine prescribed by the mission doctor that had cured his mother, she had already been seeing the *sinseh* for some time and therefore owed the traditional herbalist a large sum of money. Chinese herbs had always been expensive. As such, Dong Po subsequently offered his service to the *sinseh* as a mean to pay off his mother's debts.

On the morning of his birthday, he set off with Brother Duffy for the country's capital. It was the first time Dong Po had been to Kuala Lumpur, and the first time to a cinema to watch a movie. Like the impressionable young boy, Joey Starrett, on the silver screen, after the movie was over, Dong Po too begun idolizing the mysterious gun slinging hero, Shane, who rode in from the wilderness, appearing from nowhere as a man without a past or a future, and who, after killing the villains, got back on his horse to ride off into the sunset.

After the movie, they went to the nearby Coliseum Café. It was also the first time that Dong Po had enjoyed a western meal served by white-jacketed waiters in a real restaurant.

But it was the movie that impressed the youngster the most. Later, when they were on the long bus ride to go home to the "New Village", while Brother Duffy was snoring loudly beside him, Dong Po was lost in thought as he fantasized himself as Shane, but in his case, killing the evil Captain Neil Walker before riding away into the sunset.

☆ ☆ ☆ ☆

Earlier that morning, Captain Walker had appeared before a panel comprising Colonel Leslie Neville, Colonel Robert Stewart, and Brigadier William Bishop. The panel presided by the brigadier was set up to look into the previous month's skirmish with communist terrorists near Sintok in the State of Kedah.

"After the reopening of mining and timber logging activities at Sintok last year, the bandits became quite active in the vicinity," Captain Walker told the panel members. "My unit was thereby moved to Kepala Batas, from where we mount regular patrols to check the communist threat in the area."

He paused for a moment to survey the three senior officers before him, and was encouraged by a friendly smile from Colonel Neville and an imperceptible nod from Colonel Stewart. He was however unable to make much from Brigadier Bishop's thin sallow face other than noticing how bright his blue eyes were from behind the pince-nez he was wearing.

"Last month after getting word that several bandits had been spotted near the 15th mile Sintok Road, my unit was ordered to join Captain David Cartwright's unit to hunt them down," he said. "We pursued the bandits into the jungle and suddenly found ourselves fired upon in an ambush. Apparently the bandits had been alerted of our pursuit and were waiting for us."

As he went on to narrate the story which he had already repeated three times, first in his report, then at the debriefing for his Commanding Officer, and a third time at a Special Branch debriefing, he thought he ought to make light of the danger and impress the panel on how he had calmly led his men out of a tight spot. On a sudden impulse, he even insinuated that Captain Cartwright had probably lost his head a little.

He realized he had overstepped when Brigadier Bishop interrupted him: "Now hold it right there. According to Captain Cartwright's report and testimony, you were not moving around very much, which you later told him that you were pinned down under heavy enemy fire."

As he looked blankly at the brigadier, he felt at the same time, a blind rush of hatred welling up in him against Captain Cartwright. *That damned blighter shouldn't have reported my words,* he thought bitterly. *Oh, how I regret having had forgotten uttering those words to that bloody fellow. It's just like him to tell tales.*

Getting no response from Captain Walker, the brigadier remarked: "Well, on the whole your stories agree pretty well about being ordered to pursue the bandits and then getting caught in an ambush. But when you told us that it was you who led the men out of the ambush, it contradicts Captain Cartwright who had claimed the credit as you were said to be pinned down by enemy fire. What have you got to say to this?"

"Well, sir, as things were, it was touch and go. I was pinned down initially but as soon as the enemy fire died down, I was up and on my feet to rally our lads," replied Captain Walker, clinging to his belief.

"All right then, we'll take it that you were pinned down whereby Captain Cartwright had rallied the boys to return fire, giving you enough time to recover and join him later in repulsing the enemy," said the brigadier, sportingly offering everyone a chance out of the contradiction. "Will this conclusion be acceptable to you?"

Captain Walker grabbed at the offered straw. "Yes, sir, I accept the conclusion."

A few minutes later when he walked out of the room, he spotted Captain Cartwright talking to an air force officer in the hall. But he wasn't bothered about his colleague. He was more concerned about whatever was being discussed among the three senior officers back in the room that he had just left. He felt the brigadier hadn't really believed what he had said, especially after he had so foolishly tried to run down Captain Cartwright's credibility.

Five

*E*ight months passed by and Mao Dong Po was reminded of his favorite hero, Shane, riding away into the sunset: This time, it was Brother Duffy who was going away.

The Scotsman was retiring from the missionary service and would be returning by the end of the month to his beloved Glasgow. On the day of his departure, he came to Dong Po's home to say "goodbye" to his young pupil. On that day, Brother Duffy brought along a farewell gift.

"Seeing how ye huv enjoyed *Shane*, ye wull no doubt find this book interesting fur yer youthful imagination," declared Brother Duffy.

The book, *Casino Royale* by Ian Fleming, was released earlier that year. As Brother Duffy had predicted, the boy's rich imagination took over the moment he began reading the book and he was soon fantasizing himself as James Bond fighting Captain Neil Walker instead of LeChiffre. Reading the book helped to take away much of the sadness he felt over the jovial Scotsman's departure.

In later years, when he was older, during those rare moments that he allowed himself to reminisce his past, he would think of Brother Duffy as the first true friend and mentor whom he ever had. It was the jolly Scotsman who had taught him the importance of knowledge, and books would be the key to such knowledge. The most important of Brother Duffy's lessons was however the one about being able to laugh at oneself.

Just as he was about to board the bus at the village's bus station, the Scotsman turned to look at Dong Po. "I may nae huv enough time tae convert ye tae my faith but I think my best shot wus tae change ye frae the grave and saturnine fellow into one wha cud laugh mair easily. If a mon tak himself too seriously tae end up unable tae laugh at himself, then he wull becam most narrow-minded."

☆ ☆ ☆ ☆

Another man whose life was linked by an invisible thread to the Chinese boy had also gone back to old Blighty, in his case, England. Captain Neil Walker was home on furlough.

Home was a solidly built Victorian house in Norfolk. While it was a lovely, comfortable house as compared to the barracks he had been living most of his adult life, Captain Walker however discovered it wasn't a very pleasant home-coming.

The senior Walker had always demanded for high grades from his son during his school days. But the younger Walker was unfortunately not cut out to be a scholar. If not for his father, his mediocre grades wouldn't have got him past the Selection Board at the Royal

Military College. His father, who was then a colonel, had driven home that fact on many occasions. "If not for me, they wouldn't have accepted you. Why, you couldn't even make it as any officer's batman."

After he graduated from the prestigious military academy, and obtained his commission, he had thought his father finally would be proud of him. But he was wrong. From that moment, their relationship took a change from that of a stern father and cowering son to an entirely new level of dictatorial superior officer and subservient subordinate.

"Beginning from today, you shall address me as "sir,"" his father, who had been promoted to brigadier, had told him on his day of commissioning. "You can only call me father again on the day you attain the rank of colonel or receive a decoration, whichever comes first."

That afternoon, not long after he had come home to the family house, Albert, who was his father's former batman and had faithfully followed his master upon the latter's retirement to become his manservant, interrupted him as he was talking to his mother. "The brigadier wants to see you in his study, young Captain Walker."

Stepping into his father's study and seeing Brigadier Peter Walker sitting at his usual place behind the large desk, brought a queer feeling of awe to him. He saw before him a tall, proud man. Subconsciously, he had hoped to find his father aged, more fragile and therefore vulnerable. Instead, the sixty-year-old man still looked hale and hearty despite having lost most of his hair and his face was much lined. Captain Walker thought his father's vigor could be due in part to his fastidiousness over his food, and in part to his being an exercise freak.

The older man seemed to be reading his thoughts because his way of welcoming an only son home was an accusing bark, "You have put on weight," which was followed by a taunt, "No wonder you couldn't rise any higher than captaincy. Other than their size, fat fellows are seldom impressive."

Much as he resented his father's remark, Captain Walker was too afraid of him to retort.

Taking his son's silence in his stride, Brigadier Walker sighed. "When I was your age, I was already a decorated lieutenant-colonel. Why are you such a frightful disappointment to me?"

Captain Walker, filled with humiliation, opened his mouth as though to say something, then thought better of it and so pursed his lips together again.

"Well, you had succeeded once again to put me in a monstrous position."

This time, Captain Walker managed to say, "I don't get you, sir."

"I've heard recently from my former pupil, Colonel Leslie Neville about your yellow streak during an ambush," Brigadier Walker said. "It shamed me awfully that my son should turn out to be a frightful coward."

This time, Captain Walker couldn't restrain himself. "Is that what they think of me? That I'm a coward? Did they say I have a yellow streak?"

"Oh, Colonel Neville was too much a gentleman to pronounce those words. He merely repeated your claim of enemy fire pinning you down and so you were unable to rally your fellows in a counter-attack. The whole episode seems so ruddy peculiar, what? But knowing you as I do, I'd read the entire situation as your having lost your courage during the skirmish with the enemy. You tend to fare better when dealing with, say unarmed villagers."

For nearly a minute the younger Walker stood and stared at his father who had also chosen to remain silent as he glared at his son. Captain Walker shifted uncomfortably from one foot to the other. At first, his face was surly from hearing those humiliating words coming from his father's mouth. Then his face darkened from remembering how his hated rival, David Cartwright had been promoted to major just the week before he was due for home leave. As his father waved a hand dismissively at him, he turned to go.

Finally, at the end of a week of consistent reminders of his uselessness, he decided to cut short his stay. Without bothering to inform his father, he went to London to stay out the remaining two weeks of his furlough. Although every one of the few friends whom he telephoned surprisingly claimed the same thing – they were about to travel somewhere – he still managed to enjoy himself.

As he avoided going to clubs lest he should come across his father's friends who would surely send word to the brigadier, he spent most of his time in restaurants or theatres. On a few occasions, at the public houses, he even managed to find someone to bring back with him to the hotel he had lodged. Although his father had called him fat, and while he wasn't too tall, luckily his straight shoulders and moustache, and most important, money corresponding to his rank had helped to pass him off as reasonably attractive.

Six

$\mathcal{S}$ir Gerald Templer left Malaya in May 1954.

Two days after the departure of the British High Commissioner amidst great pomp and ceremony, Mao Dong Po and his mother made a quiet exit from the barbed-wire village which had been their home for more than two years. The sentries scrutinized the documents which permitted them to leave the village and then thoroughly went through the two suitcases containing the combined assets of both mother and son. Satisfied there was no food or medical item, they were allowed to leave. An hour later, they were on a bus going to Rawang, from where they would catch the north-bound train heading for Padang Besar in the northern State of Perlis.

Dong Po's mother had decided to migrate after the death of the uncle with whom they had put up at the "New Village". He had suddenly died of a stroke not long after the Chinese New Year.

Three months after his uncle's funeral, Dong Po's mother had said: "Much as I've wanted to stay here so as not to disrupt your schooling, now that your father's brother too has passed away, I feel we mustn't burden your aunt or your two elder cousin brothers."

Dong Po knew the enormity of his mother's decision. Much as she wanted him to be well educated, she was also distressed over having to impose on Dong Po's widowed aunt. This aunt and her daughter, Dong Fong, who was still schooling, were dependant on her two older sons. The eldest, Dong Hai, was five years older than Dong Po. He had inherited his father's bicycle repairing business and so continued to run the small shop in the village. Her youngest son, Dong Nan, who was just two years older than Dong Po, had gone to work as a farm hand as he often couldn't see eye-to-eye with his older brother.

"Don't worry about my education, mother," Dong Po had assured his mother. "One can still be educated without having to go to school. I can read books and listen to the wireless."

His mother looked at him without speaking and slowly nodded her head. "You're right. Well, in that case, I think we should go to Padang Besar to join my only brother who has written several times asking us to stay with him. There should be no problem with the authorities as he has agreed to be our guarantor."

Dong Po had met this maternal uncle only once shortly after the Second World War had ended. He remembered him as the leather goods' merchant who had presented him with a leather wallet which he had proudly been keeping all these years. Inside, was the single dollar note his father had given him. His father had said, "No wallet should ever be empty. Here, put this dollar inside for luck." Not wishing to be reminded of his father, Dong Po shifted his thought to the maternal uncle, whom he had been told to address as Elder Uncle. He recalled having heard that this uncle, who was his mother's older brother, lost his wife to illness during the Japanese Occupation when medicine was unavailable. Since then he had not remarried.

On the long train ride, Dong Po's mother wept quietly whenever she thought of the few relatives and friends she had left behind. The boy however did not feel any such sentiment. Ever since the day of his father's execution and the uprooting to the "New Village", Dong Po had avoided any close relationship with anyone.

He had been casually distant towards his two cousin brothers, cousin sister, and the other children in the new village. Although his two cousin brothers, being older, tended to ignore him, his cousin sister who was just a year younger, somehow leaned towards him. But he avoided her even though he found her, being a frail, delicate girl, with large and melancholy eyes, to be quite pretty. In later years, he realized he was afraid of any personal attachment with anyone lest he were to lose the person the way he had abruptly lost his father.

The only person he had allowed himself to feel any closeness was Brother Duffy. Even then, that came about only because Brother Duffy had been most persistent in his efforts to know him better and draw him out of his shell. From the day Brother Duffy left, there were some days when Dong Po felt himself missing the jolly Scotsman.

In recent months, he was convinced more than ever that like his heroes, Shane and James Bond, he was destined to walk life's path alone. Though he knew he still had the responsibility to care for his mother, he was determined to see to it that no one else was permitted into his life.

Captain Neil Walker was also a loner, though not by choice but rather because his fellows detested him and avoided him as much as they could.

They found him to be a fearful snob. If he wasn't sizing up a person on the basis of his rank, he would be fussing over whether the fellow was socially acceptable. With those he regarded as his equals, he would be polite although in his self-centeredness, he would secretly mistrust them, even fear them over the likelihood of their overtaking him career-wise, or envy them should they eventually surpass him. Needless to say, he tended to be obsequious with his superiors.

As for those whom he looked upon as his social inferiors, he tended to be either patronizing or coldly insolent, to the extent of being downright rude and even insulting. If a person knew about Captain Walker's relationship with his father, that person wouldn't have to be a psychologist to point out that he was unconsciously impersonating his father, thus transforming himself from bullied to bullying, from helpless victim to aggressive predator.

One evening in June 1954, Captain Walker was drinking morosely by himself in the Officers' Mess of the barracks in Butterworth. It was exactly a month from the day his unit was transferred there, coinciding with the day Sir Gerald Templer left Malaya. The bar was crowded that night as it was raining heavily, making it inconvenient for anyone to cross over to Penang.

Perched heavily on the tall bar stool, causing its springs to groan under his weight, the captain was about to order the barman to mix another gin and tonic for him when he chanced to overhear something which made him instantly see red.

Police Lieutenant Richard Smith was saying, "When Sir Gerald left, I was sad that we'd lost a competent leader."

Several things irked Captain Walker. Though the young man spoke with some refinement, Captain Walker's delicate ears couldn't miss his distinctive Cockney accent. Since arriving at the Butterworth barracks, he had seen the fellow and had wondered on a few occasions how that bounder could have made it as a commissioned officer even though a lower-ranking one than him. It riled him too that the cad seemed to have been accepted by most of the officers, especially his rival, Major David Cartwright as they were lately often seen in each other's company. And as Captain Walker was disdainful of Sir Gerald, having opined at times that the former High Commissioner was too soft on the enemy and had even gone native in his efforts to win over the locals, he felt affronted by what he perceived to be Police Lieutenant Smith's misguided hero-worshiping.

Perhaps he had one gin and tonic too many, or maybe he was depressed. But an uncharacteristic bravado seized him of a sudden and he slipped off the stool and lurched over to where Police Lieutenant Smith and Major

Cartwright were sitting. "You're a damned fool for gushing over Sir Gerald as you had. But then what to expect from your class?"

The interruption was so unexpected, and the tone so sardonic that the two men were dumbfounded. Several officers, who were close enough to hear, had also stopped their conversation to look curiously at the three of them.

It was Major Cartwright who spoke first. "You're drunk, old boy. Why don't you go back to your quarters to sleep?"

"I don't think you'll much like the truth if I tell it to you," Captain Walker said, looking right into the major's eyes.

"Get going, man," Major Cartwright ordered. "Or at least, keep a civil tongue in your head."

This time, Police Lieutenant Smith said softly to the major, "Let him have his say," and turning to Captain Walker, "Why don't you sit down, captain?"

"I don't accept favors from inferiors let alone socialize with one."

Though everyone saw the polite smile on the police lieutenant's face, the more observant ones noticed his fists clenching tight. Major Cartwright, who was white with anger, sprang to his feet. "Your behavior has been most appalling tonight, Walker. If you don't take your insolence with you back to your quarters right now, by Jove, I'll see to it that…"

"See to what?" interrupted Captain Walker. "Have you descended to Police Lieutenant Smith's level?"

The words were hardly out of his mouth before Major Cartwright's fist shot out like a bolt of lightning. Hit on the face, the captain staggered backward and then fell heavily to the floor. Several officers sprang forward to restrain the major though they didn't have to bother because the single punch had knocked out Captain Walker.

Seven

$\mathcal{I}$t was the Anglo-Siamese Treaty of 1909 that determined the border between the kingdom of Siam and British Malaya.

Padang Besar was a border town located on the fringe just inside British Malaya. It was about 35 kilometers northeast of Kangar, the capital of the State of Perlis, and the moment Mao Dong Po saw Padang Besar, he was reminded of the cowboy town he had seen in the movie, where his hero, Shane had the final showdown with the villains.

After getting off the train, Dong Po and his mother walked a short distance along the platform. Dong Po's uncle was already waiting for them at the station as he had earlier received their telegram. Although only three years older than Dong Po's mother, the tall scrawny man looked much older than the last time that Dong Po had seen him. Seeing the creases on his uncle's tanned face, Dong Po couldn't help being reminded of the creased leather wallet he carried in his pocket.

As they got out of the station, Elder Uncle – as Dong Po was told to address this uncle – pointed towards a row of wooden shop houses, saying, "My shop's over there. I live upstairs."

Looking excitedly about him, it seemed to Dong Po that life in the town moved at its own slow pace as though the people felt no reason to hurry. But there was a gaiety about the town and its residents. His young ears had already taken in the sound around him and there was an unmistaken foreignness in the people's conversations.

In the months that followed, Dong Po worked as an assistant in his uncle's shop or ran errands for him while his mother stayed upstairs to attend to household chores and prepare their three daily meals. Dong Po found his uncle to be an easy man to get along with although he was a man who spoke only when necessary.

On Dong Po's first pay day, his uncle handed three pieces of crisp ten-dollar notes to him. The youngster was surprised to hear his uncle saying: "I know you still keep the wallet I'd given you several years ago. This is your pay. If you are frugal, the money may soon fatten your wallet."

Dong Po was daily reminded of Padang Besar being a border town because each day he would come across people who spoke either Malay or Thai or a mixture of Malay and Thai. Most of the Chinese he came across tended to speak his mother's Chow Chou dialect. Within a month, his agile young mind had absorbed enough Malay and Thai for him to converse with anyone who wasn't a Chinese. At night, he would tune into BBC on the wireless to keep up with his English.

But unlike the village he had left behind where miles of barbed-wire fences separated the lawful from the lawless, he saw nothing that resembled a physical border in Padang Besar despite it being a border town. However, like everyone else, he knew there was an invisible line that sort of separated one nation from another. When he pointed out the absence of a border to his uncle, the older man laughed. "Of course, there's a border. If you step out of our back door, you are in Siam. But out the front door is British Malaya."

The observant lad noticed that like most people, his uncle had called the country by its old name, Siam. Once when accompanying his mother to the town's clinic when she had taken ill, he had read an obscure journal in the waiting room to learn that in 1939, Field Marshal Phibun Songkhram, who was still the country's military dictator, had changed the name to Thailand. When he heard other people also calling the country, Siam, he knew habits are hard to change.

But what his uncle had said about their home actually resting on the border wasn't exactly true. There was a small path to allow the night soil collectors to come behind each house to change the bucket as in those days modern toilets were unheard. The border, Dong Po reckoned to be on the fringe of the dirt path, and he often found himself opening the back door to gaze out in wonder.

And as if to confirm his uncle's words, one night in September 1954, just after Dong Po had closed the shop, he heard someone knocking on the back door. By the time he reached the rear of the house, he saw his uncle, holding a kerosene-lamp, letting a swarthy looking man into the house. The burly man was carrying a sort of violin case.

Just as his uncle was locking the back door, the stranger stared curiously at Dong Po who had by then grown into a slender teenager with wavy thick black hair atop a thoughtful, reflective face. The observant sixteen-year-old saw the middle-aged stranger switched the case to his left hand and casually moved his free hand inside the windbreaker he was wearing.

Sensing the stranger's unease, his uncle said hurriedly, "Dong Po, come and greet Uncle Somchai."

In the glow of the kerosene-lamp, Dong Po felt a chill as he looked into the stranger's glossy, depthless eyes. Instinctively, he put the other kerosene-lamp he was holding on the floor and brought both hands together to offer a *wai* – the Thai greeting – and said, "*Sawadee,* Uncle Somchai."

The stranger's teeth shone brightly as he smiled his approval. Dong Po's uncle relaxed and said, "This is my nephew, Dong Po."

After the introduction, Dong Po left the men to their business, and went upstairs to assist his mother who was preparing dinner for them. Half an hour later, as the stranger had left, his uncle came to join them for dinner.

Halfway through dinner, Dong Po couldn't restrain his curiosity and asked. "Elder Uncle, who's this man you'd told me to address as Uncle Somchai?"

"He's my friend," his uncle said non-committally.

"But why did he come at night and through the back door?"

Instead of answering him, his uncle looked at his nephew curiously for a moment. "What made you ask that question?"

"I think he doesn't want anyone to know his coming or going."

"Then don't ask so many questions," growled his uncle, putting down his empty bowl and chopsticks, indicating he had finished eating.

Catching an anxious glance from his mother, Dong Po prudently stopped talking and concentrated on finishing his meal.

☆ ☆ ☆ ☆

One evening, Major David Cartwright, Police Lieutenant Richard Smith and two other officers were playing bridge in the card-room at the Officers' Mess when one of the two, a Captain Gerald Munro passed a remark. It was directed at Police Lieutenant Smith. "Sometimes, I just cannot help wondering whether to place you as a police or army officer since you're attached to this barrack instead of a police station."

Police Lieutenant Smith smiled. "I can't blame you. Back in 1948 after several planters were killed by the communist terrorists, I'd signed on as a contract police officer and was given the rank of police lieutenant. After my three-year contract was up, I applied to be an instructor to lick the locals into shape as General Sir Gerald Templer had by then ordered the set up of the 1st Battalion which is billeted here. I was allowed to retain my rank."

"We have something in common then," said Captain Munro, a sandy-haired, raw-boned and hard-looking man who was about the same age as Major Cartwright. He was in charge of the military police in the barracks.

"Did you get to see any action so far?" asked Major Thomas Hamilton, the fourth player in their group.

"I've seen some," Police Lieutenant Smith said, in his easy, good-humored voice.

Major Cartwright chuckled. "You're asking Betty Driver whether she had sung. If only you know, Richard had been inside the jungle for longer time than any of us, Tom. Though he hasn't killed any bandit, he had wounded and captured a number of them."

Major Hamilton, who had arrived in Malaya from England just a fortnight ago, looked admiringly at the young man. He was nearly forty and was a professionally-trained accountant serving as an auditor in the Auditor-General's Office. Being a chatty player, he shuffled the cards and said, "Pray share with us an incident which you would consider to be a tight spot you've got into."

Police Lieutenant Smith frowned as if trying to remember, and then said: "Well, I suppose I could say it was that day when I went on a patrol to track and ambush the bandits operating in the Bentong area. After trekking through thick jungle, I felt a sudden tummy ache and had to stop to ease myself. To do it in the jungle is uncomfortable enough. It is far worse when a man is being laden with knapsack and gear."

He stopped, not because he had finished the story but to take a sip of his beer as his mouth was dry. "While

I was in the midst of answering nature's call, the shooting started. Squatting there in the bushes, it dawned on me that either my men had stumbled onto the bandits or they onto us. With my pants down and bullets flying everywhere, I dare say, it was the tightest spot I've ever been in."

Everyone laughed as they could imagine the awkward sight of the police lieutenant's bare bottom as he squatted among the bushes in the midst of a battle.

"And how did you all get out of that tight spot?" asked Captain Munro.

"It was the Gurkha soldiers who got us out of the tight spot. You know, those short brown fellows from the hills of Nepal?"

When all three nodded their heads, Police Lieutenant Smith said, "It was a good thing they were with us that day. With their fearful blood-cuddling yells, they scared the shit out of the bandits. I was no exception because everything in me came out in a rush, after which the firing ceased, and having had eased myself, I got my trousers back on hurriedly to join my mates."

Major Hamilton was obviously affected by the tale because he went into a laughing fit whereby everyone could see his whole body shaking with mirth. Even Major Cartwright was chortling.

The army auditor took out a handkerchief to wipe the corner of his eyes. "Any casualty?"

"Other than two heads held in each hand of two Gurkha soldiers, no one else was hurt."

That sobered them up a bit. They had all heard fearsome stories of Gurkha soldiers charging into battles with guns blazing as well as drawn *kukris* – a fifteen-inch curve-blade knife with wooden handle – which they would use later to cut off their enemies' heads.

Major Hamilton turned to Major Cartwright and asked, "And what about you, David? Have you been in any tight spot?"

Major Cartwright considered for a moment, casting his mind back to the morning after he had punched Captain Neil Walker.

Making a face, he said in his full and hearty voice, "I dare say the tightest spot I've ever got into was about three months ago when I stood before Colonel Robert Stewart, the provost marshal, for socking Captain Walker."

Seeing Major Hamilton's raised eyebrows, Major Cartwright narrated the incident where a drunken Captain Walker had insulted Police Lieutenant Smith.

"And you threw him a punch which knocked him cold?" asked Major Hamilton. "What did the provost marshal do to you thereafter?"

"Thank God, he turned out to be quite a decent chap for all the talk about him being a tartar. I got a flea in the ear."

Major Hamilton looked faintly amused. "That's all?"

"Well, apart from lecturing me on exemplary leadership, he slapped a token fine on me."

"You got off light indeed. What about Captain Walker?" asked Major Hamilton.

Before the major could answer, Captain Munro said: "He got hell from my boss who hauled him over the coals for his disgraceful behavior."

"It serves him right," Major Hamilton said. "Though I'm new here, somehow I've never seem to like that fellow at all."

"Nobody does," Major Cartwright agreed.

Eight

After Mao Dong Po's first meeting with Somchai, he saw the burly swarthy-looking Siamese a few more times.

He would either come knocking on the back door at night or sauntering into the shop's entrance just around the time Dong Po was about to close the shop. With his rich youthful imagination, Dong Po at first thought his uncle and Somchai were smugglers. That theory soon gave way to something more exciting – they were spies, or secret agents, like James Bond. This came about soon after he finished reading Ian Fleming's second novel, *Live and Let Die,* which was released that year.

In Dong Po's recollection, on the first occasion they had met and just a few days ago, he saw the Siamese carrying the violin-like case. He thought Somchai was therefore more likely to be a spy than a smuggler. If he was a smuggler, he wouldn't be empty handed as he was on those other occasions. The case was likely used for carrying a rifle.

One night just three days before the Christmas of 1954, just as Dong Po was about to close the shop, Somchai walked in. This time, he had the case with him. As had become a routine for the young man, after locking the front door, Dong Po took one of the kerosene-lamps and walked the Siamese to the rear of the house.

Just as he was about to open the back door, the lad couldn't help blurting out, "Are you a spy, Uncle Somchai?"

Somchai's eyes widened as he stared at him in astonishment. It was just for a moment and then he began to laugh. After a while, he stopped laughing and looked sadly at Dong Po before asking softly, "Where's your uncle?"

"He went to Kangar and won't be back until later tonight."

The Siamese sighed and scratched the side of his nose. "Your uncle hasn't told you about me?"

"No. All he had said was that you are his friend."

"Your uncle's a good man."

Both the middle-aged Siamese and the young Chinese stared at each other in silence for a while. As if he had made up his mind about something, Somchai said, "You really want to know about me?"

Dong Po nodded, and Somchai continued, "Some things are best left not knowing, my boy. If I were to tell you about me, I may have to remove you."

"It's true that some things are best left unknown but at times, if you keep everything to yourself, you may go crazy. Yes, if I don't find out what I want to know, I'll go crazy. Between crazy and death, I think I prefer death."

Hearing this short speech from the teenager, Somchai narrowed his eyes, looking at him reflectively. After another short silence, the older man said, "You're one of the few persons in this world who can look me in my eyes. I like that. And young as you are, you're also quite smart."

"So will you tell me what I want to know?"

"Yes, I mean no, I'm not a spy. I'm a…well, you can say, I'm a problem remover."

"You remove problems?"

"No, I mean yes, I remove those people who have become problems. In that way, the problems are also removed."

Seeing the swarthy Siamese watching him like a tiger eyeing its prey, Dong Po said, "I understand. Judging from the number of times I have opened this door for you, quite a few problems have been removed since we first met."

Somchai grunted. "Business has been good."

Pointing to the case, Dong Po asked: "Is that your removal tool?"

Somchai nodded and at the same time smiled his approval. "As I've said, you're quite smart for your age, my boy. Come, I'll show you."

Opening the case, he took out a long barrel and then a wooden butt. "This is an improvised rifle copied after the Soviet-made SVD, also known as Dragunov, which was much feared by the Germans just a decade or so ago. This one has been remodeled to fit a 3.5 powered scope, and is accurate up to eight hundred meters. The original could shoot as far as a thousand meters. Here is a silencer, and this is a clip for the bullets."

In a few swift movements, Somchai assembled the rifle and loaded the clip into it with the easy, calm grace of a professional.

"And now you are going to kill me," Dong Po said. It was more a statement than a question.

"Yes…I mean no, I'm not killing anyone. I'm just about to remove you, my boy."

"But I'm not a problem."

"Not yet," Somchai agreed easily. "But you will be when you tell others about me."

"My uncle didn't tell anybody."

Somchai who had raised the rifle, smiled. "He's different."

"Besides, you don't need a high-powered rifle like this to remove me. The pistol you carry in the right side under your windbreaker will be more suitable."

Somchai lowered the rifle and eyed Dong Po suspiciously. "How do you know I carry a pistol hidden under my windbreaker?"

"I saw you moved your hand there the first time I met you."

"Very smart, I'm impressed."

Again, there was the awkward silence as the burly Siamese and the young man looked warily at each other.

Dong Po gave Somchai what he hoped to pass as a disarming smile and said. "I don't think you want to remove me."

"No, I mean, yes, I never remove anyone who is worth keeping."

"Am I worth keeping?"

"You are a very smart young man. It will be a waste to remove you."

"Then why not be my *sifu,* or teacher? That way, my smartness won't be wasted."

"That depends."

"Depends on what?"

Somchai took apart the rifle and put the parts back into the case before answering. "Not what. Depends on who."

"Who?"

"Your uncle. It's right that he should decide."

"It's my life."

"Yes, I mean no, we will still ask him."

With those words, Somchai opened the back door and let himself out into the dark night.

☆☆☆☆

Everyone, with the exception of Captain Neil Walker, was having a great time at the Christmas party held at the Officers' Mess.

He was perched as usual on one of the tall stools alongside the bar, nursing a gin and tonic by himself. Everyone else was gathered in groups, laughing and engaging in earnest conversations. The married officers had brought along their wives, some of whom were dancing gaily after someone played music from the jukebox. The thought of asking any of the women for a dance had never occurred to Captain Walker.

He caught sight of Police Lieutenant Richard Smith saying something to Rosemary, the pretty wife of Major David Cartwright. She got up and followed the Cockney upstart – a name Captain Walker had given the young officer behind his back – to the floor. Thinking of the Cockney upstart brought a flush to his florid face.

Ever since that incident where he had insulted the Cockney upstart to be rewarded by Major Cartwright punching him in the face, they often met in the Officers' Mess. Although they would pointedly ignore each other, and he would give both the major and the Cockney upstart his icy glare whenever they passed one another, Captain Walker couldn't help seething with fury within him over the humiliation of being socked by the major. He swore to himself that he would pay back Major Cartwright one of these days.

As for the Cockney upstart, he was convinced the bounder was purposely baiting him because each time that he was within hearing distance, that vulgar cad's speech would deliberately switch into the distinctive accent so hateful to Captain Walker's delicate ears. He remembered the other night while he was having his dinner when the Cockney upstart came in with Major Thomas Hamilton and sat just three tables away.

Captain Walker could still hear the Cockney upstart's voice saying loudly, "Once, on a patrol, we 'appened to come by a secret food dump in the jungle. Someone 'ad left sacks of rice for the bandits. Me first thought was to 'ike everything 'ome...'owever, me sergeant who 'ad more experience advised otherwise. According to 'im, it ain't right to take away another guy's belongings. What 'e advised was that we scrapped the 'air from young bamboo shoots to mix with the rice. This way, those bandits would suffer 'orrible stomach pain from eating the rice as the fine bamboo 'air would 'urt their intestines. And 'e was quite right because me commander later told me the same thing."

The other officers knew Police Lieutenant Smith was baiting Captain Walker, and were expectantly waiting for the two men to come to blows. But they knew too that they would be disappointed because unlike the time when he had false courage from being drunk, in his sober state, Captain Walker was afraid of the Police Lieutenant to confront him. In Captain Walker's ostrich-like mind, he rationalized that his refusal to face the Cockney upstart was not due to fear of the cad but due to his good breeding in not stooping to the bounder's low level and also not wishing to face the provost marshal's wrath again.

After a while, realizing he wasn't enjoying the party, he slipped off the stool. Having made up his mind to catch the ferry to cross over to Penang, where he thought he could perhaps have better luck in picking up someone

at the Hong Kong Bar* in Chulia Street, he gingerly
made his way to the door.

---

* Opened in 1920, the bar was a popular hangout for military servicemen. It was
gutted by fire in the early morning of September 14, 2004. It has since re-opened
albeit without its famed mementoes of photographs, plaques, badges, lifebuoys,
etc.

Nine

*J*ust a week before Mao Dong Po's seventeenth birthday, Somchai brought the young man to Pekan Siam.

All they had to do was to get out of the back door and walk a short distance past the railway tracks, and there was Pekan Siam. Like Padang Besar, with its rectangular design comprising rows of wooden shop houses, Pekan Siam looked just like any town out of a Hollywood western movie.

By that time, Dong Po had become quite an expert on Hollywood western from having watched many movies, mostly starring John Wayne. His favorite movie however was still *Shane* even though he didn't know the actor's name. It was only many years later that he discovered the actor's name was Alan Ladd. He also couldn't tell exactly why he preferred *Shane*. Perhaps, the storyline appealed to him. Or maybe, unlike the subsequent movies he had watched, it wasn't dubbed in Thai. It was so weird to hear John Wayne speaking fluent Thai on the silver screen.

On that day, Dong Po was however very eager to embrace Thai culture. He had been to Pekan Siam a few times but this occasion was rather special because

Somchai wanted the young man to enroll in a *Muay Thai* school.

It was after Somchai had a long talk with his uncle. At first, Dong Po's uncle was not too pleased to hear that his only nephew wanted to take up Somchai's profession as it had been his intention to eventually hand over his business to his nephew. But after seeing Dong Po's eagerness and determination, he agreed on two conditions.

His uncle leaned forward to whisper into the boy's ears. "First, my sister, that is, your mother must never know the truth. And second, you must promise never to harm any woman or child."

Though he was surprised to hear so many words coming from his usually taciturn uncle, Dong Po said solemnly, "I promise to both conditions."

A shadow of relief passed across his uncle's face and he turned to Somchai who took over. The Siamese said, "Good, now that's settled, I want to see you developed physically first. My boy, you shall take up *Muay Thai*."

"*Muay Thai?*"

"Some people erroneously called it Thai boxing. It's more than that," Somchai explained. "It's a form of close, hand-to-hand combat developed over the years as my countrymen had to defend Siam in the past from covetous enemies like the Burmese."

Walking past narrow alleys jammed with people, carts, rickshaws, bicycles, and even a couple of elephants, Somchai led Dong Po into a quieter lane. After a while, they came to a courtyard where a bald-headed man, who looked about fifty years' old, was watching two youngsters going about their physical exercises. The lads were about Dong Po's age.

The moment the man turned towards them, Somchai brought both his hands together to accord him a *wai* – the Thai greeting. The ever observant Dong Po followed suit as he silently caught on the high reverence which Somchai had given the man.

"This is the young man you'd told me about?" asked the bald-headed guy.

"Yes, *ajarn*," Somchai replied with bowed head, which once again alerted Dong Po to the status of the bald-headed man. Dong Po knew *ajarn* means teacher or master in Thai, same as he had been calling Somchai, *sifu*.

"It's easy for me to accept you as my disciple so long as you do not value your life too much," said the *ajarn*, looking directly at Dong Po. "Unlike other schools, we don't use safety gear like gloves. Instead we still go by the tradition of using lengths of cords to wrap around our fists. I feel it's better to get used to pain."

Dong Po, who had earlier been briefed by Somchai on how to behave in the presence of the *ajarn*, knelt and bowed his head. From the corner of his eye, he saw the *ajarn* nodding his head approvingly and heard him say: "*Muay Thai* is sometimes called the Art of the Eight Limbs because we use eight points of contact, that is to say, the two fists, two elbows, two knees and two feet."

The *ajarn* turned to say something to Somchai which Dong Po failed to catch, before returning to the young man, saying: "All right, you will start your training the day after tomorrow as we are closed tomorrow for New Year."

☆ ☆ ☆ ☆

A week after the New Year of 1955, Captain Neil Walker stumbled by chance onto a secret.

As he was going through the paperwork on his desk, he saw a sealed envelope. Picking it up, he was about to slit it opened when the name of the addressee suddenly caught his attention. It was for Major David Cartwright. The handwriting looked suspiciously soft, and Captain Walker guessed it was by a woman's hand.

Thinking that someone had mistakenly delivered the letter to his desk instead of the major's – his office was in the next block – Captain Walker thought it served his enemy right that he should just throw the envelope into the wastepaper basket under his desk. After all, nobody would be any wiser. But immediately after he had chucked the envelope into the wastepaper basket, he bent down again to retrieve it. A thought had occurred to him that he should open and read the contents before throwing it away.

Ten minutes later, he was in his own quarters where he set a kettle to boil. Another ten minutes passed before he held the envelope against the steam coming out from the kettle's spout.

When he returned to his office – all in, he was away from his desk for not more than half an hour – he leaned back in his chair and let out a low mirthless laugh. The more he thought of the letter he had read earlier, the broader he smiled. It was a good thing that he hadn't thrown the envelope away but had opened it to read its contents. Now he had a weapon against Major Cartwright. *Haven't I said I would pay you back one of these days? And now that day has come,* he thought with savage satisfaction.

Ten

To Mao Dong Po's dismay, the training was totally out of his expectation. He had imagined himself to turn overnight into an agile fighter who would use his eight limbs to demolish his foes.

Instead the first three months were mostly spent on body conditioning exercises, such as rope skipping, limbs stretching, and body weight resistance techniques which included his being used as a "mobile punching bag" for the other two students. "Mobile" means that he was allowed to duck or swerve to avoid being hit. Even then, his body was bruised all over.

When he complained to Somchai, the Siamese shrugged nonchalantly. "That's the best way to learn to dodge your enemies, my boy, or take their blows."

"But…"

"No but," said Somchai, holding up one hand. "On the day before accepting you as his disciple, the *ajarn* said to me that you may not be able to endure the hardship. I had told him then that only losers would complain and whine. I'd also told him that had I regarded you as a loser, I wouldn't have agreed to be your *sifu*."

In the fourth month, when the *ajarn* taught him the basics of kicking, to Dong Po's surprise, he was told to practice his kicks on a banana tree in a corner of the courtyard. Even though on many nights thereafter, he had to limp home to his uncle's shop, never once had he complained to Somchai who still turned up from time to time to use the shop as his entry or exit points. Instead, he consoled himself with reading about James Bond's latest exploits in *Moonraker*.

Two months later, Somchai turned up unexpectedly one night to watch his protégé who was at the moment sparring with one of the *ajarn*'s two other disciples. It was the first time the *ajarn* had allowed Dong Po to spar.

The Siamese lad truly lived up to his name, Virote, which means power as he was tall and burly. The knowledge of his being taller and bigger than Dong Po seemed to give Virote more confidence. Without uttering a sound, he feinted with a punch, and as the Chinese lad stepped back, raising both hands to block, the Siamese quickly followed with a right roundhouse kick aimed at the Dong Po's unprotected left. Instead of backing away, the Chinese lad stepped forward and in one same movement, brought both his left elbow and his left knee up. There was a dull sound of flesh hitting flesh and having successfully blocked his opponent's kick, Dong Po's right hand shot out, slamming into Virote's face. As the Siamese staggered, Dong Po moved in to slam his right elbow into the lad's jaw. The double blows stunned Virote that he reeled about for a while until the *ajarn* caught hold of his arm to steady him. Blood was streaming from Virote's nostrils and from a cut on his bruised lips.

When the *ajarn* signaled to Dong Po that the fight was over, the young man saw from the corner of his eyes that his *sifu* was smiling with approval.

☆☆☆☆

Two days after the Alliance Party – comprising the United Malays National Organization, the Malayan Chinese Association, and the Malayan Indian Congress won 51 of 52 seats in the country's first General Election in July 1955, which saw Tunku Abdul Rahman's appointment as Chief Minister of Malaya, a party was in full swing at the Officers' Mess.

The British officers were not celebrating the political triumph of the Tunku as the man was popularly called by the locals. They were throwing a farewell party for Police Lieutenant Richard Smith who would be leaving Malaya for good the following day as he had decided not to extend his contract. All the officers, except Captain Neil Walker, were at the farewell bash. The wives of the married officers were also there.

Rosemary, the pretty wife of Major David Cartwright was smiling sweetly and chatting animatedly with whoever was speaking to her, as she stood by her husband's side. But anyone looking at the major's drawn and strained face could guess something was troubling him. Police Lieutenant Smith had noticed the strain that had built up in his friend over the past few months but as the major wasn't about to tell, he thought better than to ask.

Unknown to everyone, Major Cartwright's troubles started some six months back when he was away in Kuala Lumpur to attend a meeting. It began when someone had carelessly dropped his mail at Captain Walker's desk. The latter had secretly opened the envelope and read its contents. Determined to get back at Major Cartwright for giving him the humiliating knock-out punch, Captain Walker had resealed the letter and thereafter brought it to the married quarters where Major Cartwright and his wife lived. It was the block next to his quarters.

He had initially wanted to send someone else to deliver the envelope but fretted that the person might keep it until the major was back from the outstation meeting to hand it to him. He next thought of slipping the envelope under the door but it occurred to him that a strong wind might blow the envelope away. No, Captain Walker told himself not to take any chance now that he had such an excellent weapon.

Hence, he had personally taken the envelope to Major Cartwright's home. After Rosemary, in answer to the door bell, had opened the door, Captain Walker had a ready speech for her: "Hi, Rosemary, I was on my way back to my quarters when I chanced upon this envelope on the pathway. As it was addressed to your husband, I thought the wind could have blown it away from your doorstep and since I'm passing by, I thought I should stop by to hand it to you."

After he walked off, he chuckled to himself. Everyone in the barracks knew how possessive Rosemary could be. He was sure that she would certainly be suspicious of the feminine handwriting on the envelope to open it even though it was addressed to her husband.

True enough, Rosemary had opened the envelope and after reading the letter contained therein, came to realize that her husband had been keeping a Chinese woman in Penang. As his mistress had missed her period, she had been to a doctor who had congratulated her for going to become a mother. With Major Cartwright being away attending a meeting in the capital, he hadn't been around to see the woman. Since all military personnel had been cautioned against disclosing information on their whereabouts, the major hadn't informed his mistress of his being away. She had tried to telephone her lover and frantic from her inability to reach him, she had written the letter to him.

Though he hadn't known all that had transpired the instant Major Cartwright walked into his home and saw the look on his wife's face, he knew something was terribly wrong. Where previously, she would happily flung herself into his arms and then they would dance around the small sitting room, Rosemary just stood there that evening quietly looking coldly at him. The moment she handed the letter to him, he knew the cat was out of the bag.

After reading the damning letter, he tried his utmost to convince Rosemary that it was just a casual fling and it was her whom he truly loved. His wife had calmly listened to him but hadn't said anything. By the time he had finished talking, it was quite late and all she said then was that she wanted to go to sleep as she was tired.

But when he tried to follow her into the bedroom, she had stopped him. "I want to sleep alone."

"Why?" he cried. "I've already promised you that I will end the affair. I don't feel anything for her. It was just a casual fling."

"Casual or not, I can't bear your nearness," she said. "I feel sordid."

He flushed a deep red. As he saw that her normally warm, passionate eyes had become icy cold and hostile, he turned his own imploring eyes away to look down on the floor.

Seeing her husband looking so down, her habitual tenderness towards him led Rosemary to say: "Maybe I just need some time. You must give me time to think things over."

Her words raised his hopes a bit. "All right, may I kiss you good night?"

She leaned towards him, though without her usual zest, and when he put both arms around her and tried to kiss her on the lips, she turned her face away. After he had kissed her on her cheek, she pushed him away and went into the bedroom.

Major Cartwright heaved a deep sigh and made a shake-down of the sofa in the sitting room. That was the first of many miserable nights he had slept alone. Ever since she had come to Malaya to join him, they had shared the same bed but from that night, she kept him out of their only bedroom. It was already coming to six months and there was still no sign of Rosemary letting him back into their bedroom and her life. She was quiet most times. Whenever she had to speak to him, she was polite. Such aloofness disturbed him more than if she had been angry and created a scene. It was simply unnatural.

Once, and only once, just a month ago, he had tried to draw her out of her shell, telling her, "We need to talk. It's not fair of you to still treat me in this manner."

"Please don't talk to me of fairness," Rosemary had then snapped at him. "Isn't it enough that I'm still here with you? Can't you see I need time?"

As it was at the back of his mind that she was right, and only time would turn her around to forgive him, Major Cartwright brightened and instinctively reached out for her hand.

"Don't touch me," she cried, snatching her hand away from his. "It would be bad enough if you had been with a white woman but you had to do it with a Chink. It's simply too awful to think you could be so disgustingly filthy."

She began to cry silently as he stood watching her helplessly with miserable eyes. After that day, he had left her alone.

It bothered him too that when friends visited them, or during those times when they came to be in the eyes of the public, Rosemary would appear to be her old cheerful self, speaking to him gaily like she used to do. But the moment they were alone, she would turn cold and distant again, often retiring to the bedroom, which he knew she locked from the inside. It was like she had become two persons.

Much as he had willed himself to be patient, he knew he was at the end of his tethers. He looked terribly strained and haggard and had lost much weight from having no interest in food. And nervous too, which was why he jumped when Police Lieutenant Smith came up from behind to place an arm on his shoulder.

"I don't know what's bothering you but seeing that I shall be leaving tomorrow, please look after yourself," said Police Lieutenant Smith.

"I'll be fine. I hope you'll have a jolly journey, old boy."

Eleven

*T*unku Abdul Rahman who won the election
the previous year to become the Chief Minister
of the Federation of Malaya, returned in triumph from
London on February 10, 1956. He had just successfully
negotiated for his country's independence, which he
announced would take place on August 31, the following
year.

On the night after the Tunku made the historical
announcement, Somchai came unexpectedly to the
Muay Thai class to look for his young protégé.

After a hurried conversation with the *ajarn*, Somchai
said curtly to Mao Dong Po, "Pack up, my boy."

The young man looked at his *sifu* in surprise but
having had previously learned from Somchai that he
should at all times obey his mentor without question,
he stripped off his T-shirt, damp with sweat from his
workout. Throwing it along with a towel into a small
bag, he put on a clean shirt, and went to the *ajarn* to give
him a respectful *wai* as he sought his leave. He thought
he saw a regretful look in the *ajarn's* eyes. Without much
thought, he turned and followed Somchai out of the
school.

As they were walking towards the town centre of Pekan Siam, Somchai announced: "I have told the *ajarn* that your lessons have to cease for a while."

The eighteen-year-old lad gasped in surprise. "But I haven't yet mastered the Art of the Eight Limbs."

"Yes, I mean no, when I enrolled you in the school, it was not my intention to turn you into a professional boxer. I just want you toughened up a bit. Anyway, it's only for a short while that you cease your training."

Somchai stopped suddenly to appraise Dong Po under the light of the street lamp. He nodded approvingly. "You have developed your muscles and from what I'd seen during that one bout you had with your fellow, I should say you're now capable of defending yourself. That's enough for me, my boy."

Having said those words, he walked on in silence until they had reached the stall of a beef-ball noodle vendor, when he declared, "I'm hungry. Let's have a little supper."

After the girl brought two bowls of soup noodles to their table, Dong Po took a small spoon to scoop condiment from four different bowls. Somchai who was doing the same, lifted his head and smiled at him. "I'm pleased that you have also become quite a good marksman, second to me, of course."

"I owe it to your coaching, Uncle Somchai."

The burly Siamese nodded. "But bear in mind, my boy, a rifle is used only when it is too dangerous to go near your quarry. Even then, it's also a risk to carry a rifle around as the authorities may stop to search you."

"How come you'd dared to carry yours in Malaya where an Emergency has already been declared?" asked Dong Po as the question had been on his mind for some time.

"Ahh, should I be stopped and searched, I have a letter from a high-ranking Siamese officer, informing that I am merely a courier for him."

"Will the British accept that letter?"

"They're only after the communists. Our military are strongly anti-communists and thereby regarded as useful allies to be courted and not trifled with."

Satisfied, Dong Po abruptly changed the subject. "When will I get my own pistol, Uncle Somchai?"

"Any time so long as you have the money to pay."

Seeing the dismayed look on his young protégé's face, Somchai laughed. "I will advance it against the income you will earn later when you're ready to assist me."

"Thank you, Uncle Somchai."

The older man was thoughtful for a moment. "I haven't yet decided which pistol is suitable for you."

Dong Po who had been practicing with Somchai's pistol, a US Army Colt.45, asked, "Can't I have the same pistol as yours?"

"A pistol must suit the user. I am bigger in size than you which is why my pistol fits me perfectly. On you, my boy, it will give you an unsightly bulge in the wrong place. You must remember that in our profession, we need to conceal our tools just as we can't afford to be too conspicuous."

After finishing his bowl of noodles, Somchai gulped down his full glass of *Singha* beer. As he wiped the froth from his lips, he said. "Perhaps I should get you a Beretta M1934. Being a small-caliber weapon, it allows for better concealment and is more accurate since it has less recoil."

"How do you know so much about guns, Uncle Somchai?"

The older man, who was about to strike a match to light a cigarette, frowned and said sternly: "If you want to be a professional, you must learn your trade. Start by knowing the tools."

Seeing the hurt look on his young protégé's face, Somchai's tone softened. "There's no end to learning, my boy. I came to know about the Beretta M1934 because it was the gun that was used to remove Mohandas Gandhi in 1948."

Although Dong Po was only ten at the time the Indian freedom leader was assassinated, he had later learned from Brother Duffy how Mahatma – the name he was popularly called – had cleverly taught his people to resist the British by passive non-cooperation.

Taking a sip of the *Singha* beer in his glass, he asked his *sifu*: "From what I'd heard, he was a good man. So wasn't it wrong to remove him?"

"No, I mean yes, a man like him is worth keeping and shouldn't be removed. But not everyone thinks the way we do, my boy. To many of our competitors, it doesn't matter whether a quarry is good or bad. All they care is the money for removing a problem."

Dong Po studied the swarthy Siamese for a moment. "But, Uncle Somchai, how do we know whether those we are removing are worth keeping?"

"As my childhood friend had taught me, it is important to know yourself and know your enemy."

"You've a childhood friend?"

"He's a *taikor*, you know, the term means big brother and is used to address the head of a secret society," said Somchai, who looked like he wanted to add something more, but stopped. "Come, finish your drink. I'm taking you elsewhere."

Somchai led him to a bar, where shortly after he ordered more *Singha*, two young girls came to sit with them. They were pretty but in a cheap way. Dong Po couldn't tell whether it was the effect of their continued drinking, or the smoke as his mentor was not only puffing like a chimney but had encouraged him to smoke every now and then by pushing the round tin of *Players* towards him. And each time, he had gamely taken a cigarette out of the tin to smoke. Or was it the intoxicating presence of female company?

All he knew was that he was soon lying on a bed, not his own, and he was trying to get up but a girl who was crouching over him leaned closer until he could smell her cheap perfume. He remembered asking her, "Why are we both not wearing our clothes?" when he felt the twin globes of her dark breasts flattening themselves hard against his body. And then he felt her warm wetness engulfing him. The sound from the bracelets on her wrists and ankles was at first gentle tinkling but soon became loud rattling. Caught in the excitement, he struggled frantically against her until he felt a spasm going through him.

☆ ☆ ☆ ☆

Stretched out on his makeshift bed in the sitting room, Major David Cartwright stared into the darkness as he felt despair and at the same time, relief. A bottle of Glenfiddich was by his side.

He felt despair because his wife, Rosemary, had left him earlier that night. After sending her to the Butterworth railway station where she had taken the night train to Kuala Lumpur, and from there, would catch a plane to London, he had returned alone to his empty quarters. It was empty all right. He could even feel the emptiness deep in his heart. Instead of going to sleep on the bed in the bedroom, which before the terrible crisis, he had shared with his wife, he had by sheer habit gone to the sofa where he had been sleeping for slightly more than a year.

Strangely enough, he also felt a surge of relief flowing through him as the past year had been sheer hell. Knowing it had been just as hard, if not more, on Rosemary, he blamed himself for his folly. His affair had begun on the night after his wife had gone on a guided tour with the wives of the other officers to Singapore. He had crossed over to Penang with some of the chaps. They had gone to a nightclub in Magazine Road, and there, he had met Jenny Heng. She was one of the cabaret girls, whom the *mamasan* had sent over to entertain them.

That night he drank so much that he had passed out. When he woke up the next morning, he found Jenny sleeping by his side. She later told him that as all his friends were themselves too tipsy to bother about him, she had brought him to the Cathay Hotel in Leith Street, where they had thereafter spent the night. Since then, Major Cartwright had become a regular patron at the nightclub, and so began an illicit relationship with Jenny behind his wife's back.

As he took a swig direct from the bottle by his side, he thought ruefully that he had been a damned fool. It served him right to lose his wife. Thinking of her, in his mind, he saw Rosemary as she was before this crisis had erupted. That oval face, soft green eyes, and always that lock of hair falling over her forehead, which gave Rosemary such an alluring look. Though she was six years younger than him, she had taken charge of his household and finance as though she was years ahead of him.

I've been so beastly and foolish, it serves me right. But it has been so awfully unfair to Rosemary, he thought as his mood began to swing back to despair. *How could I have been so blind in risking it all for Jenny?*

Jenny was three years older than him. Now that he thought about the Chinese woman, she was no doubt attractive but it was more on account of the powder and rouge, unlike Rosemary's natural beauty. During those times when he saw her without make-up, she looked quite plain. However, he had to admit that her permissiveness as a woman made her most fun to be with in bed. While he had to be careful with Rosemary, who was quite prim and proper, Jenny was however game to any of his suggestions, which were things he would never dream of suggesting to his wife.

But once out of bed when the sex was over, Jenny would be most dull and boring. It was not so much her inability to converse fluently with him in his language but more over her poor grasp of general knowledge. That was why after the row with his wife had begun, he had immediately sent Jenny a cheque for a generous sum of money along with a note of apology that she won't be seeing him again. Immediately after receiving his cheque and note, Jenny had telephoned him in his office and given him an earful of rather unladylike language.

Seeing how he was able to cope with Jenny's wrath, he wished Rosemary had likewise flared up. It was not so much for his own sake but more for his wife because he knew Rosemary had suffered more strain from her attempts to contain her wrath over his betrayal. That was the reason he hadn't objected when she told him about her intention to return to England. He had also accepted her request to see her off only up to the Butterworth railway station and not follow her all the way to the Sungai Besi aerodrome in Kuala Lumpur.

Major Cartwright took another gulp from the bottle. *Her train should be halfway to Kuala Lumpur by now,* he thought. *Is she also thinking of me the way I'm thinking of her? Is she thinking with fondness the good times we'd shared or being filled instead with disgust and hatred over*

my beastliness? With those thoughts, and the effect of
the whiskey, he began to drift off into a troubled sleep.

Twelve

When Mao Dong Po woke up, it was still dark.

From the faint wedge of moonlight slicing through the blinds, he saw the silhouette of a naked woman on the bed he was sleeping. Hastily, he got up and dressed.

The moment he stepped out of the room, he tensed from sensing someone's presence in the hall. He relaxed when heard a familiar voice. "I was wondering how long it would take for you to wake up, my boy."

Turning to the direction of the voice, he sleepily murmured the Thai greeting, *"Sawadee."*

A light flared as Somchai struck a match to light a cigarette. "Did you enjoy the girl?"

Though he had difficulty finding a chair in the darkness, Dong Po was grateful for the cover of darkness as he could feel his face blushing. "I'm not sure."

His *sifu* chuckled. "You're not sure? I bet you were still a virgin until last night. Am I right?"

"I've kept away from women all these years," said the young man as he lowered himself on a chair.

"As I'd said, you're a smart lad. In our profession, we cannot afford to get emotionally entangled with any woman. But, if any time you feel the need, there are places like this where you can buy the time and body of any woman you want. Just don't get serious over any of them."

They were quiet for a while. In the darkness, Dong Po watched the red tip of his *sifu's* cigarette glowed from time to time until he grew drowsy. Somchai's next words caught him totally off-guarded. "Captain Neil Walker is now in Butterworth."

Dong Po suddenly became wide awake. "You've found him."

"Yes, I mean no, it was my childhood friend, the *taikor* who had found him," said Somchai, who immediately corrected himself, "No, I mean yes, it was Ya Loong's men who discovered the whereabouts of the captain."

As the young man sat up, Somchai continued, "From what Ya Loong had told me, this Captain Walker often crossed over to Penang to drink at a certain bar. I think it is possible for you to remove him, my boy."

Though Dong Po had fantasized countless times about avenging his father, at that moment, tried as he would, he had no idea as to what he should do next.

It was as though Somchai could read his young protégé's thoughts because he said: "You need a plan. If I were you, I'll go to Penang, say tomorrow. Tell your mother that you're going to be away for a while on business for me. Your uncle and I will back you up. Once in Penang, find a place to stay. As we have to be somewhat invisible in our profession, find a hotel or lodging house that is discreet. Best if it is located near the Hong Kong Bar in Chulia Street."

"Hong Kong Bar?"

"The *taikor* told me that Captain Walker goes to the Hong Kong Bar almost every night ever since he was posted to Butterworth."

"Shall I remove him there?"

"Yes, I mean no, you must bide your time and move only when the opportunity presents itself. Unless there's no other way, never remove a quarry where there are witnesses around as they may later finger you. Take your time to scout out the terrain until you know the area well enough to be able to strike the moment an opportunity presents itself and also to escape."

"May I borrow your pistol, Uncle Somchai?"

"Yes, I mean no, I've already told you that my gun's not suitable for you. I shall be picking up a pistol for you later today. That's why I'd advised you to set out tomorrow."

By that time, as the ray from the morning sun had begun lighting up the room, Somchai got up. "Let's go, my boy. I have to shop around for a pistol for you while you have to pack up for the trip."

☆☆☆☆

The sunlight had already come through the sitting room's open window when Major David Cartwright woke up with a splitting headache. As the bright glare in the room hurt his eyes, he felt the pulses on both sides of his forehead pounding like twin hammers.

He tried pressing his hands against his temples to lessen the pain but it failed to help. When he tried to get up, he realized a foul taste in his mouth. Glancing at his wristwatch, he saw it was already eleven-thirty. And then it all came flooding back to him. The thought that his wife had left him caused him so much distress that he had to lay his head back against the pillow. He closed his eyes and thought Rosemary, having had arrived at the Kuala Lumpur railway station some two hours ago, should now be waiting for her flight which was scheduled to take off at 12:40 p.m. from the Sungai Besi aerodrome.

Catching sight of the nearly empty bottle, he took hold of it and placed it in his mouth. After he felt the fiery liquid flowing down his throat, he sat up. His eyes went to the telephone and for a few minutes, he willed the instrument to ring. *A last reprieve for the condemned man,* he thought, before breaking into a giggle. The giggle gave way to sobbing when he recollected how Rosemary, before boarding the train the previous night, had turned to look at him. He thought then as he thought now that there was a tortured look in those green eyes, like she was torn between wanting to say something comforting to him, and yet at the same time, wanted to say something hurtful.

After his sobbing had subsided, he drained whatever was left in the bottle. He got up abruptly, swaying a bit on his feet. Looking at his watch again, he saw it was already *Tiffin* time. Knowing he would find Captain

Neil Walker at the Officers' Mess, he walked unsteadily out of his quarters.

As he had anticipated, the moment he lurched into the Officers' Mess, he saw Captain Walker in the midst of shoveling what was left of the Lancashire hotpot into his mouth. The moment Major Cartwright came near to his table, some sixth sense warned the stout man who looked up and immediately shuffled to his feet.

Major Cartwright tried to focus his eyes at the captain and wondered whether it was he or the other guy who was weaving. When he spoke, he realized his voice sounded shaky. "You've done a fine thing."

"What do you mean?" demanded Captain Walker belligerently.

"Thanks to your dastardly act, Rosemary had left me."

"I don't understand what you're talking about."

"Come off it, man," said the major, his lips quivering. "You'd to deliver that damned letter to her."

"Oh, you mean that," Captain Walker said. "It wasn't what you think. I was just doing you a service by returning a letter that I came across on the road."

"I can't imagine you to be so kind," Major Cartwright said with some sarcasm. "You're a despicable cad."

"Really, old boy, I think that's a most improper observation," exclaimed Captain Walker, and seeing his enemy's unsteadiness on his feet, he felt embolden to add "You brought it upon yourself. The thought of an officer of Her Majesty's Armed Forces cohabiting with a

Chink woman is enough for me to puke. No wonder your wife had left you."

"Why you…you bastard," said Major Cartwright who was livid with rage. "I'll kill you."

It was fortunate for the major that Captain Gerald Munro, who was among the officers having their meals in the Officers' Mess, had come close enough to grab hold of him. At the same time, Major Thomas Hamilton seized Captain Walker who was about to throw a punch at Major Cartwright. They had both seen Major Cartwright making his unsteady entry into the Officers' Mess. By now, almost everyone knew about what had happened to the major's marriage.

As Captain Munro led Major Cartwright away, the latter looked at his watch. It was 12:40 p.m. *Well, goodbye, my love,* he thought resignedly.

Thirteen

The moment he opened the small wooden box and saw the pistol, Mao Dong Po couldn't help being reminded of his long departed father.

Many years ago, just after the war was over, when he was eight years' old, his father had carved a piece of wood into the shape of a gun for him. It was his first toy. Mao Chen Lin had then gravely told him: "It was dangerous even to possess a toy gun like this last year as those yellow dwarfs may mistaken it for the real thing to shoot or worse, arrest whoever was holding it. Even now as we're still living in dangerous times, I wonder whether I should be giving you such a toy. But then boys will always be boys."

Now, as he took the Beretta out of the box, testing its weight and feel in his grip, he thought even as an adult, he was still like a boy from being thrilled over owning a gun of his own. And he also thought his *sifu* was, in some ways, like the father he had lost.

"We're living in troubled times. So be very careful not to be caught with this pistol or you may be mistakenly shot for a communist guerilla," Somchai said.

He even sounded like my father, thought Dong Po. *But unlike my father, my sifu is not one given to talking much of himself. That's why I still know so little about him.*

Somchai put a cigarette to his lips and then struck a match to light it up. After he took a long pull, he said: "I should go with you on this mission but then, it's something personal, which you have to do on your own."

Seeing his protégé nodding his head, Somchai drew a small envelope from his pocket and retrieved a photograph. It showed three men. "This photograph showed the quarry with two of his fellow officers. But my friend, Ya Loong, told me he doesn't get along well with his comrades who seemed to shun him."

"How did your friend get to know so much, Uncle Somchai?" asked Dong Po as he scanned the faces, and immediately spotted his enemy even though the guy had put on weight.

"Ya Loong is a very resourceful man. He did favors for many people, who in turn, would readily do favors for him."

"I ought to thank him when all this is over."

"Yes, I mean no, you don't have to. It is enough that I owe him for this favor," Somchai said. "No need that you should owe him as well. I rather he doesn't know too much about you, my boy."

Hearing those words from his mentor, Dong Po thought it odd and looked at the swarthy Siamese reflectively.

If Somchai knew his protégé was curious, he didn't show it. Instead, he said: "Oh, there's one more thing you should know about Captain Walker. He prefers young boys than women."

☆☆☆☆

A week later, Captain Walker did something which was quite uncharacteristic of him: He fished in his pocket for a coin to throw to a beggar.

Though there were many vagabonds waiting for the ferry commuters as they came out of Kedah Pier, the particular fellow was more persistent than the rest in following him out to the road where he hailed a trishaw. The Englishman liked to see persistence in people, something he insisted on being unable to vouch for his troopers who, he claimed were ever ready to throw in the towel.

Besides, Captain Walker was in a euphoric mood. Ever since he got his own back against Major David Cartwright, he had been walking on cloud nine. And now, as he happened to recall the good time he had with the young boy the previous night, he felt on top of the world.

For a brief moment, his face darkened as he remembered missing the last ferry to Penang due to his Commanding Officer's insistence that he finished the report which he was late in submitting. As he was unable to go to the island to drink at the Hong Kong Bar, he had instead gone to the Butterworth's red light district. It turned out to be a blessing in disguise.

After wandering aimlessly about the area, he came across The Happy Bar. When he walked into the dimly lit room, he saw a long bar manned by a Chinese bartender. He walked right up to the long bar and after perching himself on a high stool, he ordered a gin and tonic.

Casting a casual look around the room, he saw a few patrons seated on cane chairs by some of the dozen or so small round tables. The juke box was playing one of Elvis Presley's latest hits, *Heartbreak Hotel.*

When he turned to reach out for his drink which the bartender had placed on the long bar, a Eurasian girl came to sit down beside him.

"Care for some company, darling?" she asked.

Glaring at her, he said stiffly, "No."

"No problem, sweetheart," the girl smiled and went off in search of a more agreeable patron.

Captain Walker sat sipping his drink and smoking a cigarette when another girl, a Chinese this time, wearing a tight-fitting dress, walked slowly past him.

The bartender, who brought him another drink, looked meaningfully at him and raised an inquiring eyebrow in the direction of the girl.

The Englishman said brazenly: "I prefer young boys."

The bartender looked puzzled for a few seconds and then grinned broadly as comprehension dawned on him. Though he had heard from his colleagues about the strange tastes of the white men, this was the first time he had actually been asked to procure a young boy. "If you don't mind waiting a short while, sir, I'm sure my colleague can find a pretty young boy for you."

Captain Walker nodded his head. The bartender snapped his fingers whereby one of the two Chinese men that Captain Walker had seen slouching in the far corner came over. The two Chinese had a rapid exchange of words, at the end of which, the guy whom Captain Walker had figured to be a bouncer, grinned insolently at him and said, "No problem. Wait maybe ten minutes, okay?"

The ten minutes turned out to be close to an hour. But the guy had indeed brought back a sweet looking boy.

Fourteen

*A*s the trishaw crossed Pitt Street into Chulia Street, Captain Neil Walker licked his lips. The forty-five minutes' wait and the money those Chinks charged him for the drinks, the boy, and the use of an upstairs room were certainly well spent. In the dark recess of his mind, he could still hear the young boy's scream.

He had thought of going back to The Happy Bar again that night. But on second thought, considering the seediness of the joint and the absence of other white servicemen, he thought it unsafe. *Well, I may go there again one of these nights,* he thought.

Unknown to the Englishman, when he alighted from the trishaw and reached for his wallet to pay off the rider, a Chinese youth was watching him from across the street.

☆ ☆ ☆ ☆

Mao Dong Po had kept the Englishman under surveillance over the past week. Every night he had patiently stood there waiting for his quarry. Though he had learned from Somchai about the necessity of patience in their profession, it was nonetheless his good fortune that those tailors who had chosen to congregate at that particular row along Chulia Street, closed shops early. If not, he wouldn't have dared to stand there to look out for his quarry since the tailors or their workers would surely grow suspicious of him and report his presence to the authorities.

Throughout the week, it was only the previous night that the Englishman had failed to show up. But it didn't matter. Tonight was just as good as any should the opportunity present itself. As he had done on those other nights, he crossed the street to check out the bar. On entering the bar whose walls were packed with plaques, badges, framed photographs and even navy lifebuoys, Dong Po was delighted to find the bar not so crowded that night. His eyes lit up when he saw his quarry sitting alone by himself at a small table in the far corner.

He walked towards the captain, who on hearing his approaching footsteps, turned to look at him. The Englishman was delightfully surprised to find a slim young Chinese wearing a stylishly-cut silk shirt, smiling invitingly at him. Dong Po, who had been well briefed about Captain Walker's peculiar taste, had earlier made that shirt at one of the tailors across the Hong Kong Bar just for this occasion. He knew that with his boyish look, if he dressed the part, he would look even more effeminate and alluring.

Seeing the captain gawking at him, Dong Po smiled sweetly and asked softly in a low voice, "Would you mind if I join you?"

Captain Walker couldn't believe his luck – the sweet boy actually could speak his language. He gallantly stood up and offered Dong Po a chair. At the same time, the Englishman's eyes swept the room. He was relieved to find no one from his barracks there that night as it wouldn't be rum for him to be seen with a sweet young boy. Such things must be done as discreetly as possible.

And so the captain came to a decision. Smiling at the adorable darling before him, he proposed, "Why don't we go somewhere else? I know a cozy place where we can be alone."

"That sounds like a gorgeous idea."

Captain Walker felt a tingle of excitement. He quickly downed his drink in a single gulp, paid his bill, and ushered his young companion out of the bar.

Fifteen

*S*omchai had at first objected to the plan which Mao Dong Po laid before him on the night before setting out for Penang.

He had objected again on the day after Dong Po had arrived in Penang. Dong Po had telephoned his *sifu* from a public telephone booth beside the fire station* near the junction of Penang Road and Tek Soon Street. Somchai had on many occasions cautioned him about bored or inquisitive telephone operators who could easily eavesdrop into people's conversation by quoting his favorite Thai proverb, *"Kum-pang mee hu, pra-tu mee tar"* meaning "Walls have ears, doors have eyes." As such, Dong Po was most careful with his choice of words.

"Uncle, just to let you know I've arrived safely." No name must ever be mentioned over the telephone, remembered Dong Po of his *sifu's* lessons.

"Good, have you met the customer?"

"I thought I should check him out first before making contact."

---

* The fire station had made way for the 65-storey KOMTAR Tower since the late 1970s.

"That's a clever thing to do, my boy. But I still think you should have listened to me about sending a telegram to the customer instead of meeting him face to face."

Dong Po smiled, knowing his mentor was referring to the use of the rifle. Indeed, Somchai was most insistent on the night when he handed a pistol to his protégé. He had then told Dong Po: "Take my rifle instead of this pistol. That fellow's an experienced soldier. As you're still new to the business, it's very dangerous for you to confront him face to face."

His mentor's urgent tone brought him back to the present moment, and he heard Somchai saying: "It's still not too late for you to send the customer a telegram."

"No, Uncle. I really want to meet the customer to look him in the eyes."

That was the only telephone call he had made to his *sifu*.

☆ ☆ ☆ ☆

And now, on this night, seeing the sheer terror in Captain Neil Walker's pale blue eyes, Dong Po knew he had made the right decision.

They had earlier left the Hong Kong Bar. Anxious to satiate his lust, the Englishman had impatiently waved at a passing trishaw and ordered the rider to take them to a hotel in Leith Street even though the hotel was within walking distance.

The captain had often stayed overnight in this hotel to recover from his drunken stupor or to discreetly enjoy the company of any young boy he had picked up. Thus, most of the staff knew him by sight. Like those other times, a receptionist discreetly handed him a room key without subjecting him to fill this or that form. All those administrative matters could be done later. After all, the British officer was a gentleman who had all the while promptly paid his bills without fail.

After locking the door behind him, Captain Walker stood for a moment to appraise his latest find. He licked his lips and said hoarsely, "You're beautiful."

"Why don't you take a shower first?" suggested Dong Po coyly. "You will feel more comfortable. Come to think of it, the longer the wait, the more the thrill and pleasure."

The words held so much infinite promise to the Englishman that he felt himself getting an erection.

"All right, wait for me, love," he said and quickly disappeared into the bathroom.

A few minutes later, when Captain Walker hastily emerged with nothing other than a bath towel wrapped around his fleshy waist, he was shocked to see the lad pointing a silenced pistol at him.

"W-what?" gasped the Englishman as he blinked in disbelief from having been caught completely off his guard. But being an experienced soldier, he recovered very fast. "The money's in my wallet."

"This isn't a robbery."

The captain was watching the Chinese youth carefully now, his eyes wary. "Then what do you want?"

"I'm here to settle account for Mao Chen Lin," said Dong Po who could feel his own heart beating very fast.

"Mao Chen Lin?" asked the captain, frowning from trying to remember. The name however meant nothing to him though he knew that it should.

Seeing the Englishman's puzzled expression, Dong Po added, "You'd ordered his execution in a village near Batang Kali on November 6, 1951."

A look of comprehension flashed across the captain's face, and that was when he felt fear for the first time. Knowing his end was near, he stammered. "I-I was j-just doing my job. It w-was n-nothing personal."

"Indeed. As you hadn't given my father a fair chance, neither shall I," said Dong Po in a voice filled with contempt and hatred before squeezing the trigger.

☆ ☆ ☆ ☆

Since there was no moonlight that night, it was very dark when Major David Cartwright woke up from his drunken stupor. As he stirred, he found he was lying on the bed he used to share with his wife. With a cry, he hurriedly got up from the bed. *I shouldn't sleep on her bed,* he thought. *Rosemary wouldn't like it at all as I'm filthy. She won't want me to dirty her bed.*

Under his breath, he cursed those guys he had earlier been drinking with at the Officers' Mess. They were probably the ones who had carried him home after finding that he had passed out. And not knowing that he had all the while been sleeping on the sofa in the living room, they had dumped him on the large bed in the bedroom. *If Rosemary had found me sleeping on her bed, there would be an awful row,* he thought before being alerted by a sound. *It must be Rosemary coming home.*

Major Cartwright groped his way as he weaved unsteadily on his feet through the darkness towards the door of his quarters. He eagerly turned the doorknob and opened the door, expecting to find his wife had come home to him. But the moment the door opened to show no one there, the realization struck him that it was already more than a week since Rosemary had left him to return to England.

He stumbled blindly back into the house, and despite all his earlier misgivings, this time headed straight for the bedroom. Flinging himself back on the bed, he clenched his fists. What had started as the gasping of a wounded beast soon turned into loud, painful sobs. A while later, his crying subsided and the violent attack of hysterics was over. Once again he got up and went about to search for another bottle of whiskey which he kept somewhere in the house.

Sixteen

fter killing Captain Neil Walker, Mao Dong Po's immediate thought was to flee from the room.

Though he had begun trembling uncontrollably after his hated enemy tumbled to the tiled floor, he willed himself to suppress his body reaction. He took a few deep breaths to steady himself. When he felt calmer, he removed the silencer before stashing the pistol into his waistband concealed under his shirt. After that, he looked around him to try remembering any spot that he might had unwittingly touched.

Satisfied that he hadn't left any fingerprint on any object in the room, he used his handkerchief to open the door and walked out. When he reached the bottom of the stairs, he saw several sailors who were checking in. He casually walked past them.

Somchai had taught him well: "Never attract attention to yourself by running. Best is to mingle with a crowd. If not, just walk calmly away."

It was fortunate for him that the sailors were keeping the sole receptionist busy. Even then, his guilty conscience made it seemed to him that everyone was staring accusingly at him. He took a deep breath and once again, willed his limbs to stop trembling.

Leaving the hotel's courtyard, he walked a short distance down Leith Street towards Penang Road before turning left into Muntri Street to get back to the quiet hotel in Love Lane, where he was staying. The moment he entered the small shabby room he had rented, as he reached out to switch on the light, he sensed rather than saw the man sitting in the darkness on the old sofa by the window.

"So, you've finally removed the problem, my boy," a voice said pleasantly just as Dong Po pulled out his pistol, and in the same motion, cocked the pistol.

In the light, he saw Somchai grinning at him. "Put that gun away before you accidentally shoot me."

Dong Po was about to keep the pistol when he remembered. "Oh, no, I've forgotten to discard the gun."

His *sifu* scoffed. "I've never taught you that. It's what they'd taught you in those fancy thrillers you've been reading or the movies you've been watching, my boy. According to those *farang* experts, after removing someone, you must throw away the weapon lest you get caught with it and the ballistic tests pointed to you."

Dong Po knew *farang* means foreigners in the Siamese language. What he didn't understand was his mentor's logic, and so he asked: "Wouldn't it be appropriate to discard a weapon after use?"

"Yes, I mean no," Somchai said. "As our weapons are obtained from underground sources, they may already have been tainted for all we know. To discard them would be a sheer waste of money."

As an afterthought, Dong Po asked, "How did you get into my room? How did you know I'm staying here?"

The Siamese sighed, "Looks like I will have to teach you next how to pick a lock. Of course, I know where you stay since I have been following you around the past few days. You sure need to learn how to spot and shake off a tail."

"You have been following me around?"

"I was watching you while your eyes were glued on the quarry. In the day time when you weren't on the quarry's tail, I was there following you around as you familiarized yourself with the streets in the area. I even stood beside you on the day when you were browsing books at the secondhand book stalls* along Tek Soon Street but you were too engrossed to notice."

"You were actually tailing me, Uncle Somchai?" asked the younger man in amazement. "Why?"

"You don't think I would let you be in any danger, do you? And if you still have any doubt as to whether I was really tailing you, well, after Tek Soon Street, you walked towards the Great World Park* but stopped a while to look at those Indians drinking at the toddy shop*. Thereafter you had lunch in a shop in Gladstone Road and after that in seeking a shortcut across a plank over the canal* in Prangin Road, you stumbled and nearly fell

---

* All these mentioned places – the secondhand book stalls, the Great World Park, the toddy shop, and the canal – later made way for the KOMTAR Tower and the Prangin Mall.

into the foul water. At the junction of Penang Road and Burmah Road, you stopped at a book stall to buy a book. I think the title of the book is *Diamonds are Forever*. With that purchase, you came back to this room to enjoy the book."

Dong Po looked at the older man in awe. "Were you there when I shot him?"

"No, I mean yes, I was actually outside the door of Room 244. I only walked away after hearing the muffled phut of your gun's silencer."

There was a brief silence, and then Dong Po swallowed and took a deep breath before saying, "Thank you, Uncle Somchai."

For the first time, the Chinese youth saw something like embarrassment flashed across his mentor's face even though he waved a hand airily in dismissal. "Don't give it a thought, my boy. I believe you will do the same for me if it was the other way around."

Taking a puff from the cigarette he had just lighted, the swarthy-looking man grinned. "So how did you feel about removing the captain?"

"Happy and frightened," Dong Po said after a pause. "I'm glad that I have finally avenged my father's death. But after the shooting, I mean, removal of the guy, I felt scared. It came like a rush to me, like it isn't right of me to kill, I mean remove…I felt afraid of getting caught."

Somchai nodded sympathetically. "It's a normal feeling. Now you must learn to forget, my boy. Tell yourself, it's over and done with. Life has to go on, with new things to learn."

Seeing his young protégé nodding his head, Somchai said: "We'll go home tomorrow."

☆☆☆☆

Chief Inspector Robert Chuah looked with some dismay at the nude body of Captain Neil Walker. Given the police officer's fondness of food, the whiteness of the dead army officer's fleshy body reminded him of the cooked fowls hanging in a Hainanese chicken rice shop. That, plus the sight of blood and gore were enough to spoil his rather voracious appetite and keep him from his favorite food for some time.

He was also dismayed because he had just been transferred to the homicide team only yesterday. Previously, he was responsible for only those cases involving secret societies. It was a job he had held for many years which saw his rapid rise from wearing three stripes to three pips.

But his greatest dismay was to learn the deceased's identity from the papers in his wallet. As a British army officer, he came under the jurisdiction of either the Royal Military Police or the Regimental Police. This meant having to work with one of the *ang mohs*, literarily meaning red hair which the Hokkien-speaking Penang Chinese used to refer to the white men. And *ang mohs* could be quite touchy and difficult to work with, just like his boss, Superintendent John Conlay. Well, he would have to talk to him. *Better let one ang moh deal with another ang moh,* he thought.

But as he stood up to walk away, he vaguely recollected that many years ago he had seen someone who was also shot so neatly in between the eyes. Could it be the handiwork of the same killer?

Seventeen

*O*n the second morning after Mao Dong Po's return to his uncle's shop in Padang Besar, Somchai walked coolly into the shop the moment his uncle opened the shop's front door.

"May I borrow your nephew to accompany me to breakfast?" the Siamese asked, nodding casually at Dong Po who had quickly greeted his *sifu* as he walked down the stairs.

Dong Po's uncle shrugged. "It's still early. I can handle the shop myself."

Without a word, Dong Po followed his *sifu* and they walked a short distance before Somchai handed a newspaper to Dong Po. "The news of Captain Walker's removal is found in page five."

When they reached the noodle stall in the alley beside the market, the burly Siamese went to a corner table where they could have a degree of privacy and where he could have a wider view to observe the environment. The elderly lady who manned the stall took Somchai's order. Without looking at the woman, Dong Po who was busy reading the newspaper told her that he wasn't eating.

After the woman had left to prepare his meal, Somchai said, "It was reported that the captain was found shot in the face."

Noticing the accusing tone, Dong Po looked up at his *sifu's* swarthy face. "Had I done anything wrong, Uncle Somchai?"

"No, I mean yes, if you shoot a quarry in the face, you may end up not getting paid."

"What do you mean?"

"You may end up not getting paid because if you messed up the quarry's face, the client who ordered the removal may subsequently argue that you have removed the wrong guy."

"But I hadn't missed. It was a clean shot. Here, let me read the newspaper report to you, "Captain Walker was shot in between the eyes." No messing up of his face. They'd identified him correctly."

"Well, I'm just telling you, my boy, that if you were to mess up a quarry's face, you can forget about getting paid."

"Uncle Somchai, you had told me that you once removed a problem for your friend, Ya Loong, by shooting the man right in between the eyes."

"Yes, I mean no, you don't shoot them in between the eyes unless you're an experienced marksman like me," Somchai hissed. "Don't go being defensive on me, my boy. If we're going to work together, you must learn to accept criticism or we won't get anywhere."

Dong Po who was about to retort that he was as good a marksman as his *sifu,* saw his mentor's face and decided to keep his mouth shut.

Taking his young protégé's silence as having been suitably chastised, Somchai added, "At that time, I was using a smaller-caliber pistol. Had I used my Colt.45, the impact would have blown the quarry's skull apart. In that case, no face, no pay."

After that, both men were quiet as the food vendor brought a bowl of noodles to their table for Somchai.

Seizing the opportunity to change the subject, and also unsure of himself, Dong Po asked: "So what will happen now, Uncle Somchai?"

"My friend, Ya Loong, will throw some fishes to the police."

"Fishes?"

"Yes, I mean no, not real fishes," the Siamese said. "It's just something to keep the hounds off the scent. Ya Loong will misdirect the authorities by making them look at the wrong thing and in the wrong place."

The young man tried his hardest not to laugh aloud after hearing his *sifu's* explanation about the fishes. Knowing he was talking about "red herrings", Dong Po coughed a few times to cover his mirth. He quickly asked: "How will your friend do that?"

"As he knows the captain wasn't well liked, he will pass that bit of information to the police officer who is investigating the case. After all, he happened to be a friend of the *taikor,* whose information had helped to gain his promotion from a sergeant to chief inspector over the years."

After taking leave of his mentor, Dong Po returned to the shop where he showed the newspaper report to his uncle. .

His uncle read and grunted, "Your father can now rest in peace."

"Yes, he will rest in peace," agreed Dong Po as he started toward the staircase.

His uncle called out, "I don't think that's a good idea."

Dong Po stopped to look at his uncle who said softly, "If your mother read that report, she may put one and one together and realize the true nature of your recent trip to Penang."

The young man sighed.

☆ ☆ ☆ ☆

Another man was also sighing.

As Chief Inspector Robert Chuah had predicted, the British Army had sent over a Captain Gerald Munro who was in charge of the barracks' military police. At their first meeting at the Police Contingent Headquarters in Penang Road, Captain Munro had quite naturally adopted a patronizing attitude upon seeing that Chief Inspector Chuah was a Chinese. The chief inspector thought the *ang moh* was probably thinking, "These locals won't have the brains to solve cases like this one." But as he was used to such patronizing from other white men, it hadn't bothered him at all.

What bothered him was that the white man had just told him, "I shall take charge of the investigation regarding the murder of Captain Neil Walker. You will assist me by making all resources available to me."

As the captain's knowledge seemed to be confined mostly to pulling in unruly or drunken servicemen when they were let loose in town, or hauling up anyone for insubordination which the chief inspector interpreted as pissing off the higher-ranking officers, his words were enough to make him sigh.

Captain Munro misinterpreted the chief inspector's sigh because he said agreeably, "It's quite a horrid case. I mean it's awfully hard to imagine that anyone could simply go around shooting a British officer in a city which is on an island none other than Penang."

Not wishing to get drawn into a meaningless discourse, Chief Inspector Chuah decided to lead the Englishman a little.

"For every murder there ought to be a motive, as we both know," the chief inspector hastily added the last four words so as to include the white man. "So why was Captain Walker killed? Did someone envy him? Even fear him? Was it jealousy over a woman? Or was his death to do with money? Perhaps it was revenge?"

The Englishman was about to say that no one needed to envy or fear Captain Walker as his career was going nowhere but stopped himself as he thought there was no reason for the Chink to know. Instead, he said with some uncertainty. "I suppose I should jot down these possibilities and thereafter strike off those unlikely ones."

Chief Inspector Chuah pushed a writing pad across the table towards the Englishman.

"As he is not an enviable man, I guess I should strike that out," said Captain Munro, who had listed down the motives which the experienced police officer had earlier offered. "Likewise, I think I can also strike off fear."

When he looked at the next motive which he had jotted down, Captain Munro permitted himself a chuckle. Like everyone else in the barracks, he was aware of the late Captain Walker's peculiar taste. However, without bothering to explain, he merely looked at the Chinese officer and said, "Jealousy over a woman is also out of the question."

The chief inspector went to the window of his office and stood looking out with unseeing eyes that took no notice of the people walking below in the centre courtyard. He was thinking of the previous night when he had met his old friend, Chiu Ya Loong, who was a highly respected *taikor* in the *jianghu,* literarily translated as "rivers and lakes", to denote the underworld.

As had been his style, Ya Loong had come straight to the point: "I've heard about your being tasked to investigate the murder of an *ang moh* army officer at a hotel in Leith Street."

"You've heard right, my old friend," he said, nodding his head. "The manner he was killed is quite puzzling. He was shot in between the eyes, like the way Drunken Cat Tan was shot several years ago."

The *taikor* shrugged. "As I remember, you'd then thought I had something to do with Drunken Cat Tan's death since he was at the time threatening me. Well, it was a blessing that your being on the case had allowed us to subsequently become great friends. Maybe it's the same guy who'd pulled the trigger."

"Could be," the police officer said thoughtfully. "The ballistics however showed the bullets came from different guns."

"Let's see if the information I have here may be more useful to you."

And that was how the chief inspector had learned from Ya Loong some interesting things which the *taikor* heard from his sources, such as the general loathing which the late Captain Walker's fellow officers felt towards him. Though Chief Inspector Chuah had also heard about the Englishman's preference for young boys, he had deliberately included jealousy over a woman as one of the motives to Captain Munro so as not to show all his cards.

It wasn't surprising for the *taikor* to be passing information to the chief inspector since they had made a pact nearly a decade ago whereby he would close an eye to the *taikor's* gambling and protection rackets, in exchange for information. What surprised him was that Ya Loong who had all along been feeding him information on triads' activities could even access the grapevines of a British military base. And as if Ya Loong could read his mind, the *taikor* said, "Many Chinese work at the base." In saying this, the *taikor* was also deliberately keeping some of his cards to himself.

Chief Inspector Chuah was roused from his thoughts by Captain Munro's voice. "If you ask me, I dare say the late Captain Walker was killed for his money. Yes, decidedly money. He was robbed."

Not wishing to remind the Englishman that he hadn't been asked, and also, the dead captain was found with his valuables intact, the Chinese police officer decided it was time to surprise the Regimental Police Chief. "I gather the captain wasn't a likeable chap among his colleagues."

Captain Munro laid down his pen and looked up sharply. "How do you know about that?"

"I have my ears and eyes opened." Chief Inspector Chuah said non-committally. "I hear things."

The eyes of the military police officer and the civilian police officer locked. This time there was none of the smug patronizing air of the former. In its place was a wary look of grudging respect.

"From what I've heard, I was given the impression that the late captain had antagonized many fellows, two of whom were a Police Lieutenant Richard Smith and a Major David Cartwright."

"Police Lieutenant Smith had left for England long before Captain Walker's murder," Captain Munro said. "As for Major Cartwright, dash it all, I know the man and he isn't the sort of fellow to do that sort of thing even though Captain Walker had been awfully beastly to him."

"One can never really tell when it comes to human nature," Chief Inspector Chuah said softly.

"'I agree with you but in this instance I can vouch for Major Cartwright."

"How can you be so sure?"

"He passed out from drinking in the Officers' Mess on the evening that Captain Walker was killed," Captain Munro said. "I was one of those who helped to carry him home to his quarters."

"Could his intoxication be an act? I mean he could have put on an act after which he sneaked out, got on a ferry to Penang and knocked off Captain Walker?"

"I doubt it."

"Well, what's the harm in our interviewing him?"

"If he has done it…" Captain Munro broke off abruptly and threw an appealing glance at the Chinese police officer.

When Chief Inspector Chuah didn't say anything, Captain Munro shrugged. "I'll have a word with him as he's after all an officer of Her Majesty's Armed Forces."

Eighteen

*I*t was during the festival of *Ching Ming* – Pure Brightness – the Chinese version of All Souls' Day that Mao Dong Po carefully took out the newspaper which he had been keeping.

Early that morning, Dong Po's mother had placed some of Mao Chen Lin's favorite food before his altar. Although it was a tradition for Chinese families to visit the burial ground of their departed loved ones to sweep their graves, offer prayer, food and libation of wine in their memory, Dong Po's father had no grave.

His body had simply been buried, together with the other murdered villagers, in an unmarked grave. Even though Dong Po and his mother had subsequently gone back to retrieve his severed head and buried it, the burial spot was likewise unmarked. Eighteen months later, during the *Ching Ming* of 1953, Dong Po and his mother had returned to their old village to just pray for his departed soul as they were not allowed to bring food out of the "New Village". They had found jungle creepers and tall wild grasses growing all over their old village. As there was no way they could locate the unmarked grave of Chen Lin's head, Dong Po's mother had a wooden altar set up at home for her late husband.

On that warm April morning in 1956, just after Dong Po's mother had burned some paper clothing and joss paper – considered as currency in the netherworld – for the soul of her husband, Dong Po took out the newspaper, mumbled a silent prayer, and thereafter set the newspaper on fire.

Dong Po's mother looked at her son curiously. "What are you doing?"

"Burning a newspaper for Papa to read," Dong Po said easily.

☆ ☆ ☆ ☆

The Foo Heong Restaurant in Cintra Street wasn't as crowded on that night as it usually was. This was because most people had to stay home to clear the leftover food from the *Ching Ming* festival. Two men were sitting in a corner on the first floor of the restaurant by the window overlooking the street.

Just after Chiu Ya Loong had poured tea for Chief Inspector Robert Chuah, the latter casually said to the *taikor*. "As you've already made some money, it's time for you to quit the underworld. After all, unlike those other *taikors,* you're not affiliated to any triad. Your tong is your own and so you can disband them anytime you wish."

"Even so, I still owe my men a responsibility. I just can't walk out on them like that."

"I understand," the chief inspector said. "But at the rate my superiors are pressuring down, I may find it hard put to protect you any longer. This is especially so now that I've been taken off secret societies and placed in homicide."

"What happened to that case of the *ang moh* army officer who was shot in the hotel room?"

To anyone watching him, Chief Inspector Chuah's interest seemed to be on the *sar hor fun,* fried flat rice noodles served in a thick gravy with prawns and pork, which the waiter had just brought to their table. However, the *taikor* knew his friend's mind had gone back to the case. Eating was just an automatic reaction for the police officer.

After the chief inspector had eaten several mouthfuls and washed the food down with a cup of tea, he said, "We have a main suspect, a Major David Cartwright, but before we could question him, the blighter died. It seems like the murdered officer had something to do with the major's wife leaving him. The poor fellow was in a state of acute depression and just before my counterpart in the British Army could call him up for questioning, the blighter put his service revolver to his head and blew his own brains out."

After saying those words, the chief inspector gave the unfinished plate of noodles before him an uneasy look. "I've just lost my appetite."

Nineteen

*T*ime flew by. Exactly a week after it was announced that David Saul Marshall had stepped down as Chief Minister of Singapore on June 6, 1956, Mao Dong Po obtained his driver's license.

Unlike the politician who resigned after failing to convince the British that Singapore was ready for total self-rule, the Chinese lad who had earlier driven the car into a ditch in Alor Star, managed to persuade the local tester into passing him. The dialogue he had with the tester was, of course, supplemented with some money changing hands.

The next day, he proudly showed his driving license to his *sifu* who shrugged indifferently. "There's no achievement when you have to bribe your way. Well, the only good from this episode, my boy, is that you now know graft can be a useful weapon. Without corrupt officials, there will be no room for those in our profession, or for the matter, criminals, to move so freely about."

When Dong Po didn't say anything, the Siamese put out his hand with the palm facing upwards. "Let me have your driving license and some photographs. I will have to arrange for fake copies with false names for you. Use those in future when you're working for me."

By late October 1956, the Chinese Middle School riots had broken out in Singapore and Lim Yew Hock who had replaced Marshall as Chief Minister, took strong measures to crack down on the dissidents. Riots involving students were not new because in the previous year's Hock Lee Bus riots, where students came forth to support bus workers who had gone on strike, two police officers, an American journalist and a student had died while many others injured. As the British government had then felt that Marshall wasn't tough enough, they subsequently rejected his proposal for Singapore's self-rule. This could have driven the new Chief Minister towards the hard stance he was taking.

Somchai who was patiently teaching Dong Po how to pick locks, stopped to listen to the announcement on the radio: "To contain further violence arising from the riots, the government had ordered troops, supported by helicopters, to use tear gas to end the riots. Several key union leaders, including Lim Chin Siong of the People's Action Party, have also been detained under the Public Security Act…"

Returning his attention to his young protégé, Somchai shook his head. "Taking a hard stance isn't always good. For the past twenty minutes, you have been unable to open the lock which I can easily open within a minute. Why? It's because your approach is too hard and your movement's too stiff."

Unknown then to the Siamese, his words would eventually come to pass. Although Lim Yew Hock's hard stance won him the confidence of the British in the local government's ability to handle internal security, it lost him the support of the people, which allowed the People's Action Party to win the 1959 General Election and form the next government.

Long before that event, under Somchai's tutelage, Dong Po had already become an accomplished lock picker.

☆☆☆☆

For nearly fifteen minutes, Ong Lay Yong frantically tried to pick the lock which had been placed on a short chain laid across the iron grill gates to the office of the Singapore Chinese Middle School Students' Union. But being an unaccomplished lock picker, she could make no headway. As she seethed with indignation over the government's arbitrary move in deregistering the union, she muttered inaudible curses under her breath while trying to open the lock with her hair pin.

A few days ago, on a rainy afternoon, the police had come unexpectedly to order everyone out of the premise. Lay Yong who was in the committee had joined her colleagues in screaming abuses at the police officers. A Caucasian chief inspector who led the policemen had imperiously warned them, "Don't create trouble or we'll arrest you. Get out! Get out! The order has come from the Chief Minister."

"Why?" she had demanded.

The police officer gave her a bored look and short of yawning into her face, replied: "Your union has long been under suspicion of being pro-communist."

Lay Yong who was a teacher at the Chin Kang School knew too well what the police officer was saying. Just last year, she had been one of those who had organized the students from her school to join those from other schools in flocking by the busloads to the Hock Lee Bus Company in Alexandra Road to support the striking workers.

Ever since she started teaching in 1954 after graduating from the Chung Hwa Girls' High School, the petite, bespectacled schoolteacher had been very popular with her students. Young as she was, they unquestioningly obeyed her. Perhaps it was also due to the way she wore her dark hair conservatively parted in the middle and drawn over her ears to be tied in a chignon low on the nape of her neck which gave her a very matured and imposing look. Or, it could have been her zeal.

Hence, last year when she told them, "Those poor bus workers have been exploited too long. Let us go to their support so that they have a chance to fight for better wages to support their families," the students cheered loudly before boarding the buses waiting to send them to the bus company's depot.

In addition to organizing donation drives to raise money to buy food, she had also led the students to entertain the workers with songs and dances. After things got out of hand on May 12, 1955, resulting in the deaths of two police officers, an American journalist and one student from her school, she had assured the rest of her students: "By our struggles, we have scored a victory against the oppressors who have agreed to reinstate the bus workers without any loss in income. They will henceforth show more respect to workers and students." Nothing more was said about the four who were killed, including the dead student, Chong Lon Chong.

On this night, after the government, under Lim Yew Hock, whom she regarded as a colonial stooge, had deregistered her union and some other associations with the aim of suppressing anti-colonial activists and left-wingers like her, she had come back to her former office. She was desperately trying to break in because she remembered there were some documents she had left behind in a drawer.

Should they fall into the wrong hands, they would implicate a number of people including her idol, Lim Chin Siong, the charismatic and good-looking trade unionist cum politician. Her hero-worshipping of the man who was two years her senior, begun after she saw him last year when he came to her school to give talks to the students. By that time, she had already heard about the class boycotts he had previously organized at the Chinese High School, and when he joined the striking bus workers, she knew she just had to support him in rousing her students. Recently, he had once again led students' protests against the deregistering of two associations and her union.

As she still couldn't open the lock, she ruefully left the place. Unknown to her, even if she had been able to get inside to retrieve those documents, her effort would still be in vain because Lim was already arrested around the time she was fiddling with the lock. The government, exasperated over Chinese students being once again instigated into rioting which left 13 dead and over a hundred injured, gave the order for some 900 persons to be brought into custody.

It was only after Lay Yong reached her home above her father's wine import shop in Smith Street that she heard the news over the radio. About half an hour later, while she was still pondering over her next move, she heard the commotion downstairs as one or more persons were banging on the door at the side of the shop where a flight of stairs connected her home upstairs to the street below. Even without opening the door to look, she somehow sensed the police had come for her. Smiling to reassure her anxious parents who had emerged from their room, she told them, "Don't worry, I'll be away only for a while."

With those words, she walked down the dark and narrow stairs to open the door for her captors.

BOOK 2
FROM CRAFTSMAN
TO MASTER

"For victories are such, they are gained in circumstances that have not been revealed and he thus wins no reputation for wisdom; and as the enemy submits without bloodshed, he receives no credit for valor."

Sun Tzu

Twenty

*"*MERDEKA" – Independence – was heard loud and clear seven times just after the stroke of twelfth midnight on August 31, 1957.

The man who led the shouting was none other than Tunku Abdul Rahman, who had in the previous year, promised his countrymen that their nation would gain its independence from the British, and he would be the first Prime Minister of Malaya. Mao Dong Po who heard the event over the wireless, couldn't help wondering whether he was a citizen of Thailand or the newly-independent Malaya.

In the few years of living with his uncle at the border town of Padang Besar, and being influenced by his Siamese *sifu*, Dong Po spoke Thai and Malay fluently and was equally at home with the culture of each country. As such, he could be forgiven for his confusion of national identity. He even knew the history of Thailand just as well as the history of Malaya.

His knowledge of historical events in Thailand came from books and journals as he was an avid reader of anything, and not just his favorite James Bond's thrillers. Moreover, he had two good teachers in Somchai and at times, the *ajarn*, who, during those times when they were resting after or in-between practising the Art of the Eight Limbs, would talk about things that somehow connected to the history of the land.

After avenging his father, Dong Po had resumed the life of an ordinary shop assistant. As he good-naturedly haggled over prices with both locals and tourists interested in the leather wares displayed in his uncle's shop, no one realized the dangerous quality lurking behind the unassuming nineteen-year-old Dong Po who had already killed a man. On some days, he would follow his uncle to Sadao, a large town further north of the border inside Thailand. His uncle brought him along as he hoped the young man could learn how to negotiate with the suppliers. Even though he had agreed to his nephew's wish to become Somchai's apprentice, he still hoped that one day his nephew would come to his sense and so could inherit his business.

Most nights would find Dong Po going to the *ajarn* to receive further instruction in the Art of the Eight Limbs.

On the night of September 17, 1957, after class was over, he sat in a semi circle with his two fellow disciples, facing the *ajarn*, who suddenly pointed at him, saying: "It won't be long before you should become a champion. I became champion of my province when I was 25 years old."

The *ajarn*'s brow contracted as though he was trying hard to remember. "It was on June 24, 1932, the same day they pulled off a bloodless *coup d'etat* that transformed our kingdom from an absolute monarchy into a constitutional one."

Seeing his three disciples looking keenly at him, the *ajarn* who was a man with little ego, decided to tell them about the coup rather than talk about his becoming provincial champion. "Strange as this may sound but the seeds for the coup were actually planted in Paris rather than here in Siam."

When he saw that he had got his disciples' attention, the *ajarn* continued, "Seven Siamese students met to discuss the severely declining economy under King Prajadiphok who ruled as King Rama VII, after the demise of his father, King Chulalongkorn, in 1925. They agreed that the solution to this country's economic woes was to force the king to submit to the constitution and open up opportunities for capable commoners to take over the leadership. After their return to Siam, they went about influencing middle-ranking military officers to their cause."

The three young men held their breath when the *ajarn* told them that the secret police arrested some of the conspirators in early 1932,

"Fortunately for them, Prince Boriphat of Nakornsawan, who was then Minister of Internal Affairs ordered their release as he knew them personally and thought them harmless. But after the king and his family had gone to their summer palace in Hua Hin, several regiments were told to gather at Sanam Luang on the morning of June 24, 1932, under the pretext of military maneuvers," the *ajarn* said.

And so Dong Po came to learn that on the said morning, one of the coup leaders, a Colonel Phraya Pahol Pholphayuhasena read out the declaration. After criticizing the king and his ministers for the kingdom's woes, he and his fellow conspirators persuaded the troops to join the coup. On the conspirators' orders, several ministers, most of whom were members of the royal family, including Prince Boriphat, were arrested.

"Two days after the king heard about the coup, he returned to commence negotiation with the conspirators who called themselves the People's Party," continued the *ajarn*. "About six months later, a Parliament was set up with Phraya Manopakom Nititada, a lawyer, as the first Prime Minister of Siam. As factionalism continued to plague the Parliament, in mid-1933, Phraya Pahol Pholphayuhasena, who had risen to the rank of a general, led another coup to oust Phraya Manopakom and set himself up as Prime Minister. "

The *ajarn* paused for a short while as if trying to stretch his memory. "But it was not General Phraya Pahol Pholphayuhasena's destiny to occupy the central stage of our kingdom's chaotic history. Rather, it was another man who made the strongest impression."

At this juncture, the *ajarn* sighed. "That man was Phibun Songkhram, who, in the following year, forced General Phraya Pahol Pholphayuhasena to resign as Prime Minister over a scandal involving the sale of prime real estate to high-ranking officials for below-market prices. At the start of the *coup d'etat* against King Prajadiphok, Phibun was only a lieutenant-colonel. After he had taken over power as Prime Minister, he went about removing all opposition by arresting and at times, executing those he suspected of being or becoming a threat to him. In the process, he also elevated himself to the rank of a field marshal."

One of the Siamese lads, whose name was Kiet, slapped the inside of his thigh. The sharp sound caused the *ajarn* to glare sternly at him. After all, they had already been taught to sit motionless and tolerate any discomfort.

When the *ajarn* spoke again, it was a question, and he seemed to be directing it at Dong Po. "Why do you think I'm telling you this story?"

Kiet, whose earlier attempt to slap a mosquito had earned him the *ajarn's* disapproving glare, thought he should regain the *ajarn's* approval, said: "You want to motivate us so that we can be like the field marshal."

The other Siamese lad, Virote, who also thought it won't do for him to maintain passive silence, said: "I think the lesson is that to be strong, we must eliminate all our enemies."

The *ajarn* sighed. This time, it was a deep sigh that came from the innermost recesses of his person. Ignoring his two disciples, whom he had long ago dismissed as brawny but not brainy, he turned towards Dong Po. "What do you think?"

"Could it be that you're trying to tell us what goes around comes around. I say this because from what I've heard, this man, this Field Marshal Phibun was himself overthrown in a coup yesterday."

This time the *ajarn* smiled. "You're well informed. Yes, it has been confirmed that after nearly two decades, Field Marshal Phibun, who was responsible for four coups, became Prime Minister for two terms, and survived three coups while in power, was finally overthrown in a coup led by his most loyal supporter, Field Marshal Sarit Thanarat."

When Dong Po nodded his head, the *ajarn* continued, "You're right about the saying, what goes around comes around."

Around the time the *ajarn* was talking to his disciples, a woman was looking up at the ceiling of her newspaper office in Bangkok. Though it was already late, she was still in her office. After a while, she turned her gaze to the typewriter before her.

Suchin Suewonglee, who would be celebrating her thirty-second birthday in another two months' time, was no longer considered young by society's standards of the era. But she was still a very attractive woman, more so as her aloofness gave her an air of being untouchable. At her age, she was still slim with a lithe, sensuous body. Quite tall for a Thai, when she walked, there was a seductiveness of her movement hinting of much passion.

As she often caught the furtive interest in the eyes of those men she met in the course of her work as a journalist, she was well aware of her attractiveness. Indeed, earlier that evening, when she met up with her editor, he too had looked at her with that odd yearning manner. But he was too much a gentleman to make any improper suggestion.

She mused that she had once harbored a youthful hope of marrying her classmate, Vichai and thereafter bearing his children but that was thirteen years ago. Since then so many things had happened. The Japanese had arrogantly marched into her country, and the government under Field Marshal Phibun had shamelessly welcomed the unwanted guests and even embraced them as allies. Both her parents were dead. Vichai was dead. Even Madam Chettana Manoonsin, the only person who knew her shameful secret had already passed away. After the war, nothing much had changed as ordinary citizens like her continued to be trampled under the boots of a military dictatorship since Field Marshal Phibun surprisingly remained in power despite having collaborated with the Japanese.

With all these thoughts chasing one another inside her head, tried as she would, she still couldn't think of a suitable lead for the story which her editor had assigned her. Thinking it could help if she were to reconstruct the earlier meeting with her editor, she tried to recall their conversation.

The moment her editor had told her to do a story on Field Marshal Phibun's downfall, she had asked blandly in her soft husky voice: "How would you like me portray him? Set him up as a great man or a despotic tyrant?"

Her editor, Arthit Lamsam, whose thick glasses hideously distorted his eyes, was a short pudgy man in his early forties. Those who knew him had discovered that once those glasses were removed, he was really a humorous fellow as his eyes laughed along with his mouth.

When he heard Suchin's words, he laughed. "Very funny but this is no time for joking, Suchin. You're experienced enough to know the new regime will shut us down if we were to portray the fellow they had just booted out of office as a great guy."

Personally, Suchin loathed Field Marshal Phibun as he was in some ways responsible for her suffering, but as a journalist, she was duty-bound to her profession to write objectively. That was the problem. Like many of her fellow citizens, she was often baffled by the man. Good or bad, he had certainly left his mark in Thai history. After all, except for the period from end-1944 till early 1948, he had actually ruled Thailand for nearly sixteen years.

"You're right. We won't go wrong in digging up plenty of dirt about the man to please the new regime. It's timely too that after all these years, we can have some refreshing truth," she said, with her voice rising. "Yes, it serves him right that he has been toppled and forced to flee to Japan. I hope he will never ever return."

Her unexpected passionate outburst had caused the editor to look up sharply at her.

"Sorry, I got carried away from suddenly remembering the fervent nationalistic policy of the field marshal after his rise to power, which resulted in those chauvinistically anti-Chinese measures."

Arthit, who was, like her, a Thai of Chinese descent, nodded in shared understanding. "I know what you mean. Many of us had suffered those restrictions he had imposed on education, business, newspapers, and culture."

"Do you know it was on account of his segregation policy that my father was ruined?"

"What happened?" asked Arthit though he could guess she was talking about Field Marshal Phibun's determination to destroy the Chinese hold on the economy by calling on ethnic Thai to buy from fellow ethnic Thai, and to buy only Thai products.

"After the field marshal began to discriminate against Chinese businesses, my father, a fourth generation Thai of Chinese descent, was so shocked over his business failure that his health deteriorated. He died three days after Japanese troops marched into Thailand on December 8, 1941," Suchin said flatly.

She had however left out the part about her having to toil long hours in a factory thereafter to sew uniforms for the military in order to support her likewise ailing mother. She also kept to herself the bitterness she felt, which eventually drove her to join the *Khabuankarn Seri Thai* – the anti-Japanese movement in Thailand.

"I'm sorry to hear about your father," Arthit said. "But in his way, the field marshal had also saved our country from the harsh treatment which the Japanese meted out to neighboring countries during the Second World War."

"Hah! You really believe that?" she snorted with some passion flashing through her dark eyes. "If anything, that man's a collaborator for allowing Japanese troops the free passage to move through Thailand into Malaya and Burma."

The editor leaned back in his chair and looked at her reflectively.

After a short silence, her intellect, journalistic instinct, and dread of her editor's favorite criticism of her putting her heart over her head, combined to pull her back to the realm of objectivity. "No, there was no way Thailand could resist the demands of the Japanese. He had no choice but to follow the way the wind blew."

"That's how to approach the story, Suchin," the editor said encouragingly. "While we mustn't portray him as a great guy, at the same time be mindful that Field Marshal Sarit wouldn't want to be seen as leading the press to demonize his former mentor."

Suchin abruptly slapped her forehead. "Demonize him! That should be easy since he wasn't all lily white innocence. Don't forget, he had signed a secret agreement with the Japanese whereby he committed Thai troops to join in the invasion of Burma as he wanted the Japanese to reward his government by giving back part of the territory that had been incorporated into British Burma and also the four Malay States that Siam was forced to cede to the British in 1909. I dare say it was his insatiable greed for power that led him to declare war on Britain and the United States in 1942."

In her agitation, Suchin abruptly got up from her chair and began to pace around the editor's room.

"Why must you get so worked up?" asked Arthit, who found her behavior somewhat puzzling that evening.

"His pact with the Japanese had actually shamed all Thais," she said. "Though some people have been insisting for years that he was a patriot working in the interest of Thailand, it was so morally wrong. If not for the protection of his cronies in the military, people would have spoken out at the time after the war and he would have been castigated as a traitor long before this."

A chill had then gone through her because thinking of the Japanese occupiers of her country had triggered off the unpleasant memories she had been trying so hard to suppress. She remembered it was after her nineteenth birthday when she became part of the secret preparation to rise in arms against Japanese military units garrisoned in Bangkok. Unlike her male counterparts, some of whom were secretly sent to Ceylon* to be trained as radio operators, or the rest being given military training in Thailand itself, she joined the other women to be the ears, eyes, and limbs of the underground resistance movement. It was on one assignment that Vichai was killed and the *kempetai* had caught her. She shuddered involuntarily when she thought of Major Ishihara Shigeto.

This time, Arthit was truly worried. "Are you feeling all right, Suchin? Perhaps I should assign this story to another guy?"

"No, I want to do it."

---

* Today's Sri Lanka.

And now sitting at her desk, alternating her stare at the ceiling and her typewriter, she regretted having insisted on being the one to do the assignment. She felt too personal over Field Marshal Phibun to be able to think clearly and write without prejudice. But she was also too proud to reverse her decision.

To Ong Lay Yong's surprise, life as a political detainee wasn't as terrible as she had initially thought.

But even if it had been terrible, she wasn't frightened by the prospect. If anything, she was proud of the fact that she was among those being detained because she knew many people of her time considered it heroic to go to prison for a cause.

Since her arrest some ten months ago, other than being deprived of personal freedom in being confined to a Spartan-like cell, having to live according to a strictly-enforced time-table, and suffering the bland prison food, no other deprivation was imposed on her. Although the female warders went about their duties without a smile on their dead-pan faces, they hadn't mistreated her or the other detainees.

It was only on one occasion that she saw a woman detainee being forcibly overpowered and led away after she refused to obey an instruction given her and began shouting hysterically at a warder. Lay Yong had no idea what had happened to the woman as all she heard later was that she had been sent to another detention centre.

As the political detainees were not permitted to talk to each other, they met in silence for their daily physical exercise or sat down three times a day for meals in the canteen. Other times, they were mostly confined to each individual's cell. Thus, it was the solitary existence that disturbed her the most. She knew the long hours of silence had affected her because she had begun to form the habit of talking to herself.

As such, she looked forward to the twice-a-week visit by Mrs. Mary D'Souza, her case officer. But eager as she was for the opportunity to meet and talk with someone, she was still very wary. This was quite a feat considering that Mrs. D'Souza, who was in her early thirties, had a very cheerful and gregarious personality. She had the gift of making anyone she met for five minutes to think they had been great pals for years.

Lay Yong's wariness came from her suspicion that the solitary confinement was designed to play on a detainee's mind, to make her eager to seek out someone to talk, and so unconsciously might reveal something of use to the authorities. She suspected too that Mrs. D'Souza was selected for the job because she would make a perfect catalyst.

Hence, on that hot, humid day in September 1957, Lay Yong took her time as usual to carefully think over each question which Mrs. D'Souza had put to her. And each time, she would end up offering a guarded reply. By the end of the hour allocated for the meeting, seeing she had got very little out of Lay Yong, the case officer, having asked those questions as required by her superiors, retrieved her documents. After returning them to a satchel, she stood up, to indicate the interview was over.

Just before Mrs. D'Souza reached the door, she heard Lay Yong's voice. "Please...please, Mrs. D'Souza, can you get me some books? Anything to read."

The case officer, hesitating for a moment, seemed to consider her request. "Well, Lay Yong, I'll see what I can do for you."

Twenty-one

A week after the *coup d'etat* which saw Field Marshal Phibun Songkhram fleeing to Japan, Mao Dong Po heard someone knocking impatiently at the back door of his uncle's shop.

Guessing it was none other than his *sifu*, he hurried downstairs to open the door. True enough, it was Somchai who was grinning like a Cheshire cat the moment the door was opened.

"I bring good news, my boy," he told Dong Po.

The young man looked at his mentor speculatively but waited patiently for him to tell his news in his own sweet time. This was because Somchai had once chided him for his youthful impatience. As the Siamese disliked being hurried, he had then told his protégé: "As my long departed father had taught me, young people have no business to hurry their elders. All things shall come to those who wait. This is especially true in our profession, in which patience is a virtue."

By that time, Dong Po knew his *sifu's* father had been a smuggler. It was from his father that Somchai had learned some of the things he was now passing on to his protégé.

And so that night, Dong Po waited patiently for his mentor who was obviously in high spirit as he went about the motion of lighting a cigarette. After he had taken a few puffs, he said: "Now that Field Marshal Sarit Thanarat's coup has been successfully carried out, he's the most powerful man in Siam."

"From what I've read, military coups are nothing new in your country, Uncle Somchai. It's just exchanging one dictator for another."

"Yes, I mean no, Field Marshal Sarit isn't just any dictator. His loyal follower, General Thanom Kitikhachorn has been appointed Minister of Defence. More to the point, Lieutenant-Colonel Wongkot Suttharom who was my childhood friend, has been appointed Assistant Commander of the southern provinces. We both grew up in Klong Ngae, which isn't far from here. Ya Loong, the Penang *taikor*, also came from there."

Seeing his young protégé's bewilderment, Somchai laughed. "Silly boy, can't you see that this is good for us?"

"Good for us?"

"You still don't get it?" asked Somchai, cocking his head to one side as though teasing an awkward pupil. "Lieutenant-Colonel Wongkot is one of my two major clients. He will surely have problems for us to remove. Apart from jobs, we can also count on his protection."

"He has many enemies?"

Somchai who was about to use the stub of his almost finished cigarette to light another one, stopped and said: "No, I mean yes, he has problems. But sometimes I suspect he is just acting for some of those in the faction he belongs, those who are higher up and they told him they have problems to be removed."

"And as he represents them, this means less people will know, and so there will be less risk all around."

Somchai chuckled. "As I've said before, you're smart, my boy. Now, before I forget, what are you doing these days?"

"I assist my uncle as usual in minding his shop."

"I want you to take your mother away for a holiday."

Over the years that he had known his mercurial *sifu*, Dong Po had gotten used to his unpredictability. Now and then the Siamese would waltz in through the back door of his uncle's shop and then started off something unexpected that would catch the young man slightly off balance. Tonight was one of those times that Dong Po was surprised by the irrelevant suggestion. "Take my mother away for a holiday?"

"Yes, my boy, you owe her that much. Bring her to Singapore," said Somchai as he handed his protégé a Thai passport. "Thanks to Lieutenant-Colonel Wongkot, I've got you this passport bearing the Thai name, Klahan, which I've given you. When you're on mission, use those fake passports which I'd got for you. Other times, use real passport like this or the one issued by the new Malayan government."

Dong Po opened the passport and was touched to find Pattano after the name of Klahan. He knew Pattano to be Somchai's family name.

"I want you to know Singapore better because you may have jobs to do in that city some time in the future. On your way back, stop by Kuala Lumpur for the same reason."

Somchai took out a wad of crisp dollar notes. "Here is an advance for you. By the way, from now on, unless I explicitly say so, you must stay in good hotels because our cover must show us to be respectable businessmen. When you look respectable, you are above suspicion."

Seeing his protégé giving him a thoughtful look, he laughed and plunged his hand into his pocket to retrieve a box of business cards. "Here are your cards."

The young man saw his Thai name printed in gold on the simple and elegant cream-colored card which made him out to be a manager of the Pattano Pest Removal Company. As he looked up at the older man, he saw a broad grin stretching his face. It occurred to Dong Po that not only was his *sifu* totally unpredictable, but the man also had a weird sense of humor.

"In case you're wondering, my boy, the company's registered," Somchai said. "Of course, I'd used fictitious names. As you've put it, the less people know, the less the risk. It's like something out of those James Bond's thrillers you're so fond of reading, isn't it?"

The swarthy Siamese man's next move surprised Dong Po even more than his words. From inside his windbreaker, he took out a book for the young man. "Here, I've a present for you. I was told it's the latest release."

Dong Po's eyes gleamed with anticipation as he read the title on the book cover: *From Russia with Love* by Ian Fleming.

☆ ☆ ☆ ☆

Suchin Suewonglee had hardly sat down for five minutes when her editor came bouncing happily to her desk. He was excitedly waving a copy of the day's newspaper.

"That was a very good article you'd written," Arthit Lamsam cried with pleasure. "It was very clever of you to touch lightly on the man's achievements and with the same stroke of your pen, hint on his glaring flaws. I dare say it's a masterpiece."

"Please don't make my head swell," laughed Suchin as she found herself infected by her editor's good humor. But pleased as she was by her boss's praises, she hoped she would not have to write stories like this one again.

"The field marshal is pleased too," Arthit said.

"How would you know?"

"One of his aides, a Colonel Phanu Ritthidet telephoned to pass on the field marshal's congratulations to us," the editor said.

Suchin gave him a sidelong glance and wondered how he could take it. Sometimes she too felt so sickened by the system. As journalists, they wanted nothing more than the freedom to write and report on the truth. But under the military dictatorship which her country had experienced since 1932, whatever was written and published must be done with utmost care. At times, like now, she almost felt like someone's cat's paw.

"I suppose this is our lot. Ours not to question why, ours to write and sigh," she muttered.

"What? What did you say?"

"No, nothing," she replied, not wishing to pour cold water on her editor's enthusiasm.

Ong Lay Yong's eyes widened for just a second the moment she saw the book on the desk by her case officer's elbow. She instinctively knew it was for her. Much as she wanted to reach out for the book, she waited. After all, she had waited ten months, which could be considered a long time to be without a book.

Though it was a fleeting reaction, Mrs. Mary D'Souza, who was selected for the job for her sharp observant power apart from other qualifications, had caught the hungry look in Lay Yong's eyes. She was shrewd enough to proceed dangling the bait before her. She smiled sincerely. "I'd remembered your request, Lay Yong. It wasn't easy to persuade my superiors but I'm glad I could at least do something for you. I hope you will enjoy this book."

As the book was laid on its back facing her case officer, Lay Yong strained to read the single title from upside down and concluded it to be *Pygmalion*. She had heard about this book which was a play by George Bernard Shaw but she hadn't yet read it.

"Now, let's see if you can help me find some meaning to the situation we're in, Lay Yong," said Mrs. D'Souza amicably as she opened the manila file before her. "Remember the student who was killed during the Hock Lee Bus riots?"

"Chong Lon Chong?"

Mrs. D'Souza nodded. "Yes, that's the boy. How did you feel at the time after learning about his death?"

Lay Yong gave the case officer a suspicious glance. "I suppose I felt upset."

Mrs. D'Souza raised an eyebrow. "Upset?"

"Yes, upset," Lay Yong muttered. "There was no necessity at all for the police to open fire."

She suddenly stopped talking as though she thought she had spoken too much. Mrs. D'Souza, who had wisely refrained from pointing out that the students and rioting bus workers had turned unruly in pelting the police with stones, waited patiently and when the silence grew quite loud, she asked softly: "Apart from feeling upset, don't you feel any sadness or remorse over Chong's death?"

Lay Yong shrugged her slender shoulders. "I suppose you can say I felt sad. The death of any person is always felt sadly as a loss. But…"

As Lay Yong hesitated, even for just a moment, Mrs. D'Souza watched her closely and prompted, "But what?"

"No sacrifice should ever be too great or immoral for a cause as great as ours."

Mrs. D'Souza who had heard many of the Chinese schools' students quoting this Marxist philosophy marveled at the extent the communists had infiltrated into their midst and corrupted their youthful minds. Once again, as she had on many occasions asked the young girl, she repeated the question: "So what are you all fighting for?"

This time there was no hesitation as Lay Yong spoke with some passion. "We just want equality. Why are Chinese schools being discriminated? Why are our Chinese high schools' graduates deprived of any opportunity to further their education? Why are Chinese schoolteachers so lowly paid? We want answers to all these questions and more!"

Mrs. D'Souza was quiet for a while. She reflected that the girl's replies so far had been consistent with those given previously. And why should her answers differ? After all, like most of her fellows, Lay Yong believed the colonial government had treated them unfairly. But Mrs. D'Souza, who secretly sympathized with the young woman before her, was aware that while such discontent had reasonable grounds, when fanned by the communist agitators, could easily be distorted into fueling social chaos as a likely consequence.

Seeing Lay Yong's covetous glances at the book, Mrs. D'Souza decided it was time to end the day's meeting. She pushed the book across the table and rose to go. To her surprise, she heard Lay Yong saying, "Thank you,

Mrs. D'Souza. It's so good of you to take all this trouble for me."

It was the first time she received some cordiality from the young Chinese woman. Previously, they parted as though everything that needed airing had been spoken and there was no longer any need to say anything, not even goodbye let alone a thank you for coming. *Well, it was definitely an improvement, she thought. The book could be the key to open this girl's heart and reach her mind.*

Twenty-two

*I*t was the last week of October, 1957 when Mao Dong Po returned from a vacation with his mother to Singapore and Kuala Lumpur as his *sifu* had suggested.

Her mother had apparently enjoyed herself, and so had Dong Po. Only an incident gave him a wee bit of discomfort. They were at the Haw Par Villa, also known as Tiger Balm Gardens, which was built by two brothers, Aw Boon Haw and Aw Boon Par, who made their fortune in herbal medication.

When they were strolling through the ten courts of Hell, Dong Po's mother suddenly shivered at the gruesome sight of the sculpture of mortals who, after their earthly lives ended, were being punished for their sins. Without warning, she said, "One reaps what one sows. You must refrain from committing sins, such as taking another person's life, lest you'll be punished after death." He was stunned for a moment as two thoughts immediately ran through his head: *Is my mother aware of the fact that I'd killed the Englishman who murdered my father? Will I be punished for avenging my father's death?*

A few days after their return to Padang Besar, Dong Po's *sifu* came knocking loudly on the back door, and the moment Dong Po opened the door, he heard Somchai said: "It's time for you to work for me. I have an assignment for you."

Dong Po who had been eagerly waiting for this moment, asked, "Who will I be removing?"

"I've just received a contract from the Tang Kong Si to remove one of their chieftains who had become an embarrassment to the tong and may even become a potential threat to his fellow chieftains."

Dong Po had heard that the Tang Kong Si, a Chow Chou gang, was one of the two main triads in Siam. Their members had fought a bloody battle against their archrival, the Siew Li Kue, a Hokkien triad, in Yawaraj, Bangkok's Chinatown, at the end of the last century. He wondered how his mentor was involved with the powerful Chow Chou gang.

The answer was provided when Somchai said, "The Tang Kong Si is my other major client."

Since his mentor was on the subject of killing a person and as the shadow thrown by the light of the kerosene-lamp caused the older man's face to look ghostly like one of the guardians of Hell, Dong Po shuddered from being reminded of his recent visit to the Haw Par Villa. To make light of his sudden discomfort, he quipped: "What has the guy done that has embarrassed his fellows? Had he donated the tong's opium to the Red Cross?"

"Be serious," snapped Somchai. "This guy had embarrassed his fellows because earlier this year, he had allied himself with Colonel Phao Sriyanonda in the General Elections."

A chastised Dong Po asked: "Are you talking about the Chief of the Thai Police who, after the recent coup, had fled to Switzerland?"

"The very same man," said Somchai, secretly impressed by his young protégé's knowledge of current affairs. "Though General Phao openly crusaded against opium smuggling, he was secretly dealing in the lucrative opium trade, even competing against Field Marshal Sarit Thanarat on more than one occasion. It was therefore foolish of Charoen Limthongkul to back General Phao."

Dong Po was thoughtful for a moment. "From what I've heard about General Phao, any of his associates would deserve removal. But it's strange that this triad chieftain, whose family name, Limthongkul, made him out to be of Chinese descent, would take side with General Phao, who was after all, Field Marshal Phibun Songkhram's chief enforcer in his anti-Chinese policies."

Somchai smiled. "Ahh, you know that too, my boy. Well, that's the reason Charoen's fellow chieftains want him removed. Apart from the long memory of the Chinese over what General Phao had done to them, they also worry that Field Marshal Sarit might mistakenly assume Charoen's action represents their tong. At the same time, they also feared Charoen might bribe his way out to become even more powerful than them."

"But Uncle Somchai, why entrust this job to me?"

"I have to go to Burma to remove a bigger problem. And you, my boy, have got to start putting your training into practice and also earning some money."

"I suppose the job is to be done in Bangkok?"

"You'll take tonight's train for Krung Thep," Somchai said, using the old Thai name, Krung Thep, for Bangkok. Taking out a black-and-white photograph, he said, "This is how the quarry looks like. He runs the brothels, gambling dens and opium parlors in Sampaeng Lane. His front is a respectable goldsmith. It seems he is fond of meeting people at the White Lotus Hotel in Yawaraj. Remember what I've taught you: Don't make a move until you have studied him and the terrain well enough."

Dong Po studied the photograph and muttered a Thai proverb, *"Ngam tae rup, jub mai horm"*. His *sifu* agreed, "Yes, he has great looks but stank of bad breath."

"One thing I still don't quite understand is why the Tang Kong Si gave this job to us? Why aren't they doing it themselves? After all, they're not short of people to kill... I mean remove problems?"

"Yes, I mean no, some things are best left to the professionals brought in from outside. The less one knew, the less the risk. In this case, the Tang Kong Si wants to avoid an all-out internal gang war which may turn out to be more embarrassing and costly. As they see it, if they started fighting among themselves, they may fall prey to the Siew Li Kue."

Dong Po nodded thoughtfully, whereby Somchai smiled with a twinkle in his eye. "There's one more thing, my boy. Out of respect for their own fellow, they don't want the problem removed with a big bang. They said to make it look like an accident or natural cause. No blood is to be spilled. So you won't need your gun."

"What?" Dong Po jerked his head up. There was a hint of panic in his voice. "I'm not supposed to shoot him?"

"Yes, I mean no, you are to use other ways. Like all professionals, we cannot always rely on just any one tool but use what comes to hand to get the job done."

The young man stared at his mentor, puzzled. And when he realized Somchai was enjoying his role as a *sifu* who had set a most difficult test for his pupil, Dong Po laughed.

This time, it was Somchai who looked puzzled. But his surprise lasted just a moment. Like the true *sifu* he was, he knew what was in Dong Po's mind. He said softly, "This time you're on your own. So it's better to be careful than clever. Don't take unnecessary risk."

Remembering his mentor's mention of a bigger problem in Burma awaiting his personal attention, Dong Po said, "Uncle Somchai, you'll be careful too."

☆ ☆ ☆ ☆

Arthit Lamsam was looking out of the window with a thoughtful expression on his face. But the moment he heard Suchin Suewonglee walking into his room, he turned around and beckoned her to take a seat.

The short, pudgy man picked up some papers and gave them a quick glance, before handing them to her. "The most newsworthy man today surprisingly isn't Field Marshal Sarit Thanarat. It's a local triad chief by the name of Charoen Limthongkul."

"You mean the opium trader? Hasn't that scumbag fled together with his running mate, General Phao Sriyanonda?"

"On the contrary," Arthit said. "That man's a survivor. Now that he has come to realize having backed the wrong horse, he's trying hard to buy his way out."

"Will he be able to? There's no love lost between Field Marshal Sarit and General Phao. I still remember that incident in 1950 when General Phao's police surrounded Field Marshal Sarit's army convoy carrying opium in Lampang and demanded they should surrender their loot. It was fortunate that both gentlemen arrived in time before a tragic shootout between police and army could take place."

The editor took off his thick glasses and wiped them. Without them, his eyes looked less hideous. "Though the field marshal may be less forgiving towards General Phao, he may yet be generous towards the latter's associates provided they show their repentance by being more generous."

"So what do you want me to do with Charoen?"

"I hear he operates in Sampaeng Lane and hangs out quite often at the White Lotus Hotel in Yawaraj. Seeing it's not far from where you live, maybe you could try for an interview with him. It should make a good story especially now that I've got word he may be contesting in the coming General Elections."

Suchin folded up the papers. "All right, distasteful as that hoodlum is, I'll see what I can get out of him."

Mrs. Mary D'Souza was glad that she had made the effort to talk her boss into allowing Ong Lay Yong access to reading material. She discovered a subtle change in the young political detainee the moment she saw her walking into the meeting room. Thereafter, as Mrs. D'Souza was shrewd enough to subtly inject pertinent questions during her dialogue with Lay Yong, she found herself making faster progress that day.

It was the morning on the last day of October, 1957, when Mrs. D'Souza began her interview with Lay Yong. She had simply asked how the young woman felt about the book she had given her.

"Very bourgeois," Lay Yong replied.

Mrs. D'Souza, who expected that answer, chuckled. "Why do you say that?"

"Everything," said Lay Yong, shrugging her slender shoulders. "The British's class system is so decadent with the working class aspiring to attain middle class status, while the middle class is yearning for a lift up into aristocracy."

"I agree with you that a class system has its setbacks. But won't you at least agree that in the story, Eliza Doolittle, the common flower girl was given an opportunity to elevate herself to become a refined society lady?"

Lay Yong pursed her lips and gave her case officer a look of disdain. "In the first place, all men and women should be equals."

"Is that really possible?"

"The Russians had proven its possibility. Right now, it's also happening in China where Chairman Mao Tse-tung is building an egalitarian society where the proletariats would get what's due to them."

"Would you give the same marks to all your students?"

"Oh, that's different," said Lay Yong, though Mrs. D'Souza noticed she sounded a bit uncertain.

"In what way would you say different?"

"Well, I suppose some students would be born cleverer," she said. "But we're not talking about students sitting for an examination. We're talking about people, sharing wealth so that we won't have the poor working class on one side and the filthy rich on the other, with nothing better to do except to exploit their labor."

Not wanting the discourse to become too personal, Mrs. D'Souza changed track. "As you've read in

Pygmalion, after Professor Henry Higgins taught Eliza how to speak with an upper class accent and instructed her on etiquette, she changed her social standing. Isn't this what you and your fellow Chinese schools' students have been hankering after? You all wanted an opportunity in education in order to reach a higher status in life, don't you?"

Lay Yong's brow creased as though her case officer's words had somehow struck home but she didn't make any comment. Knowing it was better to leave her to reflect on her own, Mrs. D'Souza got up to leave. As an afterthought, she reached inside her valise and fished out a book. It gave her much satisfaction to see the look of surprise and delight on Lay Yong's face.

Twenty-three

*T*he slow night train from Sadao took some twenty hours to reach Bangkok.

After getting off the train at Hua Lamphong Station in the Thai capital, Mao Dong Po had to wait a while before he could find a rickshaw to take him straight to Yawaraj, the Chinese section of the city. The absence of rickshaws led him to recall that the Thai government had ceased issuing rickshaw licences in the past few years.

At Yawaraj, acting on Somchai's instruction, he checked into a nondescript hotel, a short walk from the more prominent White Orchid Hotel. Ever since becoming Somchai's pupil, Dong Po had come to realize that James Bond could only survive in fiction books. To check into a posh hotel while on a mission could possibly draw unnecessary attention to himself, which would be bad for his type of business.

Although Somchai had also taught him to ask for a room on the ground floor for ease in escaping, like jumping out of a window, he wouldn't be able to do so in the hotel he had checked in as the hotel was located atop a coffee shop. However, as the clerk had given him a room on the first floor, he had immediately after getting inside the room, opened the window and measured the height from his room to the street below. *If worse comes to worse, I can always jump out the window,* he thought grimly.

Ten minutes after he had checked in, he went down to Yawaraj Road and walked a short distance in the direction of the White Orchid Hotel. After nearly an hour of walking about to familiarize himself with the neighborhood, and getting slightly lost in the tangle of winding alleys, he eventually managed to retrace his steps to return to the main street. He found several hawker stalls on the other side of the road opposite the White Lotus Hotel.

At one of the stalls, he tried out the *kuey chap*, steam rice noodles topped with braised duck and egg in soya sauce. At another stall, he had glutinous rice dumplings in ginger syrup. He was sure he preferred such simple fare than the caviar and vodka martini that James Bond seemed to be unable to do without. And he wouldn't even have to blow a hole in his pocket like the British super secret agent.

Having satisfied his hunger, he returned to his room to sleep. That was again what his *sifu* had taught him: "Grab as much sleep as possible during a mission as you never can tell when you may be called upon to plod on without rest." When the small alarm clock he brought along rang at 10:00 p.m., he knew it was time for work.

Half an hour later, he was once again walking towards the direction of the White Orchid Hotel. He could see more lights in the distance as more food vendors had arrived. Dong Po could feel his stomach rumbling again.

He stopped at a stall. As he was enjoying a bowl of bird nest soup with ginkgo nuts, he saw a shiny black car, which he thought looked like those Ford sedans he had seen in a recent movie, arriving at the entrance of the White Orchid Hotel. A man with a livid scar on the right side of his face got out from the front passenger seat and looked around. Seemingly satisfied that there was no danger, he opened the rear door from which emerged a distinguished-looking man in his fifties, with a mane of thick salt-and-pepper hair.

After the pair had walked into the hotel, Dong Po thought how strange it was that while the first man looked every bit like a hoodlum, nature had however been kinder to the second fellow who hardly looked like a gangster. He finished his soup and went back to his hotel to sleep again, satisfied that he had sighted his quarry.

The next day, he woke up around 8:30 a.m. Though the noise from outside on the street wasn't too bad, the slanting rays of the morning sun had come in through the curtainless window. The moment he got down to the street, he hailed a rickshaw – unlike his experience in Penang, where after the war, trishaws had replaced rickshaws, one could still find rickshaws in Bangkok even though the government had stopped issuing licences – and asked to be taken to Sampaeng Lane.

To his surprise, he found the lane was not as far away as he had thought. He paid the rickshaw puller and walked the length of the narrow lane until he came to the end occupied mostly by Indian merchants. As he turned around to walk back, it occurred to him that he should also explore the side lanes. In the maze of narrower alleys branching from the lane, he found more merchants dealing in all sorts of wares.

But it was in Sampaeng Lane that he found the opium parlors. Likewise, when he passed by some shop houses along the lane whose doors were closed, men who were replicas of the bodyguard he saw the previous nights called to him, inviting him to go inside to make his fortune. At the front of some houses where green lanterns were hung, he knew those were the brothels which brought excitement to the district at night just as the traders gave life to it during the day.

Satisfied that he had familiarized himself with the district, he went into a coffee shop. He ordered a glass of *or-liang*, iced black coffee and a bowl of noodles. As he ate the noodles and sipped his drink, he casually looked at the goldsmith shop opposite the coffee shop. Although Charoen Limthongkul owned several brothels, gambling dens and opium parlors, it was this goldsmith shop which gave him the legitimate outlook of a businessman.

Half an hour later, the distinguished-looking man he had seen the previous night, came out. Just a step behind him was the same bodyguard with the livid scar on his right face. Another man who also sported a thuggish look came hurrying after them. Having paid for his food and drink, Dong Po feigned casualness as he got up to follow them. The trio walked the short distance towards the main street where they got into a car which was waiting for them. It was the same car he had seen the previous night.

While walking back to his hotel, out of the blue, Dong Po was seized with a despairing thought. How on earth was he going to remove the quarry and make it look like accidental or natural death? Without any such impossible condition, he could have simply walked up and shot the bodyguards and the quarry before trying to escape in the crowd. It could be over within a minute. But the order was clear: No blood was to be spilled. His *sifu* had certainly set him an almost impossible task.

By 10:00 p.m. that night, he was again walking towards the row of hawker stalls opposite the White Orchid Hotel. He still hadn't come up with a suitable plan. But when he was thoughtfully chewing the fish balls, he overheard a conversation that immediately aroused his interest.

The fish ball noodles vendor respectfully greeted an elderly man who sat at the table next to Dong Po: "*Sawadee, Phi-Chuan.*"

"I'll have the thick *kuey teow* with the fish balls this time."

"I'm honored that you still come to my humble stall when you can enjoy the best dishes in your restaurant."

"No one can eat the same food, no matter how good, all the time. It is refreshing at times to eat simple noodles."

"If only my two useless sons had listened to me to take up the jobs you'd offered them instead of working in the offices, they won't looked so starved each time they come home."

"Young people are impatient to wait on customers. That's why I'm very worried as I'm short of waiters and our local big shot, Charoen Limthongkul, is hosting a dinner this Saturday night, which means I only have five more nights to look for helpers. If you know anyone who wants to work, please send the person over."

"I will," the hawker promised. "I hear he will contest in the coming General Elections as the new regime has forgiven him."

"You hear right, my friend. If money can move the gods, it can move generals as well. But don't quote me."

After his hurried meal, the man whom Dong Po figured to be a supervisor of a restaurant walked across the road in the direction of the White Lotus Hotel. But he hadn't turned into the hotel. Instead, he walked on further until he came to a restaurant whose front was lighted up with rows of red lanterns.

At that moment an idea came to Dong Po. At the same time, the black Ford sedan pulled up in front of the White Lotus Hotel, which led Dong Po to marvel that the quarry was surprisingly a man of habit. Maybe, in believing himself to be invincible, it hadn't occurred to the gangster chief that he could ever be the target of an assassin.

Just a few tables away from where Dong Po was sitting, Suchin Suewonglee was also picking absentmindedly at a plate of *som tam* or papaya salad. She was trying to kill time as she had arrived thirty minutes earlier than her appointment.

When the black Ford sedan arrived at the White Lotus Hotel to discharge its three passengers, she looked across the street at them with interest. She noticed too that a young man sitting a few tables away from her, closer to the roadside and in the line of her sight, had also shown interest in the three men who had by then walked into the hotel. By the time she got up to cross over to the hotel, she saw the back of the young man as he walked down the street.

As soon as Suchin was shown to Charoen's table, the latter tried to smile. Secretly, the journalist wanted to laugh aloud from witnessing for herself the accuracy of her editor's information. In the report he had given her, it was mentioned that the secret society chief looked more impressive when not smiling. Now that the gangster was contemplating a new career as an affable politician, he had to smile more. But as he was not used to smiling, the best he could manage was a barring of teeth, which only made him looked more frightening than reassuring.

Suchin forced herself to put on a straight face and said, "I thank you, sir, for this opportunity to interview you."

Once again flashing that wolfish grimace, Charoen said, "It's my pleasure. Since I've granted you this interview, you may go ahead and ask me anything and I shall give you my frank answers to enlighten you."

Much as she disliked the man's patronizing air, Suchin smiled genially. As an experienced journalist, she decided to set him at ease by holding back the "killer questions" until later.

Hence, Charoen, in between flashing his frightful grimaces at her, was at his most gallant in fielding her initial questions. He confirmed his candidacy in the coming General Elections. And when she asked him what had decided him to do so, he gave her the all-time politically correct answer of wanting to serve the people, and do more for his country.

Her next question seemed to have caught him by surprise. "Is it true that you're one of the chieftains of the Tang Kong Si?"

The gangster scowled. This time, it was the real thing, and not the grimaces he tried to pass off as smiles. Suchin thought he was going to slap her. Thus when she saw the effort he was making to control himself by merely baring his teeth in an attempt to smile, she thought it quite admirable of him.

"Lies," Charoen growled through his bared teeth. "They're all lies. My enemies bear grudges against me and so want to prevent me from serving the people and my country. As such, they spread lies about me."

"If that's the case, the lies must have gone around because more than half of the people in Bangkok have linked you to General Phao Sriyanonda's drug deals, just as many reliable eye witnesses have claimed to have seen you in various opium dens, gambling joints and brothels."

This time Charoen went into an immediate transformation as he gave her a hard-eyed, clenched-jaw look, which was supposed to be intimidating but it somehow made Suchin thought he looked very distinguished. *Maybe I should tell him that he stands a better chance in winning votes like this than trying to smile*, she thought.

"Get out! I see now that you've been wasting my time all along," he snarled, his eyes flashing angrily. "I had thought you came with sincerity but I have been mistaken because I can tell now that you've already planned to write something bad to discredit me."

Without a word, Suchin stood up and left hurriedly. From what she had already dug up about the man, and now having spoken to him even though for less than twenty minutes, she knew deep inside her that he made her feel very uneasy. Though she had tried to make light of the situation, there was something in the way he looked at her that gave her a creepy feeling. His glare was so malevolent that it unnerved her. As she was walking out of the hotel, she suddenly realized – Charoen reminded her in some ways of Major Ishihara Shigeto.

From the White Lotus Hotel, her home was only about twenty minutes' walk away, and so she decided to walk. After passing the restaurant with the brightly-lit red lanterns, she reached the part of Yawaraj Road that was poorly-lighted. It was at the junction of a dark side alley that she sensed the presence of a man behind her.

When she turned around to face him, she saw it was one of Charoen's men, the one with a livid scar on the right side of his face and whom she had assumed to be a bodyguard.

"W-what do y-you want?" stammered Suchin, dismayed that despite trying to sound confident, her voice came out rather unsteady even to herself.

"In a few minutes, my colleague will drive over," the thug smirked at her, seemingly sensing her fear and enjoying it. "Just quietly get into the car and I won't have to hurt you."

"I think y-you have got the w-wrong person," she said, seeking to gain time and wondering whether she could outrun him.

With a mocking grin, Scar Face suddenly stretched a hand out for her. Suddenly, someone came out of the dark alley. It was so unexpected and his movement was so fast and fluid that all Suchin saw was only a blur. The person slammed into Scar Face, with both hands chopping down on the thug's neck. Before the hoodlum could recover, the man brought up a knee, possibly against Scar Face's groin because the gangster let out a high-pitched scream and then sank to his knees, moving both hands to the spot between his legs and then slowly toppling down on the road. She now saw her rescuer was the young man she had seen earlier at the hawker stalls.

☆☆☆☆

To her surprise, Mrs. Mary D'Souza had to wait nearly twenty minutes that morning before her boss's secretary finally ushered her into Mr. Raj Menon's office. Mrs. D'Souza was astonished because her boss, Mr. Menon, an Assistant Director attached to the Home Office, was a man who lived by the clock and would frown on unpunctuality.

When she went into the office, she saw papers fanned out neatly on the desk before the Assistant Director.

"Sit down," Mr. Menon barked in his usual curt manner, without looking up at her. He was still reading the sheet of paper held in his hand.

After a minute or so, he finally looked at her but his face still showed that faraway deep-in-thought look.

"This Lim Chin Siong fellow is a real pain in the neck," Mr. Menon complained. "Two years ago, when he was only twenty-two, he got elected on a PAP's ticket as a legislative assembly member for Bukit Timah. But he'd given us so much trouble that we had no choice but to take him into custody. His case officer has reported him to be a hardcore. Even now we still don't really know what to do with him."

Mrs. D'Souza knew the Assistant Director was referring to the People's Action Party, which under its shrewd and politically-savvy leader, the young lawyer Lee Kuan Yew, had in recent months been gaining much popularity among the people.

"At least, I can offer a different profile for my case," she said the moment Mr. Menon started to focus his dark eyes on her.

"Which one?"

"Ong Lay Yong."

"Oh, that young Chinese lady teacher whose agitation resulted in the fatal shooting of one of her students," Mr. Menon said.

Mrs. D'Souza had always been impressed by her boss's fantastic capacity for remembering people and events. She was wondering how a person could remember so much when his voice brought her back to her purpose of seeing him that morning. "What good news do you bring me about that woman?"

"I think she hasn't strayed too far left to cause us, as you would say, in a state of not really knowing what to do with her."

"So, what would you suggest we do with Ong Lay Yong?"

"Rehabilitate and then release her."

He gave her a hard look. "Do you really believe she can be rehabilitated?"

"I believe so," Mrs. D'Souza said, and before her boss could ask for her explanation, she offered it. "After you'd given your permission, I specially selected *Pygmalion* for her to read and I'm pleased to report it has succeeded in drawing her out of her shell. You can read the actual transcripts from this report."

When she placed the manila file on her boss's desk, the thin, tall man whose eyebrows were so fair that they could hardly be seen on his dark face said in a voice filled with incredulity, "Just one book had done so much?"

"Yes," said Mrs. D'Souza cheerfully, ignoring her boss's sardonic tone. "This is why I believe we should let her have more selected books to read. Books are the key to her rehabilitation."

"You have any title in mind?"

"I had already given her a second book," she said, and then hastily added. "Even though I haven't got your green light, I'd thought you won't mind if I let her have George Orwell's *Animal Farm*."

Mr. Menon stared hard at his assistant. "Well, at least, you seem to know what you're doing. Perhaps you may pull it off with this young woman. I wish it can be so simple with Lim Chin Siong."

"If we can turn Lay Yong around, we would have saved at least one person. If we succeed, it's only because you're a man of compassion and understanding," Mrs. D'Souza said.

Just as Mrs. D'Souza stepped out of his office, Mr. Menon couldn't help feeling flattered and at the same time, also felt manipulated and gullible. *That damned woman has always managed to put me in this position,* he thought without feeling any malice. *Maybe I should let her handle Lim Chin Siong.*

Twenty-four

*T*ried as Suna Phuwisai would, she however could not snap out of her nightmare.

Immediately after the fifteen-year-old girl arrived in Bangkok the previous night, the man who was supposed to be her agent had taken her away from three other girls who traveled with her all the way from their village near Khon Kaen in northeast Thailand. He brought her to a windowless room where she was confined. She knew she was a prisoner because she had tried to go out in the middle of the night to look for a toilet but found the door locked from outside. Luckily, she found a pot in the room to ease herself.

Early that morning, a middle-aged woman who was heavily powdered and rouged, came to look her over. Satisfied with her appraisal, she ordered Suna to follow her to a bathroom where she curtly told the frightened girl to strip and bathe under her watchful eyes. The moment Suna finished using a tin cup to scoop water from a large earthenware tub to splash over her body, the woman asked abruptly, "Are you a virgin?"

"Of c-course," stammered Suna. "Why?"

Without answering her question, the woman pointed at a pile of clothes on a chair nearby, saying, "Put these on."

She was thereafter escorted back to the windowless room. When she saw her reflection on the wall's mirror, she knew something was definitely not right. Her new clothes were too revealing for her liking and not at all like those worn by a domestic servant. And the agent had promised her a job as a domestic servant that day when he went to her village to recruit her and the other girls.

Suna looked at the woman and said timidly, "These clothes seem to be wrong..."

"What's wrong?" snapped the woman. "You must look good for the customers or they won't want you."

It took a moment for the older woman's words to register as Suna stared at her painted face. "Customers? I...I don't understand. I'm here t-to work as a d-d-domestic servant. Surely, there's a mistake..."

"No mistake," said the woman who was used to such situations. "You have been sold to us and your job is to entertain men."

After the woman left the room, Suna flung herself on the bed and cried her heart out. Every now and then she told herself it was just a bad dream and if she tried very hard, she would snap out of it. But she hadn't.

Hearing the door opened, she looked up from the bed. A distinguished-looking man with a mane of thick salt-and-pepper hair came in and closed the door behind him. A thought came to her: *Surely such a distinguished-looking man couldn't be a bad person.*

She appealed to him. "Please h-help me, sir, I've been b-brought here against my will."

Charoen Limthongkul had a standing order for all his pimps. They must let him know each time they acquired a young virgin girl so that he can be the first to try her out. And so he told the girl: "I can help you by calling the police but it can only be done later. As I've just come into this room, your captors will find it odd if I were to leave so soon."

Grateful to hear the man was willing to help her, Suna nodded her head and smiled innocently at him.

Though his face was still impassive, Charoen's eyes were alive and his voice was filled with emotion. "It will however look strange if they were to come into this room and find us the way we are. So why don't we both undress?"

Without waiting for Suna's answer, Charoen took off his shirt. When he was unbuckling his belt, he saw Suna staring wide-eyed at him. He smiled for the first time since coming into the room. "Don't be shy. Take off your clothes. As I've just said, if they were to come in and find it strange, then I won't be able to help you."

Suna's mind was in turmoil. Though she thought the man's words sounded reasonable enough but she somehow thought it odd that he was so insistent on her taking off her clothes. Besides, she was frightened by the look on his face when he bared his teeth at her. He no longer looked so distinguished but appeared quite wolfish.

And seeing him slipped off his underpants, her eyes roved to the huge rigid thing between his legs. Tearing her eyes away from the monstrosity, she looked at the man's face and was scared out of her wits by his expression.

☆ ☆ ☆ ☆

By 9:40 p.m., Mao Dong Po knew it was time for him to make his exit from the restaurant.

Throughout the evening, he had faithfully seen to it that the VIP guests seated at Charoen Limthongkul's table were never short of drinks to accompany their food. He was grateful that he had been allowed the four days' lead time to impress *Phi* Chuan of his capability and diligence to be finally assigned on that night as the waiter responsible for Charoen's table. Had he been assigned to the other tables, he would not be able to carry out the plan he had in mind.

But he was destined to serve at Charoen's table just as it was the distinguished-looking man's fate to die that night. Throughout the evening, he patiently bided his time by subserviently attending to Charoen's guests and even received praises from the man himself. Just a few minutes ago, he had managed to slip a lethal poison into Charoen's brandy without being noticed while refilling his glass. Dong Po was thankful that his *sifu* had, apart from teaching him the deadlier skills, also taught him card tricks requiring sleight of hand where nimble fingers could hide and manipulate objects.

Having taken things to that stage, it was necessary now for Dong Po to put as much distance as possible between him and his quarry. He could still recall the words of the *sinseh* during his short apprenticeship with the traditional "New Village" herbalist: "Though not harmful if consumed in small doses with other herbs, it's terrible when taken in excess. Death will occur within minutes of taking this poison. So be very careful to keep within the permitted dosage."

And should Charoen die immediately after downing his drink, Dong Po had no doubt he would be the number one suspect as the table's attendant-waiter. And having seen the way Charoen drank, he had no doubt too about the event taking place very soon. Therefore he had to make his exit fast before Charoen's thirst led him to reach for his drink. At the same time, his exit must be done casually so as not to arouse the host's suspicion.

When a guest dropped one of his chopsticks, Dong Po seized the opportunity. "I'll get a new pair for you, sir."

With those words, he walked towards the kitchen. The moment he passed the swing doors, he dropped the chopsticks, lifted a large square tin can of cooking oil and made his way past the busy cooks and helpers to the back door. This time, though his pace was faster, anyone who saw him would have thought he was carrying the can to the lane outside the back door.

In the darkness of the lane, he dumped the can and walked briskly towards the direction of the main street. As he walked, he removed the false moustache and shaggy dark brown wig he was wearing. Pushing them into the pocket of his black slacks, he removed the white waiter jacket which he had worn over a navy blue silk shirt. When he stepped into Yawaraj Road, the light from the street lamp showed him to be a different person from the one who had earlier worked in the restaurant. He walked a short distance before hailing a rickshaw and told the puller to take him to the Hua Lampong Station.

☆ ☆ ☆ ☆

At the time that Dong Po was making his escape, Colonel Phanu Ritthidet who was representing the military at the dinner turned to his host. "I heard the field marshal said you will never be short of votes as your sexual virility had you fathering many sons and daughters all over Bangkok."

Everyone laughed. Charoen, who was relieved by the colonel's presence which showed he was no longer in the new regime's black book, laughed along. Puffing with pride, he boasted, "Other than the nine children which my wife had given me, I've actually lost count of the number of children which I have had from my union with other women."

The colonel pressed on. "Is it true that you need sex every day and you only do it with virgins?"

"Yes, I'm so virile that I can't live without women," bragged Charoen, who began to feel aroused from thinking of the young girl he had enjoyed earlier that day. "And though I prefer virgins, I have to accept that they don't come by everyday. However, I'm lucky that I get them most times."

"But why virgins?" asked a man who had come from Manila to negotiate the purchase of a consignment of opium.

"I prefer virgins because they not only make for safer sex but I also believe sex with virgins can enhance a man's virility."

"Let's drink to virgins," said Colonel Phanu, who despite his skepticism and dislike of the upstart gangster-businessman-politician, was however duty-bound to his field marshal to feign friendship towards Charoen. He raised his glass, saying, "Bottoms up."

The other guests raised their glasses to join the toast led by the colonel. After Charoen had drained the content in his glass, he looked around for the waiter to refill everyone's glass. *Strange,* he thought. *Where's the guy? Wasn't he supposed to change the dropped chopsticks? Why is he taking so long?*

That was the moment he felt the sharp pain tearing at his guts. As the pain soon became very unbearable, his eyes bulged and he tried to cry out for help but choked on his bile. He couldn't understand the look of horror on the faces of his guests and what they were trying to tell him. And then his body convulsed in a painful spasmodic movement before a welcomed curtain of insensibility engulfed him.

Suchin Suewonglee fidgeted in impatience as she waited for Mao Dong Po to come to her home.

The night after the young man had rescued her from Charoen's thug, he had escorted her home. The fright and relief from being rescued had somehow loosened her tongue and throughout the walk to her home, she told him about her being a journalist and how she had been assigned to interview Charoen.

"You should stay home for a few days as it won't be safe for you to go to your office," her rescuer had told her.

"But what's the use of hiding at home for a few days? If he wants to harm me, he can still send his thugs to waylay me after I go back to work."

"Let your editor know you want to take, say, a week, off. When you report for work next Monday, everything should be all right."

"What made you so sure things will be all right by next week?"

"I can't explain. All I can say is that after this week, you should be safe." The pace of his words was hesitant as though he was mentally reviewing what could be divulged before speaking.

"Are you an undercover policeman? Has Charoen come under surveillance and about to be detained some time this week?"

He looked startled. "What made you say this?"

"I saw you," she said. "You were earlier sitting at a table by a hawker's stall opposite the White Lotus Hotel. You were spying on Charoen, weren't you?"

He laughed. "Your reporter's imagination is too much for me."

Digging into his pocket, he took out a wallet, from which he retrieved a business card. "This is my card."

She looked at it. "You're Klahan Pattano?"

"At your service, Miss…"

"Oh, I'm sorry, in the excitement, I've forgotten to tell you my name," she blushed. "I'm Suchin… Suchin Suewonglee."

"Hmm, that's a lovely name. Suchin means lovely thought, right?"

"Yes," she said, suddenly feeling shy.

Though she had subsequently taken his advice and stayed home, she was still unsure whether he was indeed the manager of a pest removal company as he had made himself out to be. Her instinct as a woman and a journalist told her that while the young man hadn't told her an outright lie, yet it wasn't the total truth either.

It was his hesitation and the veil that had come over his eyes whenever he tried to answer her questions that had alerted her. Each time she had posed a question to him, she could almost hear the clicks in his brain as he thought over the most appropriate answer to give her. Besides, though he seemed to have the time to come over to her house to accompany her in the past few days, once it turned dark, he would leave, giving the excuse that he had work to do. She suspected he had gone back to Yawaraj Road to spy on Charoen.

In the past few days that they were together, she had found it a daunting task to place him. First, she thought him too young to be a manager of a firm unless he was working for his father since the company's name was Pattano. And yet, from their conversation, she found him to be quite intelligent and well informed even though he had little formal education. In some ways, he reminded her of Vichai. They both shared the same youthful look and cheerful disposition. But unlike Vichai, there was a hard edge about him, something dark, dangerous and mysterious, despite the air of easy confidence about him.

Who was he really? Was he an undercover cop as she had initially suspected? Perhaps he worked for the American government. After all, she had heard that the Central Intelligence Agency had recently become very active in her country. And he had proven himself to be well-trained from the way she had seen him handling Scar Face.

Whoever he was, she knew that despite their age difference, she was somehow being drawn towards him. It was the first time ever since Vichai that she had felt any deeper emotion toward a man. Just the day before, when they were both sitting on the sofa discussing the future of Thailand, Suchin had suddenly felt a yearning to touch him and also for him to feel her. On that sudden impulse, she had reached her hand out to stroke his face, and he had responded by taking her in his arms to kiss her. It was only a momentary weakness on her part because she suddenly pushed him away.

Though his eyes registered surprise, he had very cannily asked her: "Are you bothered by my age or upset by something from your past?"

"I'm older than you."

"Does it matter?" he asked. "I think it has more to do with your past."

Taken aback by his perceptiveness, she said curtly: "The past is gone and forgotten."

"Yes, unpleasant things are best left behind. Well, it's time for me to go to work," he said as he got up from the sofa.

She somehow felt very low after he had left and was unable to sleep much throughout the night. Early in the morning, when she heard him ringing her doorbell, she was filled with elation. As in the past few days, he had brought her breakfast. Earlier that evening, just as he was about to leave, he had turned around and asked her: "Will you wait up for me tonight? I will come by later though I don't know when."

And so she had been eagerly waiting.

Putting down her book, Ong Lay Yong rubbed her tired eyes.

As she stretched out on the bare bed in her cell, she replayed the conversation she had earlier that morning with Mrs. Mary D'Souza. It was on account of that dialogue that she had re-read *Animal Farm*, whose author, George Orwell told the story of how the pigs led the other animals in Mr. Jones's Farm to revolt against their human masters and after their victory, decided to run the farm themselves on egalitarian principles.

"Is Mrs. D'Souza right in saying that I resemble Boxer?" she asked herself aloud as she had developed the habit of talking to herself.

She still remembered Mrs. D'Souza's words: "Like Boxer, the hardworking horse who was so brainwashed by the pigs, your only contribution to your cause would be allowing the pigs to become more powerful to establish a new tyranny which will eventually corrupt them."

"But it was only a fictitious tale…" she had tried to argue.

"A fictitious tale?" asked Mrs. D'Souza. "Wake up, young lady. It is a fiction no doubt but it is also a satirical allegory of the Russian Revolution. Just the other day you were praising the Russians. Surely you can recognize Stalin or shall we say, Napoleon as one of the pigs is called in the book? Or even Trotsky who is none other than Snowball the other pig?"

"But Boxer is such a fool…" and realizing she was admitting to Mrs. D'Souza's earlier comment that she resembled the hardworking albeit gullible horse, she stopped. A flush came slowly over her face, which also showed horror from being dismayed that she could harbor such thoughts.

And now as she recalled the earlier day's conversation with the case officer, Lay Yong shook her head slowly from side to side. "It couldn't be like what has been written in the book. Our cause is good. Colonialism has already been proven to be oppressive and rife with corruption and suffering. Our only hope of salvation is in sacrifice and dedication to our cause. I mustn't waver."

Twenty-five

After the rickshaw-puller had dropped him off at the Hua Lamphong Station, Mao Dong Po went to sit on a bench for a few minutes. Sure that no one was on his tail, he got up and walked briskly to the west gate

At the west gate, he got into another rickshaw and told the puller to send him to the Ratchawong Pier. From there, he crossed the Chao Phraya River over to Tha Din Daeng where he waited ten minutes, carefully scanning the faces of the few travelers who came later in three other boats. Assured that everyone was genuinely going about their normal business, he boarded a boat to return to the Ratchawong Pier. He repeated his observation until he was satisfied that he was not being followed. His *sifu* had taught him well. He started walking the short distance to the home of Suchin Suewonglee, a few houses away from the junction of Chakrawat Road and Songwat Road.

On nearing her home, he realized his heart was beating quite fast. He knew it wasn't the exertion from the walk. He was actually looking forward very much to see her again. Though he had gone to brothels in the past whenever he felt the need, and it had been quite a while since he had a woman, yet the feeling he now felt towards Suchin was different. At those brothels, it had been like animals mating with one another. Other than physical lust, he had felt nothing deeper for those women whom he paid for their time and access to their bodies. But with Suchin, even though they hadn't been physically intimate, Dong Po however felt an inexplicable force pulling him to her. He realized he had enjoyed those conversations with her.

When Suchin opened the door in answer to his ringing her doorbell, his very first words caught her by surprise. "Will you allow me to stay in your home tonight?"

"Of course, not only tonight but any number of nights" she said eagerly and then flushed. "I'd thought of asking you to move out of your hotel and come to my home but..."

"But what?" he asked with a mischievous grin, knowing fully well how conservative people were in those days in their part of the world. Men and women in Asia wouldn't behave so liberally like those characters he read in the James Bond's novels unless they were oblivious or uncaring of their neighbors' gossips.

Seeing his cheeky smile, she was again reminded of Vichai and the memory brought a pang of sorrow to her heart. Dong Po caught the fleeting sadness crossing her eyes. "If it isn't convenient, I'll leave."

"No, no, it's all right," she protested hurriedly, and with an effort, pushed the past out of her mind. "But where's your luggage?"

"I travel light," he said non-committally. "And may I use your telephone to place a call to Sadao?"

"Please go ahead."

Dong Po walked to the living room and picked up the telephone.

He gave the operator a number which he had long ago committed to memory. As he waited, he remembered his *sifu's* caution to call the number only when it was absolutely necessary.

Somchai answered on the fifth ring. "Who is it?"

"This is Klahan," Dong Po said. "Just to let you know the client's problem has been removed."

"That's good, my boy," the gruff voice came from the other end sounded hollow. "I too have removed the other client's pest."

Dong Po marveled that even though they weren't seeing each other face-to-face, his *sifu* seemed to know why he was making the call – the young man was worried whether his mentor had made it safely back from his assignment in Burma.

"When will you be back?" asked the Siamese.

"Maybe in a day or two."

"There's no hurry, my boy. It may be good for you to explore Krung Thep a bit as there may be requests in future from our Bangkok's clients for pest removal services."

After he replaced the receiver, he turned and caught Suchin studying him. One of her eyebrows was raised as

195

though she was expecting him to explain something that was puzzling her. He thought she looked very attractive as the expression made her high cheekbones stood out even more.

"I was just telling my boss about the completion of one of our pest removal jobs," he said, reaching out for her hand.

She was about to lean towards him but the feeling lasted only for a moment because she pulled her hand abruptly away the moment their hands touched. Her mind flashed back to the night of January 3, 1945.

Nearly thirteen years ago. Vichai and she were carrying secret documents for the *Khabuankarn Seri Thai*, the underground resistance movement. To allay any suspicion, they were holding hands like lovers, something they wouldn't have to feign as they were indeed in love. Just as they were crossing the Rama VI Bridge, the Allied bombers chose that moment to fly overhead to drop their deadly cargo. Vichai who was just a year older than her were killed during the bomb raid. She miraculously escaped unhurt though unable to evade her Japanese captors who took her thereafter to a worse hell – Major Ishihara Shigeto.

"Are you all right?"

Suchin was drawn back to the present by Dong Po's question. She stared at him for several seconds and then blinked. "Yes, I'm fine…I guess I'm tired as it's late. Your room is that one. If you'll excuse me, I shall say goodnight."

He gave her an odd look. Just as she was about to walk up the stairs to her bedroom, he said: "By the way, I don't think you need to worry about Charoen anymore. On my way here, I passed by a restaurant in Yawaraj Road and saw a commotion. It seems he has died in the midst of a dinner party he was hosting."

"How did he die?" she turned around to ask. "Was he shot?"

"Oh, nothing as dramatic as that," he said easily, his eyes were totally void of any expression. "If he had been shot, the police would have been swarming all over the place."

Again, she searched his eyes. "Then what caused his death?"

He shrugged his shoulders. "Perhaps, he had a heart attack."

As she stood there, staring at him, she felt the tingling feeling up and down her spine. *Has Klahan something to do with Charoen's death? She wondered. Is he an assassin? Perhaps he's avenging the death of someone dear to him and whom Charoen had harmed?*

"Goodnight," he said, walking towards the room she had earlier indicated.

☆☆☆☆

That night was particularly hot and humid. Ong Lay Yong, who was sweating, was unable to sleep. She suddenly thought of her home and her parents.

Ever since her incarceration, she had tried not to think of them and had even refused meeting them on those few visits they had initially made to the detention centre. As she used to tell her pupils, "A true revolutionary must be willing to sacrifice even parents, family, or home for a cause."

But that night, her mind somehow went back to the time when she was studying at the Chong Hwa Girls' High School. She remembered the mornings when she would get up early to eat breakfast prepared by her mother before going to school. As she normally took a bus to Bartley Road, she was surprised one morning when her father, who usually got up an hour after her, also rose early to join her for breakfast, saying, "I'll send you to school today."

At first she had thought her father was eager to show off the new Morris Minor he had recently bought but when they passed the Cathay cinema heading towards Selegie Road, he suddenly said, "Lately, you've been coming home or sneaking out at odd hours, trying not to be seen."

Her voice stiffened, like hackles rising. "Are both Ma and you spying on me?"

"Ma doesn't know as she sleeps early and very little can rouse her once she has fallen asleep," her father said. "As for spying on you, well, I'm just worried about you."

"There's nothing to worry about," she said. "I was just attending meetings…"

"That's why I'm worried," her father interrupted. "I know what sort of meetings you've been going to."

"What do you mean?" she asked suspiciously.

"Many of my friends also have sons and daughters your age. It seems to us that communism has an appeal not only for the irreligious and fanatics but also young students like our children."

"If there isn't poverty, corruption, injustice, excessive greed of landlords and bosses who would exploit the people, then there's no need for communism."

Her father sighed. "Well, as Ma and I have already lost a son, I hope you'll be careful. The government isn't going to tolerate any dissident."

Hearing her father's mention of her only and elder brother who was one of the thousands of victims of the *Sook Ching* – purification by elimination operations – carried out during the Japanese Occupation, she held her peace and stared out of the window.

After a short silence, as the car neared her school, she said, "Please drop me off here as I don't want to be seen in a motorcar."

And now, years later, as she was locked up in a prison cell, she wondered whether she had done the right thing in making her parents worried over her. Since she had refused any meeting or communication with them, they wouldn't know how she was faring. She remembered her mother used to lament, "Maybe Heaven is using you to punish me for my not being filial enough to my own father."

And then to her surprise, Lay Yong spoke out loudly, "What a silly woman my mother is in thinking she has been unfilial to her father! My grandfather is such a useless man."

In her mind's eye, she saw an old man who preferred to live a profligate's life than to work. That was why after inheriting a grain business and a shop house in Penang from an uncle, Lay Yong's grandfather had sold away the business though he kept the shop house where he lived alone and rented out the front to other businessmen. On the few occasions that Lay Yong's mother had brought her to Penang, she found herself disliking that surly-looking man whom she was told to address as "Grandpa". Lay Yong disliked him because he was not only full of complaints but also seemed indifferent towards his grand-daughter. And from her communist viewpoint, he was a landlord – an enemy.

Twenty-six

*M*ao Dong Po's eyes widened when he saw the thick wad of currency which his *sifu* had just handed to him. He had never seen so much money before in his life.

It was in early December 1957, two weeks after Dong Po's return from Bangkok. That night, without warning, Somchai came knocking on the back door of Dong Po's uncle's shop just after the lad had helped his mother cleared the dishes from their earlier dinner.

After Dong Po gave Somchai a quick account of how he had removed Charoen Limthongkul, the Siamese chuckled: "Your apprenticeship in the Chinese herbalist's shop hadn't been a waste after all. Here, you've earned $8,986 after deducting the money I had advanced you and also for buying your Beretta pistol.

"I didn't know we can make so much money from removing problems," Dong Po said in awe. "My father had once told me that the most a doctor can make was about $400 a month and those are the really good ones."

"Your father was right. It takes a doctor at least two years to earn this much money," agreed Somchai. "Considering that a simple meal at the famous Hoy

Tian Lao in Krung Thep costs only around 50 Bahts, or at most 100 Bahts, you've just earned a princely sum."

Hearing Somchai mentioning the popular Chinese restaurant at Sua Pa Road in Yawaraj, Dong Po smiled as it reminded him of the night not long ago when he had taken Suchin Suewonglee there to celebrate her birthday. The dinner had cost him nearly 160 Bahts, which showed his mentor was not always right.

Pushing Suchin from his thoughts, he turned to his *sifu*. "I suppose people are willing to pay much money for problems to be removed?"

Somchai who was about to lit a cigarette, stopped and looked at his young protégé. "No, I mean yes, only a few can make much money in our profession. There are many problem removers out there but only the few good ones who excel in removing the really serious problem can demand more money. In a country like ours, in such violent and uncertain times, where life is held cheaply, many will even remove problems for just a few dollars or even for free."

"We are among the few good ones?"

"Yes, I mean no, I am among the few top ones, my boy."

Dong Po tried hard not to show his displeasure. "I don't understand, Uncle Somchai. If I'm not considered as among the few top ones, then why have you given me so much money?"

"No, I mean yes, you're good in what you do. After all, you have been personally taught by me," said the

Siamese with some pride. "But if you were to offer your service on your own, the clients will either laugh at your face or they will pay you very little."

"Oh, I understand," said Dong Po as his face brightened considerably. "You mean the clients knew *your* reputation and so are paying you the highest fees."

Somchai grinned. "As I've said many times before, you're smart, my boy."

"And they are paying so much for my removing Charoen because they think *you* are the one who has done the job."

"Right again, my boy."

"Tell me, Uncle Somchai, how am I ever going to build my own reputation since the clients don't know about my existence? Come to think of it, how do the clients know about people like us?"

Somchai took a long pull of his cigarette before saying: "People like us cannot just post an advertisement in the newspaper about our services. Therefore, those who want problems to be removed won't know exactly who to turn to."

"Then how come you are seldom short of orders, Uncle Somchai?"

"As you already knew, my orders come from just two clients."

"A faction within the military for whom Lieutenant-Colonel Wongkok Suttharom represents and someone in the Tang Kong Si. Who's the guy, Uncle Somchai?"

Somchai hesitated for a moment as though deliberating whether he should tell his young protégé. Then, choosing his words carefully, he said: "Some things are best left without knowing."

Somehow Dong Po knew he was walking on thin ice and so he merely nodded his head. But he felt a bit hurt that his *sifu* hadn't seemed keen to take him into his confidence.

And then he heard Somchai saying softly: "Back to your original question, I think it's better you get your assignments through me because the less my clients know about you, the less risk you face. Besides, they won't pay you as much as they will pay me."

Again, Dong Po didn't say anything, and the Siamese continued: "My friend, Chiu Ya Loong, the Penang *taikor,* once gave me a book called the *Art of War* which was written around 500BC by a military strategist called Sun Tzu. He wrote that the true warrior win victories, which won't earn him any reputation for wisdom or valor because his strategies are too secret while his enemy submits without any need for him to draw out his sword to spill blood. You must strive to be such a warrior."

Both men sat in silence for a while and then the Siamese suddenly yawned and pulled out a pocket watch. After a quick glance, he ended the conversation with, "It's late. I'd better get going. One thing though. Now that you've got a lot of money, don't be carried away into spending like there's no tomorrow. You must learn to save for a rainy day. Moreover, the authorities may become suspicious as to where you have got the money."

Two weeks went by and still Suchin had not heard from Klahan, which was the name Dong Po had given her. Several times she nearly reached for the telephone but each time she hesitated.

She sat staring at the sofa where he used to sit during those few days he had spent with her in her home. *It's strange that sometimes the people whom you get to see a lot mean so little to you, but the one whom you have so little time to be with, could yet mean so much,* she thought. *Am I in love?*

But when she thought of the day she last saw Klahan, she felt a sense of hopelessness welling up in her. Instead of staying just a night or two as he had told his boss over the telephone, Klahan had stayed at her home for two weeks.

On reflection now, it had been the happiest time of her life since the war. She had begged her editor for an additional week off. They had thereafter spent the days exploring the city by tram and in the evenings talking about anything that came to their minds.

Those times when they were alone at home, she had often caught the strange look in his eyes – the same look she often got from other men. There had been suitors in her life though none was permitted into her home as she knew what men had in their mind when alone with an attractive woman. Thus, she marveled that Klahan, despite being allowed access to the privacy and intimacy of being alone with her in her home had not once tried to take advantage of her. She could however sense his desire for her. On her part, she felt just as keenly for him but she held herself back the way she knew he too was holding back.

In the past two weeks, she had asked herself many times, "Why?" And the answer had unfailingly pointed to Major Ishihara Shigeto. Even now, she involuntarily shuddered from recalling the name of that demon in human form.

Her nightmare had begun not long after the Japanese soldiers had taken her to a cell. She cringed from recalling how they had forcibly torn away her clothes and throughout her ordeal, whooping and leering at her terror. Though she was initially surprised that they hadn't raped her, she was however smart enough to suspect that they were keeping her for someone more important and thereby more terrifying.

All that had happened some thirteen years ago, but she could still hear the iron door creaking open on its rusty hinges for the Japanese officer in white shirt and khaki pants to stride in. As she huddled in a corner, using her knees and arms to cover her nudity, she instinctively knew he was *kempeitai*.

The stocky man looked about thirty and was of average height, which made him shorter than Suchin. But at that moment, he seemed tall and menacing. As his hair was cut quite short, he appeared bald unless he came close to you, which was exactly how the terrified girl came to find out as he squatted and leaned within inches of her face. She saw his eyes were hard and dark, and the expression on his face was simply inscrutable.

"Despite what you may have heard about the long history of enmity between the Chinese and Japanese, we're really not an unreasonable people," he spoke, surprisingly in Thai, albeit in a halting and gruff manner, which somehow spoilt the soft, melodious flow of the language. "Though you're of Chinese descent, you're still considered Thai. Therefore, if you cooperate with us by telling me what you were doing on the King Rama VI Bridge, and give me the names of your accomplices, we can still treat you as a Thai and let you go."

"My boyfriend and I were crossing the bridge when the bombing started," she said, trying to sound confident. "We weren't doing anything wrong."

"Come, come, pretty one," he smiled for the first time, apparently relishing the hint of fear in her voice. "Don't take us for fools. We have found some interesting papers on your dead boyfriend and from your clothes. Won't you want your clothes back?"

"I'm telling the truth, we were just crossing the…"

She didn't finish the sentence because he hit her face hard with the back of his hand, causing her head to jerk and knock against the wall. Stunned as she was, she could feel the warm sticky blood seeping from her lips and nostrils. Dazedly, she looked at his still smiling face and saw his thick fingers had already unbuckled the belt of his pants. And that was when her nightmare had begun.

The distant bleat of a boat's horn snapped Suchin back to the present. *Maybe Klahan is still angry with me,* she thought miserably. *That could be why he hasn't called me. Oh, why hadn't I told him what had happened to me? If I had, then maybe, he could have understood.*

It was on the night of her birthday, and before she was due to report for work the following morning. They had just got back from dinner at the Hoy Tian Lao, and were sitting in her living room when he suddenly said, "Don't move."

She sat still as he had ordered. Suddenly his hand shot out in a blur to slap her bare shoulder. When he showed her the mosquito he had killed, she was surprised that he had hit the insect without causing her any pain. Having seen him made short work of Charoen's thug, she knew he was capable of defending himself. But tonight, she was sure he was in the same league as those martial art experts she had once interviewed. Like them, he knew how to focus his force and moved with lightning speed.

Perhaps she was moved by his gesture of care towards her, but without realizing it, she had leaned against him. When he moved both his arms around her, she felt very safe and contented. However, the moment he bent down to kiss her, she was once again seized by blind panic, causing her to frantically break away from his embrace. Once more, her mind flashed back to the Japanese monster and the shameful things he had done to her and forced her to do for him.

When she glanced quickly at the young man sitting on the sofa beside her, Suchin forced herself to push the past out of her mind. She thought Klahan looked bewildered. At the same time, she saw his eyes were full of hurt

"Suchin," he called to her, reaching both hands out for her again.

"No, Klahan," she pleaded, huskily. "Leave me alone."

It was the way he had narrowed his eyes and set his mouth in a thin line that told her that his youthful pride had been badly injured. For the first time, she noticed how pale and drawn his face had become.

They stared at each other for a while and then he broke the silence, saying, "All right, I'll leave you alone."

She had sat there by herself, with bowed head, feeling lost, inadequate, ashamed of her past, and unsure what to do with him when she suddenly saw his shadow on the floor. Quickly raising her head to look at him with tear-filled eyes, she saw he wasn't looking at her as he said, "Thank you for your hospitality."

And those were the last words she heard as he walked out of her home. She was so stunned that she hadn't stopped him. By the time she recovered enough to rush to the door, he was already gone.

☆ ☆ ☆ ☆

That night Ong Lay Yong woke up gasping for air. She looked up at the small window high up on the wall and saw darkness beyond the iron bars, telling her dawn was still several hours away.

Perhaps it was the narrowness of her cell, or maybe it was her frustration over the only window being too high up for her to look out. But that night, she felt claustrophobic. Feeling the air becoming more and more oppressive, she struggled to push herself up on the bed and sat upright till her breathing grew easier.

It was at that moment when she suddenly thought of her parents again. Both of them had come to her school graduation ceremony. On that day, she was filled with both sadness and elation. She was sad to be leaving school and having to say goodbye to her teachers and schoolmates. At the same time, she was elated because it would be the last time she was wearing the black-and-white uniform and she was eagerly looking forward to starting a new life as a working adult. Thanks to her father's connection – he was among the principal donors to the Chin Kang School – she had got a job as a trainee teacher at the school.

When her mother was talking to another parent, her father had asked her: "Are you sure you really want to teach? I mean there's always a job for you in my wine import business."

She knew her father had expected her reply even before she answered him because she had seen his eyes narrowed a fraction. Annoyed by his words, she had told him: "I prefer to be a teacher than to…to help you make alcoholics out of people."

This time, it was her father's turn to be annoyed. "You seem to have forgotten it was money from my wine import business that has nurtured your growth since you were young and got you through schooling all these years."

Though she said nothing but turned away with something like a sneer on her face, he added with some malice: "Well, if you want to teach, then teach. Just don't go about teaching your pupils to shout slogans the way you and your friends just did on stage."

Realizing he was criticizing her for her role that day in leading her classmates on the stage to shout their rehearsed appreciation for the teachers, she bristled. "What's wrong with our showing appreciation for our teachers?"

"It's all right to make a speech or sing a song but when I saw the lot of you shouting slogans, I can't help feeling how mindless you all appear to me... like a flock of parrots."

"It may seem mindless to you but that was how Chairman Mao Tse-tung had mobilized the masses to bring about reforms to China."

Twenty-seven

*E*arly one morning, just a week after the Chinese New Year in 1958, Mao Dong Po's mother woke him out of his sleep.

"Your boss is waiting for you downstairs," Madam Mao told her son who shook his head to clear his sleepiness.

"My boss?" he asked sleepily and then realized who his mother was talking about.

Not long after Dong Po had begun working for the Siamese, his uncle, after consulting with both of them, had told his sister, Madam Mao that Somchai had taken her son into his pest removal company as a part-time manager. Madam Mao was at first doubtful until Somchai himself had told her that her son would be paid commissions each time he successfully carried out the assignments given him. Somchai had even asked Dong Po to show his mother the business cards carrying the name of the Pattano Pest Removal Company. His *sifu* had added, "Of course, Dong Po will still help out his uncle in the shop when I don't have any assignments for him."

After a hurried wash and a quick change of clothes, he ran down the stairs to find the swarthy Siamese about to stub out a glowing cigar. Seeing his young protégé, Somchai grinned and waved the remnant of his cigar at him. "You should try this, my boy. After smoking one, you won't want cigarettes anymore."

Dong Po had lowered himself on a rattan chair facing his *sifu* who turned sideway on his chair to fish out two more cigars from his pocket. "Try it."

As it was the first time the young man held a cigar, he carefully watched his mentor who had also put a cigar to his own mouth. He saw Somchai bit off the end, spit it sideways onto the cement floor, and then lit it with a gold-plated lighter. Dong Po did the same though instead of spitting the end onto the floor, he put it into his pocket. Somchai then offered him a light.

After both men had taken a few puffs and savored the rich tobacco, Somchai leaned forward. "How was it?"

"You're right, Uncle Somchai. A cigar sure tastes better than a cigarette."

A satisfied smile appeared on the swarthy Siamese's face. "The ones we're smoking are Montecristo from Cuba. Without doubt, they're very expensive but worth every cent, my boy."

Dong Po was about to take another puff when his ears pricked up at his *sifu's* words. "Remember I'd told you that you may have jobs to do in Singapore?"

When the younger man nodded without saying a word, Somchai continued. "Well, now that Field Marshal

Sarit Thanarat has gone abroad for medical treatment, his right-hand man, General Thanom Kittikachorn is running the show."

Dong Po waited patiently for his mentor, who was puffing furiously away at his cigar to rekindle his cigar's smoldering tip, to come to the point. "I've been asked by Lieutenant-Colonel Wongkot Suttharom to remove a problem. It seems one of the members in the coalition government, a former military judge whose switch to politics has been largely financed by the Siew Li Kue, is proving to be a nuisance."

"You mean the Hokkien triad, which is the Tang Kong Si's archrival?"

"That's right," Somchai nodded. "The moment Lieutenant-Colonel Wongkot told me about the quarry, I'd contacted my client at the Tang Kong Si. It seems the Chow Chou triad chieftains too are baying for the quarry's blood as he had on many occasions in the past tried to get legislations passed to run down the Tang Kong Si's influence and also sent some of their members to jail or before a firing squad. They too wanted me to remove him."

"A corrupt judge certainly deserves removal," the young man passed sentence. "Can I assume we'll be paid twice for this job?"

"You assume right, my boy. We'll get payment from both clients."

"Why don't I do this job in Bangkok instead of Singapore?" asked Dong Po who was hoping for an opportunity to see Suchin Suewonglee again as it was already more than two months since he last saw her. He too had missed her and there were times he had thought of telephoning her but had hesitated from doubting whether she would welcome his call. "I'll be glad to remove him with a bang as a warning to all."

"Yes, I mean no, the job is to be done in Singapore, not Krung Thep and both parties want it to appear like an accident. So, there shall be no bang, my boy."

Dong Po's face clouded. "Strange, why don't they want a big bang? Come to think of it, since the military is so powerful, why don't they get rid of this fellow themselves?"

"Like the triads, the military…even if only a faction within the military, can't afford to be seen as too high-handed. As such, they need professionals like us. They want the removal to be as low key as possible. After all, this guy, having been a military judge, still has his supporters with the other factions of the military."

Hearing his young protégé sighed, Somchai said, "The reason the job is to be done in Singapore is because the quarry will be carrying something illegal for the Ghee Hock Tong, another Hokkien triad operating in Singapore and affiliated to the Siew Li Kue. As he has diplomatic status, the Customs in Singapore won't search his luggage."

"When should I leave?"

"You shall leave the day after tomorrow, giving you two days' head start to familiarize yourself. The quarry will be there for only three days. Here's his photograph and details of his schedules, including places he will be going, and the hotel he will be staying."

"How come you have such detailed information, Uncle Somchai?"

"When the military and triads combined their resources, they can be very formidable, my boy."

"After this job, may I take a couple of weeks off?"

"Where are you going?"

"Bangkok."

Somchai looked at Dong Po shrewdly but he saw his young protégé's eyes were veiled, revealing nothing. *Strange*, he thought. *Ever since Klahan came back from Bangkok, he looked sadder and older, not at all his usual youthful, exuberant self.*

After a while, the older man grunted. "Do as you please, my boy, so long as you don't let me down on this assignment. And since you will be in Bangkok, get in touch with this man," said Somchai, taking out a business card from his wallet. "He's a real estate agent. Tell him that you're my nephew, and I've told you to seek his advice. He'll help to grow your money which shouldn't be left idling. Use some, not all, of your money to buy land or property that he will advise. I will tell you how to invest the rest later in Malaya and Singapore. All right, I've got to go."

Dong Po sat alone, studying the photograph of a man who had a rather enormous nose which seemed to take up most of his ferret face. He looked more like a crook than a judge-turned-politician, even a corrupted one. Apart from his bulbous nose, the man had a mole on his right cheek. *He won't be difficult to recognize,* Dong Po thought. *That should make the removal a bit easier since I won't have to waste time trying to make him.*

The only thing bothering the young assassin was that it wouldn't be easy getting near the quarry since he would surely be protected by the Singapore gangsters. How then to stage an accident? And then he remembered his *sifu* had once taught him: "It will be futile to come up with a plan unless you have some idea of the final outcome. This means having some idea of the end result and then working backwards to find the mean to do the job. To do this, you must first study the quarry's schedules and habits carefully."

It also occurred to Dong Po that even if he could pull it off, getting away wouldn't be easy either. Once he had removed the quarry, he would have to move fast without drawing too much attention to himself. Perhaps, with luck, he could steal a car, with which to drive to the Causeway and after abandoning the car in Johor Baru, he would catch a train back to Padang Besar, and onwards to Bangkok.

But he hesitated because it would be risky to steal and thereafter be caught driving a stolen car. If news of the removal leaked within the hour, the police could very quickly set up road blocks along Bukit Timah Road or at the Causeway which would put an end to his escape plan. Of course, that could be the case if they knew who to look for. If the removal was well-planned, then no one would be any wiser and so the police wouldn't be looking for him at all. As Somchai had said, they wanted an accident, and so an accident it would be.

☆☆☆☆

After two months of waiting for Klahan (as she knew Dong Po) to call, Suchin Suewonglee couldn't take it anymore. She had willed herself to forget him and tried her utmost to forget him, but it was futile.

At last, she decided to call him and so one night after she returned home from work, she took out the business card he had given her and gave the number to the operator.

Three rings after the operator had put through the call, Suchin heard a gruff male voice. "Who is it?"

"My name is Suchin. May I speak to Klahan?"

There was a short pause before the man said: "He's not in."

"When will he be back?" she insisted. "It's important I talk to him."

The man's voice sounded hushed and guarded. "There's no telling when he'll be back. He's away on business."

"Is there a way I can reach him? Maybe, I can telephone the hotel he's staying?"

"I'm sorry but I have no idea which hotel he's putting up."

Suchin hesitated a moment. "Well, in that case, can you please let him know Suchin's looking for him?"

After putting down the telephone, she leaned back in the sofa. *I should have told him about what had happened to me during the war,* she thought. *But now, it's too late. Well, maybe, it's better this way. I'm after all, too old for him.*

☆ ☆ ☆ ☆

Ong Lay Yong's lips trembled with emotion. "It's happening as Karl Marx had predicted. The working class will take over all aspects of society and eliminate all the other classes to create a classless society."

Mrs. Mary D'Souza silently kicked herself for having told the young girl about how Ong Eng Guan, the recently appointed Mayor had derided the British and the English-educated civil servants. After Mrs. D'Souza came to the part about how the new Mayor had refused to wear the official wig, or use the gold-and-silver mace, saying those items were relics of colonialism, like the Mayor's working-class supporters, Lay Yong let off a cheer.

She declared, "It's time the English-educated running dogs of their colonial masters wake up to the fact that change is imminent. It takes courageous fellows like Ong Eng Guan and Lim Chin Siong to start the ball rolling."

Realizing her hard work had suddenly reverted to square one, Mrs. D'Souza sighed. She decided to try once more to move the young woman away from her leftist stance. "What about Lee Kuan Yew?"

"Oh, that fellow," Lay Yong said. "I'm not sure about him."

"Why?"

"He's English-educated."

Mrs. D'Souza waited.

"I once read a report in the newspaper about how his mother had wanted to raise him as a professional gentleman in the best English tradition," the young woman went on. "He and his family are all Anglophiles."

"But he had done a lot for the workers, the University of Malaya's Socialist Club, and it was he who had cultivated the two courageous fellows you'd named earlier."

Lay Yong shrugged. "I'm still not sure about him. He may try to be one of us but perhaps he isn't really one of us."

Mrs. D'Souza raised her brows. "What do you mean by us?"

"We're the masses," she said, averting her case officer's eyes. "We're the working class."

Twenty-eight

*E*ven though Colonel Prapass Oanorn had a most enjoyable night with his new, sexy secretary, who had accompanied him on this trip to Singapore, he was nonetheless in a bad mood when he got out of the chauffeured car at Boat Quay.

Earlier that morning when he awoke in his suite at the Raffles Hotel, he was already feeling lousy. It was a good thing for his secretary that Colonel Prapass was a man who insisted on sleeping alone. After their romp in her bed, he had returned to his suite. That morning, he felt rotten because he had dreamt of Chakraphan Choonhavan. As in all those past dreams, Chakraphan was crying, "Give me back my life…give me back my life."

During his tenure as a military judge, he was accustomed to passing the death sentence on many men. Though he could only vaguely remember some of those condemned fellows, it was Chakraphan whom he could recall with any clarity. Chakraphan was also the only one who had the temerity to haunt him in his sleep.

Sometimes Colonel Prapass wished he hadn't sent the fellow before a firing squad. After all, it hadn't really been proven that the young baker was a communist.

Besides, Chakraphan's family had sold off the family's bakery business to raise the sum Colonel Prapass had demanded for his release. But Colonel Prapass had ultimately passed the death sentence on the unfortunate baker despite having pocketed the bribe. He had done so in order to please then Field Marshal Phibun Songkhram, who after narrowly escaping trial as a war criminal at the end of the war, had tried to win the trust of the Americans by cracking down on the communists in Thailand. Besides, Chakraphan's family was of Chinese origin, the target of the field marshal's discrimination policies.

Now as Colonel Prapass stood, clutching the attaché case and sweating profusely, under the hot midday sun, he couldn't help shivering from recalling the bad dream. From where he stood, the Singapore River was on his right, while a row of double-storey shop houses were on his left. It was a busy street with many coolies trotting about, each one carrying a heavy sack on his shoulder. Some were heading for the shop houses while others were going towards the bumboats wedged up against one another along the quayside. A short distance away, two lorry-cranes were parked on the quayside, each dangling a large square wooden box at the end of a cable hook.

He stood still and squinted, uncertain which of the shop houses he was supposed to go. To his relief, the chauffeur, who had parked the car, came to his side and pointed at one of the shops where strangely, unlike the other shops, nothing was on view, leaving one to wonder whatever it was they were selling in that shop.

As he walked towards the shop, Colonel Prapass saw three Chinese men behind the counter staring suspiciously at him. Suddenly from somewhere inside the shop, a corpulent man wearing a thick gold chain across his equally thick neck waddled out smiling broadly. He spoke in Thai. "Colonel Prapass, welcome to Singapore. I'm Goh Lau See. Sorry, I wasn't able to meet you personally when you arrived last night. But I trust my chauffeur had been most useful."

Though he bristled inwardly that the obese man had failed to *wai* him with the respect he deserved, Colonel Prapass forced himself to smile. It was really beneath him to deal with scumbags like this one. But he had no choice since he owed the Siew Li Kue too many favors. *Well, let's get it over with,* he thought. *After this, I can get back to more pleasurable things, like my new secretary.*

Unknown to Colonel Prapass, just a short distance away, Mao Dong Po who was pretending to be an art student, was sitting on a foldable canvass chair by the river side, seemingly engrossed in his sketching. Wearing a wig of long, unkempt hair, and round glasses, he certainly looked the part of a bohemian art student. From where he sat, he saw the quarry handing over a briefcase to the fat Chinese guy. After a short conversation, fatso shook hand with the Thai and turned to go back into the shop. Just then, the chauffeur came along to ask the quarry to follow him to the car.

If there hadn't been any specific instruction like "no big bang but low key" such as an accident, Dong Po knew it would have been a perfect time to draw out a pistol and shoot the quarry. But since he had strict instruction of making it looked like an accident, he had reluctantly left his pistol behind in his uncle's house in Padang Besar.

As he sighed in frustration, he heard the grating sound from one of the lorry-cranes' motors. He turned to look at the source of the sudden din and saw the driver-operator jumped down from the cabin to walk to the back to look at the boom, presumably to check whether something was caught in the boom or if the cable was jammed. *This could be the opportunity I'm looking for,* Dong Po thought.

That night, Suchin Suewonglee dreamt Klahan was making love to her. He was lying beside her, at first using his hands to stroke her body, exploring those tantalizing places and moving closer to kiss her on the lips. Before long, he had rolled on top of her.

Just after he had joined with her to become one, he whispered in her ears: "Cooperate with us. Tell me what you were doing on the King Rama VI Bridge, and give me the names of your accomplices and I shall let you go."

Suchin opened her eyes and saw the hard and dark eyes of the Japanese as he began pushing faster and harder inside her, hurting her.

She screamed and woke up. After that, she sat up in bed, fighting to steady her body from trembling violently.

☆☆☆☆

Apart from having little opportunity to speak to anyone except her case officer, Ong Lay Yong also found it grating on her nerves at times to spend so much time being left alone in her cell. Hence, she also looked forward to her daily exercise and meal times even though the inmates were not allowed to talk to one another.

Earlier in the morning, when Lay Yong was doing physical exercise, it was possible that enough blood got into her brain to jolt her into getting a so-called brain wave. Thereafter, she was so deep in thought that the instructor had to shout at her a few times when she failed to follow the instructions given her.

After she was back in her cell, she began talking to herself as had become her habit. "I've been so foolish. Yes, I've been a fool for too long."

She sat still on her bed for a few minutes, holding her breath and hearing her heart thumping softly. The morning exercise, followed by a cold shower, had done her a lot of good that day. She found herself possessing the clarity of mind to think better.

Everything appeared so clear to her now. From the first time, Mrs. Mary D'Souza had given her *Pygmalion* to read, the case officer was subtly trying to subvert her from her cause. After *Pygmalion*, she was given *Animal Farm*. As Lay Yong's beliefs seemed to be shaken by George Orwell's anti-socialism satire, Mrs. D'Souza gave her another of Orwell's work, *Nineteen Eighty-Four*. This was followed by Friedrich Hayek's *The Road to Serfdom*.

"What a cunning devil Mrs. D'Souza is," she said aloud. "Well, now that I know the tricks she has up her sleeve, I shall play the game with her by pretending that she has succeeded in turning me around."

Hearing a door being slammed shut somewhere outside her cell, she stopped to listen intently for a while. After the sound of footsteps receded, she smiled happily. "Yes, I mustn't argue with her anymore but will play along and convince her that I've abandoned my cause. Only in this way will I be able to secure my freedom."

Twenty-nine

*I*t was the first time that Mao Dong Po had been on an airplane. He thus found the flight from Singapore to Bangkok to be an exciting beginning.

Though he was filled with anticipation, he did not relax until the Malayan Airways Limited's Vickers Viscount took off from Kallang Airport. Despite it being already dusk, he was glad he had asked for a window seat as he craned his neck looking out of the small window, taking in the sight of the flickering lights below. In those places where the lights were concentrated, he knew they came from the city. As for the scattered lights, he guessed they were from the many ships floating on the dark expanse of the sea.

He was thinking what a good idea it was to fly instead of going by his original plan of stealing a car to drive to Johor Baru to catch a train. Apart from the comfort, flying would also be faster than taking a train. He was looking forward to seeing Suchin Suewonglee again. And just when he was pondering over whether she would be as glad to see him, an air stewardess offered him a glass of iced water. *It's cool to fly*, he thought happily. *Like James Bond.*

He was happy too that in the end, he got his "big bang" without going against the instruction he had received. A smile came to his face when he recalled his slipping unnoticed into the lorry-crane's cabin to hit the lever releasing the cable. What followed was a loud crash – the "big bang" he wanted – as the large wooden crate dangling at the end of the cable hook came tumbling on top of the car carrying the chauffeur and the quarry. By then, Dong Po had already jumped off the cabin to slip unseen into a side alley linking to Chulia Street since everyone's attention was diverted towards the accident.

At the time he was making his escape, from the corner of his eyes, he saw enough of the badly-crumpled rear section of the car to know the passenger could hardly survive. If Colonel Prapass had sat in front, then it wasn't his fate to die yet. But having studied the man's profile, he knew the colonel was too pompous to be found sitting in front next to the chauffeur.

The droning of the aircraft's engines caused him to close his eyes to catch some sleep. After all, it had been an eventful day. Dong Po stirred again when he felt the Vickers Viscount banking sharply to get into position for the approach to Bangkok's Don Maung Airport. He knew he had dozed off because the flight attendant was announcing that they would be landing shortly. A glance at the Rolex he had bought in Singapore showed it was 11:10 p.m.

After the nightmare, Suchin was unable to fall asleep again.

For a while, she tried to read but her mind was too disturbed to concentrate. As the night was very humid, she decided to take a shower and washed her hair.

The moment the water sprayed on her body, she regretted her decision. Against her will, her mind drifted back to the day when Major Ishihara Shigeto made her performed a sexual game, using the water pumps he had set up in her cell and which his sadistic mind had then invented. After her ordeal, he had asked her: "Why are you so stubborn? You think we don't know about the *Khabuangkarn Seri Thai*?"

When she remained silent, the Japanese *kempetai* officer laughed. "They're just youngsters playing games. So far, have they launched any attack against us?"

And when she still refused to answer, he had sneered: "Do you know on the night the Allied bombers attacked the King Rama VI Bridge, it was your countrymen, Thai pilots, who flew up to intercept those bombers?"

She hadn't wanted to believe him but somehow his words got to her, nearly breaking her resolve.

The chimes of her doorbell snapped her back to the present. *Who could it be so late at this time of the night*, she thought after a glance at the clock saw it was already way past midnight. She hurriedly wrapped a towel around her, and grabbing another towel, a smaller one, to dry her hair, she went to the peep-hole to see who was at the door.

The moment she saw who the visitor was, Suchin's eyes immediately misted with tears. Though she tried to blink them back as she opened the door, they slowly trickled down her face. But they were tears of joy – Klahan had come back to her.

"Is it really you, Klahan?" she asked as a sudden thought came to her that she might still be in the midst of yet another dream.

"Why don't you believe it's me?" Dong Po asked, trying to keep his voice from showing the elation he felt from seeing her again, and also from knowing she was just as eager to see him.

"I never thought I would see you again. Well, if it's really you, then please come in."

After Suchin had closed the door, they stood staring at each other for a while, each unsure as to what to do. Dong Po could sense from her body language that though they were somehow treading on very sensitive ground, she was yet delighted to see him. Perhaps it was the smell of her hair and the mildly intoxicating scent of the perfumed soap she used earlier. But being so close to her and having had missed greatly, and being a man who was used to taking risk, he took her hand and drew her close to him.

As they stood hugging each other, she murmured: "Why hadn't you telephoned me all this while?"

"I'd wanted to," he said truthfully. "But I wasn't sure whether you would welcome my call. Besides, in Padang Besar where I live with my mother and an uncle, there's no telephone line yet."

"But your business card shows…"

He interrupted her. "Yes, though my office is in Sadao, my boss doesn't like his employees to use the telephone for private matters."

"No wonder he sounded quite curt when I telephoned two nights ago."

He broke from their embrace to stare at her. "You did?"

"Yes, he'd told me you were away on business. Is your boss your father?"

"No, my father's dead. But in a way, my boss is like a father to me."

She saw his eyes shone brightly, and then he said with obvious pride, "I was in Singapore. I flew into Bangkok this evening because I'd wanted to see you again."

Her eyes widened. "You flew in just to see me?"

"Yes, I've missed you," he said, hugging her close to him once more.

"I thought a lot about you too," she murmured.

"What about?"

"I realized how little I know about you," she said. "I didn't even know your father's dead and your boss is like a father to you. In fact, I don't know anything about you at all. For all I know, you could have been married."

"I'm not," he laughed. "You would have seen I don't wear any ring."

"Many married men took their rings off when they went chasing after other women," she snorted.

"I'm not them," he said simply, which led her to pull away to stare intently into his eyes before taking his face between her delicate hands to kiss him softly on the lips.

The morning after Ong Lay Yong had wised up to her case officer's strategy, she was scheduled to meet Mrs. Mary D'Souza.

The alert case officer immediately sensed the change in the young woman before her. Not only had Lay Yong greeted her cheerfully but she even said, "I guess I've been quite muddled up in my belief to think that a classless society is the answer to our current problems."

"Oh, what led you to think so?" asked Mrs. D'Souza softly.

"I've been thinking over the things I've read in those books you gave me. Somehow I cannot help feeling those authors could be right after all."

"Right in what way?"

"Well, a totalitarian state may not necessarily be a good thing," Lay Yong said. "As Hayek has put it, a centrally-planned system may end up incapable of delivering the promised reforms or worse, become tyrannical, which in George Orwell's words, "All men are equal but some are more equal than others." Hence, I guess the British isn't that bad after all since they still allow Mayor Ong Eng Guan to do things his ways."

Mrs. D'Souza listened with her head slightly turned on one side. Though the young woman's words sounded reasonable to her, she couldn't help wondering how sincere she was.

As she scrutinized the case officer's face, Lay Yong felt a surge of confidence. *Though Mrs. D'Souza isn't too convinced as to whether I mean what I've said, she's not disbelieving either,* she thought. That's good. If she isn't sure, then she most probably has doubt too as to whether I'm too far off into the left. Let me convince her of my turnaround though I must be careful not to overdo it.

Clearing her throat, she continued: "The fact that the Mayor hasn't been arrested means there's still hope for a return to democratic reforms in this country."

Looks like I was right about using selected books to influence her, Mrs. D'Souza thought happily, in her wanting to believe that she had made a breakthrough with this young woman in her charge. Aloud she said, "Let me see if I can get you *The Fountainhead* by Ayn Rand."

Thirty

*O*n the night of October 20, 1958, Mao Dong Po heard the announcement over the wireless that Field Marshal Sarit Thanarat had staged a second *coup d'etat*.

He knew the field marshal had just recently returned from the United States where he was receiving medical treatment. Considering that Prime Minister Thanom Kittikachorn was the field marshal's right-hand man, whom he had appointed to head the caretaker government, Dong Po was surprised. By the time the news broadcast was over, he had grasped the situation. Field Marshal Sarit had not only declared himself the new Prime Minister but had declared a state of martial law, banning opposition parties and newspapers, and suspending constitutional rule.

His first thought was Suchin Suewonglee. Was she all right? Though he was halfway reading James Bond's latest adventure in *Dr. No*, he thought of borrowing his uncle's bicycle to go over to Somchai's home in Sadao to telephone her. But he changed his mind because he wasn't sure whether the telephones would still be working. He looked at his watch and saw he still had time to catch the night train for Bangkok provided the trains were still allowed to run. As it was, there was no mention of curfew being imposed.

Even so, Dong Po did not relax until he felt the train lurched under him as it pulled out of the station. As he leaned back against his seat, his mind wandered back to that night early in the year when he had flown from Singapore to Bangkok to see Suchin. On that night, they had talked until the early hours of dawn before falling asleep in each other's arms.

Suchin had told her about her capture during the war and the worse-than-torture humiliations she had suffered at the hands of the inhuman Major Ishihara Shigeto. There were times when her narration was done in a flat, wooden voice, and times too when she had broken down, sobbing her heart out.

When she had told him in a trembling voice, "He did s-such terrible t-t-things to me, and m-made me performed those shame…shameful things for him, I…I couldn't help t-t-thinking I won't be able t-to feel clean again…", he felt a blind rage seizing him. He was so angry that he silently prayed that the Japanese would still be alive, and he could have the opportunity to remove him one of these days. That man should not be allowed to live. Even though there would be no payment for the job, he would gladly do it for free.

He had also learned that Suchin managed to escape on the night of April 14, 1945, when B29s bombed Bangkok again. As the Wat Lieb and Samsen Power Plants were destroyed, the city was plunged into darkness. After a part of the wall of her cell collapsed due to the shock, Suchin, who was once again miraculously unhurt,

crawled out. In the darkness and confusion, she somehow
found her way safely through roads clogged with military
vehicles, bomb craters, tangled tramway cables and
telephone wires to the home of Madam Chettana
Manoonsin who was a friend of her mother.

Though at first she had no idea where she was, a
kindly passer-by told her that they were in the Patunam
area. After he had shown her the shortcut to the Saen
Saeb Canal, she managed to beg a boatman to send her
to Madam Chettana's home in the Nonchok area. The
first words that Madam Chettana uttered to her were:
"Thanks to the Buddha, you've come here instead of
going to your home because that will be the first place
the Japanese will go to look for you. But I'm sad to tell
you that your mother passed away a few months ago
after a short illness."

Suchin had shown him the photograph of her parents.
He had seen it several times as it was placed in a leather
frame on top of the living room's mantelpiece. The faded
and yellow photograph showed a man and a woman in
old-fashioned clothes standing arm in arm. Until she
took the photograph down to show him, Dong Po had
already guessed they were her parents.

As the train chugged its way laboriously through the
night, Dong Po fretted. He was impatient to see Suchin
because he yearned to hold her close so as to reassure
her that he loved her and would protect her. He was glad
that in the past eight months he had traveled to Bangkok
to spend a week or two each month with her.

Dong Po also knew that Suchin had made considerable progress in getting over her shame and guilt – over the deaths of Vichai and her mother – as she no longer suffered those bad dreams. Besides, she had allowed him to make love to her. Though initially, she had showed signs of distress by turning frigid, during his last few visits she had become more participative and shown more passion.

He realized there were two more huddles he had to cross – first, asking Suchin to marry him, and thereafter he had to seek his mother's blessing. His worry was that both Suchin and his mother would object in view of the fact that she was thirteen years' older than him. The second huddle was his *sifu*, which ultimately meant a decision whether to continue or not in his chosen profession.

Somchai had once dryly commented, "I can see you're in love, my boy. Don't forget what I had warned you before. Those in our profession cannot afford to get emotionally entangled with any woman. Attachments can prove to be fatal as they put your mind in the wrong place at the wrong time."

Since then he had spent a lot of time thinking over Somchai's words and realized there was some truth in them. It was fortunate that ever since the last assignment in Singapore, for which he received a total of $19,867 – a lot of money at the time – there had been no other assignment. *Well, at least I've made a lot of money in recent years,* he thought. *Maybe, I shall use the money as capital for a business venture. Even if I left the money alone which has, in accordance to my sifu's advice, been invested in*

real estate, stocks, and high-interest deposits with several
banks, Suchin and I can still live comfortably

☆ ☆ ☆ ☆

When the doorbell rang, the noise startled Suchin into
dropping the book she was reading. As she had nothing
to do ever since Field Marshal Sarit Thanarat banned all
newspapers in Thailand, she had stayed at home, fretting
over what to do next when not catching up with her
reading.

Once she saw who it was at her doorstep, she could
hardly contain her joy.

"You're back," she said as a matter-of-fact statement
than a question.

He told her the simple truth. "I'm worried about
you."

"But you shouldn't have come," she said. "It's
dangerous to travel at times like this."

"There's no danger. Although there are soldiers all
over, they actually made it safer to move around."

At that moment, as though to prove his words, a
convoy of military trucks rumbled by.

"I think you'd better come inside," Suchin said
hurriedly when she realized they were still standing at
her doorway.

After he had taken a sip of water from the glass she
brought him, he stretched out on the familiar sofa,
laying his head on her lap. Suchin was stroking his head

lovingly when he told her: "After all these months, I've finally come to realize last night while on the train how much you mean to me. From the moment I heard the news of this latest coup, I was filled with worry for you."

She smiled happily down at her lover. "Silly, what's there to worry? By now, we're so used to coups and military dictatorships."

"When I was on the train, I'd made the decision to propose to you upon finding you safe and sound. Now that I've found you so, I must ask if you will marry me."

He knew his worry of the possibility of Suchin objecting his proposal due to their age difference was not unfounded because he saw a frown coming to her face.

"I can't marry you," she said. "It won't work as I'm thirteen years older than you."

"Even if you're twenty years older, we can still marry so long as we're truly in love with each other."

She shook her head. "It won't work because our society won't accept it."

"I don't care a damn for society's acceptance of what is essentially our choice," he said, raising his head angrily from her lap and using his hands to push himself up into a sitting position.

"What about your mother? Do you think she will accept me?"

Since he had no answer to her questions, he shifted his eyes to gaze down at the floor. As an afterthought, he said, "I'll talk to her. I'll convince her how we truly feel for each other. She'll understand."

It seemed a long time before he heard her voice. "I don't want you to tell your mother about us. Let us be contented with the way we are."

When he didn't respond, Suchin, with her years of maturity and experience, laid her hand over his. "You may not know this, but you've actually brought me a lot of happiness in recent months."

Though he turned to smile at her, she could see the fleeting sadness in his eyes.

After walking up the familiar flight of stairs, Ong Lay Yong was puzzled by the sight before her.

There was an iron wok on the floor of the living room and some joss paper beside it. Her mother who hadn't accompanied her father to the detention centre to fetch her home that morning, beckoned to her to go near the wok. Without uttering a word, her mother held up the joss paper, arranged like a fan, and began to use them to sweep all over Lay Yong, starting from her head and down her body to her feet. After repeating this several times, the older woman set the joss paper on fire and placed them in the wok. Her father who had also came into the room stood beside them to watch the joss paper burned itself out.

"Now that I have completed this ritual of washing away all your bad luck, I can speak," her mother said.

"Welcome home, Lay Yong. You understand now why I couldn't go with your father to fetch you?"

Lay Yong nodded though she regarded the superstitious practice of her parents with some disdain as she had heard such superstition had long been banned by Chairman Mao Tse-tung in China. She had nonetheless silently endured the ritual as she knew it would be futile to protest. *No wonder Chairman Mao had said that such archaic customs must be stopped if China was to progress,* she thought. But even though she would never admit it, she was yet touched by her mother's gesture despite it being so anti-revolutionary.

Her mother's voice broke her reverie. "You must now go and bathe yourself with the water from the tub where I've already put in seven different flowers. After you have undressed, hand the clothes to me so I can burn them as well. Thereafter, you shall put on the new clothes I have placed in the bathroom for you."

Lay Yong wanted to scream in exasperation but again she restrained herself. Despite her parents' old-fashioned ways, it was still good to be home. *One day, we, the young, as Chairman Mao has predicted, shall create a new age both for ourselves and for the world*, she thought.

Thirty-one

*A*fter his twenty-first birthday, Mao Dong Po began to take a keen interest in the political wind of change blowing through his country and the southern State of Singapore.

Perhaps it was the boredom from having little to do. It had been a year since Somchai gave him the job of removing the Thai politician in Singapore. Thereafter, he had got no further instructions from his *sifu* though they still met regularly.

Once when he had casually mentioned about not having any job for a long time, Somchai had stared hard at him before asking: "Have you run out of the money I'd paid you?"

When he retorted that he had invested most of the money as Somchai had advised, the Siamese said softly, "It would be suicidal to send you on any mission now that you're head over heels in love."

While Dong Po still kept up the pretence of working at his uncle's shop in the day and spent most evenings with his *ajarn* who had taken him to the highest level of *Muay Thai,* he felt very lethargic from the inertia. As such, now and then he would travel to Bangkok to visit Suchin Suewonglee.

Last November when he first heard she had got a job as a copywriter, working for her former editor who had started an advertising firm, he was glad for her. But early this year, when he heard she was tasked with a second job after her boss had revived his newspaper following the government's lift of the ban on the press, he wasn't quite pleased. First, he couldn't help wondering about her relationship with her boss even though Suchin had assured him there was nothing intimate between them. Second, as a copywriter, she seemed to work longer hours and so had lesser time to spend with him whenever he was in Bangkok. Now, in holding two jobs, he knew he might as well stay away because she would certainly have little time for him.

Apart from his boredom, his interest in politics could also be due to the election fever that seemed to infect almost everyone around him. Wherever he went, people talked of nothing else but the coming General Election and the possibility of a merger with Singapore. Almost everyone already knew about the talks between Lee Kuan Yew of the People's Action Party and Tunku Abdul Rahman. Having been to Singapore twice – once when he brought his mother there for sight-seeing, and the second time on Somchai's mission – he felt a bonding with the island-State.

Hence, on May 15, 1959, he went to Penang to catch a flight to Singapore. For two weeks, he idled in the day, often sleeping till noon in his room at the Majestic Hotel until night time when he joined the hordes of excited people in following the PAP campaigns, often adjourning from one venue to another. He heard Goh Keng Swee spoke about Singapore's grim economic position, while Toh Chin Chye assured the electorate that the PAP was the only party capable of giving them a stable, honest and just government.

Somehow their words led Dong Po to think of his *sifu*.

Once, in a rare mellow mood, Somchai had told him, "When I was sixteen, the economy was so bad that I'd dropped out of school to assist my father in his smuggling activities. We were so poor and desperate that we were beyond any honest work. Besides, why should we be honest when the government isn't?"

It was on that occasion that Dong Po learned how his *sifu* and his father had smuggled opium, which was then a government monopoly, cigarettes, liquor, and at times firearms. But when he unwittingly asked what had happened to Somchai's father, the Siamese abruptly clammed up. Somehow Dong Po sensed he and his *sifu* had something in common.

☆ ☆ ☆ ☆

From where she sat in her office, Suchin could get a good view of her boss, Arthit Lamsam, without him knowing she was looking at him.

As she looked at him that day, she saw a short pudgy man in his early forties, whose thick glasses hideously distorted his eyes. Perhaps that was why Arthit was still single since few women could regard him as good-looking. Suchin was one of the few who could see beyond the man's facade. If Arthit hadn't taken her into his employ ten years ago, she would probably be among the hordes of underpaid workers struggling for survival in any one of the factories sprouting up in Thailand over the past decade.

She remembered that day when she had turned up at his office in response to the advertisement he had placed in his own newspaper. As his newspaper was distributed only in Bangkok and its circulation was then small, his office occupied just two rooms as he hired only three reporters who also handled the photography, sub-editing, layout and production.

Arthit had looked at her through those thick glasses, causing her to tremble slightly at the sight of his hideously distorted eyes. "Why hadn't you written in but come in person?"

"I know I won't stand a chance against all the other applicants since I don't have any experience as a reporter. But unlike them, I am desperate enough to come personally to ask for the job."

He regarded her wordlessly for a long time with those sinister eyes before asking, "But can you write?"

"Why don't you try me?"

And that was how she had come to marvel at her boss's ingenuity as she saw the newspaper grew over the past ten years to more than a dozen times its original circulation since it was now also distributed in nearby Pattaya, Khon Kaen in the northeast, Chiang Mai in the northwest, and Hua Hin in the south. She had also found him to be a kind man despite his looks.

Once again, she marveled at Arthit's ingenuity and resourcefulness. After Field Marshal Sarit Thanarat's ban on newspapers at the time when he staged his second coup, Arthit had switched his resources to advertising, doing copy writing, and printing and distributing pamphlets, brochures and flyers for the advertisers of his former newspaper. Now that the field marshal had lifted the ban, Arthit simply revived his newspaper. As a result, he actually emerged from the crisis with two businesses instead of just one.

Likewise, she now held two jobs, alternating between being a copywriter and a journalist. But she wasn't complaining since her boss had generously increased her pay. Even if he hadn't given her the raise, she would happily worked both jobs for him as she felt grateful to him for keeping her employed all these years.

Her only worry was not being able to spend as much time as she would like with Klahan – the name by which she knew Dong Po – whenever he came to Bangkok. She was thus grateful that he had stayed away the past few months as his presence filled her with much guilt for neglecting him. But on the other hand, she missed him terribly. Though he had written several letters to her and recently, even sent a postcard to her from Singapore, she had only written to him once as her job left her little time. They had however spoken often over the telephone.

Thus, she was relieved when she learned about his interest in the politics of Malaya and Singapore. *At least, I believe I'm right in thinking he's a spy,* she thought. If not, why should he be so interested in the two countries' politics? Or for the matter, why is he so fond of reading James Bond's thrillers? And then she remembered having bought Ian Fleming's latest release, *Goldfinger, which she had meant to surprise him.*

"Do I pay you to day-dream?"

Startled, she looked up at the smiling face of her boss. "Now that I've awoken you from your day-dreaming, here's an assignment for you."

She took the note from him, and frowned. "You want me to accompany His Majesty to the province again?"

Arthit nodded. "What else can we, journalists, write about these days?"

Ever since Field Marshal Sarit's move to revitalize the monarchy, Arthit had sent Suchin on two occasions to report on King Bhumibol Adulyadej's tour of the provinces, and countless times to cover the king's launching of government development projects. He knew that much as Suchin revered the king, she wasn't too keen to cover such assignments. But having heard about the fate of fellow journalists who dared to write "feel-bad" news, he had warned Suchin to toe the line.

And that day, not for the first time, she told her editor: "The field marshal's just clever enough to exploit the pomp and ceremony of the monarchy to give himself the legitimacy to rule from behind the throne."

"I know what you mean," Arthit smiled, taking off his glasses to clean them with a handkerchief. "By portraying himself as a loyal servant of the king, he can exercise power without being seen as dictatorial. Instead, he is now looked upon as a strict but benevolent "father" of the people."

"Well, at least, he's still somewhat better than the previous dictator whose neglect of the king had failed to bolster national identity."

"Yes, nowadays, Thais are beginning to feel a national identity through the increased presence of the king," the editor agreed. "This is where we can play our part too. Besides, the field marshal seems to be sincere about wanting to stamp out the opium trade and end police corruption."

"Considering his past involvement, I'm not so sure about his wanting to stamp out such a lucrative business," Suchin retorted. "Even though he had personally gone around, wielding an axe to smash opium dens, I think he's merely trying to impress his American allies."

"Well, at least he had gained a reputation for getting things done," Arthit said. "You'd better go and pack up for the trip."

☆☆☆☆

Four days after the PAP won 43 out of 51 seats, Ong Lay Yong was surprised when she heard over the radio that the triumphant party had demanded the release of eight political detainees, one of whom was her hero, Lim Chin Siong.

Early the next morning, she was among the crowd waiting outside the Changi Prison. As pigeons were symbolically released and the crowd cheered, she managed to catch a fleeting glimpse of Lim among a few others coming out from the prison before he was whisked off in a waiting car. A day later, she heard with mixed feelings over the wireless that the new Government had appointed Lim as Political Secretary for Labor and Law.

Lay Yong who still refused to work for her father in his wine import business, had took up the job of a nurse at the General Hospital. One of the conditions for her release the previous year was that she was barred from teaching. Again, it was her father's connection that had got her the nursing job.

When she left for work after listening to the news broadcast, as she walked along New Bridge Road towards Outram, she reflected on the words of Goh Keng Swee who had been tasked to manage the State's finance. During the victory speech at City Hall, he had urged the English-educated voters, most of whom had rejected the PAP, to brace themselves for racial and language equality.

Though she thought his words were reasonable enough, she couldn't help feeling suspicious as eight of the nine members of the Cabinet were themselves English-educated. When she thought of the appointment of Lim as one of the political secretaries, while she was glad for his having become a person of some account, she wondered whether he was being used by the PAP. After all, she still wasn't sure about the new Prime Minister Lee Kuan Yew even though he had assured the people that their joys and their sorrows were also the government's joys and sorrows.

It's all rhetoric, she thought cynically as she stepped into the General Hospital's entrance. Only Time can tell whether Lee is for real.

Thirty-two

After the General Elections in Singapore ended, Mao Dong Po flew to Kuala Lumpur where he stayed until August 19, 1959, when it was the turn for his fellow countrymen to cast their votes.

Since he hadn't registered as a voter, he could only regretfully watch from the sidelines but it was nonetheless a heady experience for him. On August 20, he awoke around 9:00 a.m. in his room at the Federal Hotel after having stayed up late into the night to keep pace with the votes' counting. By the time he sat down to lunch at a coffee shop in Jalan Bukit Bintang, he knew the Alliance – comprising the United Malays National Organization, the Malayan Chinese Association, and the Malayan Indian Congress – had won a two-third majority of the votes. He knew Tunku Abdul Rahman would be sworn in as Prime Minister for a second term.

After lunch, he returned to his room, with the intention to catch up on his sleep. As he passed by the reception desk, a clerk called out to him: "Mr. Mao, here's a telegram for you."

The telegram came from his *sifu*, with a short message, "Your presence is requested to discuss a potential business."

Tired as he was, he packed up, checked out of the hotel, and hired a taxi driver to drive him to Padang Besar. It was just after 11:30 p.m. that he walked into his uncle's shop to see his uncle in earnest conversation with Somchai. After greeting both of them, he hurried upstairs to greet his mother. By the time he came down again to meet his mentor, his uncle had discreetly excused himself so as to leave them to their business.

The Siamese looked at Dong Po and grinned. "So, are you thinking of taking up politics, my boy?"

"It's too late for me as the election's just over," Dong Po said, "Besides, I shudder to think how many people I may itch to remove if ever I should become a politician."

Somchai nodded, "Yes, I mean no, I think you're more responsible than that."

They sat in silence as Somchai reached for his cigars. After offering one to his protégé, Somchai produced his gold-plated lighter to light for both of them.

"I've received a request for the removal of the leader of the Malayan Communist Party."

Though he was exhausted, Dong Po sat up. "I can't see why the Thai military or the Tang Kong Si would be interested in removing Chin Peng."

"Yes, I mean no, there's no direct interest. It's just a matter of someone requesting a favor from someone or someone owing someone else a favor. Incidentally, it has nothing to do with the Tang Kong Si."

"I see," Dong Po said. "But from what I've been hearing, the communists aren't such a terror these days. They're losers who are on the run. So why make such a fuss?"

"Have you heard of C.C. Too?"

Dong Po thought for a moment and shook his head.

"C.C. Too or Too Chee Chew works for the British, then the Malayan government, and possibly the American. He's the head of the Psychological Warfare Section. He has a theory that as communist terrorists based their actions on the opinion of the populace, without the people, the communist cause would be a lost one. And should the masses be sufficient impressed, they would come over to the side of the authorities, thus dashing the hopes of the rest of the rebels."

"And killing, I mean removing Chin Peng will do the trick?"

Somchai shrugged. "That seems to be the idea. As part of the mopping up and consolidation phase, it was thought that the removal of this guy is appropriate. After all, the communist terrorists think nothing of removing anyone who stands in their path. It's time for them to be at the receiving end."

"Sounds like poetic justice. Besides, I have no love for the communists. It was partly because of them that I lost my father. But am I supposed to go into the jungle to hunt down the selected quarry?" Dong Po asked, feeling somewhat queasy over the prospect as he had no knowledge of jungle warfare.

"Yes, I mean no, I'm sending you on a job, not asking you to commit suicide," Somchai said. "You're a hunter, my boy, not a jungle fighter."

Though a sense of relief flooded through Dong Po to hear those words, he nonetheless watched his *sifu* with some wariness.

"People think of hunting as a chase, like tracking the quarry all over until the ultimate kill. In reality, the truly good hunters loathe to waste energy in such a haphazard manner. Instead, they use their cunning to know their quarry, know his pattern, then plan ahead, like setting up an ambush to patiently wait for the quarry to show up."

"Know yourself, know your enemy."

"Ah, you've read Sun Tzu's *Art of War*," said Somchai before drawing on his cigar and letting the smoke out slowly. "You're a good hunter, my boy. This is why I'd thought of you the moment they gave me the assignment."

"But I thought you have qualms in assigning such jobs to one who is head over heels in love?"

"Yes, I mean no, you're no longer so possessed as before," Somchai said with a knowing wink. "If you can tear yourself away from Krung Thep all these months to follow the politics in Singapore and KL, then I think you're no longer overly enamored and so it's safe to give this job to you."

When Dong Po remained silent, Somchai leaned toward his protégé, his voice lowering. "The bounty for Chin Peng's head is \$125,000."

As much as Field Marshal Sarit Thanarat tried to project an image of himself as a strict yet caring fatherly figure to his people, there were those like Suchin Suewonglee who felt mistrustful towards him.

She was especially bitter whenever she thought of the government's violent suppression of any opposition, be they from politicians, students, journalists, writers, or other intellectuals, some of whom were jailed or summarily executed without trial.

Knowing her deep resentment towards dictatorship, her editor tried hard to impress her of the progress made, such as allowing the presence of the revered King Bhumibol Adulyadej to be felt through public ceremonies, tour of the provinces, and launching of development projects.

Arthit Lamsam also told her: "Apart from trying to build up traditional Thai values and promote Buddhism, the field marshal will also be remembered for his economic reforms, and strong promotion of education, especially in the rural areas."

Though Suchin smiled politely each time, Arthit couldn't tell whether her smile was genuine or not.

☆☆☆☆

As far as Ong Lay Yong was concerned, the installation of the first Malayan-born *Yang di-Pertuan Negara* or Head of State on December 3, 1959, was yet another show staged by the Singapore government. In her mind, although the 49-year-old Yusof bin Ishak had replaced Sir William Goode, she couldn't help regarding Lee Kuan Yew as the master puppeteer in this political *wayang kulit* or shadow play.

"Scalpel."

Immersed in her thoughts, Lay Yong stood without moving, which prompted the surgeon who was performing a kidney operation to demand irritably a second time. "I say scalpel, nurse!"

Startled by the surgeon's sharp voice, she quickly handed him a scalpel.

A while later, the surgeon said, "Sponge."

This time, she dutifully handed him a sponge.

Thirty-three

*I*n later years, Mao Dong Po would regard the period from August 1959 to December 1963 to be the most wasted period of his life. History was being made locally and internationally but he was either too preoccupied to notice or too phlegmatic to bother.

In early 1960, after challenging the collective leadership of the People's Action Party, Ong Eng Guan was dismissed from the Lee Kuan Yew-led Cabinet and expelled from the PAP. Not long after that, Lim Chin Siong defected to join Dr. Lee Siew Choh in forming the Socialist Front. Throughout the crisis within his own party, Lee still worked with Tunku Abdul Rahman to further the merger between Malaya and Singapore. But Dong Po wasn't paying attention as he was too busy sniffing around the towns and villages along the Thai-Malayan border for news of Chin Peng.

He knew that after the failed meeting with the Tunku and David Marshall in Baling on December 28, 1955, Chin Peng had fled to South Thailand, leaving his deputy, Shan Ru-hong, more commonly known as Ah Hai to take over as acting Secretary-General of the Malayan Communist Party.

Towards the end of February 1960, he finally got news that the elusive Chin Peng was going to Ban Nang Sata to meet Che Anjang Abdullah who was better known as Abdullah CD. Despite his misgiving over the remoteness of the place, which made it risky for him, he still traveled all the way to Ban Nang Sata in pursuit of his quarry. Dong Po took great care as he knew the communists' way of sending in an advance party in disguise to scout the area. But either his informant was himself misinformed, or the quarry had changed his mind, or had been alerted, Dong Po spent two days in the village without sighting both men, let alone the advance party.

On the third day, knowing it wasn't safe for him to linger, he beat a hasty retreat to Yala where he caught a train to Hatyai, and from there another train to Bangkok, as he decided to spend a week with Suchin Suewonglee. In Bangkok, his spirit was slightly lifted when Suchin presented him the copy of *Goldfinger* which she had bought for him. In his preoccupation, he had even forgotten to buy his favorite author's latest release.

It was six months later, just when he thought the communist leader's trail had turned cold that another informant told Dong Po that Chin Peng was going to Ban Phru to meet Rashid Maidin in Sala Thung Lung on the day after the mid-Autumn festival. As Rashid was one of Chin Peng's most trusted comrades, having been chosen by him to lead the Malay-dominated 10th Regiment, Dong Po believed the information enough to go three days ahead.

He rented a room on the first floor of a house beside the village's main road overlooking the coffee shop where the two Communist leaders were supposed to meet. Again, he was careful to watch out for any of the advance party. On the said day, cradling Somchai's sniper rifle which he had borrowed, he positioned himself by the rented room's window to keep watch. Again, Chin Peng and Rashid failed to show.

As such, Dong Po couldn't be blamed when he sunk into a deep depression in December 1960 from finding out that his quarry had already uprooted from Thailand for resettlement in Peking. Had the wily Communist leader found out that he was the target for an assassination? Dong Po was so depressed that he took his *sifu's* advice to go to Bangkok to lick his wound.

Suchin was most surprised to find Klahan (the name Dong Po used in her presence) at her doorstep on January 1, 1961. Though she was delighted to see him as it had been a long while since she last saw him, she could tell from the look on her lover's face that he was an unhappy man.

However, despite her concern, she wisely refrained from asking him. She knew he would have to work through for himself whatever was troubling him. After all, she knew he had kept a lot of things from her. If he had wanted to tell her, he would do so one of these days. But meanwhile, she would try her best to be supportive of him.

And so she embraced him passionately after he got into her home. As the fire of love engulfed them, she hurriedly led him to her bedroom. Later, after the fire was extinguished, as she lay contented on her bed, caressing the back of her sleeping lover's head, Suchin couldn't help thinking that his lovemaking had become less tender than the last time. It was as though he was starved and also on his guard against her. Being older than him had its advantage because she was matured enough to guess this was one of the ways where men differed from women. Despite their long absence, while her feelings for him still saw to it that making love to him was the most natural thing in the world, he was however less sure and so was more wary.

But when she handed him a copy of *For Your Eyes Only*, which was Ian Fleming's release for that year, his eyes lit up. She knew then that he was assured again of her love for him. And knowing how fond he was of those James Bond's thrillers, she was sure something was distracting him to the point of even neglecting to buy the book.

For three years thereafter, Dong Po elected to live an idle existence in Bangkok. But his decision gave Suchin some happiness as they lived like a truly married couple albeit a strange one. Each morning she would set out for work while he would sleep until the time for him to go to her office to join her for lunch. Each evening she would happily hurry home where they would at times eat in when she cooked and other times went out for dinner. Most evenings, they would cuddle on the sofa in the living room, or each of them would be preoccupied with a book.

The first two years passed by quietly. In the third year, on the night of September 16, 1963, when Suchin heard over the wireless the announcement about the merger of Malaya, Singapore, Sarawak and Sabah to become Malaysia, she turned to look at her lover who appeared indifferent. He was engrossed in Ian Fleming's latest book, *Thunderball*.

He didn't respond even when Suchin remarked, "I'm surprised that despite the Malayan leader's misgiving over the left-wing PAP, he still agreed to include Singapore in the merger."

Although Dong Po hadn't said anything, he was thinking: *Does the merger mean anything to me? Am I a Malayan, Thai, or Malaysian? No, I'm really nothing if I can't even do my job well. I'm certainly no James Bond.*

Five days later, when the PAP was returned to power in Singapore's second General Election, Suchin, recalling her lover's enthusiasm in the previous election to the extent of going all the way to listen to the candidates' pre-election speeches, turned to look at him. As she surreptitiously watched him, she realized that his eyes had a faraway look even though he seemed to be reading *The Spy who Loved Me. If anything could distract him from his favorite hero, something is indeed wrong*, she thought.

For the rest of 1963, when the Indonesians, who opposed the merger, were flexing their muscles, in first threatening a policy of Confrontation, and thereafter sending agents to infiltrate Sarawak and Sabah to conduct raids and sabotage, Dong Po wasn't at all bothered. And when President John F. Kennedy was assassinated on

November 22, 1963, he was nonchalant about it. Then in 1964, when Indonesian paratroopers landed in the southern State of Johor, he began to show some life.

To Suchin's relief, he said: "It was fortunate for my countrymen that we have the support of British, Australian and New Zealand troops to help deflect the Indonesian aggression."

Suchin, who had all long thought her lover to be a Thai of Chinese descent like herself, was surprised. "Which countrymen are you talking about? Aren't you a Thai?"

"Although I hold a Thai passport, I also hold a Malayan one. That reminds me I ought to go back to change my passport now that my country is called Malaysia. Besides, I haven't seen my mother and uncle for quite some time though I'd spoken to them over the telephone from time to time."

After that, he lapsed into silence, and seeing he was not about to elaborate further, Suchin also kept quiet. *He will tell me more when he's up to it*, she thought.

Unknown to Suchin, her lover was thinking of his *sifu*. Though Dong Po had now and then telephoned Somchai to let him know he was fine and at the same time, to assure himself that his *sifu* was also all right, the young man knew he was also anxious to know whether his mentor had a job for him. It wasn't that he needed the money as his investments were doing well to increase his wealth and his bank deposits earned him high interest. It was more the case of being assured of his own usefulness.

And so on the morning of December 8, 1963, Dong Po left for Padang Besar. As for Suchin, when she got into her office, she felt a bit moody from knowing her lover won't be coming later that day for lunch with her, and he also won't be home that night. She decided to work on an advertising copy to keep her mind busy. It was then that her editor sprang the news of Field Marshal Sarit Thanarat's sudden death on her.

"How did you know?" she asked.

"A few minutes ago, one of my sources telephoned me to say the field marshal's dead," Arthit Lamsam cried excitedly. "That was all he could tell me. Thus, I need you to find out more."

Thereafter, she spent the entire day being blocked by bureaucratic officials, threatened by overbearing ones, and chased away by those who thought journalists were nothing more than pests.

By the time Suchin finally got back to her office around 5:00 p.m., a frenzied Arthit asked: "What did he die of?"

"A variety of ailments aggravated by hard work and high living," she said.

He stood there open-mouthed as Suchin sat down at her desk to fit a piece of paper into her typewriter. Arthit asked, "What's next?"

"His body will be placed inside a pagoda-shaped golden urn for 100 days of mourning before being cremated."

"No, I don't mean that," her editor said. "Who will take over?"

"General Thanom Kittikachorn has taken over as Prime Minister."

As he thought of the avuncular-looking general with his iron-grey hair and toothy grin, Arthit shuddered involuntarily and muttered, "From the frying pan into the fire."

About two hours later, having filed her story, a thoroughly exhausted Suchin finally got home.

☆ ☆ ☆ ☆

Ong Lay Yong was a furious woman. Her anger which began as a simmer had turned into a boil. It was largely directed towards one person: Lee Kuan Yew.

She began seething earlier that year after it was announced on February 3, 1963 that Lim Chin Siong and a hundred or so pro-Communists were arrested. According to one report, they were involved in an armed rebellion led by a guy called Azahari to overthrow the Sultan of Brunei. As Lay Yong regarded Lim as a revolutionary seeking to turn Singapore into an egalitarian utopia, she was sure it was just an excuse cooked up by the government to lock him away. After all, Lim couldn't be involved in the politics of Brunei, which was some distance away from Singapore.

Like those members of the Socialist Front, she was further upset when she heard the speech by Lee over the radio on September 16, 1963, that Singapore had merged with Malaya and the two Borneo States of Sarawak and Sabah to form Malaysia. She had loudly exclaimed: "That man has sold us out."

But the limit to her restraint was when the PAP romped home to power in the General Election. *No wonder Lim and the others had been put away on those trumped-up charges*, she thought fiercely.

And then on December 18, 1963, after she heard over the wireless the details given by both Lee and the Tunku about Indonesia's opposition to Malaysia, and that Indonesian agents were planning acts of terror and subversion against Malaysia, a thought came to her. In her agitated state, she recollected that the Chinese word for "crisis" is made up of two other words – "danger" and "opportunity".

"Yes, this latest crisis has awoken me to my life's path," she said aloud to herself. "As Chairman Mao Tse-tung had once written, a revolution isn't like inviting people to dinner, writing an essay, or painting a picture. There's no kindness, gentleness, courtesy or restraint. A revolution is simply an uprising, an act of violence, which one class shall adopt to overthrow another."

She looked out of the window of her room located on the first floor at the back of her parents' house for a long while before she smiled dreamily and said: "Now that I know my true purpose in life, I must however be patient. What I intend to do may not take place now but the opportunity will present itself by and by so long as I am patient. Even if I have to wait ten or twenty years, Time will be on my side."

Thirty-four

*M*ao Dong Po couldn't help gaping the moment he saw Somchai walking into the foyer of the Oriental Hotel in Bangkok.

The swarthy Siamese was wearing a well-cut dinner jacket and bow tie. To complete the picture of a sophisticated gentleman, he was blowing clouds of smoke from a cigar. No wonder the two smartly-uniformed doormen hurried to open the door for him.

Earlier that day on January 6, 1964, as Suchin Suewonglee was rushing off to her office, she had told Dong Po not to wait up for dinner with her as she would be working late. This suited Dong Po fine because the previous day, shortly after arriving in Bangkok, he had received a telegram from his *sifu*, asking him to dinner with him at the Oriental Hotel. Since Dong Po had forgotten to mention to Suchin, he kept quiet and later in the evening went to the hotel which was founded in 1876 on the banks of the Chao Phraya River. He was looking forward to seeing his *sifu* again as the last time he was back in Padang Besar, his uncle had told him that Somchai would be away for some time.

After the waiter had taken their orders, Somchai offered his protégé a cigar.

"No, thank you, I have my own," Dong Po said, fishing one from his pocket.

Both men took a few puffs and then Somchai turned to look at Dong Po. "Don't you think it's time to stop gaping at me like an idiot?"

"I'm s-sorry, Uncle Somchai," Dong Po said. "But you look so smart. In fact, you look like James Bond."

Somchai who, like his protégé, had grown to enjoy James Bond's movies though not the books since he couldn't read English, snorted but Dong Po could tell he was pleased by the compliment. The older man said, "It's also time for you to learn to dress smartly."

They were quiet for a while when the waiter returned to lay out their drinks. After the waiter had walked away, Somchai raised his glass of red wine. "Happy birthday, my boy."

Dong Po was stunned but only for a moment. He quickly raised his glass in response to his mentor. "Thanks."

"I'm glad to see you look much better than the last time I saw you."

Somchai's words led the twenty-five years' old man to remember that day, slightly more than three years ago when he reported his failure after Chin Peng had left for Peking. Seeing his then crestfallen face, Somchai had gently told him: "In our profession, there are bound to be some guys who are too elusive to be removed. Perhaps it's not their time to go yet."

Dong Po had cried, "But I've let you down", to which his *sifu* had surprisingly replied, "There's some good from your failure, my boy. At least, you're now more humble and so won't get carried away by a false sense of invincibility in yourself."

And as an afterthought, the older man had wisely added: "Why don't you go to Bangkok? At times like this, it takes a woman's touch to set you right again."

And now looking at his *sifu* across the table, Dong Po felt grateful to have this eccentric man's guidance all these years. Indeed, Somchai was like a father to him. Caught up in his sentimentality, he was about to say something mushy when the Siamese blew out a cloud of cigar smoke and asked: "Are you ready for another job, my boy?"

Dong Po stared at him, astonished. "Of course, I am, Uncle Somchai. I've been idle for too long."

"I have a friend who is a legitimate businessman. He's in the construction business and has been facing unfair competition ever since one of the Siew Li Kue's chieftains bought over a construction company with the aim of laundering their dirty money. My friend has asked for my help."

"He wants us to remove the problem."

"Yes, after one of his sons was killed recently, he decided he had enough of the strong arm tactics and he's prepared to pay $30,000 to remove the problem.

I'm sure you'll be delighted to hear there's no condition as to how to do it."

Dong Po who had throughout the entire meeting sensed something was not quite right about his mentor, frowned. And then he brightened. "Uncle Somchai, how come you no longer say, "Yes, I mean no" or "No, I mean yes"?"

For a moment, Dong Po thought his mentor would throw the rest of the wine in his glass at him. But Somchai made a face instead. "So you'd noticed. Well, I went to Hong Kong for lessons on how to dress, behave in upper-class society, and of course, not forgetting how to speak. Times have changed. Finesse and style could command more respect and of course, higher fees."

It was not for the first time that Dong Po thought his mentor was a puzzle to him. But then what he said made sense. All he said to his *sifu* was, "No wonder my uncle had told me that you would be away for a while."

☆ ☆ ☆ ☆

It was nearly 11:00 p.m. when Suchin Suewonglee came home.

Dong Po was already curled up on the sofa, smoking a cigar and reading the latest of Ian Fleming's novels, *On Her Majesty's Secret Service*, which he bought from the Oriental Hotel's bookshop earlier that evening. He smiled at her as she came in.

"It takes a spy to read about another spy," she teased him the moment she caught sight of the book's title.

"I'm not a spy."

"Then what are you? You have more money than I've ever seen anyone else earning. And you've so much time on your hands to travel here and there, or hang loose, unlike me who have to work like a slave for a living."

"Marry me and then you won't have to slave for a living anymore," he said though he instinctively knew she would refuse his proposal just as she had refused on many occasions to accept his money.

"No, for all I know, I may end up a widow," she said with a broad smile so as to take the offence out of her words. "If you're not a spy, then what are you? An assassin?"

Had she been paying attention, she would have seen a flicker in his eyes. But her mind was elsewhere. When she used the word, "assassin", she was recollecting the conversation she had with her editor earlier that day in her office.

"You're a character assassin, Suchin Suewonglee. Yes, that's what you are." Arthit Lamsam had accused her. "Go on and kill Field Marshal Sarit Thanarat's reputation even though he's physically dead."

The accusation had come about because after the death of the field marshal, rumors begun when his eldest son, Major Setha Thanarat, applied to the courts to appoint him as executor of his late father's estate. According to him, his stepmother, the thirty-something and comely Thanpuying Vichitra Thanarat had deliberately under-declared the field marshal's assets at

$650,000 after stashing away millions of dollars in cash, jewelry, and land deeds, for her own use.

Although the late field marshal had kept a tight rein on the press, Prime Minister Thanom Kittikachorn appeared to close an eye. As such, Suchin had gleefully joined her fellow journalists to dig up records which showed the late dictator had owned or held interest in a trust company, a brewery, at least 50 automobiles, and 30 parcels of land, most of which were doled out to a score or more of mistresses. From there on, not a day passed without some stories being published about the field marshal's amorous flings with various women.

"I'm anything you want me to be," Dong Po said as he stubbed out his cigar in a crystal ashtray.

Her lover's voice brought her back to the present. Looking at him, she smiled happily, all her earlier exhaustion gone. "I prefer to think of you as a spy...the spy who loved me. I'm going to take a shower, after which, as I'm for your eyes only, show me again that you do love me."

He grinned cheekily at her, "As I'm on Her...I mean Your Majesty's service, I shall obey most willingly."

☆☆☆☆

Ever since the day Ong Lay Yong thought she had discovered the real purpose of her life, she seemed to become a changed person. There was a renewed determination about her, which even surpassed her zeal for her covertly subscribed revolutionary cause. And as she also changed her wardrobe and took an interest, like other girls of her age, in how to blow and comb her hair and make up her face, she began to look even more attractive.

At home, her parents soon noticed the new zeal and change in her, which led her father to ask hopefully, "Have you found a boyfriend?"

Thinking how odd that people seemed to think having a boyfriend would get a girl excited about life, she gave her father a pitying smile. "No, I haven't got a boyfriend."

Her father shook his head sadly. He and his wife had long ago given up all hopes of seeing their daughter getting married. He muttered to himself, "At her age, my daughter won't be able to interest any man."

At work, her colleagues also found her a changed person. Where she used to regard work as a dreary chore, she suddenly seemed more passionate in her job. She not only volunteered for this or that but also took more interest when the doctors around her talked shop, about the drugs they used, or the way to handle the sharp instruments when opening up a human body.

Thirty-five

lthough most of the Burma-Thailand border threaded through dense jungle and difficult, impassable terrain, it was very easy for those who knew the topography, or were desperate enough, to cross to and fro the two countries.

After driving nearly twenty minutes through rough jungle track, which often caused the jeep's occupants to bounce, and wince each time the outgrowing branches slapped the sides of the vehicle, the driver suddenly stopped. As a bruised and shaken Boonrwad Wanglee had enough of being bounced up and down on the bumpy ride, he breathed a sigh of relief. If not for Khun Sa's insistence to meet him in person, Boonrwad would prefer to let one of his lieutenants made the tedious trip.

Although Boonrwad was twenty-two years older than the thirty-year-old Khun Sa, he deferred to the younger man for two reasons.

First, despite being so young, Khun Sa already had his own private army of nearly a thousand men, who were outfitted by the Burmese government and thereafter left alone to lord over his area in the jungle of Burma. Second, and the most important reason, Khun

Sa was rapidly catching up with Lo Han Hsing as a major supplier of opium to his tong. It was sound strategy to secure more supply lines than relying on just a single source.

After another hour of trekking on foot through thick jungle, Boonrwad, his two bodyguards, and the driver-cum-guide sent by Khun Sa, arrived at a camp. It looked like any logging camp except that it was surrounded by high barbed-wire fence and tall sentry-towers manned by men armed with automatic rifles and machine guns.

Seven hours later, Boonrwad was back in his room at the Sripragard Hotel in Chiang Mai. He couldn't wait to take a shower and then change into new clothes as that would mean feeling human again. Having had concluded a good deal with Khun Sa for several consignments to be delivered over the next few months, which his friends in the military had assured they would close their eyes, he felt good. He licked his lips when he recalled Khun Sa's revelation that he had started laboratories to manufacture the new heroin which promised more profits than opium. All these pleasant thoughts aroused his appetite and he decided to go out for supper.

After stripping off his clothes, he was about to reach for the door knob of the bathroom when the impossible happened. He neither heard nor saw the wire loop over his head. He only realized his danger when the thin wire bit into his thick neck and he heard the faint breathing of the assassin behind him. Instinctively, he tried to claw off the wire which was already cutting into his skin, drawing blood. Just when he thought he was about to black out, he fell back heavily against the assassin, lifted both his feet up to plant firmly against the wall, and kicked out, causing both of them to fall backwards. As he rolled sideways, he shouted hoarsely at the top of his lungs, "You fools, come in quick. I'm being attacked."

That same night in April 1964, a thoughtful expression came to Suchin Suewonglee's face just after she heard the radio broadcast about Malaysians casting their votes in their country's General Election.

As she knew her lover had spent weeks in Singapore and then in Kuala Lumpur to follow the 1959 General Elections, and missed the one in Singapore the previous year, she thought it strange that Klahan had chosen to go to Chiang Mai instead of Kuala Lumpur this time. Three days ago just when he was about to set out, she had reminded him about the General Election in Malaysia. "Haven't your superiors assigned you to go to Kuala Lumpur?"

He gave her a long amused look before asking, "What are you implying, my dear?"

"As I still think you're a spy, I can't help wondering why you're not going to Kuala Lumpur for the country's General Election this time."

He had laughed good-naturedly. "I'd told you so many times already that I'm not a spy but just a manager of a pest removal company. My boss has just asked me to meet a client in Chiang Mai."

"Won't it be more convenient for the client to simply call in a pest removal firm operating in his own town?"

Her lover had merely shrugged. "Maybe he prefers our personal service."

That night, after thinking over his words, she got up from the sofa and went to the drawer where she kept all her diaries. She found the 1957 diary and turned the pages to November.

After a while, she muttered to herself, "Hmm, not long after Klahan had rescued me from Charoen Limthongkul's thug, the triad chieftain died, presumably from heart attack."

She next searched for the 1958 diary, and after flicking through some pages, let out a low whistle. "It was after he had flown in from Singapore in February 1958, that the former military judge and aspiring politician, Colonel Prapass Oanorn was reported to have died in an accident in Singapore."

She went back to sit down on the sofa again. After a long silence, she sighed. "I hope I won't get to read about another person's death in Chiang Mai this time."

☆ ☆ ☆ ☆

If she had died that very night, Ong Lay Yong wouldn't have minded death at all so long as she could die in Dr. George Teng's arms.

Earlier that evening, they were having dinner at the Swee Kee Restaurant in Middle Road. After dinner, when George suggested driving her to Changi Beach, where he knew a secluded spot by the sea that they could sit and talk, she agreed. After all, she was in good mood having had learned that except for one candidate, the other eight fielded by Lee Kuan Yew to contest in the General Election in Malaysia had lost.

Lying on the beach, she remembered it was her who had made the first move when she unbuckled George's belt and unbuttoned his pants. After that, there was nothing to stop him from doing the same to her. Their lovemaking was both wild and animal-like, and at the same time, slow and tender. Though it was a bit painful at first, considering it was her first time, it was nonetheless a most wonderful feeling for Lay Yong since her lover was very experienced.

Now that they were both spent, as she snuggled contentedly against George's lean and hard body, she recalled how they had met each other.

It was in late January 1964 when George was among the group of newly-graduated doctors posted to the General Hospital. Though Lay Yong had turned down several doctors who had tried to date her over the years, she somehow couldn't resist George when he approached her the week after the Chinese New Year. Perhaps, it was his good looks as he had a tall, athletic body. Or it could have been his boyishness that had tugged at her heart strings.

On their first date, they dined at a coffee shop in New Bridge Road before crossing the street to catch a movie at the Majestic cinema. The simple night's outing gave more pleasure to Lay Yong than if George had taken her to a posh club or a five-star hotel for fine dining. After that first date, the next three months were filled with outings for the two lovebirds, whereby they found out more about each other.

It pleased her to discover the anti-establishment inclination of her boyfriend. He had once told her: "In clinging to the old ways, the so-called senior doctors have become complacent. If I have my way, they should all be ordered to sit for examinations again." But she was careful not to reveal too much of herself to him.

Though they initially flirted with words, a month later, she had allowed him to kiss her. After that, they indulged in some petting and necking but she would stop him each time he pleaded with her to go all the way. But tonight, she wantonly stepped beyond the conservative norm of their times.

Lying in her lover's arms, she wondered whether she had given herself to him out of her inability to resist her own basic desire as a woman to be loved. After some thought, she concluded that her action was really in keeping with Chairman Mao Tse-tung's observation that as times had changed, today's men and women were equals. Therefore, whatever the male comrades could do, female comrades could do as well. In this way, she believed she had taken a bold step albeit an insignificant one in furtherance of her revolutionary spirit.

Thirty-six

$\mathcal{S}$omchai was sitting at the Riverside Terrace sipping a gin and tonic, and as usual, polluting the air with his cigar.

It was on account of the cigar smoke that Mao Dong Po located him so easily when he came to the Oriental Hotel in Bangkok to look for him. Ever since Somchai had ordered Dong Po to head west to await an opportunity to remove Boonrwad Wanglee who was going to sneak across the Burmese-Thai border to meet his opium suppliers, the *sifu* went to the Riverside Terrace each evening to wait for his protégé's safe return.

The moment he saw Dong Po's face, he knew but he still asked. "How did it go, my boy?"

Though the young man averted his eyes to look down on the floor, Somchai saw his lips twitched. "I've failed, Uncle Somchai."

Somchai didn't ask further because the waiter had come over to take Dong Po's order. After the waiter had left, Dong Po wasted no time in giving his mentor an account of what had happened since they last met.

They were both silent for a while and then the *sifu* said, "There's nothing wrong with your strategy of stealth instead of going for the quarry with a blazing gun. In fact, it's brilliant to pick the lock to enter and hide in his room and then wait for the opportunity to remove him quietly so as not to alert his bodyguards waiting outside the room. What went wrong was your over-confidence. You should have simply plunged a knife into him instead of trying to garrote him with a wire. That guy's a mad man, and insane people are exceedingly strong."

Seeing his protégé's crestfallen look, Somchai said gently, "But lucky for you, my boy, that you had enough sense to make a run instead of trying to finish the job after he broke away from your strangle. Lucky too that his room was on the first floor instead of higher up, thus allowing you to get to the balcony to slither down the knotted rope you'd prepared before his bodyguards broke in."

Dong Po shook his head, looking like he wished the earth would swallow him up. "I've failed you. I can't tell you how sorry I am…"

"Well, what matters most is your safe return, my boy. Moreover, I must say I'm proud of the fact that so far, you haven't fallen into habit patterns but would change your *modus operandi* each time. Just remember next time, don't try garroting a guy especially if he's bigger and stronger than you. Well, as they say in the West, he who runs away lives to fight another day."

Distressed as he was with himself, Dong Po couldn't resist a smile to hear his mentor mouthing two English words like *modus operandi* and that quotation. "How did you come by the words, *modus operandi*, and the saying, Uncle Somchai?"

Somchai reached for an ashtray with which to stub out his cigar. "I learned from one of the Hollywood movies I was watching. It's important to keep on learning new things. So, what's your next plan, my boy?"

"I haven't thought of it yet."

"Whatever you come up with, be mindful that you've lost the element of surprise. Boonrwad will be harder to remove as he will now be on his guard."

They sat watching the river traffic for a while and then Somchai said, "By the way, I won't be returning to Sadao as I have relocated to Krung Thep. As for you, my boy, my advice is that you should move to either Kuala Lumpur or Singapore."

Dong Po looked at him in surprise. "Why? I thought we're doing just fine in the south."

"You thought wrong, my boy. Times have changed. We should now move to where the action is."

"How about I also move to Bangkok?" he asked hopefully.

Somchai didn't say anything but fished inside his pocket for two cigars. After offering one to Dong Po, he held the light for him, and then lit the other for himself.

After taking a few puffs, he said: "I don't want you in Bangkok, my boy. First, you may bring unnecessary risk to yourself as you may be distracted by your woman. Besides, I don't know whether your relationship will last. Second, I need someone to take care of future business in both Malaysia and Singapore."

After a short pause, he added, "Third, after tonight, we should only meet whenever it's absolutely necessary. I don't want people to link us together. Open a bank account here and also in Kuala Lumpur and Singapore. Since I have an account with the Hong Kong and Shanghai Bank, I suggest you do the same as it will make it easier for me to transfer any payment for future jobs to you."

☆ ☆ ☆ ☆

When Suchin Suewonglee read the report filed by the correspondent for North-west Thailand, she was filled with trepidation.

Busy as she was with an advertising copy for a major chain of retailers, she still spent the next two days doing research on Boonrwad Wanglee, the man who was hospitalized with a badly lacerated neck after an assassin nearly garroted him in his hotel room. From the correspondent and a few other sources, she unearthed some interesting information on Boonrwad.

Boonrwad's father, Wang Li-wei, a textile merchant in Amoy, was one of those who had joined the Revive China Society. After the Ching government discovered a coup being plotted in 1895, the plotters, including the leaders, Dr. Sun Yat-sen and Wang, fled for their lives. Wang was fortunate in that he was in a restaurant with some friends when he heard government troops had gone to his home as well as the homes of the other plotters.

His wife and three sons were less fortunate as they were arrested and subsequently executed.

Wang came to Thailand, where he set up a textile shop near the Klong Ong Ang Market. With his connections to the anti-Ching secret societies in China, he soon became a respected leader in the Siew Li Kue triad. In a very short time, he came to own several opium dens, gambling houses and brothels.

Like those Chinese who had taken Thai names after making Thailand their home, Wang grudgingly changed his surname to Wanglee though he continued using his Chinese name, Li-wei. But after he had taken a Thai wife who gave him a son in 1911, he named the boy, Boonrwad.

Even though Wang, being involved in the unsavory triad business, could be extremely ruthless towards his enemies or strangers, he was however generous to his friends or relatives. But the same couldn't be said about Boonrwad. Immediately after he took over his father's tong in 1937 when Wang died of illness, he ordered some of his thugs to go to the house of his late father's mistress. Since that day, no one heard about her or her two teenage sons – Boonrwad's half-brothers.

A medium-height plump man, with a pair of slightly protuberant eyes on a cherubic face and slender fingers and fair skin, Boonrwad looked more like a scholar than a gangster. Suchin thought that was why Boonrwad was known as the Iron Pen Scholar until she found out more.

It was the North-west Thailand's correspondent, a former crime reporter in Bangkok, who told her this story. When Boonrwad was ten, his father introduced him to Chinese calligraphy, saying he mustn't forget his roots. Three years later, the young boy found a sharp iron spike which he used to practice his calligraphy, scratching out bloody words on stray animals that he caught in the neighborhood. He stopped only after his father gave him a severe thrashing when some neighbors complained about the fatal mutilation of their pets.

It was his combined cunning, ruthlessness and viciousness that gave him the strong grip over the men in his tong. It was rumored that his late father's right-hand man, Sondhi, had initially tried to usurp Boonrwad's position. No one could prove the rumor because Sondhi's badly-mutilated body was later found inside a gunny sack floating on the Chao Phraya River. People whispered that Boonrwad had resumed his deadly calligraphy with the iron spike.

After the Japanese Occupation, one man came forward to accuse Boonrwad of being a secret informer for the *kempeitai* and had sold out many unfortunate Chinese. The man's body was subsequently recovered from a gunny sack floating in the Chao Phraya River. Multiple cuts were also found all over the man's body. After that, now and then whenever a mutilated corpse was found in a gunny sack in the river, people would whisper that the Iron Pen Scholar was practicing his deadly calligraphy again.

There's no doubt the world is better off without the likes of Boonrwad, Suchin thought fiercely. *But in what way is Klahan involved? How much of Klahan's story of being an ordinary business executive is true?*

Her love for Klahan had her wanting to trust him but her journalist's instinct was forcing her to consider the possibility that there was a side of him she knew nothing about. Suchin was so engrossed in her deep inner conflicts that she did not see her editor until he spoke: "You're still here. What are you working on?"

"I'm thinking of doing a follow-up on that Boonrwad fellow who was nearly garroted in his hotel room in Chiang Mai, like what was he doing there. It should make an interesting story for our readers," she said.

"No, leave that guy alone," Arthit said, suppressing a shudder. "That gangster is too dangerous to cross. From what I've heard, he's quite glove-in-hand with some of our generals."

☆ ☆ ☆ ☆

Unaware that two journalists were discussing him, Boonrwad was at the very moment climbing on board a helicopter which had been chartered to fly him back to Bangkok.

Earlier that day, he was discharged from the hospital where he had spent three nights under observation. His neck, especially his throat was still sore, and he was yet unable to speak properly.

Ever since that night when the assassin tried to kill him, he had felt both fear and fury. It was the first time in his life that Boonrwad no longer felt safe, and the recollection of the night when he had nearly died at the hand of an assassin frightened him. But Boonrwad being Boonrwad, he was furious that such a humiliating incident could happen to him. His cunning told him that if he wanted to get rid of the fear and the humiliation, then he must get rid of the assassin.

Throughout the flight, he brooded on his next move.

The day after Ong Lay Yong had sex with Dr. George Teng, she was scheduled for the afternoon shift.

From the moment she went into the hospital, she knew something was wrong. As she hurried towards the stairs, Dr. Ernest Wong, who was just walking down, winked at her. "Good afternoon, Miss Ong." Apart from the cheeky wink, there was also an odd note in his voice.

Once she got to her floor, as she walked along the corridor, a doctor whose face she recognized but couldn't remember his name, gave her a leering smile.

It was only later in the evening when she went to the cafeteria for her dinner that a suspicion came to her mind. Several doctors who were seated at a table were watching her, and all of them were smirking broadly.

Her face turned red and she turned around to walk out of the cafeteria as she had lost her appetite.

Thirty-seven

*I*n early July 1964, Mao Dong Po went to live in Singapore in accordance with his *sifu's* direction.

After his failed attempt to assassinate Boonrwad Wanglee, he spent three months in Bangkok, hoping to get another opportunity to finish the job. But as Somchai had anticipated, it wasn't going to be easy since Boonrwad would be on his guard. Dong Po saw the triad chief had increased the number of his bodyguards from two to five.

Somchai advised him to shelf the contract for a while, to allow the quarry to regain his confidence and so hopefully lower his guard once more to provide the opportunity he was looking for. This was his mentor's advice: "Instead of wasting your time here, go to Singapore or Kuala Lumpur, and once there, look around for a house or apartment. If you like it, buy it rather than rent. As I've always been telling you, property makes good investment. After all, you're rich enough provided you haven't squandered off the money I'd paid you."

"No, Uncle Somchai, I've already invested some of the money as you have advised. In fact, I have in recent years already owned two houses and an apartment in Singapore, which my agent had, on my behalf, rented out to people."

"That's good," grunted the Siamese.

Taking his *sifu's* advice, within a week of his arrival in the island-state, Dong Po bought a small walk-up apartment in the Cairnhill area, near Orchard Road. He lived there alone as his mother had declined his invitation to join him. As she had told him, "Your uncle needs me more than you do. Over there, I have no friend and so shall be lonely."

Having had installed a telephone in his apartment, he telephoned Suchin Suewonglee almost every night. Though Somchai had told him to spend more time in Singapore to familiarize himself with the country, and make friends with the people, Dong Po knew he was by nature, too restless, and so would be traveling to Padang Besar once a while to see his mother and uncle, and more often to Bangkok to be with Suchin.

He was mindful of his mentor's doubts as to whether his relationship with Suchin would last. Thus, on the flight to Bangkok on July 19, 1964, he resolved to prove Somchai wrong. But he was nonetheless worried. Though he wasn't sure but ever since his last trip to Chiang Mai, he sensed that Suchin was unusually tensed whenever they were together.

While his eyes took in the ocean of clouds floating outside the small window of the aircraft, his mind however drifted back to one evening not long after his return from Chiang Mai.

He remembered he was watching the news on the new television set she had just installed in her house. It was the night when he saw the South African anti-apartheid leader, Nelson Mandela, declaring his willingness to die for his ideal at the opening of the Rivonia Trial.

Suchin, who had come into the living room just after the newscaster made that report, had abruptly asked: "For the right price, will you kill people like him?"

Though he was taken aback by the sudden question, he had managed a nervous laugh since she had come too close to the mark. "Ahh, tonight you're assuming I am an assassin, not a spy."

"Whatever," she said looking intently at him. "Will you kill people like him?"

He recalled having told her: "Even if I have the ability to kill people, I don't think I will kill indiscriminately. I will kill only those who deserve to die."

Her eyes softened but not her words. "Well, well, what have we got here? It's rare to find an assassin with a principle like yours, or at least, a conscience."

Later that night when they made love, he had a strange feeling that she seemed somewhat distrait.

He returned to the present upon hearing the chief stewardess's voice over the intercom, requesting all passengers to fasten their seat belt as they would be landing soon.

Two nights after his return to Bangkok, Dong Po was having dinner with Suchin at the hawker stalls along Yawaraj Road where they had first met, or to be exact, where Suchin had seen him for the first time. The hawker had just brought them their bowls of noodles when the burlier and nastier-looking of the three men sitting two tables away swaggered over to their table.

"What are you looking at?" he demanded

"No, nothing in particular," Dong Po said softly.

Suchin saw a slight smile curling on the bully's lips. He was obviously a bully who was relying on his bigger size and the company of his two companions to pick a quarrel. She glanced anxiously at her lover who smiled calmly as he averted his gaze away from the bully.

"You were looking at me," the bully insisted. "Am I nothing?"

To Suchin's astonishment, her lover brought up his hands together to offer the bully a *wai*, the traditional Thai greeting. "I apologize if I have offended you."

The bully smirked. "I don't want words of apology. You shall pay for our dinner."

"Yes, I'll do that," Dong Po said meekly, whereby the bully turned to wink at his two companions, and at the same time, shouted at the hawker, "This boy is paying for our dinner."

After the bully and his companions had strutted off, Suchin who had once seen her lover made short work of a thug when he had tried to harm her many years ago, asked softly: "Why?"

"Well, you should believe now that I'm not a secret agent like James Bond or an assassin as you'd made me out to be," he chuckled good-naturedly. "You've been watching too many movies."

To her own surprise, Suchin was indignant that her lover had allowed the bully to have his way. She was sure that he could handle the guy. Klahan's meekness however convinced her all the more that he was merely putting on an act to fool her into thinking he was less dangerous than she thought him to be. Somehow this made her more furious.

On the stroll back to her home, she was unusually silent as she seethed with humiliation. Dong Po too walked with his own thoughts. He was glad he hadn't allowed his anger with the bully to break his resolve. After killing Captain Neil Walker to avenge his father, he had promised himself that he would only kill to protect himself or those whom he loved, or kill only those who deserved to die, and even so it had to be a business deal. Besides, he was thinking that his *sifu* was right. Somchai had once told Dong Po, "Only remove a problem which is worth the effort. Otherwise, you're no better than those who would accept peanuts for just any job. Always remember you're in a class of your own."

✩ ✩ ✩ ✩

Not far away, two men seated in a restaurant at the junction of Songwat Road and Ratchawong Road, were having an earnest conversation. Nearby, at another table, five men sat watching them and also looking around them from time to time.

One of the two men, a cherubic-looking fellow with a pair of slightly protuberant eyes was asking with some irritation, "What do you mean you don't know? Someone is trying to kill me, and all these months you still can't tell me who's trying to kill me."

The other man, who was burly and at least half a head taller than Boonrwad Wanglee, ignored the implied accusation and asked almost insolently, "What do you expect from me if you can't even answer me when I last asked you whether you had enemies?"

If you have been anyone else, I would have done you in with my iron pen, thought Boornrwad maliciously but aloud he said, "I've so many enemies, I won't know which one to suspect."

"Well, whoever's trying to kill you will surely try again. You have better be on your guard."

"I've increased my bodyguards from two to five."

"Six," the burly man corrected him. "Ever since you'd told me about the attempt on your life, I have been around, mostly in the shadows watching out for you. I hope to spot him before he gets to you."

Boonrwad managed a grunt, the closest he ever got to thank a person. Even though it had been some three months, his throat still felt dry and painful.

Ong Lay Yong was surprised when Dr. George Teng intercepted her in the corridor of the hospital. "I really need to talk to you. I'm off this Friday. I know you're also not on duty that day. Can we have dinner together?"

Throughout the month of May, she had declined all his attempts to date her, and at the same time, had worn a stoic mask as she went about her duties at the hospital with an aloof attitude. By June, he had stopped asking, and her colleagues had ceased gossiping about her as new scandals had arisen for them to talk and laugh over.

When Lay Yong gave him a cold stare, George pleaded earnestly, "All I'm asking is that you join me for dinner so that I can explain things to you. Please…"

A thought came to her and she nodded her head. "All right."

George's face lit up. "Splendid, I'll fetch you from your house at 6:00 p.m."

True to his word, George was waiting in his car at 6:00 p.m. sharp on July 21, 1964.

After she got into his car, he said, "I know a lovely seafood restaurant in East Coast Road."

"Anywhere is fine," she said.

After that they drove in silence. She could sense George was fidgety as he twisted his head as though he had a stiff neck. Though it was quite breezy as George had turned both triangular-shaped windows in the front to allow air to flow into the car, she saw from the corner of her eyes that he was perspiring. Now and then he cleared his throat as though he wanted to say something but thereafter remained silent.

Unknown to her, George had felt some regrets for having boasted to his fellow doctors about his having deflowered her. Once he had started bragging the morning after he had sex with Lay Yong on the beach, there was no stopping as everyone pressed him for the lurid details. But since then, George who was an experienced hand in the game of seducing nurses and the occasional patients had surprisingly been unable to get her out of his mind. After Lay Yong had refused to go out with him when she realized what he had done, George felt himself desiring her even more. He was hoping to convince her of his remorse and so get them to resume their relationship.

As they neared Rochor Road, to break the silence, she reached out to turn on the car radio. An anxious male announcer's voice told them: "Rioters had set fire to houses and vehicles in the Kallang and Geylang Serai areas. People are advised to stay off the streets as the government has declared a state of curfew."

They both instinctively looked towards the direction of Kallang and Geylang Serai, and true enough they saw black smoke in the distant skyline.

"Oh no," George said. "I should send you home."

No wonder there's so little traffic today. Well, this crisis will suit my plan perfectly because the danger has presented an even better opportunity, she thought happily as she opened her handbag.

He turned right into Rochor Road, with the intention to turn back into North Bridge Road. The moment he swung into North Bridge Road, which was already deserted, she pointed towards the junction of Liang Seah Street. "Please pull over there."

He obediently stopped where she had indicated. Just as he turned to ask for her reason, the last thing he saw was Lay Yong's malevolent eyes when she turned towards him and then he felt the sharp pain slicing across his throat.

Thirty-eight

The year 1965 turned out to be quite a historically significant one for Malaysia and Singapore albeit a fruitless one for Mao Dong Po.

First, on March 10, Indonesian saboteurs planted a bomb near the Hongkong and Shanghai Bank at Orchard Road in Singapore. The explosion killed three persons and injured more than 30. Thereafter, Indonesian soldiers clashed openly with those who were defending the Malaysian State of Sabah. It was only in October that the Confrontation came to an end after General Suharto seized power from President Soekarno.

The day after the bombing, Mao Dong Po was back in Bangkok, partly to see Suchin Suewonglee and also to try completing his unfinished assignment.

For nearly a month, while Suchin went to her office, he would hang around the Klong Ong Ang Market where Boonrwad Wanglee maintained his legitimate front of a construction company in an imposing office next to the textile shop which used to be his late father's cover. Several times he spotted his quarry but unfortunately, no opportunity presented itself. Boonrwad always had his five bodyguards surrounding him, and he had picked them well because their alert eyes never failed to look constantly around them.

A disappointed Dong Po left for Padang Besar on April 9 to spend a quiet week with his mother before returning to Singapore. After that, he visited Bangkok at least once a month but each time he felt his frustration growing as his quarry never relaxed his vigilance.

Then on August 9, when he was in Singapore, he heard an announcement on the radio which brought a loud sigh from him: Singapore had separated from Malaysia to become an independent state. Though he shook his head sadly, he had long before that day known the split would be inevitable.

He was aware that for some months already since the failed attempt by the People's Action Party to enter mainland politics, the squabbles had intensified, especially between the PAP, the Malaysian Chinese Association and the United Malays National Organization. To end the bickering, UMNO leaders, Tunku Abdul Rahman and Abdul Razak, MCA chief, Tan Siew Sin, met up with the PAP leaders comprising Lee Kuan Yew, Toh Chin Chye and Lim Kim San on September 29, 1964 whereby all agreed on a two-year truce during which everyone would try his best to defuse the communally sensitive issues and put aside party differences.

However, relationships continued to sour, especially after Lee mooted the concept of a "Malaysian Malaysia" in March 1965, which was taken up by the opposition. From then on, accusations and counter-accusations were hurled, and calls for Lee's arrest were made.

From his *sifu*, who seemed to have an inside source of information, Dong Po learned that the moderate Tunku, after considering the futility of the situation, had reached a painful decision on June 29 that Singapore would be cut loose from Malaysia. Somchai had also told him that while Abdul Razak continued with his efforts to heal the rift, preparations had been made in Kuala Lumpur for the Separation Act. By August 7, Lee met the Tunku who confirmed his decision, to which the former agreed and accepted albeit with great reluctance.

As Dong Po mulled over the uncertainties in politics, it struck him that, like him, politicians such as Lee actually trod a very thin line, between safety and danger. Lee, who nearly got himself incarcerated, had however by a stroke of luck, emerged instead as Prime Minister of his city-state. *As for me, it's either death or imprisonment should I ever get caught,* he thought. *I hope my luck holds.*

The moment Suchin learned about the separation of Singapore from Malaysia, she placed a long-distance telephone call to her lover.

It rang several times but there was no answer. Suchin jiggled the hook impatiently and when the operator answered, she gave her another number to call. The previous year, Klahan had told her that his uncle had finally installed a telephone in his shop house.

He had by then loosened up enough to tell her a little about the time when he was a boy until the murder of his father. He spoke too about growing up in the barbed-wire "New Village" before moving to Padang Besar with his widowed mother. Though he stuck to his story of working as a manager of a pest removal firm owned by a man who was like a father to him, she still couldn't bring herself to believe that story. Incredible as it may seemed, her intelligent mind let her to suspect that he was an assassin.

But having come to accept that guys like Charoen Limthongkul, Colonel Prapass Oanorn and Boonrwad Wanglee were society's scumbags, she no longer felt afraid *of* him. Instead, she was afraid *for* him, knowing his chosen profession was one that was fraught with danger.

A woman's voice answered. Suchin, who remembered that Klahan had also told her that he was known as Dong Po at home, asked in the Chow Chou dialect. "May I speak to Dong Po please?"

The woman, whom Suchin guessed to be Klahan's mother, said, "Dong Po is in Singapore."

"What? I can't hear you," she raised her voice as there was some static on the line, "Can you please say that again?"

"I said Dong Po is in Singapore."

After replacing the telephone, she made a mental note to call him again later that evening when she got home. But two hours later, the moment she stepped inside her house, her telephone began to ring. Instinctively, she knew the call was from her lover.

True enough, it was Dong Po. "What's up, darling? I heard you'd telephoned Padang Besar for me?"

"Yes, I was thinking of you after learning that Singapore has separated from Malaysia," she said. "What do you plan to do now?"

"As usual, my plan is to convince you to marry me. Now that my mother had heard your voice, she too is pressuring me to settle down."

She laughed. "I'm already your wife as there's no other man in my life."

"I know we're already living like husband and wife. Why don't we make it formal?"

"The answer is still no. We're doing fine as we are."

She heard him sighed, and then he said: "Well, even if a formal marriage isn't acceptable to you, at least consider taking a holiday with me because you've been working too hard and I want to show you Singapore and Malaysia."

"I'm afraid I won't be able to take a vacation for some time to come as I have many uncompleted assignments."

"Well, to your original question as to what I plan to do, I think it's better for me to move to Kuala Lumpur since my mother and uncle are both staying put in Padang Besar. Moreover, my boss thinks business for us will be better in Malaysia than in Singapore."

"I agree with him too," she said aloud though she kept her thoughts to herself. From what she had read about Lee Kuan Yew, his stand for efficiency, law and order would by and by give little room to those outside the law, and she knew her lover was certainly outside the law. "When will you move?"

"I'm not sure. I still have some loose strings to tie up here. Once I'm settled there, I'll let you know."

"Hurry up, and come home soon," she said huskily. "I've missed you."

☆ ☆ ☆ ☆

In a soundproofed room in the basement of his textile shop, Boonrwad Wanglee was gloating at the terrified shirtless man whose muscular chest was pressed tightly against the back of a chair from being secured by thick ropes.

Boonrwad went behind the chair to look at the young man in the face. In his hand was a sharp iron spike. "You want to kill me? Well, here, I am. Are you going to kill me?"

After saying those ominous words, Boonrwad giggled as the hapless man squirmed and struggled but to no avail since the ropes securing him to the chair was very tight. And then the cherubic man stopped giggling. His face turned into a snarling mask as one hand went involuntarily to massage his throat while the other gestured with the iron spike. "Who are you? Why had you tried to kill me?"

"You'd murdered my eldest brother."

There was genuine surprise in Boonrwad's voice. "I murdered your eldest brother? Who's he?"

Frightened as the captive was, he still had enough sense to realize he had spoken too much. He knew his words could endanger his family and so decided not to say anything more.

"Who's your brother?" repeated Boonrwad as he walked around to the back of his captive. "If you think you can ignore my question, then you'd better have the courage and strength to endure the things I'm going to do to you."

This time the captive knew the fear he had felt ever since he was spotted and captured by two of Boonrwad's bodyguards, was nothing to be compared with the terror he suspected he was about to find out. A panic began to build in him.

☆ ☆ ☆ ☆

Although Ong Lay Yong was Singapore-born and was not close to her Malaysian relatives – an aunt and an uncle, both of whom were her mother's surviving siblings, and their children – across the Causeway, she however chose to join those who had opted to resettle in Malaysia. Her grandfather, she learned from her mother after her release, had passed away in Penang at the time she was under detention.

From the night she slashed Dr. George Teng's throat with a scalpel which she had earlier removed from an operating room, Lay Yong was filled with both elation and dread.

She was elated from having had extracted vengeance from the man who, in receiving her precious gift of virginity and trust had however treated her so shabbily and shamefully. *But I've proven Chairman Mao Tse-tung's words in that I can do what men can do,* she thought. And to her surprise, her elation continued to soar beyond the pleasure of getting even with someone who had wronged her. Soon she felt even more. The realization that she held the awesome power of life and death over others actually gave her a grandiose sense of power and so made her feel tremendously good about herself.

She was however fearful of being discovered. She was afraid that the police wasn't fooled so easily into thinking that George was killed by rioters. While she was confident that should the police come around to ask about George's love affairs, there would be enough jilted girls to keep them busy, she wasn't so sure whether he had told anyone about going out with her that fateful evening. After all, she had already found out the hard way that her late lover had a big mouth.

The police however had too much on their hands. Forty-three days after the July riot, where many people were killed or injured, another riot broke out again. Due to the vehement opposition from the Soekarno-led government in Indonesia against the formation of Malaysia since Soekarno coveted the North Borneo states of Sarawak and Sabah, and resented a strong and united Malaysia, the authorities had all along suspected Indonesian agents were behind the riots. As such, the police was directed to focus their investigations on political agitators – Indonesian agents who had infiltrated into the country and the local Communists. Subsequently some 240 suspects were arrested.

Much as Lay Yong thought their detention was hogwash since she blamed the riots on what she chose to regard as the Prime Minister's ineffectual leadership, she was however glad to have those political agitators taking the heat away from her. Even so, she remained on her guard.

By Christmas 1964, she felt certain that George's death had been written off as a casualty of the riots. It was then that someone from her past literarily bumped into her. In later years, she suspected the accidental meeting could have been a deliberate one, considering the whole episode had an air of unreality about it.

It happened like this.

She was walking home after work at the hospital. After turning into Smith Street, a car she had earlier seen parked by the roadside came up near enough for its left bonnet to graze her thigh. She thought it was lucky that the car wasn't going at fast speed and she had heard the sound of the engine in time to step up onto the pavement.

As she turned to glare at the driver, the man hurriedly got out, saying, "I'm so sorry... I..."

He broke off to gape at her, causing her in turn to gasp from having taken a good look at him. The man was the first to speak. "Well, now, who would have thought of it? After all these years, I'm seeing Ong Lay Yong again."

She too was delighted to see the short, thin and wizened man who was her tutor when she was in secondary school. As Wang *Lao-su* – Teacher Wang –

was strongly recommended as a mathematic genius to her father, he was hired to be her tutor. Wang *Lao-su* turned out to be more adept in brainwashing young minds as it was he who was responsible for her indoctrination into communism. The last she saw him was during the Hock Lee Bus Riots.

After the day when he nearly ran her down in his car, they often met for meals at hawker stalls in the Chinatown area as she was eager for news of their clandestine movement, which she knew, could only be obtained from Wang *Lao-su*.

One night in July 1965, after the People's Action Party won the Hong Lim by-election, she had asked Wang *Lao-su*: "Why have the people rejected Ong Eng Guan? Is this the end of our struggles?"

"It's the end for Ong Eng Guan as he has never been a true believer of our cause, but our struggles shall never end. Right now, the action has shifted to Vietnam but one day, we will resume our struggles here in Malaysia and Singapore."

"But I thought our comrades fighting in the Malaysian jungle had been routed when it was announced five years ago that the Emergency had ended?"

He gave her a genial smile, "Poor girl. That comes from having no contact with our comrades. You must join a cell which will see you have the continuous guidance and support of our comrades as well as information."

From him, Lay Yong learned that although most of the guerillas in the jungle had retreated to the Thai-

Malaysian border, and Chin Peng had gone to live in Peking, they were merely lying low to await another opportunity to rise again. Meanwhile, some of the guerillas in the central and south of Malaysia were still waging hit-and-run warfare, and the *Min Yuen*, or underground movement comprising sympathizers who lived in the cities but secretly supporting the cause, was also just as active.

After it was announced that Singapore had separated from Malaysia, Wang *Lao-su* suggested to Lay Yong that she should relocate to Kuala Lumpur where she could play a greater role as a cell leader. As her revolutionary spirit had been revived, she readily agreed.

"Good, I will get in touch with our people in Kuala Lumpur who will help you get a job in a hospital there," Wang *Lao-su* promised. "Once you have settled down, you will recruit and indoctrinate your own cell members to prepare them for the day when we shall rise again."

Both her parents had objected to her migration to Malaysia but it was to no avail as her mind was already made up. Seeing there was no way to dissuade her daughter, Madam Yap Bee Wah told Lay Yong, "If you must go to live in Malaysia, then at least go to Penang where my sister, Yap Bee Eng, and my brother, Yap Chin Kooi, can look after you."

"Spy on me, you mean?" she asked defiantly.

And so, on the last day of 1965, she was on a bus heading for Kuala Lumpur.

Thirty-nine

*O*n January 7, 1966, a day after Mao Dong Po and Suchin Suewonglee had celebrated his twenty-eighth birthday in Bangkok, they were on board a Malaysian-Singapore Airlines aircraft bound for Kuala Lumpur.

It was the first time that Suchin was flying, and also her first trip out of Thailand, having been persuaded at last by Dong Po that she deserved a vacation. Hence, earlier when the big Skymaster taxied along the runway at Don Muang Airport, she was filled with excitement. And when the engines roared louder and louder as the aircraft surged forward faster and faster, she gripped her lover's hand, muttering under her breath: "The plane will never go up. We'll all crash."

Once they were off the ground and rising higher and higher until the houses below looked like doll's houses and the cars on the roads like toy cars, a thought occurred to her, which she spoke aloud to her lover, "Though the governments of Malaysia and Singapore weren't able to work together as one government, it's a wonder that they can still cooperate in running a joint airline."

"Only Time can tell whether this cooperation will last," Dong Po said, raising his voice a little to make himself heard above the din. "Now that the Malaysian and Singapore governments had wrestled control from BOAC and Qantas to become major shareholders, they had changed the name from Malaysian Airways Limited to Malaysian-Singapore Airlines. But I really doubt if this joint airline can last."

"Why do you say that?"

Dong Po was silent for a while and then he sighed. "Though we both don't have siblings, as you can see of those who have, they inevitably ended up squabbling. As the saying goes, close as the teeth and lips, the former are known to bite the latter."

"I see what you mean," Suchin said, and after a while, lulled by the drones of the engines began to doze off.

In the silence that followed, Dong Po thought to himself that while envy and squabble were common with most siblings, a few were however quite close to one another. He felt sad when he recollected how his failure to assassinate Boonrwad Wanglee had caused the client to lose yet another son. He was actually there at the time the young man was spotted by one of Boonrwad's bodyguards. Dong Po still seethed with frustration when he recalled his helplessness in watching two of Boonrwad's bodyguards cornering and knocking the hapless young man unconscious. He was unable to intervene because to do so would have exposed him.

It was later when his *sifu* had told him the young man was another of the client's son who was trying to avenge his eldest brother's death that Dong Po felt some regret.

"Then I should have intervened, at least to save an innocent life even though that would mean I may no longer be able to remove the quarry since my identity would be exposed," he told Somchai.

His *sifu* however disagreed. "It won't do much good. You'll endanger yourself and your dear ones by exposing yourself. A greater good lies in removing the evil once and for all."

As the plane flew onwards to Kuala Lumpur, Dong Po sighed and pushed all depressing thoughts out of his mind. He took out *The Man with the Golden Gun* to read, having had finished *You Only Live Twice* the previous night. Though he looked forward to reading the novel, he felt inexplicably sad that its author, Ian Fleming had died in August 1964, which made him treasure all the more his collection of Ian Fleming's novels, including his final work, *Octopussy and the Living Daylights,* which Suchin had airflown all the way from London for his birthday.

☆ ☆ ☆ ☆

For nearly a week, Suchin stayed at a small walk-up apartment which her lover had bought, not far from the junction of Treacher Road* and Weld Road*.

---

* Treacher Road is today's Jalan Sultan Ismail, while Weld Road is today's Jalan Raja Chulan.

On the morning of the second day after Suchin's arrival in the Malaysian capital, Dong Po showed off the Vauxhall sedan he had recently bought by taking her to the Lake Gardens. Many people were there as it was a Sunday. Despite the crowd, they had a fabulous time rowing a rented boat on the lake until afternoon when they went to the Race Course at Jalan Ampang. Later that evening, he took her to the Ampang village, where they had *yong tau foo*, bean curd cakes, bitter gourds, chilies, and egg plant, all of which were stuffed with fish paste.

Although Dong Po brought Suchin to the Coliseum Café at the lower stretch of Batu Road the next day, she wasn't really keen on western meals. She however relished the moment in the Coliseum Cafe when Dong Po told her about the time when he was a boy and Brother Duffy had brought him to Kuala Lumpur to watch *Shane*, enjoyed a hurried meal at this same restaurant, and then rushed back to the "New Village" before the evening curfew.

"Are you still in touch with this Brother Duffy?" she asked. "He sounds like a wonderful guy."

He shook his head sadly. "No, we've lost contact. He's indeed a most wonderful guy, next to my Uncle Somchai."

"But you don't seem to know much about this Uncle Somchai," commented Suchin, who had only heard bits and pieces about her lover's boss though she had long ago suspected he was Dong Po's teacher in his deadly profession.

"He tells very little about himself, like as though he isn't comfortable about revealing too much."

Just like you, she thought.

When he found out that she preferred the dried beef noodles at an old restaurant at Cross Street*, he took her there on each of the next three days. They went after their afternoon naps just before sunset. Dong Po told her that on most days he preferred to stay home after lunch as it would be too hot to venture outdoors.

As her country had never been colonized, Suchin was fascinated by the Selangor Club, when Dong Po told her about the "spotted dog" story, whereby a member used to leave her Dalmatian in front of the clubhouse.

Her eyes lit up when she saw the unique architectural design of the Railway Station and the National Mosque, which was completed the previous year.

During the second week of her stay, Dong Po drove her to Malacca where they stayed for two days to explore the old town. She was mesmerized by the descendants of the Portuguese and Dutch they came across. From Malacca, they drove south to Johor Baru and across the Causeway to Singapore.

Suchin was ecstatic after he checked them into the Raffles Hotel. Dong Po was glad he had decided to stay at the Raffles Hotel instead of bringing Suchin to his apartment. From the colonial-style hotel, on most evenings of their week-long stay, they would walk to the

---

* Cross Street was renamed Jalan Silang until 2003 when the name was changed again to Jalan Tun Tan Siew Sin.

Esplanade where they would eat *satay,* pieces of meat on sticks barbequed over charcoal fire, and dipped in spicy peanut sauce. From the Esplanade, she would gaze across the Padang to admire the grandness of the City Hall. On the third day, he took her to the Clifford Pier where they boarded a boat for a short romp around the bay.

Time flew so fast that soon, they were back at the Subang Airport in Kuala Lumpur to catch a flight that would take them back to Bangkok. When they were walking up the metal steps about to board the aircraft, Suchin said to Dong Po: "Malaysia and Singapore are such interesting countries."

☆ ☆ ☆ ☆

"This country is so boring."

"The food's most unpalatable too. When the hospital administrator gave me the transfer order to head north to Butterworth, I'd thought the food would be more enjoyable since I've heard so much about Penang hawker fare from my mother but it turned out to be so disappointing. How I've missed the *char kway teow* back home in Hock Lam Street."

"Yes, those flat rice noodles ought to be fried with sweet sauce rather than the salty variety of soy sauce they used here in Penang. And they fried it so dry up here. As for Penang *laksa,* I've never tasted anything so vile. I really can't understand why the locals would go so crazy over a bowl of rice noodles served in a spicy soup of tamarind paste, shredded fish, chopped-up cucumber and mint leaves."

"Well, even though the country's so boring and the food's quite insipid and unpalatable, at least, my job is important."

"Of course, I think it's quite a feat to recruit three nurses, a hospital attendant, and an ambulance driver to our great cause. To lead a cell is certainly a most important job for the cause."

"But I think recruiting cell members and leading them isn't as important as having used my feminine wiles to ensnare a senior officer of the Special Branch as I have done."

"Of course, haven't Wang *Lao-su* been so generous with his praises the moment he heard about the hook-up with an Inspector from the elite unit which have been responsible for the deaths and imprisonment of so many of our comrades?"

"Yes, Wang *Lao-su* has been most insistent that I should try drawing out as much vital information as possible from the inspector. But until we get orders to start a full-scale revolution, everything's so boring."

Anyone who had heard the words being spoken aloud would have thought a conversation between two persons was in progress. Actually, it was Ong Lay Yong talking to herself. That night when she talked to herself, she had even alternately changed her voice so that it appeared like two persons were engaged in a conversation in her rented room at a house located a short distance from Bagan Luar Road.

"What do you mean I've got the wrong guy?"

"From what you'd told me about the assassin who'd tried to garrote you in Chiang Mai, I think the one you'd caught wasn't the same fellow. This one got caught too easily."

Boonrwad Wanglee stared open-mouthed at the tall burly man with some skepticism. "No, we'd caught the assassin. And I must say, it was no thanks to you that we'd caught him."

As usual, the man ignored Boonrwad's insulting tone. "Did you get a confession out of him?"

Those words stopped Boonrwad who was about to say something rude to the tall man. The tall man smiled as he knew the captive wouldn't have a chance to say much once the secret society chief got started in his hobby. He would simply be too eager to go all the way with his deadly calligraphy using the sharp iron spike.

Seeing he had got Boonrwad's attention, the tall man continued, speaking with more confidence now. "If I were you, I won't lower my guard. Not yet."

Forty

*T*hroughout 1967, Mao Dong Po was unable to make any move against Boonrwad Wanglee as the gangster remained on his guard. Then on April 5, 1968, a day after Martin Luther King was assassinated, Somchai summoned Dong Po to Bangkok.

His aircraft landed at the Don Maung Airport around mid-morning. From the airport, he went straight to the Oriental Hotel. He found his *sifu*, who was stylishly dressed, wearing a pair of khaki slacks and a matching short-sleeved khaki shirt with military-style epaulettes, sitting at a table at the Riverside Terrace. Dong Po just couldn't resist a cheeky, "Going on safari?"

Ignoring his protégé's cheek, Somchai asked Dong Po whether he would like to join him for coffee since it was still too early for his usual gin and tonic.

The moment the waiter left with the order, Somchai frowned. "That was a bad thing they did in America, my boy."

Knowing his mentor was an Americanophile, from his craze over American movies even though in Thailand, most of the Hollywood offerings were dubbed in Thai – something Dong Po couldn't accept as he found it extremely ludicrous to hear Sean Connery speaking in fluent Thai – he waited for the older man to tell him what the Americans had done that was so bad.

"It is bad that someone had removed Martin Luther King, who I feel doesn't deserve removing," Somchai said, shaking his head sadly. "This sort of thing gives professionals like us a bad name for which we don't deserve at all."

In trying to suppress an urge to laugh over his *sifu's* weird way of reasoning, Dong Po ended up coughing. Taking no notice of his protégé's amusement, Somchai fished out a cigar from his breast pocket. After lighting up, he puffed out smoke and sighed contentedly. "But the Americans have need for professionals like us."

Seeing the waiter coming back with his coffee, Dong Po silently shook out his napkin and threw it across his lap. After the waiter had left, he asked: "Are we talking about an individual American client or something bigger and more organized?"

"The request came from Wongkot Suttharom… remember my childhood friend? He's now a full colonel and he has been asked to recommend one or more private contractors to assist the Americans," said Somchai.

"I see. But I would have thought the Americans have all the resources to handle their own jobs. So why do they need us?"

"Well, the Americans are busybodies, my boy. With the on-going Vietnam War and their fingers stuck in most pies, they have need of independent jobbers. Come to think of it, there are also jobs where they can't risk any embarrassment of fingers pointing back to them."

"I suppose there's a job on hand, Uncle Somchai?"

"Yes, we…I mean I have been asked to remove this fellow," Somchai said, taking out a small envelope from his pocket and retrieving from it, a photograph. "You, of course, will do the actual removal."

Dong Po immediately felt uncomfortable the moment he glanced at the photograph which showed a man, a woman, two young children, and a cat. It was obviously a family photograph. Turning the photograph, he could see handwritten words on its back: "Tim, Jennifer, Derek, Jo and Kitty."

"Am I supposed to remove the entire clan, including the cat, whose name I bet is Kitty?"

"No, only remove the guy."

"I take it that this family photograph has been provided by the Americans?" demanded Dong Po sourly. Before his mentor could nod his head, the younger man complained: "Can't they just hand over a photograph of just only the quarry himself?"

Somchai sighed. "I can understand your feelings, my boy. Now that you've seen the man's family, it sort of complicates the removal…like the job has become somewhat personal."

"You bet," Dong Po said. "I wouldn't mind knowing the man has a pet because if it comes to breaking into his home, the knowledge that he has, say a dog, may be useful since a dog could bark or even attack an intruder. But…"

He left the sentence unfinished. They both sat in silence for a while watching the river traffic, and then Dong Po asked. "Have they told us why they want the removal?"

"It's on a need-to-know basis."

"That means we're not supposed to know."

"The clients have however agreed to our recently revised fees though payment is on a first-hit-first-pay basis because they have also opened the job to other professionals."

"I don't like not knowing the reasons for removing this quarry," Dong Po said stubbornly. "What if the quarry should turn out to be another Martin Luther King?"

Once again, they sat in silence. Dong Po was unhappy because he had caught the fleeting look on his *sifu's* face when he mentioned Martin Luther King. It was a look filled with deep sadness. And then he heard Somchai's words which confirmed his worst fear, "I'm under deep obligation to Colonel Wongkot, who is in turn obligated to the Americans."

Just after Dong Po had gulped down all his coffee and was about to take his leave, Somchai said: "By the way, the client who wants to avenge his two sons had doubled the fee and promised an additional $10,000 bonus if the job can be completed within this year."

It was the second time after so many years that Suchin Suewonglee had seen her lover in such lousy mood.

As soon as Dong Po had finished his meeting with Somchai at the Oriental Hotel that morning, he took a taxi to Suchin's office. The previous day, he had already telephoned her to let her know he would be coming to Bangkok, and promised that as soon as his meeting with his boss was over, he would drop by to take her out to lunch.

Even though he had been looking forward to see Suchin, he was still suspicious and upset over the deal which the Americans had forced upon Colonel Wongkot, who in turn, forced onto Somchai. He knew he had every right to be upset and suspicious because ultimately he would be the one tasked to carry out the assignment. He didn't want innocent blood on his hands. The sight of the quarry's family unnerved him.

Having seen the dark frowns on Dong Po's face as he sat in the outer office waiting for her, Suchin quietly went to see Arthit Lamsam. Thereafter, she went to where Dong Po was sitting.

"I've just asked my boss to let me have the rest of the day off," she told Dong Po and was glad she had made the last-minute decision because his face had immediately lit up. "Seeing it is such a lovely day, and as it's still too early for lunch, why don't we go to visit my parents?"

He was about to protest jokingly about her refusal to visit his mother and yet here she was asking him to visit her parents. However, seeing the pleasure lighting up her face, he just nodded his assent. Besides, having had previously accompanied her on a few occasions, he found the place peaceful and soothing. It was something he needed that day.

Half an hour later, the taxi dropped them off at the temple located on the west bank of the Chao Phraya River. They walked into the temple's ground and went inside one of the buildings, where the ashes of Suchin's departed parents were kept in separate urns and placed in an alcove in one of the walls. After paying their respect, Suchin led Dong Po by his hand out into a side garden.

All of a sudden, Suchin turned to Dong Po. "Unlike prominent or wealthy people who often kept the bodies of their departed loved ones in a temple for a long period of time before cremation to show they are loved and respected, my parents were simple folks and so opted for a speedy cremation. Should anything happen to me one day, will you do the same for me? I mean arrange a speedy cremation for me?"

He frowned and then admonished her. "Why are you talking like this?"

"Don't be angry with me. I'd just thought if I don't tell you, in the event something should happen to me, then you won't know what I want. After cremation, please keep some of my ashes in the temple beside those of my late parents and scatter the rest in the Chao Phraya River."

When he made no reply, she smiled and said. "I'm older than you and so your chances of outliving me are better. Moreover, I actually prefer to go before I appear like an old hag to you. This way, you'll still retain a pleasant memory of me."

Though he smiled back at her, deep within, he could feel the morning's uneasiness returning to engulf him.

☆ ☆ ☆ ☆

If Boonrwad Wanglee had felt any unease after being warned that he had probably caught the wrong guy, time had erased all his fear.

Moreover, ever since he first set eyes on the dancer with the most sensuous and exciting body he had ever seen, performing at the Chez Eve Nightclub, he began to throw all caution to the wind. Almost every night, he would go to the nightclub to watch Marisa as the nightclub's guest dancer was called. Her erotic style of dancing seemed to give him endless pleasure. Although he had arranged for flowers to be sent her everyday, he was surprisingly bashful about ordering the manager, who fawned on him, to ask her to join him on all those nights when he was there watching her performance.

His awkward bashfulness probably came about because Boonrwad was unable to dance. Once, when he had turned down a dance hostess accompanying him, saying gruffly, "I don't dance," the girl had cheerfully told him: "Then I won't lose you to that sexy Marisa. Do you know our nightclub's guest dancer has a peculiar eccentricity in that she refused to entertain anyone who couldn't dance properly?"

After a week's deliberation, he decided to take up dancing lessons as he was determined to woo the professional dancer. But that very night when he came to the nightclub, to his surprise, the dancer was not performing during the cabaret's show time. Boonrwad quickly summoned the manager who told him that Marisa had left that morning for Singapore as her contract with his nightclub was over.

"Which nightclub in Singapore has she gone to?" he demanded.

"If I'm not wrong, she's performing at the Tropicana."

☆ ☆ ☆ ☆

Having had previously worked in the hospital in Kuala Lumpur, Ong Lay Yong knew the administrator's habits.

Although Dr. Aminah binte Kuntom was a vocal critic against the British ways when they were running the hospital, once she landed the coveted position, she did a full 360-degree turn to insist on continuing the British tradition of faithfully observing tea time. Thus, Lay Yong knew that each afternoon for half an hour – Dr. Aminah had even lengthened the tea break – the hospital administrator would refuse to see anyone in her office.

That very afternoon, Lay Yong sneaked back to the hospital. As her lover, Chief Inspector Chris Ng – he was promoted recently – had asked her to accompany him to the Malaysian capital where he was attending a briefing, she agreed as she thought of the possibility of picking up some useful information from him. At the same time, she decided that having been away from her previous workplace for more than a year, it would be safe for her to carry out something she had long wanted to do.

Dr. Aminah, who was dozing on her sofa in the corner of her office, sat up the moment she heard someone entering her office. "I thought I'd said no one is to enter my room…oh, it's you. What do you want?"

Ignoring the disdainful look on her former boss's face and her unfriendly tone, Lay Yong said pleasantly, "An eye for an eye, a tooth for a tooth. You'd given me a bad time previously when I was attached to this hospital. And you'd thought you could get rid of me by booting me to Butterworth. Well, I'm back."

Dr. Aminah appeared slightly taken aback. As Lay Yong's ominous words sank in, she got up and tried to work her way around Lay Yong, who was standing with her back to the door. All of a sudden, Lay Yong's hand reached out to clasp something firmly over her former boss's nose and mouth. The two women struggled but the Chinese woman's strong grip kept the pad in place. The sweet, sickly smell of ether soon took effect on Dr. Aminah.

Moving her limp body back on the sofa, Lay Yong took out a hypodermic needle and gave the inert hospital administrator an injection.

Forty-one

*D*isturbed as Mao Dong Po was from having seen the photograph of Tim Lane's family including even the family cat they owned, he was more upset over having to kill a guy who may probably not deserved to die. Hence, he hadn't given much thought to the contract. Instead his mind was on Boonrwad Wanglee, who he found out had lately become a regular at the Chez Eve Nightclub.

Around 7:20 p.m. – about three hours before Boonrwad came to learn that the sexy dancer he was smitten with had left for Singapore – Dong Po went to the nightclub to scout out the vicinity. He was standing in the shade of a big tree across the street surveying the place and trying to figure out the best way to ambush the quarry later that evening when he heard a slight sound behind him. He whirled around just in time to see a tall, burly man raising a snub-nose.38 Colt to aim at him. Just as quickly as he had whirled around, Dong Po's right feet moved in a blur, kicking the gun out of the man's hand.

"It's you," the tall burly man gasped in surprise.

Dong Po's eyes too had widened in astonishment. It had been many years since he had last seen Virote, who trained with him under the *ajarn*. Recovering quickly from the shock, the Chinese asked. "Why?"

The Siamese had also recovered his composure. "Surely you know why."

When Dong Po shook his head, Virote said, "As a detective sergeant with the Royal Thai Police, it's my duty to arrest you."

"For what?" Dong Po asked in a casual and innocent tone. "Have I done anything wrong?"

"You're after Boonrwad Wanglee."

Dong Po's voice was soft. "Now, why should a police detective sergeant like you be so anxious in watching out for a crime boss like Boonrwad? Moreover, I don't think you want to arrest me. You were about to shoot me in the back."

Virote at least had the decency to blush. But he still insisted: "You've better come quietly with me or…"

"Or what?" asked Dong Po, studying his former sparring partner warily. "You take me in so that you can later remove me at your convenience or hand me to Boonrwad in return for a handsome reward? No, thank you."

"Looks like I shall have to use force since you are so…" said Virote without finishing his sentence which was a tactic to catch an opponent unaware at the time of making his move.

Instead of waiting politely, like most people, to hear out someone's speech, Dong Po knew the instant Virote lunged at him. He didn't back away as Virote had expected him to do. Instead Dong Po moved forward to slam his right elbow against the Siamese. He followed this strike with his left fist, hitting Virote on the side of his mouth. But the Siamese seemed immune to the pain, which would have floored another man because his left hand was already grabbing Dong Po's right hand and raising his right knee, aiming at the Chinese lad's left rib cage. Anticipating the attack as he had seen the slight movement of Virote's shoulders, Dong Po raised his left knee to block the Siamese. With both hands, he pushed Virote away and at the same time, kicked out, slamming the ball of his right foot in the Siamese's solar plexus.

The moment Dong Po pulled back his right leg, his left leg swung up to connect with the side of Virote's head. In those days when they were sparring before the *ajarn*, Dong Po had controlled his force. That night, he went all out without any restraint. Hence, when he heard the sickening thud, after which Virote crumpled like a discarded rag doll, Dong Po knew the Siamese cop was already a corpse even before his body hit the ground.

Having killed the police officer, Dong Po looked around and was assured no one was about as it was still much too early for the nightclub to commence business. He embraced anonymity by walking further down the road and then hopping onto a passing bus. Ten stops later, he got off at Petburi Road where he hailed a taxi to go to Suchin Suewonglee's home. After all, he had promised to take her out for dinner later that night.

Ever since the first evening when his *sifu* had invited him to dinner at the Oriental Hotel, Dong Po had wanted to take Suchin there but she had always declined as she preferred eating at the roadside vendors more than in a posh hotel's restaurant. That morning before she set out for her office, he had insisted that they dined that night at the Oriental Hotel. To his surprise and delight, she had agreed to try out the food at the hotel.

☆☆☆☆

Around 6:45 p.m., Suchin reached her home but Dong Po wasn't back yet. She had a shower before putting on the clinging wine-red dress which Dong Po had bought in Singapore for her previous birthday. Taking one final look at her image on the full-length mirror, Suchin was pleased with what she saw. Despite her being already forty-two years' old, her figure was perfect and she still looked her best. And tonight, she certainly looked most dazzling in that alluring dress.

Just as the clock hands showed 8:10 p.m., Dong Po came in. He gave her an approving nod and smiled. "You're beautiful, darling."

Unlike many women who indulged in self-deception, Suchin's attractiveness was again proven the moment she walked with Dong Po into the Chinese restaurant at the Oriental Hotel. Several heads turned as a waiter ushered her and her beau to their table.

"What's recommended?" she asked happily after they were seated.

"Me."

"Silly," she laughed. "That will be later tonight."

"I'm serious…I'd discovered there's a dish named after me," he chuckled, and pointed to an item in the menu. "Here, look for yourself."

True enough, she saw the words "Dong Po Rou" printed on the menu.

"*Rou* is Chinese for meat and this is a Hangzhou's specialty dish describing a cube measuring five inches by five inches by three inches of succulent combination of lean and fat pork," he explained.

"So you're famous."

"No, not me," Dong Po said modestly. "The dish is named after a famous poet by the name of Su Dong-po also known as Su Shi, who lived during the Song Dynasty. According to legend, he was an honest official whose outspokenness often led to his being banished to remote places. In one such remote post, he came out with the recipe. My father admired him so much that he named me after him."

"You're a strange man, Dong Po," she said. "Yes, I think I shall call you by this name now that I finally knew the story behind the name. You're really a strange man."

"Why do you say that?"

She didn't reply as the waiter had come to take orders. A smile came to her lips when she heard her lover speaking fluently in Mandarin to the waiter.

"How is it that you can also speak Mandarin so well?" she asked after the waiter had left. "I thought you speak Thai, English and our Chow Chou dialect."

"I also speak Malay," he said. "I learn to speak Mandarin from watching Shaw Brothers' movies when I was growing up in Padang Besar. Well, you still haven't answered my question as to why you think me strange."

"You're a killer," she said, quickly raising a slender hand to stop him as she saw he had tensed up and was about to protest. "I have never been able to shake off this instinct as I can feel the danger vibes about you but…"

She saw him staring intently at her with an amused albeit wary smile though he didn't say anything. She continued, "But you're still quite learned. Besides…"

"Yes?"

She was about to say that those whom she believed he had killed deserved to die but instead, she said: "You're also good looking, at least to me. That makes you a lady killer."

He laughed, and as his laughter was infectious, she joined in. She could feel the tension evaporating.

If only you knew what I've done earlier this evening, Dong Po thought with some sadness. Though he willed himself to smile and act normal, deep within he felt an inexplicable sadness for having to kill Virote. But he knew he had no choice since Virote had chosen to be a rogue cop and with an effort, he blotted out the unpleasant memory.

A scowl appeared on Chief Inspector Ali bin Abdul Karim's face. Not for the first time he thought: *They should have posted me anywhere but homicide. And certainly not under that slave driver, Assistant Superintendent Ahmad bin Kassim.*

This was the result of his candid self awareness. While Chief Inspector Ali prided himself on his stamina for any sexual romp in bed with the ladies, when it came to leg work to investigate a homicide, he somehow lost interest very quickly. As for ASP Ahmad, he was not only a workaholic but he also insisted his team members put work before everything else.

He had just emerged from ASP Ahmad's office after having been told in no uncertain terms about the unsatisfactory outcome of his investigation into the questionable death of Dr. Aminah binte Kuntom. Chief Inspector Ali had tried to convince his boss that after Dr. Aminah was found dead in her office, a doctor had been quickly summoned, and he had thereafter given the verdict that her heart had stopped beating.

"It was a case of cardiac arrest," the chief inspector had told his boss, glad that he remembered the exact words provided him by the doctor.

But ASP Ahmad insisted: "It's hard to believe that a vibrant young woman like Dr. Aminah with no health problem could suffer a sudden heart attack."

Now that he was outside his boss's office, Chief Inspector Ali muttered unhappily under his breath. "If you're so clever, why not you handle the case yourself? Yeah, why did you assign it to me?"

Some 250 miles away in Butterworth in the north, a woman happily made a little moue in front of the mirror as she put on her lipstick. Her lover, Chief Inspector Chris Ng, would be coming in about half an hour's time to take her out to dinner.

Ong Lay Yong was in extremely good mood. Ever since her return from Kuala Lumpur, she had been feeling extremely pleased with herself. That day after she had injected her unconscious former boss with a lethal dose of potassium chloride, she felt the same surge of gratification she had first experienced from slitting Dr. George Teng's throat. And throughout the seven-hour drive from Kuala Lumpur back to Butterworth, she had picked up bits of information about Operation Whitewash from Chris, who was always so eager to impress her of his importance in the Special Branch.

"If Chris was really that important, how come it took him so many years to be promoted to chief inspector?" she posed the question to her image in the mirror.

Using a different voice, she answered, "Of course, he has given the excuses of not having powerful patrons and how one of the underworld chieftains whom he had antagonized, had bribed his superiors to stall his promotion."

Putting down the lipstick on the dressing table, she leaned closer to the mirror to check her mascara. "Well, he's still useful enough because it was thanks to his information that I've managed to strike a blow for our cause."

The recollection of what had happened three days ago brought a smile to her lips. It was due to her lover's indiscretion that a Police Field Force convoy which set out to hunt a group of Communist terrorists operating in the Kroh-Betong area was ambushed. As the Communist terrorists had the advantage of surprise, they killed 16 troopers and wounded 17 others. Apart from seizing firearms and ammunition, they also left three badly-damaged police vehicles.

When she thought of Wang *Lao-su's* subsequent praises for her contribution to their cause, Lay Yong muttered: "That blabbermouth Chris is still useful to us after all."

The thought of him led her to recall the first time they had met. At that time, Chris was still only an inspector though from the way he behaved, one could be forgiven into thinking he was the State's police chief, or at least, in command of the district. He had been admitted to her hospital for removal of piles. As the night nurse, Lay Yong had looked in on the patient. He was propped up on the bed.

Seeing his forlorn look, she had, for want of nothing better to do, pulled up a chair to chit-chat with him. After all, she remembered Wang *Lao-su* having had once told her: "If you can befriend any police officer or make him enamored with you, so much the better. It will help our cause greatly."

From the moment she caught him glancing surreptitiously at her chest, she knew the police officer who already had a wife and three young children – she had seen them coming to the hospital two days ago – was interested in her. Chris may not be that great looking as he was a thin man with sharp features like a long sallow face, small beady eyes and a pursed mouth lined at the top with a wispy moustache, but he was still interesting enough in bed.

With this last thought, Lay Yong giggled. "Having Chris is still better than being alone playing with myself."

Another man who was at that moment stepping out of the Paya Lebar Airport was also giggling to himself as he thought of how he was going to win the affection of the sexy dancer he had recently became so enamored. He was so preoccupied that he didn't even notice the uneasy glance from the single bodyguard accompanying him.

Boonrwad Wanglee thought he was very clever for having come up with the plan. He had told his wife that he had to go to Singapore for business. As his wife had long ago given up on his philandering ways, she knew there was a woman involved but so long as she was given free rein to run the textile business and help herself to the money from the till, she couldn't care who her husband was bringing along or going to see in Singapore.

It was part of Boonrwad's plan to join a crash-course in Singapore to learn quickly how to dance. After that, he would pursue Marisa, who, he found out had a three-month contract to perform at the Tropicana, and after that, another three months at the Neptune.

Even though he had read about the death of Detective Sergeant Virote Boonmi near the Chez Eve Nightclub, his mind was so engrossed with the dancer that it hadn't occurred to him that the sergeant's death could have something to do with him. All he could think of at the time was having one less corrupted cop on his payroll.

Forty-two

To Mao Dong Po's surprise, more men than women seemed to be into dancing. He counted eleven men including him and Boonrwad Wanglee in the dancing class he had joined. There were only five ladies.

Three months earlier, he had used a fictitious name to enroll himself as a pupil at the Juanita Pereira Dance Studio. That came about after an excited Somchai tipped him off a day after Boonrwad left for Singapore with only a bodyguard to protect him. It hadn't taken Dong Po too long to pick up Boonrwad's trail. After the triad chief had signed up for the intensive evening lessons at the dance studio located in Tanjong Katong, Dong Po too had joined the class, arranging it in such a way that he was in the same class with his quarry.

As there were more men than women in the class, he often found himself partnering with other men as they tried to learn the dance steps from the instructress, a vivacious Eurasian woman about his age by the name of Juanita Pereira. Tried as he would, he somehow couldn't get himself paired off with Boonrwad as his partner for the evening.

Not wishing to draw attention unnecessarily to himself by insisting on having Boonrwad as his partner, he bided his time. His patience paid off one evening in September when to his delight, he found the Iron Pen Scholar was to be his partner for the evening's lesson.

"You have all been doing the Argentine Tango in the past few weeks," began Juanita. "So you should know by now that it is the most exotic and passionate of all dances, for which I must once again remind you that it is characterized by intricate leg work, walking steps and turning figures. The movement must be spontaneous and there must be communication and expression between the leader and the follower. We'll practice for the last time tonight before moving to another dance in tomorrow's class."

And turning on the music playing from the gramophone, Juanita shouted, "Let us begin," the moment the lively tune of *La Cumparsita* came on the air.

It was just a few more minutes to nine – the time the class usually ended – that Dong Po spotted the opportunity. They had just finished the routine known as *lady's gancho*, and shifted to the routine called *parade with arraste,* when Dong Po's leg swung forward. The moment he saw Boonrwad stumbled on a step, Dong Po knew the tiny poison-tipped needle he had inserted in his dancing shoes had struck home.

Dong Po mumbled an apology. "Sorry, I still can't get used to the steps."

Boonrwad grunted as he glared malevolently at the younger man. Dong Po ignored him as he was thinking: *This is an easy death for you compared to what you'd done to most of your victims but I'm still glad I've finally got you. All it takes would be another thirty minutes or so for the poison to work.*

☆ ☆ ☆ ☆

Having received her lover's telegram earlier that day, Suchin Suewonglee went directly from her office to Don Muang Airport to meet his arrival from Kuala Lumpur. Having read a dispatch about the death of Boonrwad Wanglee in Singapore, she was surprised that her lover was flying in from Kuala Lumpur.

Unknown to her, the previous night after Dong Po left the dance studio in Tanjong Katong, he had taken a taxi directly to the Paya Lebar Airport where he caught the last flight to Kuala Lumpur. Had any of his classmates from the dance studio gone to the airport, he or she would not have been able to recognize Dong Po. This was because after leaving the dance studio, he had immediately removed the wig and moustache he was wearing all those times he was faithfully learning to dance.

As soon as Suchin saw him emerging from the customs checkpoint, she waved happily to him. "Welcome home, my dear."

"Hey, darling," he said, hugging her. "You're beautiful."

From the airport, they went straight to the Oriental Hotel for dinner as they had agreed. To Dong Po's delight, Suchin had developed a liking for the ambience in Bangkok's oldest hotel.

By 7:50 p.m. just as they were strolling hand in hand into the hotel lobby, she stopped abruptly in her stride. Dong Po turned to look at her in surprise and saw her face had turned deathly white. As her eyes were wide with terror and she was cringing right before his eyes, Dong Po quickly put his arm around her and whispered softly in a low, comforting voice, "It's all right, dearest. I'm here by your side. There's nothing to fear."

He knew she had made a great effort because her feet began to move again. Having earlier seen her looking towards the reception area, he guided her away to a quiet corner and at the same time kept an eye on the only man who was talking to a receptionist.

"It's him," she whispered. "It's that monster. Please take me home."

Without a word, he led her out of the hotel where they got into a waiting taxi.

☆ ☆ ☆ ☆

An uneasy thought flashed through Dr. Padmanathan's mind that night as he walked out of the hospital and made his way to the car park.

He couldn't understand why earlier when passing by Ong Lay Yong on his way out, she had smiled so sweetly at him. *If anything, the damned woman hates me to the core*, he thought. *So why the hell was she smiling so sweetly at me?*

Right from the day she was posted to the hospital, the tall, bearded anesthesiologist had taken a deep dislike of the Chinese nurse even though it was really his fault. At first, Dr. Padmanathan who fancied himself a ladies' man, had tried his usual crudity with newly posted nurses, telling her: "When I'm not sending my patients to sleep, I like to take beautiful women like you to sleep…with me."

She had not only given him a frosty glare but had also later reported him to the hospital administrator for having sexually harassed her. As the other nurses had merely suffered his crude proposals in silence and ignored him, it being the first time that he was being reported made him see red even though the hospital administrator hadn't done much except to relay the report to him. Thereafter, he tried to give Lay Yong a bad time whenever he had an opportunity. She, in turn, had always been silent, stoic and cold towards him.

Hence, that afternoon, to find Lay Yong actually smiling sweetly at him made him feel somewhat wary and uneasy. But by the time, his car turned into Chain Ferry Road, she was no longer in his thoughts. Instead he was feeling very sleepy, yawning loudly from time to time as he tried to keep his concentration on the road. *What's wrong with me today,* he wondered. *Why am I suddenly so sleepy?*

And then he saw the headlights of the huge trailer looming up before him and heard the loud blare of the horn. Though he hit the brakes hard, he knew it was too late as he felt an agony shooting through him and heard his own scream as a ton or so of metal crashed into his car, sending him into a darkness experienced by his past patients. However, unlike them, he won't have a chance to wake up anymore.

Forty-three

As soon as he had sent Suchin Suewonglee home, Mao Dong Po told her that he would have to go out for a short while as he had to see his boss.

Suchin, who had by then regained her composure from having got over her fear asked: "Won't you have dinner with me before going out again? It won't take me long to prepare a simple meal for us."

"I'm not hungry as I've earlier eaten a little on the plane. If I'm hungry, I'll have something light with my boss," he said. "After I've updated him on our business, I shall hurry home to you."

"All right then," she said, wearing a concerned expression on her face as she watched him rummaging inside his valise for something which he quickly slipped inside his pocket. He moved too fast for her to see whatever it was. Something told her that Dong Po wasn't telling her the truth but she also knew she was unable to stop him. Hence, she told him huskily: "Please be careful."

"Of course, dear," he laughed easily.

Once Dong Po got out of Suchin's home, he hailed a taxi and told the driver to send him to the Oriental Hotel. Once back at the hotel, he first went to the restroom where he extracted a fake moustache – taken earlier from his valise – out of his pocket. He adjusted it above his lips and then took out a pair of gold-framed spectacles from another pocket. Using the hair gel generously provided in the hotel's restroom, he combed his hair, all straight back. When he looked again at his image on the mirror, he was pleased to find it was a different person from the one who had earlier entered the restroom.

Thereafter, he went to the reception counter and asked a clerk: "Can you please check for me whether a guest by the name of …"

He paused in mid-sentence because he sensed a man walking near to him. When he turned to look, he saw it was none other than former Major Ishihara Shigeto, the man whose name he was about to say. Smoothly, he continued addressing the clerk, "Michael MacDuff has already checked in?"

While another girl hurried forth to attend to the Japanese, the clerk attending to Dong Po checked the register and then looked at him with a puzzled expression, "I'm sorry, sir, but we don't have a guest by the name you've given me…"

Seeing the Japanese had walked away towards the hotel's entrance, Dong Po mumbled an apology to the clerk and turned to follow his quarry. The Japanese raised a hand as though to hail a taxi parked along the driveway but at the last moment seemed to change his mind. He walked along the pavement down the driveway leading to the street.

Outside the hotel, a cool breeze was blowing. It thus occurred to Dong Po that was the reason why his quarry had decided to walk instead of taking a taxi. He smiled as it suited his purpose but the moment he turned from the hotel's driveway into the busy street, Dong Po's smile vanished as he realized the Japanese was no where in sight. He had lost him. Perhaps the Japanese had jumped into a taxi at the main street. And then an uneasy thought struck him: *Could it be that he was aware I was tailing him? After all, that man was an intelligence officer, a spy-catcher during the war. As my sifu would have chided me, in underestimating my quarry, I have been careless.*

Without breaking his stride, Dong Po walked on and turned left, heading towards the direction of Sathorn Road. He could detect nothing unusual. Despite the bustle and confusion, there was no jarring note and apart from some street vendors shouting to him about their wares, no one else seemed to show any sign of interest in him.

And yet, his instinct – whether one was a hunter or hunted, both shared the same gut feeling – was one of uneasiness like there was a menacing danger lurking around. As he had learned to trust his instinct, he stopped in front of a shop that had copper wares on display. Holding up a big copper coffee pot that had recently been polished, he pretended to examine it. He smiled grimly when he saw the reflection on its shining rounded surface. Although the entire view was distorted, the image of the man was reflected there.

Now that he knew the Japanese had reversed their roles to be the hunter while he was the hunted, he put

the pot back on the table and walked on. When he came
to a junction and seeing the side alley was deserted, he
turned into it. He heard rather than saw the man
following him into the alley. In a flash, Dong Po wheeled
around to face the Japanese.

"Ishihara Shigeto?"

"Who are you?" asked the Japanese in Thai as he
walked nearer. "Why have you looked twice at me tonight
in the hotel and then trying to follow me?"

"I'm here to send you to hell for what you'd done to
a young girl named Suchin Suewonglee during the war."

"I've enjoyed so many young girls during the war
that I can't remember which one you're talking about,"
the former *kempetai* officer said with a sneer as he
continued to walk nearer still.

When they were just a few feet apart, they faced each
other and Dong Po attempted to lock eyes with Ishihara.
He willed himself to project his spirit in such a way that
his opponent's confidence would give way from knowing
he had no chance of winning. That was the way the
ajarn, and the other masters of the Art of the Eight Limbs,
and even those masters of other martial arts, had all
along been instructing their pupils: Take the initiative
to make the opponent know he was as good as defeated.

It was at the very moment when the Japanese blinked
and turned from their eye-lock that Dong Po's right leg
lashed out. He still remembered the *ajarn's* instructions
– use legs when an opponent is out of range; use hands
when at close quarters. Ishihara sensed the threat because
he took a step back. But the young Chinese quickly

snapped his right leg back to place a step forward so as to follow Ishihara's retreating step.

The moment his right foot was in place, his left leg swept upwards. Surprisingly, instead of retreating, the Japanese moved forward and slammed his body against the Dong Po. Caught on just one foot, the Chinese lost his balance. The Japanese followed up to kick him in turn but Dong Po had nimbly rolled away only to knock his head against the handle of a cart which a peddler had left by the roadside.

Ignoring the pain, he sprang back on his feet but was unable to dodge Ishihara's right hand which came down hard on the left side of his neck. It was lucky for him that he had seen it coming and had tensed his neck muscles. Even then he still felt the shock that went through his body. To keep the Japanese from following the momentum of his attack, Dong Po's right hand shot out to punch Ishihara's face. But the Japanese easily blocked it with his left hand and to Dong Po's surprise, simultaneously brought his right foot up and then down to stomp Dong Po's left foot.

The Chinese was glad for those months spent kicking the banana tree at the *ajarn's* school to develop his capacity to withstand pain. Gritting his teeth to bear out the pain, and seeing they were very close to one another, Dong Po reached out both hands to grab his enemy's head. Ishihara tried to pull away but Dong Po stood on his uninjured right foot and brought up his left knee against Ishihara's ribs. He knew his left foot had been avenged when he heard one of the rib bones breaking. Ishihara was a tough opponent because he didn't go down as others would. Instead, he shuffled back, clutching his injured side.

Now as both men circled each other, a thought came to Dong Po: *If not for my ability to take pain, I would be worse off by now. I should have kept my anger at bay as it had caused me to make mistakes. And I must not underestimate this man.*

True enough, this time it was Ishihara who came at him. Dong Po anticipated correctly that Ishihara's left hand cutting through the air was a feint. Before the Japanese could move his right hand to deliver the real blow meant for the soft spot below his Adam's apple, Dong Po had stepped forward on his left foot and with his right foot slammed up hard between Ishihara's legs. He heard a hissing sound escaping from the Japanese and saw his face had turned white.

Dong Po knew it was folly to allow Ishihara the time to recover. Being younger gave Dong Po the edge because he had by then slipped behind the Japanese. Though Ishihara was still able to put up a short albeit feeble struggle, Dong Po managed to loop the former major's neck inside his right elbow. As he had long ago promised himself that he would kill this war criminal to avenge Suchin, he unhesitatingly jerked his arm back, hard, and heard the satisfying sound of his enemy's neck bones at the top of his spine snapping.

Being a professional assassin, his first thought was to remove the quarry without any fuss. After all, he wasn't sure how formidable the guy could turn out to be. But he had wanted to inflict some pain on the quarry the way he had hurt Suchin. Now he was glad he had done it.

☆☆☆☆

Suchin Suewonglee was initially unable to sleep. She couldn't even contemplate closing her eyes as she was too disturbed by the sudden reappearance of the Japanese after all these years. She could still feel that petrifying moment when she saw him and felt all her blood draining from her as a sudden overwhelming fear seized her.

It had also occurred to her that her lover had gone back to the hotel to look for that monster. She could never think of Major Ishihara Shigeto as a man. After all that he had done to her, he was indeed a monster, a demon. But was her lover able to handle that monster? She had no doubt if Dong Po was what she thought him to be, he would be able to handle that fiend. But what if Dong Po wasn't a trained agent or assassin? What if he got hurt, or worst, even got killed?

She had wanted to stay up, to wait for Dong Po to come home, determined to find the final answers to end all her speculations. But with so much questions swimming around her mind, her spent emotion and her exhaustion, before long, her eyes closed, much against her will.

She was still asleep at slightly past midnight when Dong Po let himself into her bedroom. Noiselessly, he undressed and crawled into bed beside her.

☆☆☆☆

Early in the morning when Ong Lay Yong came to work in the hospital, she found everyone else talking excitedly about Dr. Padmanathan who was killed in a head-on collision with a trailer along Chain Ferry Road the previous night.

I'm becoming more and more adept in walking my life's path, she thought, filled with an inexplicable rush of exhilaration. *Though Chairman Mao Tse-tung had talked about power growing out of the barrel of a gun, I don't even need a gun. All I'd to do was to slip benzodiazepine into his coffee. Yes, I'm turning into a formidable killing machine for the Revolution. Cross me at your peril.*

Forty-four

*I*t was not the first time that Somchai thought his childhood friend looked very smart in his military uniform.

"May I offer my congratulations on your recent promotion, Wongkot?" offered Somchai, addressing the silver-haired man by his first name, a privilege accorded to only those few who were close to him. As children, the two of them had often answered nature's call by squatting side by side along the part of the canal near the village of Klong Ngae in southern Siam. This could count as being close.

Brigadier-General Wongkot Suttharom waved the hovering waiter away and smiled a thin smile. "There's no need for congratulations so long as a job's still unfinished."

"What do you mean?"

"The Americans aren't pleased," the brigadier-general said. "Don't forget I'd recommended you very strongly to them."

Somchai's eyes narrowed. "Surely you don't think I'll let you down?"

"Certainly not," said the brigadier-general, raising one hand placatingly. "But the Americans are getting a bit impatient. As it is, the quarry was one of them but due to his crave for the good things in life, he began siphoning off some of his operating funds to support his expensive habits. After that, he even does some business for himself, like dealing in narcotics, contraband, and firearms. But he became a real naughty boy when he started selling information to the Russians and the Chinese."

Somchai lit a cigar, without offering one to his childhood friend whose vices were limited to liquor and women. He was thinking: *At last I'm being taken into confidence.* But aloud he asked: "How come the Americans can't get him themselves?"

His childhood friend waved a hand dismissively and half smiled. "Though they're gunning for him, don't forget he was one of them and so knew their ways. As he's so elusive, the Americans have no choice but to enlist a few hitters on a first-hit-first-pay basis. Here, they have provided a fact sheet for your use as they are anxious the job's done as fast as possible. Be careful. From what I've read, he was a former Special Forces' officer who had served in Korea and therefore quite a tough guy to handle. I hope you get him first."

"Thanks, I'll see to it," Somchai said, exhaling a cloud of smoke.

After the brigadier-general had left, Somchai remained sitting at the Oriental Hotel's Riverside Terrace looking out at the Chao Phraya River. His mind went back to the previous evening when Mao Dong Po briefed him on how he had removed Boonrwad Wanglee.

"I must compliment you, my boy, on the novel way you'd removed the problem. Fancy dancing Boonrwad to his death," Somchai had chuckled gleefully. "After your telephone call, I'd informed our client immediately and the next day, he'd transferred the money in full to us. It included the promised bonus. I've already wired your share to your Kuala Lumpur's bank account. Make sure you invest the money wisely."

And just when Dong Po was about to take his leave, Somchai had reminded him, "Don't forget to concentrate on our American client's job."

Now sitting at the Riverside Terrace, Somchai thought it was a good thing that his protégé could start working on the American quarry. He had meant it when he told Brigadier-General Wongkot about not letting him down. He owed his childhood friend too much.

It was 1940 when he was twenty years' old that his father was fatally shot when customs officers caught them in an ambush. Somchai was hiding in a monsoon drain, panting with fear and exhaustion when a customs officer spotted him. The customs officer was grinning sadistically at him as he cowered there in trepidation. Pointing his pistol at Somchai, he said, "Having killed the old fellow, now it's your turn. This way, there's no need to make lengthy reports and my fellows and I can share the seized loot ourselves."

A shot had rung out but not from the pistol of the customs officer who fell dead before his eyes. To his surprise, it was Wongkot, then a second lieutenant in the Army who had shot the customs officer. Over the years, it was Wongkot who had cared for him like an elder brother as he was two years older, and provided him with firearms as well as taught him how to use them.

☆ ☆ ☆ ☆

Immediately after she read the morning's newspaper, Suchin Suewonglee's face lost all color. She telephoned her home. Almost ten rings later, her lover answered the telephone and Suchin said excitedly: "It's reported in today's paper that the Japanese monster's dead. He was found badly bruised in an alley and his neck was broken."

"You woke me up," accused Dong Po, who proceeded to yawn loudly. She knew whenever he was back in Bangkok, he would sleep until noon before coming over to her office to join her for lunch. This morning when she got up to prepare to go to her office, he was sleeping so soundly that she hadn't the heart to wake him.

His easy voice continued, "I guess the late Major Ishihara Shigeto had plenty of enemies."

"You didn't… I mean it wasn't you…?" she sounded uncertain.

She heard him chuckling. "Ahh, my dearest Suchin. Your imagination's working overtime again. Well, he has got what he deserved."

When she replaced the telephone, anyone could see she had a thoughtful expression on her face. Despite some lingering doubts, she was yet quite sure Dong Po was a professional assassin. A chuckle escaped her when she thought of the ironic humor of his cover as an executive of a pest removal firm. All those who had died, including Boonrwad Wanglee and the Japanese monster, had indeed been pests. And then she shuddered. *I'm only afraid that Dong Po may one day come across someone who's more ruthless and stronger.*

☆☆☆☆

After the third victim had died by her hands, Ong Lay Yong was smart enough to lay low even though deep within, she was really itching to kill again.

And so the months flew by uneventfully. At the time when racial riots erupted throughout the country on May 13, 1969, Lay Yong held back her urge to make use of the mayhem to kill the fat nursing sister in her ward.

On the evening of July 28, 1969 she was in Singapore, having returned to spend her week-long annual leave with her parents. That evening in her old room that looked out the back of the double-storey shop house in Smith Street, she suddenly heard over the radio that Lim Chin Siong had been released from prison earlier that day after he renounced politics.

"Has it been that many years already?" she asked aloud to herself and made a rapid mental calculation. "He has been imprisoned for six-and-half years."

Suddenly a look of contempt twisted Lay Yong's lovely face. "But that man has no stamina. If he can serve six-and-half years in prison, why not make it sixty-five years?"

She shook her head in disgust and told herself: "That man's certainly not one of us. How can he be when he gives up so easily? When I was released, even an insignificant revolutionary like me hasn't agreed to renounce politics. As Chairman Mao Tse-tung has said, even if half of China may have to die for the cause, then so be it. I'm ashamed now to think that I'd once looked up to that Lim fellow."

It was perhaps fortunate for Lim that Lay Yong was scheduled to return to Butterworth early the next morning or he may possibly ended up as her fourth victim.

Forty-five

*J*ust before dawn on October 14, 1973, Mao Dong Po awoke breathless and in a cold sweat. His heart was thumping loudly.

Unlike those recurring nightmares of his father being taken away to be shot, this one was rather abstract. And it also refused to fade away with the darkness of the night or the early light of dawn and so the dream he just had of Suchin Suewonglee still disturbed him.

In the dream, Suchin was leaving Bangkok for a far and unknown destination. Somehow, Dong Po who was not with her in Bangkok was yet able to see vividly the sadness on her face and he felt an urgent need to telephone her. But Dong Po was out there on the streets of Kuala Lumpur (or was it Singapore?). He was racing about from one place to another in a desperate attempt to get hold of a telephone.

Each time he came across a public phone booth, to his chagrin, he found the telephone to be out of order or the static was so bad that she was unable to hear him. And so, he was rushing around frantically once more trying to find a telephone that worked. And it was in such a frenzied state that he woke up panting.

Looking at the luminous dial of his Rolex, he saw it was twenty minutes to five. He got up and took a cigar from the humidor on top of the sideboard. Though he normally didn't smoke until after lunch, he felt he needed to smoke that morning to calm his frayed nerves. The abstractness of the dream was more fearsome than the ones regarding his father. It had somehow unnerved him.

Half an hour later, knowing it was the time that Suchin usually got up, Dong Po telephoned her.

A sleepy low, throaty voice answered. "Hello?"

"Darling, it's me," Dong Po said. "Did I wake you up?"

"Doesn't matter," she said. "It's time to get up anyway. Are you calling to say you're coming home?"

"Yes, I'll see if I can catch a flight later today. I've missed you terribly. I wished I had gone back with you instead of staying on here."

"I've missed you too," she chuckled. "Anyway, you'd got to complete the transaction regarding your newly purchased apartment."

In a flash, Dong Po's mind went over the lovely month of August when Suchin had taken leave to come to Kuala Lumpur to help him with the furnishing and decorating of the new apartment he'd bought in Damansara Heights. In the past few years, at his request, she had flown to Kuala Lumpur several times to assist him to look for a new apartment. It was not until they came across the one in Damansara Heights that they both agreed unanimously that he should buy it.

After buying the apartment, he had told her, "I want this new apartment to have your personal touch, together with mine. It's going to be our home whenever you have time to spend with me in Kuala Lumpur. Even if I am here without you, I will still be able to feel your presence in the furniture and items we would both plan and buy together."

He had not sold the old apartment he owned when he first moved to Kuala Lumpur. Instead he had rented it out. It was the legal transactions in the purchase of the new apartment that had kept him from returning to Bangkok with Suchin the previous month.

Suchin's voice brought him back to the present. "Do you love me?"

"I love you though you'll never know how much."

"I know which is why I love you so much. So have a safe flight, my dearest. Call me again in the office to let me know which flight you are on and I'll meet you at the airport."

After that, Dong Po put back the telephone receiver with a pleased smile. But as he was subconsciously still uneasy, he thus looked forward all the more to be back in Bangkok by Suchin's side later that day.

☆☆☆☆

Two hours later, Suchin came into her office with the intention to work on an overdue advertising copy. Just as she started working, the telephone on her desk rang.

It was from one of her paid sources in the military who informed her that Field Marshal Thanom Kittikachorn had finally lost his patience. For nearly a week, thousands of student protesters from Thammasat University, joined by members of the public, had gathered at the Democracy Monument in Bangkok's Ratchadamnoen Avenue. They were protesting against the military dictatorship headed by the "three tyrants", namely the field marshal, his son, Colonel Narong Kittikachorn, and Colonel Narong's father-in-law, Field Marshal Praphas Charusathien. At the same time, they were demanding for the release of thirteen students who had earlier been arrested by the military.

"As the field marshal is very upset, he had just ordered his troops to move in to disperse the students. They're beginning to leave the barracks," the source said hurriedly. "I can't tell you more, I've got to go."

After replacing the telephone, she looked towards her editor's room. But as Arthit Lamsam still hadn't come in, she thought there was no time to lose. The other reporters had already left for other assignments. Grabbing her camera, she hurried out.

About twenty minutes later, she arrived at the Democracy Monument, which had been built in 1939 to commemorate the 1932 coup which ended absolute monarchy in Thailand.

A few minutes after she had begun shooting off several frames with her camera, the soldiers arrived. She was in the midst of focusing her camera on the soldiers to catch them in the act of leaping off their jeeps and trucks when the protestors behind her began to throw stones and Molotov cocktails at the soldiers. All of a sudden, there were shouts of command and several soldiers raised their rifles and opened fire at the crowd.

Suchin, who would have turned 47 years old in a week's time, was wondering what had caused her to fall down. Lying on her back, as she stared upwards at the steeple of the monument, she knew she mustn't lay there. There were many things to do that day. She had taken the photographs, spoken to a few persons and so had to file the story before going to the airport to meet Dong Po. As she tried to get up, she felt the pain spreading all across her chest and found it hard to breathe. Her last thought was that Dong Po still hadn't called her to tell her what time he was arriving later today.

☆☆☆☆

That night, as Ong Lay Yong was wearing a skimpy light-green dress, cut low and short, it didn't take Chief Inspector Chris Ng too long to maneuver her out of it.

They had earlier checked into hotel which was one of her lover's favorites. Its layout and design allowed them to sneak about discreetly. Chris had told her the first time, "You wait in my car at the rooftop car park. I'll go downstairs to get us a room. When I come back, we can both go up to our room from the elevator at the rooftop car park level without being seen by the reception staff downstairs."

Once again as she waited in the car, she thought it a splendid arrangement. That was, of course, before she discovered her lover had also brought women, other than herself, to the hotel as well as other hotels all over the island.

The moment they went inside the hotel room, he came up from behind her and nuzzled her neck. "You're good for me. You really are, Lay Yong."

A short while later, they were both in the nude and riding the waves together with their entwined bodies. It took them a long time as both were quite adept at holding back until they finally reached orgasm in perfect unison.

After it was over, and they were lying exhausted on the bed in the dark, she tried tentatively to get her lover to talk about the new Inspector-General of Police. She was cunning enough to begin like this: "Some of the girls in my hospital said there is a restaurant in Yan in the State of Kedah which serves better seafood than the ones here in Penang. They said they have soft-shelled crabs fried in a light batter which we seldom get in Penang."

There was a distracted look on her lover's face as he lit a cigarette. "The restaurant is not in Yan. It's in Kuala Kedah. I'll take you there one of these days."

"Oh, that will be lovely," she squealed in delight though deep inside her heart, she knew her lover far better than to expect that day. "Speaking of Yan, wasn't that the birthplace of your new IGP?"

He nodded his head absentmindedly and she pressed on, this time working on his ego. "As a senior officer, surely you get to see the IGP and know him well?"

Chris began to show some interest. "Of course, the IGP travels a lot to seek the advice of his senior officers all over the country and at times, we would also meet at briefings held at the Federal Police Headquarters in Kuala Lumpur."

Lay Yong smiled. From experience, she knew only two things could interest her lover. Apart from his obsession with sex, he was very inclined towards impressing people of his importance, which Lay Yong guessed was due to a suppressed inferiority complex. After they had become lovers, through her subtle questioning, the Special Branch officer often inadvertently fed her a steady stream of information, which she would dutifully pass on to Wang *Lao-su*.

Even Wang *Lao-su* had once expressed his amazement at the ease she managed to extract information from her lover. "That man must be very besotted with you because as a Special Branch officer, he ought to know better than to shoot his mouth off like this. He's really a most unusual Special Branch officer indeed."

Forty-six

or two terrible years, Mao Dong Po was a tormented soul.

First, he had to return to Bangkok to claim the body of Suchin Suewonglee from the mortuary, and then see to her cremation as she had once requested. After that, he suffered a series of long, dark and lonely nights. He found it so hard to believe she was no longer among the living. And yet he had to believe since she wasn't there. He couldn't help asking whether it was retribution from his having killed so many people.

On each of those nights he had obstinately stayed in her home instead of moving out into a hotel. It was as though he wanted the pain, to punish himself. And on those long, lonely nights, Dong Po would replay his last conversation with Suchin. Played it once, played it again. And then the replays of those wonderful evenings he had spent with her in her home would return to torment him. He could even visualize what she looked like, and how she sounded like.

Once, he came across a pair of shoes she had bought but not yet worn. Seeing the high-heeled shoes lying inside the box, gave him such a turn that tears came to his eyes. The shoes looked so pathetic. He had held them close to his chest, knowing she surely had tried them before telling the shop assistant to put them into the box for her. Through eyes blurred with tears, in a voice filled with agony, he had cried aloud: "So now, where are you? Are you able to hear me and feel my grief?"

Although Suchin hadn't wanted to meet his mother and therefore was not formally wedded to him, she had nonetheless accepted him as her husband just as he had thought of her as his wife. In essence, they had been a married couple. That was one of the reasons he forced himself to stay in her home. It would be remiss of him to just pack up and leave. He tried very hard to convince himself that Suchin's spirit was there in her home. It was like the nightmare he had the morning before she died – he knew she was there somewhere but somehow he was unable to establish communication with her.

Now that circumstances had forced him to lose her, he found the experience entirely different from the time when he was a bachelor prior to having known her. Being alone was now so unpleasant. Tried as he would, he just couldn't take the loneliness and emptiness he felt. It was all so unreal. He could still feel Suchin's presence everywhere as the entire house was alive with memories of her. When he took to the streets, he could likewise feel her presence from being reminded of her. But it was the silence of the long nights which was especially unbearable and each night he would cry himself to sleep. He wept for himself and the wife he had lost.

He began to understand what it was like to be insane because he found himself laughing through his tears at the memory of those funny moments with her, and the jokes they shared. The moment both tears and laughter had subsided, came the anger from his guilt of being away from her. And he raged against those responsible for her death. He blamed those students who should have stuck to their studies than indulge in politics. And while he cursed the government, even though the "three tyrants" had already been driven into exile, he knew nothing would bring Suchin back to life.

He tried to escape his loneliness by going to places where crowds of people mingled, such as bars. But an odd realization struck him: The more people could be found, the lonelier he felt. Their laughter meant nothing to him. And on those few occasions when women approached him, he saw them as strangers, with nothing in common at all to share.

And the worst realization was that other than his *sifu*, he had no one else to turn to. But even if he could, he knew he would be unable to tell his mentor about the unbearable ache he felt inside him. Thus on those occasions when Somchai forced Dong Po to meet him, the desolate man kept much of his grief over his personal loss to himself. He knew his *sifu* would simply look at him with contempt and disgust at his weakness and would probably tell him, "I'd told you so." Even the thought of turning to Somchai filled him with shame.

It was Somchai who had first brought him the news of her death. On that terrible day, Dong Po arrived back at his new apartment in Kuala Lumpur at four o' clock. The moment he opened the door, he heard his telephone ringing. Unknown to him, it had been ringing every few minutes throughout the day.

He hurriedly put down a gift-wrapped box containing a string of pearls which he had bought for her birthday, and the air ticket that he had earlier collected from the travel agent before picking up the receiver.

His *sifu* had, in his usual style, gone straight to the point: "I've bad news for you, my boy. Your woman's dead."

A part of Dong Po stoically accepted the unexpected news as he knew Somchai was not given to making practical jokes. And the man had very reliable sources of information. However, another part of Dong Po refused to accept the shocking news.

Somchai at first thought the connection had been broken as the silence on the other end of the line was so complete. "Hello? Hello, my boy, you still there?"

With an effort, Dong Po said, "Yes, I am. What happened?"

"She went to the rally this morning. The soldiers began firing and I guess she was caught in the shooting."

All that was two years ago. Now on the morning of the second anniversary of Suchin's death, Dong Po was sweating profusely from the long walk and the hot sun. He had earlier gone to the temple where Suchin's ashes contained in a small urn were kept next to those of her departed parents. As he walked down the road, he went to a shady spot under a tree where he stood for a while to rest.

For nearly fifteen minutes, he was refreshed by the cool breeze as he watched some schoolboys shouting gleefully and trading insults as they played with their *pakpao,* kites. Though much skill was involved as those schoolboys would rein in or let go the strings according to how each of them would feel the pull of the wind, ultimately the fate of those kites would be left to the wind buffeting them.

A sudden thought struck him: *Like the wind, circumstances had dealt me a cruel blow by taking Suchin away from me. But I mustn't allow my life to carry on drifting aimlessly and being buffeted all over by the wind like those kites. I have both the skills and knowledge which ought to be put to good use to get my life back on track. Yes, Suchin would have wanted that. I know what I shall do. I shall return to Malaysia and since there's little in Penang to remind me of Suchin, I shall arrange to move there so as to make a new start for 1976.*

☆ ☆ ☆ ☆

While the New Year held new hopes for Dong Po, it was not so for Ong Lay Yong.

The first week of January 1976 found her sinking into a deep depression from being caught up in conflicting situations and moods.

On the political front, she was upset over the re-establishment of diplomatic ties between China and Malaysia. That was a blow for the communists in Malaysia. But she was pleased that her comrades had in the past two years scored two significant victories – assassinating the Inspector-General of Police, *Tan Sri* Abdul Rahman bin Hashim on June 7, 1974, and the

Chief Police Officer for the State of Perak, *Tan Sri* Khoo Chong Kong just two months ago on November 13, 1975.

She was however upset because she felt she hadn't contributed anything to the two assassinations. This was because her lover, Chief Inspector Chris Ng either knew nothing or was avoiding all those questions fed her by Wang *Lao-su* to put to him. More likely it was his ignorance from having been suspended pending investigation of corruption.

But what infuriated her most was the discovery that her lover, while taking his pleasure with her, was also sleeping with another woman, a certain Wu Hsiao Ling, ironically a woman from China. After stumbling by accident – she found in his car, a birthday card where he had penned a most disgustingly intimate message to that woman – she realized he was stringing her along to satisfy his insatiable lust. As such, she decided to catch him red-handed in the act.

It was on account of this discovery that she trailed her unfaithful lover to a hotel room on the night of January 16, 1976. Angry as she was, Lay Yong lost courage at the crucial moment about confronting the chief inspector. Instead of bursting into the room to create a scene, she went home to a sleepless night. She was unable to sleep from being torn between conflicting emotions, such as her rage over her lover's unfaithfulness, and her shame from her sudden refusal to confront the couple. And though she kept telling herself she hadn't any feeling for the man, yet she couldn't explain her seething jealousy and fear of loss from the prospect of not seeing each other again.

The next morning, having finally convinced herself that she should be a strong woman, a true revolutionary, as expected in the sight of Chairman Mao Tse-tung, she returned to the hotel. This time, she unhesitatingly knocked on the door, where after a short wait, she saw the peephole darkened and heard her unfaithful lover's low voice growling, "Go away."

"No, it's better the three of us have a talk," she insisted.

She knocked again and then the door opened. Lay Yong found herself facing her faithless lover. He was already dressed. Though he tried to prevent her from entering the room, she slipped past him with a pivot and a pirouette, moving her slender frame lightly on her toes like a ballet dancer, and in the same quick motion, reached behind his back to pull out the revolver she knew he tucked in his waistband.

"Go on, get back inside the room," she ordered, pointing the gun at him.

Having seen the wild look in her eyes, the chief inspector did as he was told. But despite his compliance, all came to nothing. As he was unable to conceal the mocking look in his eyes, an incensed Lay Yong, who had pointed the revolver at his head, suddenly drew back the heavy hammer, and pulled the trigger. Even before his body slammed against the wall from the impact of the bullet, she had turned to fire at the woman.

Knowing she had very little time before someone reacted to the gunshots, Lay Yong hurriedly wiped clean the gun with her dress, crossed over to the chief inspector's body and placed the revolver into his hand. She pressed his forefinger against the trigger.

As she slipped out of the open door and calmly walked away, she thought, *I can at least report to Wang Lao-su that I have removed another enemy of our cause.*

Forty-seven

For nearly a week in early 1976, Mao Dong Po stayed in Padang Besar, where he celebrated the Chinese New Year with his mother and uncle. This came about because he felt guilty for not having spent enough time with them over the years. After that week, he moved to Penang.

The moment he arrived on the island he checked into the Palm Beach Hotel, preferring its quietness to the bustle of its larger and posh neighbors like the Golden Sand Hotel or Rasa Sayang Hotel. After that, remembering his *sifu's* nagging, he engaged a real-estate agent to help him look for a beach-front property.

When he had first mooted the idea to his mentor, though Somchai was still uneasy from failing Brigadier-General Wongkot Suttharom's American clients, he had said, "Penang is a good place to make a fresh start. You're now in a sort of twilight zone as your past holds wonderful yet painful memories and your emotions are still in turmoil. Go and stay by the sea because I'm sure the sun and the beach will heal you. Listen to the sound of the waves. They can give you a calming effect."

The real-estate agent was an eager beaver. Within a week, Dong Po, who loved the smell of salty sea breeze, and listening to the sound of sea waves, had purchased a small bungalow by a secluded beach in Tanjong Tokong. Not long after he moved in, some of the people in the vicinity began speculating about him. They were curious to know what he did for a living. By and by, as he patronized the same shops as his neighbors, he heard some of the rumors being circulated about him.

The unflattering ones ran like these: "The strange, quiet man living alone in that bungalow is a drug smuggler from Thailand's Golden Triangle. I know because I've heard him speaking Thai. He's here in hiding" and "He had served ten years for killing an unfaithful wife. That's why his eyes looked so sad and haunted." The less malicious ones were: "His wife was killed in an accident which explains why he doesn't drive", and "I think he's an undercover policeman with Interpol watching out for drug smugglers from Thailand." One came close to the mark – "He's a professional assassin."

Unflattering or not, he had laughed all the same and were secretly pleased that he had acquired a status of being mysterious. He had seen the pretty wives of two of his neighbors eyeing him speculatively, attracted by this aura of mystery surrounding him. He only felt uncomfortable over the gossip about him being an assassin as he could still remember his *sifu's* words: "The great military strategist wrote that the true warrior win victories, which won't earn him any reputation for wisdom or valor because his strategies are too secret while his enemy submits without any need for him to draw out his sword to spill blood. You must strive to be such a warrior."

He also felt uncomfortable when the brassier of the two neighbors' wives, whose name was Shirley, tried a few times to waylay him during his evening stroll along the beach, engaging him in conversation and then dropping hints of her availability. As a red-blooded man, he was naturally tempted. But something held him back. Even though Suchin Suewonglee hadn't been to Penang with him, he felt enough of her presence to worry that her spirit would disapprove of his action. Besides, he had no wish to end up using his skills to remove any enraged husband who found he had been cuckolded. And so he had feigned ignorance whenever he was being proposed. After a while, Shirley decided he was either an idiot or gay or both and so she stopped bothering him.

☆☆☆☆

Sitting at his desk, Deputy Superintendent Robert Chuah looked at the headline of one of the newspapers. It screamed COP SHOOTS MISTRESS AND COMMITS SUICIDE. The headlines of several other newspapers scattered across his desk told almost the same thing.

By now, he had already known the story by heart: "A chief inspector under suspension on charges of corruption was believed to have committed suicide after fatally shooting his mistress. Wu Hsiao Ling, 35, and Chief Inspector Chris Ng, 44, were both lying in a pool of blood when police burst into a hotel room after the staff had reported hearing gun shots. Ng was still clutching the weapon, a Smith & Wesson.38 revolver in his hand. Two spent cartridges were recovered from the chambers. Senior CID Officer, Deputy Superintendent

Robert Chuah said initial investigations showed the two were lovers who had often used the hotel, and they had been quarreling since checking in the previous night…"

What bothered DSP Chuah most was the fact that the dead chief inspector was indeed found clutching his gun at the crime scene. From his experience, DSP Chuah knew the recoil from a fired gun would cause it to spin or fling away from whoever had used the weapon on himself. As such, the deceased couldn't be holding the gun in his hand.

It also bothered the senior officer of the Criminal Investigation Department at the Penang Police Contingent Headquarters that a most inept assistant had recently been pushed to him, and he had no choice but to assign the investigation to that fellow. If he had his way, he would make sure Assistant Superintendent Ali bin Abdul Karim would never be assigned to investigate any murder case. Tracking down missing pretty women would be more his cup of tea.

But being the pragmatic man that he was, DSP Chuah wasn't about to rock the boat. Let the public, and especially his inept assistant, believed it was the late Chief Inspector Ng who had shot his mistress and thereafter turned the gun on himself. That should go down better than having an unsolved murder on his lap. Moreover, with regards his hopeless assistant, well, it had all along been DSP Chuah's philosophy to "live and let live."

This also explained why he hadn't bothered to respond to his wife who had received several requests from her sister in Singapore to help keep an eye on her daughter who worked in a hospital in Butterworth. *All these over-indulgent mothers*, he thought contemptuously. *As if a grown-up middle-aged woman couldn't look after* herself. *And as though I've not enough work to keep me busy.*

☆ ☆ ☆ ☆

Live and let live had never been a philosophy of Lim Hoe Peng. He was a thin faced swarthy man of average build, with deep-set brooding eyes and glossy black hair. His trade mark was a pair of sunglasses which he wore day and night to match his dark clothes. It was rumored that this former bodyguard, driver, and enforcer of Snake Eyes Siang, the chieftain of the Khong Si Tong, or Zero-Four Gang, operating in Butterworth, even wore those sunglasses when having sex with the girls working in the tong's brothels.

In the Penang's underworld, few people knew him by the name of Lim Hoe Peng. He was simply called Lim-*kor*, meaning Elder Brother Lim, by the thugs in his tong. Although many thugs in Malaysia sported fanciful nicknames like their counterparts in Hong Kong, after he had sent one of the thugs in his tong to hospital for nearly six months for calling him Black Sunglasses Lim, no one had dared to do the same except for those from other tongs.

Ten minutes after Snake Eyes Siang was pronounced dead at the hospital from a stroke suffered while having sex with a prostitute working in one of the tong's brothels, Lim proclaimed himself the new chieftain. For Lim, who grew up in the Lim Jetty area, near Weld Quay on the island of Penang, as the son of a trishaw man and a seamstress, it was considered an achievement. He soon went on to prove his mettle as he expanded his territory to Penang and the tong's business to include the white powder – the locals' slang for heroin – until he was caught two years ago.

As he was able to bribe his way, and also agreed to make himself useful to the police, he was released just before the Chinese New Year. But given the profitability in white powder trafficking, he was soon back to his old business though he was careful to pass scraps of information of minor importance to the police, and offer the occasional scapegoat for them to put behind bars.

Since his youth, Lim had been contemptuous of the "an eye for an eye, a tooth for a tooth" dogma. He believed in collecting a hefty interest with all his debts, meaning two eyes for an eye, or two teeth for a tooth. Live and let live was definitely not his nature. And so that evening, in a house in Perak Road where some of the tong members were busy weighing and packing white powdery substance into small plastic packets, Lim was determined to take eyes, teeth, and more. Groveling before him on the floor in a soundproof room was Foo Kwang Lin, one of the thugs working for his gang.

"*Lin lau boo*," Lim cursed. Though the three words in the Hokkien dialect simply mean "your mother", used in Lim's tone, it implied an insult. "You think I'm too stupid not to find out that you were the one to tip off the police, eh?"

Anyone watching the scene would have thought he or she had been transported back in time because Kwang Lin who was on his knees, was repeatedly knocking his head on the cement floor as though he was kowtowing a Chinese emperor. But judging from his horribly distorted face, after being savagely beaten, anyone could tell the worse was to follow.

"I didn't betray you, *Lim-kor*," Kwang Lin cried pitifully. "I wouldn't dare…"

Lim spat at the groveling man. "You really think I'm a fool, don't you?"

Turning to two of his thugs, one of whom was Ah Sai, his chauffeur-cum-bodyguard, Lim ordered: "Tie him to that chair."

After the two had tied Kwang Lin to the chair, Lim walked towards him and asked, "Do you know how traitors were executed by those Chinese emperors in the past?"

"Please, *Lim-kor*, please, I beg of you…"

But Lim wasn't listening. There was a faraway look in his eyes. Many years ago, Snake Eyes Siang had taken him to Bangkok to visit a fellow triad chieftain. The fellow by the name of Boonrwad Wang-something was a real tough guy in the Thai underworld. At the time of their visit, that Thai chieftain was about to punish one of his tong members over a betrayal. At Snake Eyes Siang's request, the visitors were allowed to watch. That was the first time Lim saw for himself the ancient form of execution called lingering death by slicing or death of a thousand cuts.

"All right, you two get out of the room and see that no one is allowed to come in until I say so," Lim told his two henchmen after suddenly producing a sharp, wicked-looking knife.

Ah Sai and the other man, known as Kam Choon, quickly left the room, closing the heavy door behind them. Despite the soundproofing, the first scream came through to send chills down their spines. Several more piercing screams followed and Kam Choon's face turned ashen, while Ah Sai ran off to the toilet to vomit.

Forty-eight

*A*t around 7:30 p.m. on December 6, 1977, two days after the hijacked Malaysia Airlines aircraft crashed in Tanjong Kupang in the southern State of Johor, killing a hundred passengers and crew on board, Mao Dong Po saw him.

Dong Po was sure it was none other than Tim Lane. Ever since his *sifu* had shown him the photograph of the tall, powerfully built man with a head of unruly hair, together with his family, and a cat, Dong Po had committed that face to his memory. In his profession, good memory is a must-have as it would be dangerous for him to go about carrying photographs. The American had grown thinner but it was definitely him.

Earlier, Dong Po had finished his dinner of fried oysters' omelet in a coffee shop at the junction of Kimberley Street and Carnarvon Street. He was walking towards his car parked along Carnarvon Street when he saw the American in a gleaming black Mercedes Benz passing by.

As soon as it dawned on him that the American was his quarry, he hurriedly got into his car and gave chase. The Mercedes Benz went to the ferry terminal in Weld Quay where it went on board a ferry. Dong Po followed.

During the short crossing across to Butterworth, the American and a Chinese man wearing a pair of sunglasses, even though it was already night time, got out of the Mercedes Benz and walked towards the front of the ferry. From where he sat, flanked on both sides by two large trucks, Dong Po put on the wig and false moustache which he had retrieved from the glove compartment. After glancing at his new image on the mirror, he returned his attention to both men who were talking animatedly as they stood on the deck at the front of the ferry.

Dong Po was elated that by chance he had spotted the American who had a hefty price on his head. Three months before the fall of Saigon on April 30, 1975, Somchai, in a bid to get Dong Po out of his depression over the death of Suchin Suewonglee, had forced him to go to Saigon to track down the American as he was said to be in that city.

For nearly two weeks, Dong Po stayed at the Continental Palace Hotel, from where he would sally out everyday to hang around Rue Catinat, and at times, strolling about Le Loi Square, hoping to catch a glimpse of the quarry. The only place he couldn't be bothered was Thong Nhut Boulevard as he doubted the quarry would go near the American Embassy since his fellow countrymen were also gunning for him. But the trail turned cold and without fresh lead, he was forced to give up the hunt.

Now sitting in his car on the ferry, he also felt pleased that he was able to think of Suchin without the usual rancor, guilt and self-pity over his loss. The previous year when he heard over the radio about students clashing once again with police and the army at Thammasat University in Bangkok on October 6, he could still feel the anguish from losing Suchin.

Twenty-five minutes later the ferry arrived at the Butterworth terminal. Again, Dong Po followed the Mercedes Benz discreetly until it came to a stop in front of a place whose lighted signboard declared The Happy Bar. Both men alighted and went inside. Dong Po remained in his car. After nearly an hour, he got out. As the area was quiet and deserted except for the occasional passers-by, he went to a dark lane a short distance away to relieve himself of the water building up in his bladder. *I doubt James Bond can ever be caught doing things like this*, he thought sardonically. *Even if he does things like this, author Ian Fleming, or movie producers like Harry Saltzman and Albert Broccoli would never tell.*

After he had done his thing, he went back to wait in the car.

☆☆☆☆

To anyone who was watching, Ong Lay Yong had just taken out a small hand mirror from her handbag to study her face. It was really a fairly common behavior with most women. Only one thing was amiss. She did it at a busy street junction, or to be precise, the junction of Victoria Street and Chulia Street Ghaut.

But vain as Lay Yong was, her action came about because she had just been to a meeting with her cell leader, Wang *Lao-su* at a house in Bridge Street*. When she and five other comrades were about to leave, Wang *Lao-su* had reminded them: "Do watch your back to make sure you aren't being followed. It pays to be careful as the Special Branch has many informers all over this city."

Just as she was making sure that no one was tailing her, she was also recalling what her cell leader had told them earlier. Dropping his voice melodramatically as was his nature, Wang *Lao-su* whispered: "It was one of our brave comrades from the Japanese Red Army who tried to hijack the MAS aircraft but unfortunately something had happened on board, causing the plane to crash. But our Japanese compatriot died a glorious death."

Puzzled, she had asked, "Aren't the Japanese our enemies?"

Piqued that his cell members hadn't looked too impressed, Wang *Lao-su* had at first glared at her, but his irritation lasted for only a moment because his eyes softened just as sudden as they had hardened. "As long as we believe in the same cause, there shall be no divide amongst men and women of this world. We share a common cause against what Chairman Mao Tse-tung has identified as monopoly capitalist groups in a handful of imperialist countries which depend on aggression for their profits. Otherwise, we stand united worldwide as international communists."

Wang *Lao-su* was smart enough to know that agent-running was often about motivation, and if his cell

* Today, it is called Jalan C.Y. Choy.

members would ever be of any use to him, they needed plenty of encouragement from time to time. This was especially necessary because with improvement in relationship between China and Malaysia, their cause to overthrow the Malaysian government no longer seemed as legitimate as it once was. To motivate his cell members, Wang *Lao-su* had to narrate some "feel good" stories of successful revolutions, but such were sadly lacking in recent times. Hence, he thought a sprinkling of quotations from Chairman Mao and the recent fatal hijacking would do the trick.

But as Lay Yong walked towards the ferry terminal, she was still unconvinced about the things Wang *Lao-su* had spoken earlier that night. Had the hijacker been any race but Japanese, she would have hailed him as a hero as she hoped she could pull off such a spectacular feat one day. However, considering her brother was murdered by the Japanese, she couldn't accept any Japanese to be a compatriot. She was also bothered that earlier in July that year, the purged anti-revolutionary Teng Hsiao-ping was restored to power while the Gang of Four, one of whom was Chairman Mao's widow, was expelled from the Communist Party of China. What exactly was China coming to?

With those troublesome thoughts, she walked up the ramp to the ferry terminal.

Forty-nine

*F*rom the way the traffic policeman was waving frantically at him to stop, Mao Dong Po knew there was going to be trouble.

Earlier, when the American came out from The Happy Bar with the Chinese man who wore dark sunglasses even though it was already night, Dong Po saw one more guy had joined them. After the three of them piled into the same Mercedes Benz, which the chauffeur had driven to the front of the bar, Dong Po followed them at a discreet distance.

As Dong Po pulled up at the road block, the policeman who wore the two stripes of a corporal, asked him: "You want to kill someone?"

He was momentarily stunned by those shocking words. A chill went through him that he had been discovered when the corporal continued. "Without any light, you will kill someone soon if I hadn't stopped you. Get out of your car and see for yourself."

Dong Po felt a surge of relief when he realized what the corporal meant. In his haste to follow his quarry, he had forgotten to switch on the lights. Though he was chagrined over losing his quarry, he obeyed the corporal and walked with him to look at the car lights. Knowing most low-ranking officers basked in whatever little authority they had, Dong Po tried to look suitably awed and said in an ingratiating tone, "Thank you, *Tuan*. I'm so sorry, *Tuan*, for having forgotten to switch on my lights…"

"I'm not *Tuan*," the corporal crossly corrected him on his use of the salutation, equivalent to sir, as accorded to senior officers. "I'm Corporal Ramasamy."

A second policeman, a sergeant, came over. "What's the problem?"

"He's driving without a light, Sergeant Awang."

The sergeant's eyes immediately lit up. "Now it would be very inconvenient if we were to issue you a ticket as it means you will have to appear in court. But…"

He left the sentence unfinished. Knowing what the sergeant was hinting, Dong Po was about to reach for his wallet when the corporal, who seemed to look rather unhappy from hearing the sergeant's words, judging by the frown on his forehead and tight lips, interrupted curtly, "Let me see your licence."

And then it happened. The pistol, which Dong Po had kept hidden in his waistband, slipped out and fell with a loud clatter on the road. Perhaps, when he reached for the wallet in his back pocket, either his arm or the windbreaker he wore had tugged it out. *But it doesn't matter anymore*, he thought. *James Bond wouldn't have been such a clumsy oaf like me.*

Dong Po's reflex action was to throw a punch at Corporal Ramasamy who had instinctively reached for the revolver in his holster. As the corporal fell down, the sergeant was either too smart to try any heroics or too dumb to react other than standing still with his mouth gaping. Two other policemen, like the sergeant, had also turned into statues. Ignoring them, Dong Po jumped into his car and drove off. Just as he was about to turn into a side road lower down the main, he heard the corporal shouting, "Stop, or I'll shoot."

☆ ☆ ☆ ☆

After Ong Lay Yong got down from the ferry ramp, she walked briskly to the bus station to catch a bus. To her relief, she saw the bus was still there. If she had missed that bus, which was the last one to her area, she would either have to take a taxi or walk nearly half an hour to reach her home.

Getting up on the bus, for the first time in many years, Lay Yong suddenly thought of her parents. She recalled the time before her father started his own wine import business. He was then working as a clerk for another wine importer. As the family didn't own a car then, her mother would accompany her in taking buses to and fro the primary school she was attending. In those days, though buses in Singapore were old, they were quite clean, unlike buses in Butterworth now, which were both old and dirty.

Somehow, her mind switched from buses to the old dilapidated house in Johor Road where her parents had once rented a room. What frightened her most living in that run-down hovel overcrowded with other tenants, far more than the stinking pit latrine was the horde of cockroaches. They were everywhere, sometimes even crawling into her bed.

That was when she began to resent those schoolmates who lived in clean, lovely homes, and came to school in private cars or taxis. Now that she thought about it, she knew she still envied them. And yes, she quite pitied herself that her mother had to walk daily with her to the bus stand, and then spend a lot of time waiting for the stuffy and hot buses, while those children from better-off families were spared such suffering.

As the self-doubts assailed her, Lay Yong began to wonder whether this was what it all bore down to. Could her cause be nothing more than petty envy? Was it a case of resentment by those who haven't much possession against those who seem to have plenty? Like sort of having a chip on the shoulder kind of thing? Whatever you have should also be mine?

No, I mustn't think like this, she thought. *This is the contradictions among people that Chairman Mao Tse-tung had warned. Just because we have won victory, we mustn't relax our vigilance. Whoever relaxes vigilance will be disarmed politically and be landed in a passive position. I mustn't relax my vigilance. Like a true revolutionary, I must stop thinking of my parents and the past.*

A minute after they had passed the roadblock, Tim Lane turned to his host: "I'd thought a car was following us, Lim."

"Oh, is that so, Tim?" asked Lim, who then leaned forward to speak rapidly in the Hokkien dialect to his chauffeur.

The chauffeur grunted and pulled the car to the side of the road. Together with the American, Lim turned around to look back. They were too far down the road to see the police roadblock.

"We'll wait a while. When that car passes by, it will be our turn to follow," Lim suggested.

They waited for nearly five minutes, and then Lim shook his head. "You're probably too keyed up, Tim. I'll take you to a place where you can unwind."

"I hope it will be an interesting place with many pretty young ladies," Tim said, giving Lim a leering wink.

Fifty

It was the corporal who had fired two shots at him. Mao Dong Po heard the shots, one of which shattered his car's rear window and pierced the seat to hit him in his left shoulder. He felt the impact of the bullet like having been punched. When he looked down at the crimson patch spreading on the front left of his shirt, he felt the numbness in the shoulder where he was hit though it wasn't painful. The pain, he knew, would come only later.

He kept his foot down on the accelerator until a junction where he turned into a maze of side alleys. Time and again, he swung left and right, then right and left, until he even confused himself as to where he was. Finally he braked and got out of the car to start running on foot as he knew they would be looking for a car with a shattered rear window.

Lucky for him, he had registered the car with a driving licence and identity card under one of his many aliases conveniently provided by his *sifu*. Somchai had taught him, "Never allow anything to be traced back to your real identity. Use an alias. That's why I'd given you those fake documents."

There was also a possibility that the police might think he would try using the car as long as he could in order to lengthen the distance between him and them. *Well, if they think that way, then they may give me a good head start as they won't search for me here*, he thought. *While I still have the strength, I've better start running fast.*

Soon, Dong Po guessed, very soon, a massive manhunt would be underway for him once the policemen reported the incident. By then, the police would have gone to many hotels. This meant he had to try making his way back to his house over on the island. He must avoid any hotel or boarding house. He knew too detectives would also be questioning taxi drivers, keeping the Railway Station in Butterworth under tight surveillance, and also poring over the manifests of flights operating out of the Bayan Lepas Airport. *How I could have been so careless?* he wondered.

But he couldn't afford to panic. As he was beginning to feel the pain, he knew he had to forestall a panic-induced blackout by breathing slowly from the diaphragm and at the same time, tensing and relaxing his muscles. Likewise, he had to stop the bleeding by pressing the edges of the wound together with his fingertips. Accordingly, as he ran, his hand worked on his wound while he ordered himself to breathe.

☆☆☆☆

Ong Lay Yong's initial thought was to walk away. But she had a natural instinct to side with the hunted against the hunter.

Earlier, she had alighted from the bus and walked the short distance to the house where she rented a room. From the moment, she saw the man staggering past her before collapsing on the road, she sensed he was hurt. Out of curiosity, she went over to the man's side to look at him.

She saw a man in his thirties with a moustache and thick, curly salt-and-pepper hair. To her surprise, when she looked more carefully, in his unconscious state, he seemed quite young, even boyish-looking. After a quick glance at the wound on the front of his shoulder, she turned him over to confirm from the smaller entry wound that it was a bullet that had done the damage. Her experience told her the man was lucky in that the bullet had missed any vital artery or organ.

Satisfied that it was only a flesh wound though he had lost a lot of blood which was why he had fainted, Lay Yong made an instant decision. Since the man had been shot, whoever had injured him was likely to be hunting for him. Carried away perhaps partly by her romantic nature and partly by her dislike of government – who else carried guns to shoot people? – she lifted him. Those who had worked with her at the hospital knew there were reserves of strength in her surprisingly slender body.

Forty minutes after passing the police roadblock, the Mercedes Benz carrying Lim and his guest had returned by ferry to the island of Penang.

As the car came to a halt at a bungalow in Tanjong Bungah, Tim Lane thought there was nothing special about the place. Getting out of the car, he resigned himself for an evening of boorish entertainment. *One can never trust any of these Chinks as they are either too tightfisted with their money or simply too backward to lay out a real good time for their guests*, he thought dourly.

But the moment he stepped into the house, he was immediately dumbstruck. Several girls came forward to greet them and the amazing thing was that the girls were really pretty. The ones he had seen earlier that evening at The Happy Bar were nowhere compared to these gorgeous ones before him.

Lim gave him a knowing smile. "These girls are part-time models and part-time hostesses. They used to work for an agency ran by a very smart woman. Unfortunately, her lover, a chief inspector with the Special Branch, fatally shot her. It turned out to be my good fortune because I took over the agency."

Out of curiosity, Tim asked: "What happened to the chief inspector."

"Oh, he blew his own brains out."

Though the American had cheered up considerably, especially after one of the girls, the one with a captivating smile, came to link arms with him, he still thought his host was too crass for his liking. *But what the heck, he's going to help me make a lot of money,* he thought benevolently. *And I'm gonna have a great time as well.*

Fifty-one

*A*lthough Mao Dong Po's body was still soaked in perspiration, luckily for him, Ong Lay Yong was there to sponge him off with a wet towel. She was up throughout the night to watch him and sponge him whenever she thought it necessary.

Once they got back into her rented room, she had immediately boiled a pot of water, with which to clean the wound and thereafter dressed it up with the bandage she kept handy. To ease his pain, she had also given him a mild shot of morphine.

By that time, she had discovered two things about the stranger she had rescued. First, the moustache was a false one as it had slipped off. Second, when she deliberately tugged at his hair, the wig came off as well. Having discovered the moustache, she wasn't surprised to find the stranger was wearing a wig. It was when she was removing the wig that the man stirred and opened his eyes. As she looked at him, she saw he looked distant though his eyes were a bit too bright. And then he closed his eyes again and soon she heard a faint snoring.

Now, sitting there watching him, she wondered who he was. Was he a criminal on the run, or a subversive like her? From what she had seen of his clothes, his taste was too bourgeois to be a revolutionary. Even if he was a criminal, she knew he wasn't an ordinary one. He was certainly not a hoodlum because there wasn't any tell-tale tattoos on his body. The thought of his body excited her because she saw he was well-built and muscular. This was a man who watched his fitness. Besides, she quite liked his angular face.

While he was sleeping, she went through his pockets and found only a wallet stuffed full of money, some business cards bearing the name of Klahan Pattano, a manager with a pest removal firm. She also found an identity card with his image, giving his name as Mao Dong Po. There was however a driving licence with his image albeit another name, Tan Kim Huat on it. She also found three cigars which confirmed her suspicion of his bourgeois tastes.

At dawn when the chicken, which the neighbor's wife reared in their tiny plot of land next door, started crowing, Dong Po stirred. His left shoulder was stiff and throbbing. At the same time, his lips were parched. But he didn't move. From where he lay, he saw thick black hair atop a soft oval face from which a pair of large black eyes was trying to concentrate on a book.

The moment she looked up and caught him looking at her, she smiled. Though she looked to be in her late twenties, he saw that she still had the shy smile of a little girl. Dong Po smiled back because he could guess that if not for this lovely woman, he would already have died on the streets, or worse, been captured alive.

"Where am I?"

"My rented room," she said, handing him a glass of water. "You're really a lucky man. First, it was I who found you on the street. Second, today's my rest day and so I was able to nurse you throughout the night. Third, I am a nurse and so knew what to do. Fourth, the bullet went through your shoulder without hitting any vital artery or organ. Finally, my landlord has brought his wife to Kuala Lumpur for a few days to visit their daughter. If they're around, they would have reported you to the police by now."

"You know I'm wanted by the police?"

She nodded. "You were shot. I've also heard the sirens of police cars rushing about in the vicinity last night. Besides, I'd discovered you were wearing a disguise... though I like your real face better."

"My real face?" asked Dong Po, his eyes twinkling with amusement, and then he suddenly looked serious. "You aren't afraid of me?"

She stared right into his eyes as if daring him. "No, I'm not afraid of you. And you don't have to fear me either. So you'd better go back to sleep because you've lost a lot of blood. You need rest."

He nodded. "Thank you for what you've done."

☆ ☆ ☆ ☆

The previous night, Deputy Superintendent Robert Chuah stood behind the army truck while a team of soldiers and police officers searched the area. As it hadn't been established whether the fugitive was a communist agent or a criminal, he had rushed to the scene where an officer from Special Branch, an Assistant Superintendent James Lau was already present to organize a manhunt.

The Special Branch officer briefed him, "We have sent the pistol, a Beretta M1934 for tests. Our guys have found the car, which they had gone over most thoroughly but found nothing. We will try to establish to whom the car was registered."

Ten minutes later, one of the men called out to them, "*Tuan*, there are some blood stains here."

It was Corporal Ramasamy from Traffic Police who had called to them. When they walked to where the Indian stood, DSP Chuah borrowed the torch from the corporal to shine on the spot where dark blood stains showed.

"I may be wrong but I think he was still able to flee on foot even though he had been shot."

"Good thinking, corporal," said DSP Chuah, who was different from many of his fellow officers. While they seemed to think those members of the rank-and-file had no brain, DSP Chuah often praised his men whenever they bothered to share their thoughts with him.

"Could he have gotten far?" asked ASP Lau.

"Maybe," DSP Chuah replied. "Depending on how badly hurt he was, or whether he had managed to hail a passing taxi or even hop onto a bus at the nearby main road."

"Maybe we should embark on a door-to-door search," suggested Corporal Ramasamy.

ASP Lau shook his head. "He's unlikely to be in the vicinity. If I were him, I wouldn't linger but would try putting as much distance as possible between me and my pursuers. Moreover, I doubt if anyone would stick their neck out to help a stranger with gunshot wound. They would have reported him by now. Check out hospitals and clinics instead."

Corporal Ramasamy spoke rapidly into a walkie-talkie, telling whoever was on the other end to check out hospitals in case someone with a bullet wound was brought there. He added, "Have someone to ask around the taxi stations too."

Watching the Indian and remembering he was the same man who had earlier stopped and shot the fugitive, and noting his quiet competence, DSP Chuah made a mental note to ask for his transfer to CID. *This man's wasted in doing traffic duties,* he thought.

☆☆☆☆

At the time when Lay Yong was talking to her unexpected patient, Lim was already up and running with his illegal deals. No matter how late into the night or more accurately, how early in the morning he got into bed, he slept very little and would be up by the first light of dawn.

Though his first thought on waking up that morning was about how much money he would make from selling the batch of heroin to Tim Lane, his smile of satisfaction was ended by the ring of the phone. He picked up the receiver, half expecting to find the American on the line but it turned out to be one of his sidekicks, Kam Choon.

"*Lin lau boo,*" he screamed the Hokkien swear words after listening to what Kam Choon had told him. "Last night when you talked to that gaming outlet boss, didn't you make it clear to him that our tong will not take no for an answer?"

He paused, waiting for a response. As he listened, he stubbed out his cigarette forcefully in the ashtray.

"All right, you make sure he understands the consequences of crossing me. And don't you let him get away with it. If you do, the other outlets' bosses we have under our control may follow suit and then we won't be able to launder our money. Should that happen, I shall hold you responsible," Lim said, and then slammed down the receiver with the same agitated force he had used to stub out the cigarette earlier.

For some years, Lim had been buying winning lottery tickets through the less scrupulous agents or those who had somehow ended up in his clutches for one reason or other. The real winners were paid in cash, which included a small commission. Likewise, the agents also earned a small commission. By using these bought winning tickets, Lim was able to launder some of his ill-gotten money from his illicit businesses. In this way, almost every member of his family appeared blessed in winning lotteries each week.

To hear that one of the agents was backing out was most displeasing for him, especially so early in the day.

Fifty-two

*T*he loud roar of a fighter jet flying overhead woke Mao Dong Po up from his troubled sleep.

"As the air force base is not far away from here, we're used to the noise of the planes flying above us," said his rescuer the moment she saw his eyes had opened.

With his right arm, he pushed himself up on the bed, and then flexed his left arm. Though his left shoulder still ached, he felt much better than the last time he was up. At least, he no longer felt feverish. Gratefully, he accepted the glass of water and the four pills she handed him.

"Pain killer and antibiotics," she declared.

"I may not know your name but I'm in your debt," he said, looking around the room, and saw the blanket on the floor, which told him she had been sleeping on the floor."

"My name is Lay Yong...Ong Lay Yong," she said. "Who are you, Dong Po?"

"Since you already knew I'm Dong Po, I guess what you meant is, "What are you?" Am I right?"

She smiled but he noticed the little girl he saw earlier that morning was gone. This was a woman's smile, a smile driven by the female vanity to attract attention and also driven by the female inquisitiveness to extract information.

"If you'd already been through my things, then you should know I'm a manager with a pest removal company."

"Klahan Pattano? Does a manager of a pest removal firm carry a pistol?"

"What?" he asked, suddenly feeling his heart stopped beating and momentarily struggling to breathe.

Lay Yong shrugged. "It was on the news. The police said they have shot a man who dropped a pistol at a roadblock along Jalan Bagan Luar last night and appealed to the public to report anyone with a gunshot wound."

Dong Po closed his eyes as his mind raced over the events of the previous night and the plan for his next move. "Can you get me a clean shirt?"

"That will be no problem," Lay Yong said. "But you still haven't answered my question."

"There are some questions which are better left unanswered. I'm grateful to you for saving me. All I can tell you is that I'm not a bad man."

"All right," she said. "I believe you'll tell me more in your own sweet time."

A few miles away, in a room at the Butterworth police station, two men sat across a table facing one another.

"I guess it's my show after all," Assistant Superintendent James Lau said gloomily. "The pistol's ballistics matched with the one from a shooting of a British army officer some years back. So it's likely that the fugitive is a communist agent."

Deputy Superintendent Robert Chuah nodded. "You're referring to the case of Captain Neil Walker, if I remember the name correctly?"

The man from Special Branch lifted an eyebrow in surprise.

"I was the investigating officer at the time but subsequently was forced to hand it over to a British officer attached to the Provost Marshal's Office," the CID man explained. "The case was closed after a colleague of Captain Walker blew his own brains out. It seemed the deceased captain had something to do with that guy's wife leaving him. So my counterpart in the British Army assumed the bloke shot Captain Walker and later committed suicide."

ASP Lau sighed. "We've checked the car registration. It was registered to a man by the name of Soon Tiong San."

"Ahh, then you can send someone over to his home to pick him up for questioning."

"No way," ASP Lau said glumly. "The Birth and Death Registry's records showed Soon Tiong San died on September 21, 1947."

☆☆☆☆

Despite the initial lousy start that morning, the rest of the day surprisingly turned out to be a good one for Lim.

Just before lunch time, Kam Choon reported that the gaming outlet boss, who had earlier tried to wriggle out of their deal, had been sufficiently threatened to return meekly to their fold. Lim was thus able to enjoy a reasonably delicious lunch with Tim Lane at the Eden in Hutton Lane.

"How was last night?" he asked the American.

"It was fantastic," Tim gushed. "I owe you one, Lim. Though I've been around Asia, the girl last night was the best."

The Chinese watched the American's face and smiled. He knew the man meant every word because Lim was confident in his girls. They were very well trained, thanks to the late Wu Hsiao Ling. No matter how ugly or undesirable a male client would be, those girls could always make a man walk away believing himself to be the most attractive and virile guy in the world. And the girls were also very well-trained in the various ways to please a man in bed as Lim himself had long ago found out.

The last thought got him thinking of his latest mistress. As he was out entertaining the American the previous night, he was unable to go to her. Well, he would definitely see her tonight.

Fifty-three

*T*he "own sweet time" which Ong Lay Yong had mentioned for Mao Dong Po to tell her more about himself, didn't exceed two days.

On the morning of the second day, she went to work, leaving him alone in her room. Later that afternoon, she stopped by an emporium to buy him a shirt. When she handed it to him, she also told him that she had applied for an additional three days' leave in order to spend time with him.

"I'm truly grateful for all that you've done for me," Dong Po told her and he meant every word.

"If you're truly grateful, then tell me who you really are. You can trust me. If I'd meant you any harm, you will be in the police lock-up by now."

And then, Dong Po had an inspiration. His *sifu* had once instructed him on how to effectively use disinformation to turn a truth into a lie in order to mislead, and at times, to twist a lie into a truth. According to his mentor, the trick was to combine a half lie and a half-truth. "Such combination is lethal because they tend to be more credible than either an outright lie or truth," Somchai had said.

"Well, if you really want to know, my name isn't Mao Dong Po," he confided. "But as I've already used this name a long time, I think of myself as him. For your own safety, please think of me as Mao Dong Po."

He saw she was fascinated, and he continued. "I'm also not a manager for a pest removal company. That was my cover just as Klahan Pattano is one of the many aliases I assumed. After a civil war in my country had ended disastrously for my side, I was forced to flee to this country. I have no other skills except to kill."

"I understand now," she said, pleased that she could always get men to tell her the truth. "I supposed you're Vietnamese, and you are either a mercenary or an assassin."

"Yes, I hope you will keep my secret to yourself," he pleaded with beseeching eyes and was startled to find her cool and amused eyes appraising him.

"Your secret's safe with me."

"Thank you, Lay Yong," he said. "Another thing is that I cannot stay here much longer. I have to go."

"Where do you want to go? Do you have a home?"

"Yes, I have a house in Penang. I feel safer there."

"But what about your car? Won't they be able to trace it to you and your home?"

"I'd registered it under another alias and I've all along kept it parked some distance from my home so that no one knows the car belonged to me."

"You sure know your business," she said with admiration. "Come, let me help you get into your shirt. It won't be easy and might be painful. After that, I'll accompany you to your home."

For a moment, he hesitated. It was bad enough that he had told her about his being an assassin. Would it be going too far to allow her to know where he lived? Should he reveal his sanctuary to her? But he mustn't forget, she had saved his life. Besides, it helped to have her around him since the police would be watching out for a lone man. Having decided, he said: "All right, please help me wear the new shirt."

All that had taken place a year ago. On this December evening in 1978, Dong Po was sitting on his living room sofa with Lay Yong cuddling against him. For the first time, they were watching TV programs in color as technology in Malaysia had moved out of the black-and-white phase. They had also moved from rescuer-stranger to become intimate lovers.

It had begun a month after she had been to his beach-front home in Tanjong Tokong. She had by then become a frequent visitor, especially during her rest-day when she would use his home to change and swim in the sea. One day after a swim, she came into the house wearing a flimsy two-piece bikini swim wear. Instead of going into the bathroom to shower, she lingered around engaging him in casual talk.

It hadn't taken her long to make the first move as she shifted nearer to him. He was watching her with an expression that hovered between fascination and caution, like he desired her and yet was holding himself back. Finally his hands reached out to pull her towards him. She hadn't fought him off and instead even helped to remove his clothing.

Though they had since become lovers, Dong Po had no idea that Lay Yong often thought him not as exciting in bed as the departed Dr. George Teng or the late Chief Inspector Chris Ng. Of course, she too had no idea that after Suchin Suewonglee's death, Dong Po had felt an odd sense of guilt over being too passionate in bed with another woman and hence his lovemaking tended to be perfunctory, almost like an impersonal release of his physical tension.

Initially, Dong Po's lovemaking hadn't bothered Lay Yong as she hero-worshipped him after being taken in by his story. She was especially impressed when he had shown her a South Vietnamese passport – no longer valid since the fall of Saigon. Thereafter, she ceased pestering him with questions about his identity. On the other hand, Dong Po was however a bit disturbed when he found out Lay Yong's intense leftist idealism. Her political leaning was too stifling for his comfort. Though she had at first tried to conceal it from Dong Po, he was sharp enough to deduce her belief in the communist cause.

For example, she had once told him, "There's really no need for you to flee your country. A united Vietnam under the communists is better than a split one, especially when the south was a corrupt regime and a puppet of the Americans."

Like his father, he was non-political and thus felt uncomfortable with those who would display any frenzy over a cause. Besides, he had seen enough of communism to know it to be a lost cause. Even communist China had earlier that year started economic reforms to enable its peasants to sell part of their crops on the free market.

However, Dong Po was canny enough not to let on that he knew her leftist leaning or reveal his own critical view of communism. After all, he too had his dark side and he hadn't been exactly truthful with her. And as he closed an eye to her political inclination while she harbored hopes of recruiting him, they were able to remain lovers.

☆☆☆☆

Deputy Superintendent Robert Chuah had long ago given up trying to understand the facts of life.

Eight months ago, to his surprise, his inept assistant was given a promotion – Ali bin Abdul Rahim was now holding the same rank as him – and posted to Kuala Lumpur as one of the district chiefs. *That guy surely has a guardian angel watching out for him*, DSP Chuah thought.

The thought also led him to think of Assistant Superintendent James Lau. Although ASP Lau's investigation of the fugitive gunman, believed to be a communist agent, came to a dead end, he was more fortunate in that he had also been promoted to deputy superintendent and posted to Commando 69 – an elite force in the Police Field Force – as its Commanding Officer.

As for me, I guess my promotion prospect right now is rather poor considering that I was one of those who came under suspicion for graft by the National Bureau of Investigation, he thought sadly. *But my conscience is clear. Though I may close an eye in the case of illegal gambling, for which the grateful gambling dens' operators would give me gifts or money, which I have never solicited in the first place, I won't tolerate serious crimes such as robberies, rapes, dealing in the white powder and murders.*

The last thought brought a frown to his forehead. He was still unable to successfully close the case of the 32-year-old man, identified as Foo Kwang Lin, whose badly-mutilated body was found dumped at the Mount Erskine Cemetery three years ago. He was particularly fascinated by this case because of the numerous mutilations all over the body. Although investigations revealed the man to be a drug pusher who had served time in prison, it irked DSP Chuah that he was unable to establish the motive, with which to nail the murderer or murderers.

Even when he asked his friend, Chiu Ya Loong, and the retired *taikor* had told him that the deceased was a minion of Lim Hoe Peng, DSP Chuah knew he hadn't much evidence to pin the murder on Lim. Thinking about the baffling case, he let out a long sigh. It looked like he had no choice but to file it in the thick folder containing the files of other unsolved cases.

Even if Lim had access to DSP Chuah's private thoughts and inside knowledge that the CID detectives had been unable to link the murder of Foo Kwang Lin to him, he would still suffer no remorse.

As far as Lim was concerned, he had done no wrong in making Kwang Lin suffered a terrible death as a result of wrongly suspecting Kwang Lin of betraying him and so had caused him to suffer a short term of incarceration. Lim would simply reason that if that guy hadn't betrayed him then, he would probably betray him one of these days.

It was the same warped reasoning he employed in carrying on his illicit business. As far as he was concerned, so long as none of his own family members were hooked on the habit, it was all right for him to deal in heroin. After all, if he wasn't supplying the white powder to those losers out there, and making a tidy profit since drug addicts were prepared to fork out a lot of money to indulge in their habit, others would. So why should he be bothered?

Fifty-four

*T*he year 1979 could be said to be quite an unexciting one for Mao Dong Po unless he considered the attempt by Ong Lay Yong to indoctrinate him to join her cell.

At first, she was subtle about it. But as he ignored her, she became more insistent. He didn't know that Lay Yong was afraid of Wang *Lao-su* faulting her inability to recruit a new member to replace a nurse who had been transferred away. Her persistence however irritated him as he had other things on his mind, such as the lack of jobs coming his way. Though he had asked his *sifu,* all the latter would say was, "Patience, my boy, patience. After all, we still haven't satisfied our American clients." Thus, there were times when Dong Po and Lay Yong got into heated rows but they always managed to make up in bed.

Then on the evening of December 27, 1979, Dong Po felt his adrenalin pumping again. Fate had once more led him to bump into Tim Lane by chance. It began to shower the moment Dong Po, after meeting his lawyer in Beach Street, came around to the Mariners' Club at Light Street. Although he was feeling down from having to alter his will now that Suchin Suewonglee was dead, his gloom vanished the moment he saw the American waiting to cross the street to go to the open clearing beside Fort Cornwallis where some cars were parked.

Seeing the American sprinting across the street, Dong Po instinctively followed. He knew that if he failed to catch up fast with his quarry, the latter would drive off and he might not get another chance like this. As the rain gave Dong Po an excuse to break into a fast trot after his quarry, he managed to close the distance very quickly.

The American, who had opened the car door, was about to turn at the sound of Dong Po's racing feet. The young assassin's right hand moved very fast to pull the door wide open and with the same hand, struck the right side of the American's head just as he was turning. As the man crumpled, Dong Po pushed him down into the driver's seat. As the man appeared unconscious, Dong Po grabbed him by the hair to lift his head up. He placed a finger of his free hand under the quarry's nostrils and was amazed that his quarry was dead from just that single hard blow to the head. The young assassin quickly looked around him to make sure no one was watching.

He was thankful that it had already turned quite dark. Moreover, due to the rain, few people were out and he guessed any passing motorist would be too intent on watching keenly the road ahead through the moving windshield wipers. A sudden realization struck Dong Po. It was really quite reckless of him to chase after the American since he, Dong Po, was not carrying any firearm. He moved his hand under the man's jacket and sure enough, pulled out a Browning automatic pistol. If that man had been faster, Dong Po could have been fatally shot.

Although a little shaken on hindsight, he gamely went over to the other side of the car, opened the door and pulled the man over to the passenger seat. Luckily the American wasn't that heavy. After slamming the door shut, he hurried over to the driver's side as the rain had begun to turn into a downpour. He lifted the man's legs and slid them over, before getting behind the wheel.

Throughout the drive, he could hear the rain drumming overhead on the roof of the car. After driving a short distance, he passed Millionaires' Row as Northam Road* was popularly called by the locals. After he had circled the small roundabout to turn into Kalawei Road, he pulled over to the roadside to wipe away the mist that had begun forming on the interior surface of the windshield. Though the rain had helped him to take his quarry unaware and kept away prying eyes, it also caused him some inconvenience.

He soon came to the roundabout at Bagan Jermal, which he circled and turned into Tanjong Tokong Road. He slowed down due to the poor visibility caused by the heavy rain. Very soon, he turned left towards Fettes Park, and then right into the Vale of Temp. When he finally arrived at the spot he had in mind, he pulled the car into a clearing. The rain had by then dwindled into a light sprinkle. Knowing traffic was infrequent on this stretch of road, he confidently got out to cross over to the passenger's side, opened the door and dragged the corpse out.

---

* Today, it is known as Jalan Sultan Ahmad Shah.

411

Lay Yong was beginning to lose her patience with Dong Po.

Although she had initially been excited over her discovery that he was a killer, now she was beginning to have her doubts. If Dong Po was really capable of killing anyone, it would, of course, be a feather in her cap to recruit him to her cause. Wang *Lao-su* would be most pleased if she could talk him into working for them.

"Yes, if only he is willing to help us knock off a few important persons, such will instill a sense of insecurity amongst the populace and so destabilize the country, creating an opportunity for us to renew our armed struggles," Lay Yong said aloud to herself within the privacy of her rented room.

"But despite my having tried so hard, he has pointedly been ignoring me," she murmured.

And then she thought of the previous night when Dong Po had the temerity to laugh at her.

"How dare he tell me to my face that I have neglected my parents for the cause? This is simply too much," she hissed through gritted teeth.

But she felt better when she remembered how she had screamed at him: "My parents? Don't talk to me about them. They understand nothing. My father's just a greedy wine importer who couldn't care a damn for the drunkards he'd created so long as he could amass his profits. As for my mother, she's a weakling, always so submissive to my father."

He had then looked at her in that aloof and condescending manner before walking away.

That December night, as she brooded further over Dong Po, another thought occurred to her.

"Actually, Dong Po hasn't been much of a lover. Though he was gentle and understanding in bed, he was hardly passionate or exciting," she muttered to herself.

And the more she thought, the more she felt the late Chief Inspector Chris Ng was a more preferred lover since he was both passionate and exciting. Unlike Dong Po, the late chief inspector was certainly more fun. Why is Dong Po so straight-laced? Why couldn't he be like Chris who was so game for trying out different ways of love-making? She suddenly regretted her impulsiveness in killing him.

Again, she said aloud: "Perhaps I should have exercised more self restraint at the time to shoot only that damned bitch instead of both of them."

Well, it's too late, she thought. *But no, maybe it's not too late to start a new affair. After all, there are a couple of good-looking fellows among the new batch of doctors posted to my hospital. I bet they would make better lovers than Dong Po any time.*

☆☆☆☆

That same night, several police officers were combing a clearing in a hilly part of Penang that went up and down steep slopes, and consisting mostly dangerous bends and corners. As the officers searched, Chief Inspector Mohamed Fauzi bin Abdullah stood looking down at the corpse of a middle-aged white man. It had been raining the whole evening, which was why there was a great deal of mud everywhere.

"As you can see, *Tuan*, everything's messed up. The reporters were tipped off before us and so they got here well ahead of our men. Now there are footprints all over the place, including ours and everyone else's," Sergeant Ramasamy (formerly of Traffic Police) said.

Chief Inspector Fauzi who was recently posted to join the CID team in Penang, nodded absentmindedly, and looked away from the corpse. As usual, he felt somewhat nauseated by the smell of death. He searched his hip pocket for the packet of cigarettes he carried.

"When the head is turned, you can see the livid, ulcerous bruise at the side of the skull," Sergeant Ramasamy pointed out. "I think that was the only place he was hit and likely the cause of his death. I've told our men to comb the area thoroughly to see if they can find the murder weapon."

"Good job, Ramasamy," the chief inspector said, taking a puff of the cigarette he had lighted. "Too bad the year will end with one additional murder statistic. It will spoil the record."

The sergeant shrugged. After two attendants from the ambulance had removed the body, Chief Inspector Fauzi walked over to his car. Since there was nothing more he could do other than to wait for the forensic report, he should go home and return to the sleep from which he had earlier been awoken.

Oblivious to the disco music blaring from the overhead speakers, Lim glared at his trembling chauffeur-cum-bodyguard.

"*Lin lau boo,*" he opened with his favorite swear words. "Why am I feeding you and your family when you cannot even perform a simple job as I've given you?"

Although Ah Sai couldn't see his boss's eyes behind the sunglasses, and especially under the dim lighting of the lounge, he sensed Lim was glaring at him. He shivered and answered in a quivering voice. "I…I have t-t-tried asking around b-but am getting conflicting reports."

Lim shook his head impatiently. "I shall give you until tomorrow night to get me the answers I want. As it is, I'm tired of waiting. I have already waited a long time to take over Wah Chye's territory. I can't make my move unless I know how strong he is, how many men he has got, and who are his allies, especially in the police department. So get me those answers by tomorrow night, okay?"

The unhappy minion nodded before slinking into the darkness, leaving Lim to turn his amorous attention to the pretty hostess by his side. Though Ah Sai wasn't a big shot in his tong, he knew too well there would surely be trouble ahead if his boss really were to wage war against Wah Chye's tong. He hadn't dared to tell his boss but from what he had heard, Wah Chye who used to be a former lieutenant of the independent chieftain, Chiu Ya Loong, whom they called Loong-*kor,* was capable of defending his turf.

Fifty-five

*M*ao Dong Po was in high spirit.

He had several reasons for being so. For starter, he was the first to remove the elusive American, who was sought after by his own fellow Americans and other freelance assassins. Thus, it was natural that Dong Po felt some professional pride. After his *sifu* had claimed credit for Tim Lane's removal, the American clients who had learned from Interpol about the death of an unidentified man fitting Lane's description, had promptly paid up. The bounty had increased over the years, thus causing Somchai and Dong Po to naturally be in the best of mood.

He was still feeling great when on the last day of 1979, he got a telephone call from his mentor suggesting they should meet at the bar in Pekan Siam where Somchai had so many years ago arranged for his young protégé's first sexual encounter. At the appointed time Dong Po arrived to find his *sifu* waiting outside on the street. The Siamese, who was wearing white duck suits, including a pair of matching tall socks and white tennis shoes, looked like a navy captain or colonial planter. He smiled expansively the moment he caught sight of his protégé.

"Come, my boy, we have the entire floor upstairs to ourselves."

Wordlessly, Dong Po followed his *sifu* up the stairs. The swarthy Siamese went to a closet where he took out a bottle of Mekong, the fiery local whiskey, and two glasses.

After they had drunk the first glass, Somchai said, "I have need of your skills again."

"So soon, Uncle Somchai?"

"When there's no work, you complained. Now that there're jobs to do, you still complain," Somchai chided his protégé. "As it is, there're two jobs to be done."

"Two jobs?"

"Yes, there're two men to be removed. One is a triad chief who does terrible things to people apart from being a major distributor of the white powder. From what I've heard of this man, whose name is Lim, he's the worst scumbag you could ever come across. The other man is a communist agent who has no qualm about accusing innocent men in order to get himself off the hook."

After that justification speech, Somchai took out two cigars, which he offered one to Dong Po. He lit his and took a puff. "You're the only one who can remove those two guys who aren't easy to handle."

"That's what they said too about Tim Lane. According to them, he was a tough Special Forces officer but I took him out with just one punch."

"Don't be conceited, my boy," said Somchai sternly, and seeing his protégé making a slight bow, he smiled.

"Reality is very different from reading the exploits of James Bond and watching John Wayne charging into battle as a tough Green Beret."

They sat in silence smoking their cigars. After a while, Somchai said in a stronger voice: "Our success depends a lot on the element of surprise, my boy. From what I've seen so far, I know I haven't groomed you in vain. All these years, after each of your assignments, you would tell me how you had removed those problems. After the first few jobs, I've known then that you're a natural, like those predators who hunt at night."

The older man's words somehow caused Dong Po to reflect on his past jobs. True enough, except for the removal of the Thai judge-turned-politician, all the other removals had been nocturnal ones. He was surprised that he hadn't noticed until now that his *sifu* had pointed out.

"I think you're born for it. That's why when you'd first asked me, I'd decided to take you on as my pupil," said Somchai. "If you remove Lim and Chea Song, you will also be repaying an old debt."

"What do you mean, Uncle Somchai?"

"You remember Ya Loong, my childhood friend?"

When the Siamese saw Dong Po's eyes widening a little, he nodded. "Yes, the one who'd provided us the information which allowed you to remove Captain Neil Walker so many years ago. We still owe him this debt, my boy. Thus, we won't expect payment for Chea Song the communist who had wronged him. But for Lim the white powder supplier, Ya Loong's henchman, Wah Chye, who has succeeded him as a *taikor*, has offered to pay $30,000. That sum we shall accept as Wah Chye's in the position to pay."

"I'll do the jobs, Uncle Somchai, but I shall need an additional pistol, say a Beretta with a silencer. Can you also get me a silencer to fit this Browning pistol?" asked Dong Po, producing the gun he had taken from the late Tim Lane.

"Ahh, I understand," Somchai said approvingly. "I see you already have a plan."

☆ ☆ ☆ ☆

At the time that Dong Po was talking with his mentor, Ong Lay Yong had already taken a new lover to amuse herself.

There were two good-looking guys from the new batch of doctors posted to the hospital where she was working. Once she had made her choice, she went after the unsuspecting fellow like a tigress that had already spotted a deer.

Like the tigress, she started off employing stealth as she casually stalked Dr. Alfred Ling who unsuspectingly attended to his duties in the hospital. Somehow or other, she seemed to be always bumping into him at work, or be coming across him outside after work. What he couldn't know was that she had a girl from Administration who provided her with information of his movement.

As she was already an accomplished actress, capable of projecting an image of herself as a weak and helpless, yet attractive and young (surprisingly she still looked like she was in her early thirties despite being already forty-three) lady, Alfred, a well-built, rugged, yet extremely bashful fellow was soon head over heels with her.

And then like the tigress, she finally pounced on the doctor who ultimately was only too glad to be eaten alive. It was again thanks to the girl in Administration, the one who was always complaining about how unfair the world was, and whom Lay Yong was cautiously courting to join her cell that she was assigned to the same clinic and shift as Alfred. As their shift was coming to an end that afternoon, she casually remarked: "It's so hot and humid today. How I wish to go for a swim."

"Sounds like a marvelous idea to me," Alfred said enthusiastically. "Why not join me for a swim at the Penang Swimming Club as I'm a member?"

"I have an even better idea," she said, brushing a stray strand of hair out of her eyes. "A friend of mine has a bungalow by the sea. As my friend has gone outstation, I was given the key and told to help keep an eye on the place. We could go there to swim in the sea and later tonight, I'll cook New Year Eve dinner for us."

"That will be fantastic," the doctor gushed happily.

Dong Po had earlier told Lay Yong that he would be away from New Year Eve until the second day of the New Year. Thus, she knew it was safe to take Alfred back to the seafront bungalow with her. Having been Dong Po's lover for slightly more than two years, she knew he kept very little personal things in his home. No photograph of himself, and all his personal belongings were kept locked in a closet. And since she had used vague terms like "my friend", she knew Alfred had assumed the friend was another lady.

And so the couple had a lovely time together, swimming in the sea, and thereafter, she whipped up a reasonably appetizing meal for Alfred. Afterwards, as they sat together on the sofa in the living room watching TV, she decided it was time to make her move.

Alfred, who had been rattling on and on for the past half an hour about his family in Sitiawan, was saying: "And so on that day, my mother passed away."

"Oh, how terrible that must be for you," she purred, snuggling closer, and then kissed his cheek. Though he appeared stunned for a moment, she ignored his astonishment and pulled him closer to her as though he was in need of solace. One thing quickly led to another and before long, they were both naked on the sofa, and so Lay Yong got herself a new lover.

☆ ☆ ☆ ☆

"Ahh, Fauzi, here you are," Superintendent Robert Chuah said. "Come and sit down."

Since he had given up on his own promotion prospect, the unexpected elevation to Superintendent gave the Chinese officer much pleasure. The pleasure was however short lived as he was worried over the latest murder case. "Any break-through regarding that Caucasian fellow whose body was found at the Vale of Temp?"

"Not yet, Sir," Chief Inspector Fauzi said. "It's odd that the guy carried no paper on him at all. It makes identification so difficult. We have also been to the hotels and lodging houses but no one knew him. We're still waiting to hear from Interpol whether they have anything for us."

"I can understand an unidentified local but an unidentified *orang putih* doesn't seem to make much sense," said Superintendent Chuah, using the Malay words, *orang putih* meaning white man. "It's really odd that even Immigration has no record."

"I'm not surprised," said Chief Inspector Fauzi, whose tone was quite contemptuous. "From what I've heard, our border checkpoints aren't as secured as they should be."

Superintendent Chuah thought about what his chief inspector had said for a few moments and finally growled, "That's an oversimplification. Well, keep me posted."

☆ ☆ ☆ ☆

When Tim Lane who had become a major buyer of the white powder from Lim didn't turn up with the money on the night he was supposed to meet with Lim to do the exchange, Lim decided not to linger after five minutes was up.

He decided it was too dangerous to wait any longer. Upset as he was, he knew the American would have a good reason for not keeping the appointment. After all, they had done a lot of exchanges in the past year. Early the next morning when he read in the newspaper about an unidentified white man's body being found murdered and dumped in the Vale of Temp, he involuntarily exclaimed, *"Lin lau boo!"* He knew instinctively the corpse was his missing buyer. Knowing he had lost an opportunity to make a lot of money, he was naturally in a foul mood.

Another man with whom Tim Lane had also agreed to meet was just as dismayed when he read the same news report about the murder of an unidentified white man. He had actually met Lane the previous afternoon at a quiet coffee shop in Union Street where they had agreed on a deal whereby the American would deliver a cache of explosives to the man in South Thailand.

Unlike Lim whose concern was profit, the man whose name was Chea Song was upset because he was planning a revolution and any failure to get the explosives would mean no revolution. A beetle-browed and swarthy-faced man with heavy-lidded eyes that had a curiously dreamy quality, Chea Song was born in Penang on May 14, 1937. The Malayan Communist Party recruited him while he was still schooling at the Chung Hua Middle School. Before his arrest by the late Chief Inspector Chris Ng in 1974, he was working as a manager for a charcoal kiln in Sadao in South Thailand. After he agreed to work secretly for the Special Branch, he was released.

But being a true communist, he was merely using disinformation to mislead his case officer in the Special Branch by fingering those people who weren't communists but forced to make financial contributions at one time or another to the Malayan Communist Party. One of them was the retired *taikor*, Chiu Ya Loong who owned the charcoal kiln in Sadao. Meanwhile, Chea Song was working on a grand scheme to incite some radicals in South Thailand to rise against the Thai government in a bid to turn the South into an autonomous State. Given that the communists were atheist, they were merely pretending to support the religious belief of the separatist groups, trying to make use of them for their own ends. Those communist guerillas who had previously moved from Malaysia to South Thailand were already on stand-by, waiting for the right moment to seize advantage of a chaotic situation.

As he put down the newspaper, Chea Song's face was filled with unhappiness.

Fifty-six

The next day, Somchai walked into the shop of Mao Dong Po's uncle from the front. Ever since the two countries had set up tall barbed-wire fences along their long border, Somchai was no longer able to slip in and out via the back door as before. Instead, he had to cross at the official checkpoints. But Somchai being Somchai, he had already managed to befriend the officials who would simply wave him through without checking his passport or belongings. After all, the Siamese was known as a most generous fellow.

"Happy New Year, Uncle Somchai."

"Happy New Year to you too, my boy. Here's the pistol you'd asked me to get for you. It's a newer model than the one you formerly carried," said Somchai as he opened a wooden box to take out a Beretta automatic. "Here are the silencers."

He watched in fascination as Dong Po dexterously took apart the pistol and then reassembled the parts before slipping a 9-millimetre clip into the weapon and pulling the slider to chamber the first round. Something about the way his protégé handled firearms so effortlessly had always caused him some envy. After all, he was the *sifu* while Dong Po was only his pupil. But secretly, he knew the younger man was better at it than him. *The old must always learn that at a certain stage in life they have to make way for the young,* he thought. *And I need not have to feel envy since a good pupil is simply a reflection of his master.*

After Dong Po had finished checking the gun, Somchai handed him a photograph. "This is Black Sunglasses Lim."

Dong Po's eyes widened. "I've seen him before. Yes, he was with the American."

"Not surprising," Somchai said. "As Lim's in the white powder business, most likely, the American was a buyer."

"Where's the other guy's photograph, Uncle Somchai?"

"I'd burnt it the other day after Ya Loong had shown it to me," said Somchai sheepishly. "I'd thought that would impress him on how professional I am."

Seeing the look on his *sifu's* face and hearing his grudging admission, Dong Po nearly wanted to laugh aloud but he restrained himself. As the bond between mentor and protégé was similar to the relationship between father and son, he knew he had to toe the line at times. But he secretly marveled that all these years, he still hadn't found anyone whose ego could match Somchai's. "How am I going to make Chea Song if I haven't any idea how he looks like?"

Somchai sighed. "I'll have to ask Ya Loong again on the excuse that I need to study him more."

☆ ☆ ☆ ☆

By noon on New Year Day, Ong Lay Yong felt she had enough of Dr. Alfred Ling.

Although he had a voracious appetite and plenty of stamina for sex – they did it four more times in the guest room where Lay Yong at least had the decency to bring him to spend the night with her – he was however too selfish for her liking. He cared only for his own gratification. And he was a sloppy kisser and exceedingly clumsy in bed.

But the worse was that when he was not busy pawing her body in his clumsy way, he was bent on shooting off his mouth non-stop about his extremely large and seemingly close-knitted family. Just an hour before noon, he was already telling a bored Lay Yong about his having a cousin whose niece's sister-in-law had just bagged a government scholarship to study in London.

Hence, by noon, when the talkative doctor was going to tell Lay Yong about the eccentricity of his mother's grand-aunt, she just couldn't take it any more. She told a disappointed Alfred that she had to go back to Butterworth to keep another appointment with a friend. Even though he insisted they should at least have lunch together as it would be a shame to miss that frightfully funny story about the son of his mother's granduncle, she fled immediately.

By the time she got back to her rented room, she decided to give the other doctor a chance to know her better.

"And if Dr. Alfred Ling isn't too happy about my dumping him for Dr. David Ooi, or if he starts

badmouthing me, well, he will then end up with a
funeral attended by his large clan," she muttered to
herself in her room. Once again, the knowledge of her
holding the power of life and death in her hands gave
her a thrill.

☆☆☆☆

The disappearance of Tim Lane put Chea Song in a tight
spot. They were supposed to meet a second time whereby
the American would advise him on the date, time and
place for the explosives to be handed over. Without the
American who was believed to be dead, Chea Song was
forced to drop his plan. He knew he would have a hard
time trying to explain to his superiors in the Malayan
Communist Party.

Lim had no one other than himself to answer. Even
so, he too was in a tight spot. Lim knew he had to quickly
find another big buyer to replace the missing American,
presumably murdered by person or persons unknown.

He cursed the American. He cursed whoever had
killed the American. He cursed the market for the white
powder. He even cursed the gods for sending this problem
to him since he had spent much money throughout the
year giving donations to temples all over the island of
Penang and even in Province Wellesley on the
mainland. He however neglected to curse his greed,
which had led him to increase production ever since he
got to know the American.

Caught in that position, Lim was understandably annoyed when his chauffeur-cum-bodyguard came forth to give his report.

"*Lim-kor*, I've found out that Wah Chye is still enjoying the protection of his former *taikor*, Chiu Ya Loong whom people called Loong-*kor*," Ah Sai said. "This means *Loong-kor's* friends, Scar-Face Wong of the Loong Foo Tong and No-Smile Khor of the Pa Hsien Tong would naturally become Wah Chye's allies. Likewise, Loong-*kor's* buddy in the police force, Superintendent Robert Chuah would probably be backing Wah Chye as well."

"*Lin lau boo*," screamed Lim, who was silently seething as he listened to his henchman's narrative. "Must you spoil my day with all these bad news?"

As Lim angrily stalked away, the luckless Ah Sai stared unhappily at his boss's back, wondering what he had done wrong. Hadn't he gone around collecting the information his boss wanted?

Fifty-seven

On his forty-third birthday which fell on January 6, 1980, Mao Dong Po decided it was the right moment to act. In the past few days, he had already familiarized himself with the terrain and the movement of his two quarries.

That evening, after using one of his many aliases to rent a Toyota sedan, he drove to Lim's house in Cantonment Drive to carry out his stake-out. While sitting in the car to wait for his quarry to show, he admired the houses and thought Lim had sure made it from his Lim Jetty days. After ten minutes, he knew his quarry would show any time now.

At eight-fifteen, the gates were opened by a servant and a gleaming black Mercedes Benz rolled out. The quarry, who was wearing sunglasses, was sitting at the back of the car driven by Ah Sai, his chauffeur-cum-bodyguard.

Dong Po smiled. Many people lived according to a habitual routine. After observing Lim in the past three days, he was amazed to find Lim was one such predictable creature. Being a major player in the underworld, surely Lim ought to know better than that? As his *sifu* had taught him, Dong Po's personal rule for himself was to assume the worst – that he was being watched – and so he would vary his routes of travel and daily timetable. This was what Somchai had once told him, "Don't presume that I always come here to the Oriental Hotel. I only do so when I want to see you. Even then, if you've noticed, our appointment varies in time, and I always use different doors to come and go."

Knowing his quarry's next destination, unless he broke from habit, Dong Po didn't bother to follow the Mercedes Benz. Instead he overtook Lim's car and using several short cuts, went ahead. In less than fifteen minutes, he was already parked along a quiet tree-lined section of Perak Road, where again, he waited most patiently.

When the Mercedes Benz finally came, Dong Po glanced at his watch and smiled again. As he knew from his previous surveillance, Lim would get out of the car and go inside the house. Lim simply couldn't resist stopping by that building each night to ensure everything was all right before proceeding to the home of any of his string of mistresses whom he visited by turns. And why not? The illicit activities going on in that house with people weighing and packing small packets of white powder was the spring of Lim's illicit wealth.

Just as he had predicted, Lim got out of the car and entered the house. Dong Po also got out of his car to walk over to the Mercedes Benz. He knocked softly on the driver's window and waved a street map for effect. Ah Sai rolled the window down and asked irritably, "What do you want?" He shut up when he found himself staring into the muzzle of a silenced 9mm Browning automatic.

"Get out," ordered Dong Po, and as soon as a terrified Ah Sai got out, he pushed the chauffeur-cum-bodyguard against the car, and frisked his body.

After recovering a small Llama pistol, which he quickly slipped into his own pocket, Dong Po whispered into Ah Sai's ears, "This is none of your business. So don't get killed for nothing. Go as far away as you can. You understand me?"

Ah Sai, who had come to an instant decision that his abusive boss wasn't worth dying for, nodded. When Dong Po barked, "Go," the chauffeur-cum-bodyguard scurried off like a frightened rabbit.

After that, Dong Po stood in the shadows of a tall tree to wait. Five minutes later, Lim returned. He was about to get inside the car when he realized Ah Sai wasn't in the driver's seat. Straightening up, he stood bewilderedly looking around him. That was when Dong Po stepped out from behind the tree. As soon as Lim saw Dong Po, his hand went for the pistol he kept in his waistband. Dong Po calmly raised the silenced Browning pistol and shot him in the right eye through the sunglasses he was wearing.

He opened the rear door of the car, lifted and pushed Lim's body onto the back seat. Looking at his watch, he saw it was just after nine, giving him enough time to catch up with the other quarry.

Ong Lay Yong was worried. She had been feeling uneasy ever since the previous evening when her landlady knocked on her room, telling her there was a phone call for her.

At first she thought it was Dr. Alfred Ling, whom, she had been avoiding the past few days. Annoyed, she raised the receiver to her ear and was surprised to hear a woman's voice asking, "How can the whole world be transformed, Jasmine?"

She was immediately on the alert because the woman had addressed her by her code name, Jasmine. In the cell which she belonged, the members were each given a code name after a particular type of tea. And the question was part of their secret ritual. Without hesitation, she replied, "Only with fire."

"I can't talk long," the woman said. "I call to tell you that *Pu Erh* has been detained in Singapore."

"Who are you?"

"It doesn't matter," the woman said. "Just pass the word to the others. After that, everyone should go to ground and stay alert. Although it is unlikely that they can make *Pu Erh* talk, we must still be prepared for the worst."

There was a click and the line went dead. As she walked back to her room, her mind was in turmoil. Pu Erh, the name of an old tea found only in Yunnan in China, was the one adopted by her cell leader, Wang *Lao-su*.

Fifty-eight

*T*he clock tower at nearby King Edward's Place chimed ten times.

Mao Dong Po knew that if Somchai's information was correct, any time now his quarry would arrive at the car park located near the ferry terminal. He felt an unexpected gratitude towards the city councilors for their laid back attitude. Had they been more diligent in putting up and maintaining more street lamps, night predators like him would find it more difficult to go about their illegal activities.

His *sifu* was right about him being a night predator. Like all those who hunted in the darkness of the night, he needed the shadows to hide in. He glanced at Black Sunglasses Lim's corpse lying on the ground beside him. And then he heard the footsteps. His quarry, Chea Song, was walking towards the car.

The moment he heard Chea Song fumbling with the door, Dong Po stood up, raised the silenced Beretta automatic pistol and pointed it at Chea Song's face. He hesitated just for a split second, and after that, a small, neat hole appeared between Chea Song's startled eyes. Quickly, Dong Po, thanking whoever had invented the silencer, removed it, bent down and placed the Beretta in Lim's hand, pressing his limp fingers to make sure his finger prints were on the gun. It was a good thing that *rigor mortis* hadn't yet set in.

He then crossed over to do the same with Chea Song, this time using the Browning which he had used earlier to shoot Lim. He had also already removed the gun's silencer. Satisfied, he smiled and got into Lim's Mercedes Benz and drove back to Perak Road where he had left his hired Toyota sedan.

Leaving the Mercedes Benz, he drove away in the rented car to stop briefly at a telephone booth in Burmah Road, near the Top Top Café, to make a call to the police, alerting them about the shooting. Before the police operator could ask him more, he hung up and walked back to his rented car. With luck, nobody would stumble upon the two bodies as yet and the police would probably arrive at the conclusion that the two had shot at each other. As his *sifu* had taught him, misdirection and disinformation were powerful tools in their deadly trade.

☆☆☆☆

That was indeed the conclusion of Probationary Inspector Mazlan bin Othman when he came to the crime scene. He also thought it odd that one of the deceased was wearing sunglasses since it was already night. And then he smiled and said in his "I-am-quite-a-smart-fellow" voice to the corporal standing beside him: "They must have shot each other during the day when the sun was still bright. It's only now that the case has been reported."

S I F U

But when he told the same to his boss, Chief Inspector Mohamed Fauzi bin Abdullah, he got a dressing down. "Use your head, man. After all, you came up from rank-and-file before being selected for officers' training and so ought to know better. Could the two bodies remain undiscovered so long until now? And if you'd bothered to keep your ears and eyes open, the guy who was wearing sunglasses was none other than Lim Hoe Peng also known as Black Sunglasses Lim who controlled the Khong Si Tong in Butterworth and despite being convicted on a narcotics rap a few years back, had continued to expand his operations in Penang."

Later that night when the resentful probationary inspector went out of the Police Contingent Headquarters to the 24-hour tea kiosk in nearby Transfer Road for a cup of tea, a stray puppy wandered into his path. In his lousy mood, he lashed out viciously with his right foot at the hapless puppy.

As the puppy yelped in pain and scurried off into a dark lane, an *imam* – Islamic cleric – who was also having a cup of tea at the kiosk shook his head sadly. The cleric was thinking: *Kindness to animals is an exalted virtue since animals are also God's creations. Even Prophet Muhammad himself had once narrated the story of a prostitute who, on seeing a panting dog by a well, about to die of thirst, took off her shoe to draw some water for the animal, and so the Prophet told his followers that God had forgiven the woman for her good deed. It's so sad that some of my fellow clerics, being human, have injected their personal beliefs to preach against dogs, thus causing many Muslims to forget the Prophet's kindness to these helpless animals.*

He was about to open his mouth to share his thoughts with the uniformed police officer but on seeing the look on the latter's face, he wisely decided to keep his counsel to himself. As he watched the police officer, he thought: *If only Muslims care to read the Quran more. In Surah 5:4, it is written: "They ask you what is halal (clean and permitted) for them? Say "Halal for you are all things that are good for you and those things that are caught for you by the dogs." Doesn't this prove that dogs are clean since what is caught in a dog's mouth is permitted to men?"*

☆ ☆ ☆ ☆

Just before midnight, Ong Lay Yong came to a decision. She emerged from her room to find the living room in darkness as her landlady and her family had gone to bed.

She made her way to the telephone and dialed Dong Po's number. Hearing Dong Po's voice, she asked: "Will you be free tomorrow?"

"I can be," he said non-committally. "What's up?"

As her eyes roved to a calendar hanging on the wall, showing the Penang Hill's funicular train, on an impulse, she suggested: "I was thinking why don't we both go hiking up to Penang Hill early tomorrow morning?"

He laughed, thinking she was always coming up with all sorts of weird ideas. Besides, she had been avoiding him since his return from Padang Besar. He hadn't minded since he had work to do. Now that he had carried out his mission, he cheerfully asked her: "How early is early?"

"Why don't you fetch me from the island's ferry terminal at 6:30 a.m.?"

"All right, I'll see you then."

Once she was back in her room, Lay Yong began muttering to herself: "I'm not going to ground as the mysterious woman has advised. Should Wang *Lao-su* rat on me, I won't be able to keep on running. And I won't want to go to prison again."

She poured a glass of water from the carafe. After taking a few sips, she said: "The time has come to do something spectacular to avenge for all our comrades who had been killed or arrested. I will have to convince Dong Po tomorrow. If I can get him to help me, I won't fail."

She set the alarm clock and switched off the lights.

Fifty-nine

*T*he next morning, Ong Lay Yong missed one ferry. Hence by the time she arrived in Penang, it was 6:50 a.m. Mao Dong Po was already waiting in his car for her.

Throughout the drive to Waterfall Road, she was surprisingly quiet and Dong Po, thinking she hadn't slept well the previous night, left her alone. Half an hour later, they started their hike up the hill from the Moon Gate. After walking for what seemed to be several hours, the sweaty couple came to an escarpment. As they stood near the edge of the rocky cliff, they discovered they could get a panoramic view of the city of Georgetown. They could even see the tiny ferries crossing the channel in the distance. The splendid view and the strong wind induced them to stop for a rest. They knew in a short while their sweat-soaked T-shirts would dry.

As they stood there admiring the scenery, for some reason, Lay Yong felt an urge to get Dong Po into her confidence. Since meeting him that morning, she had desperately wanted to launch into a speech that had gone round and round her head throughout a sleepless night. But she held back as she thought the timing wasn't right.

Now, standing on that escarpment, she thought it was time to begin.

Tentatively, she began her opening gambit. "Do you believe that everyone has a destiny, a sort of life's plan?"

"Maybe," he said absentmindedly, looking out at the magnificent view, and thinking: *If only I had brought my wife here when she was alive. Knowing Suchin, she would have loved the scenery.*

Lay Yong's voice, which had raised one notch, startled him. "I'd stumbled on my life's plan a long time ago. It led me to realize the truth of Chairman Mao Tse-tung's words in that power grows out of the barrel of a gun. You'd once told me you have no other skills except to kill. I think that's your life's plan. I believe too that you knew it."

She saw she had his attention, and so she pressed on. "But there's really not much purpose in killing the insignificant nonentities. For a person like you who has the skills, you ought to set your sight on someone who really matters."

Somehow, her words caused Dong Po to recall his conversation with his *sifu* last night after he had killed the two men. Somchai, who had come to Penang to await his report, had told him after the briefing: "I'm proud of you for giving Ah Sai an escape route, my boy. By not being trigger-happy, you've set yourself up to be a true professional."

Dong Po had shrugged. "From what I'd found out, Ah Sai is a misfit of a hoodlum. Though he carries a pistol, I doubt if he ever could bring himself to shoot anyone.

Killing... I mean removing him, actually serves no purpose."

And his mentor had agreed. "You're right, my boy. Not anyone can use a gun even if he carries one. In a way, we're the misfits because unlike most people in the world, we're able to forget once a job is done. For most people, they can't and as they know they can't, they won't dare to remove anyone in the first place."

Lay Yong's voice was raised another notch louder when she asked him: "Will you live up to my hope that you will kill someone of significance?"

Jostled back to the present moment, Dong Po managed to ask, more out of idle curiosity: "Have you anyone in mind?"

For the first time that morning, Lay Yong smiled. Encouraged by the headway she thought she was making, she said: "There's a man in Singapore. His followers think very highly of him. They believe him to be a patriot. But when I thought about how my elder brother and those other young men died during the *Sook Ching* carried out by the Japanese during the war while this man managed to escape, I felt it's all so unfair."

A strong gust of wind blew her hair all over. She paused to pull them back in place, and then continued. "He survived to live a life of deceit, pretending to be one of us. But once he no longer has any use for us, he chucked us aside. It's my intention...my life's plan to kill him. I hope you will join me in this great cause. He is..."

Intrigued as he was, Dong Po interrupted her abruptly: "I don't want to know who he is. I'm not joining you."

She blinked in surprise. "Why not?"

At that moment, everything became quite clear to Dong Po. He thought how extraordinary it was that so much could flash through a person's mind in just a few seconds. All of a sudden, without any of his foolish sentiments, he saw Lay Yong as she truly was. He knew the overwhelming gratitude he felt towards her for having saved his life had to some extent, blinded him. And the fact that she was an attractive woman had added to his blindness. But Lay Yong, being what she was, could never feel anything for anyone. She was merely using him, or to be more precise, trying to use him the way she said of the person whom she wanted him to kill.

Indeed, her words stung him, causing him to bridle with resentment. *How dare she presume I will become her cat's paw to kill somebody?* In his agitation, he told her harshly, "Put out of your mind any thought you may have of using me. I'm a professional, not an amateur like you."

From the expression in her eyes, he knew she was stung by his words. Her face suddenly took on a crumpled, little-lost-girl look. As he still felt some obligation towards her for having saved his life, he was immediately ashamed of his harshness towards her. But it was too late because she suddenly glared at him and was about to raise her hand to slap him. He was however too quick for her.

After he caught her hand, he held onto it, preventing her from pulling it away.

"Stop it," he said. "I don't want to hurt you. If you carry on like this, I may have to."

The moment Dong Po released her hand, he knew he had made yet another mistake. Lay Yong, her mind deranged by her fear since hearing about Wang *Lao-su's* arrest, the lack of sleep and disappointment over Dong Po's rejection to her appeal, suddenly felt that anyone who wasn't an ally was an enemy. Since she had divulged her secret to an enemy, her paranoia told her it won't be long that he would betray her. And having lost her senses, she appeared not to realize how precarious the place was.

"You bastard!" she hissed, and hurled herself at him, as though she couldn't care or even would welcome the idea of them both being thrown into the abyss below.

His well-honed reflexes led him to shift his body. But when she stumbled past him, he instinctively reached out to catch her. Unfortunately, he wasn't fast enough. All he saw was the woman tumbling in a tangle of arms and legs down into the void. Then he heard a shout, "Lay Yong!" only to realize he was the one who was yelling.

It was several hours later in the sanctuary of his beach-front home in Tanjong Tokong that Dong Po lifted his tear-streaked face from the floor to look at the two suitcases he had spent the entire afternoon packing. He was leaving Penang. It was time for him to return to his apartment in Kuala Lumpur, which he and Suchin

Suewonglee had once regarded as their home away from home.

After Lay Yong's fatal fall, he had made his way back to the foot of the hill and found a public phone to make an anonymous call to the authorities about a climber having fallen down a cliff slope. Thereafter he had gone home where he finally allowed the dam welling up inside him to burst. At one point when he was sobbing bitterly, he still had enough sense to wonder briefly at the degree of despair and self-loathing he felt.

I'm not a human being, he thought as he cried. *I'm a beast. She'd saved my life and I've repaid her by causing her to fall to her death. And the worst is that I couldn't even do the decent thing like joining the search team to recover her body and giving her a proper burial. I'm worse than an animal.*

As he sat sobbing hysterically on the floor of his bedroom, he wished he could turn the clock back. Everything had happened so fast. If he had held his peace, refraining from answering Lay Yong the way he had, she would probably still be alive. After all, she was just a silly, misled woman, with fanciful ideas of herself as a revolutionary.

And then he calmed down a bit. But when he went to the bathroom to wash his face and blow his nose, the sight of his image on the mirror filled him with rage. In his craziness, he threw a punch at the mirror, shattering it to smithereens. Not caring anymore, he continued punching until his blood ran down his arm.

After that, he blacked out. When he woke up, he was sitting on the bathroom floor, with shattered glass and aluminum around him. He saw it was already twilight. Oddly enough, now that the tears and his rage had all been spent, and as his hand throbbed, he felt relieved.

Just as he was about to get up, from outside, Dong Po heard the amplified voice of the muezzin from the nearby mosque calling the faithful. He had once read somewhere that the singsong voice was actually proclaiming:

> *God is most great.*
> *I testify that there is no god but God.*
> *I testify that Muhammad is the Prophet of God.*
> *Come to prayer, come to success.*
> *God is most great.*
> *There is no god but God.*

Strangely, the muezzin's sonorous voice filled Dong Po with a sense of calm and peacefulness.

It was at that moment he came to the decision. The killing must stop. It dawned on him that he had been trying to play God. But unlike God, there was nothing just in his action. It had been purely personal and criminal because murder ought to be regarded a crime. He had either foolishly or deliberately mistaken greed of money for justice. Whatever, he knew now that it was so easy for any man like him to take a life. But only God has the power to give and restore life. He had once read a booklet about the death and resurrection of Jesus Christ. God has even come to this world to suffer, die and rise again so that sinners can be saved. With that thought, Dong Po decided he no longer had any desire to kill.

He made up his mind to stop while he still could.

BOOK 3
RETIREMENT

"For none of the five elements – water, fire, wood, metal and earth – is always predominant; none of the four seasons can last forever; the days are sometimes longer and sometimes shorter; and the moon sometimes waxes and sometimes wanes."

Sun Tzu

Sixty

*S*ince the day he returned to his apartment in Kuala Lumpur, Mao Dong Po had, for the first time in his life, begun to drink heavily.

Previously, each time after he had removed a quarry, he had no problem purging the person from his conscience. As he had judged each one of those he had killed as deserving death, he hadn't suffered any remorse after each job. But the death of Ong Lay Yong disturbed him so much that he felt as though her ghost was haunting him.

At the time of Suchin Suewonglee's death, he had blamed himself for not being there with her by her side, and also castigated himself for not being decisive enough to insist that they should get married and she should stop working. Thereafter, in his grief, he had drunk in order to induce sleep.

But Lay Yong's death was different. Somehow, he felt directly responsible. It was like he had killed her with his own hands. And the fact that Lay Yong had once saved his life didn't make it any easier on him. Thus, he found he even had to drink in the day as well, failing which he found it hard to pass each conscious hour.

Early one April morning, two days after the US military screwed up in a mission to rescue American hostages in Iran, Dong Po woke up feeling like his head was being squeezed in a tight shrinking iron head-band. When he was a kid, he had watched a Shaw Brothers' movie and later, as an adult, read the Chinese classic, *Journey to the West*.

It told the folktale of how the Goddess of Mercy charged the immortal Monkey with the task of escorting Priest Sanzhang to travel to the West to fetch the Buddhism scriptures. But knowing the Monkey's unruly character, she gave him an iron head band to wear, and thereafter instructed Priest Sanzhang to read the words carved on a piece of jade should the Monkey misbehave. The reading would cause the head band to shrink, causing tremendous pain to the Monkey, thus putting a stop to his unruliness.

Dong Po went to the bathroom to get some panadols from the medicine box, and when he saw his reflection on the mirror, he was shocked. He looked pale and haggard, while his eyes were red and puffy. Even after he took the panadols, the headache still refused to go away and his throat felt as dry as before. As the rays of the morning sun came flooding into his apartment, he felt the pressure increasing in his head.

He was about to pull the curtains when he heard the door bells chimed. Looking through the peep hole, to his surprise, he saw it was his *sifu*. The swarthy Siamese seemed to be as fastidious as ever, wearing a three-piece gray suit, white shirt, and red silk cravat. At first, the thought of not answering the door bell fleetingly crossed

Dong Po's mind. But he couldn't do that to his mentor and so he opened the door and wordlessly stepped aside to let the older man in.

Once inside the apartment, Somchai, who had seen what Dong Po himself had already seen of himself earlier, was also quick to notice the empty whiskey bottle on the coffee table. He shook his head angrily and frowned. "What's the matter with you, my boy?"

Dong Po lowered his head, ashamed even to look at his *sifu* in the eyes, and mumbled. "I seem to see her ghost everywhere. Always she looks at me with that accusing look in her eyes. I can't bear it unless I drink till I'm blissfully unconscious."

As Somchai didn't say anything and Dong Po was somewhat relieved to have someone to talk to again – the last time, he spoke to Somchai, he had only briefly mentioned over the telephone about Lay Yong's fatal fall, before announcing his decision to quit – he felt the tears coming to his eyes and he cried, "I can't take it anymore. What can I do? Oh, what can I do?"

But the sympathy he expected didn't come. Instead, Somchai looked at him coldly and this time he spoke with unmistakable contempt, "You're a man. So behave like one."

Without warning, the *sifu's* face contorted with anger and he grabbed Dong Po's shoulder, half pulling and half pushing until he dragged his protégé into the bathroom and shouted, "Look! Look at yourself in the mirror. Is this the guy who had asked me to take him on as my apprentice years ago? Is this the fearless problem remover I had molded? A tough man who could now only weep and beg for pity? Who cries like a woman, "What can I do? Oh, what can I do? Had any of your quarries ever cried to you and beg for your pity?"

Dong Po was shocked and yet amused by his mentor's outburst. He was shocked to find Somchai roughing him up like this and stung by his words which struck him as true. At the same time, his mentor's mimicry appealed to his sense of humor, which, suppressed as they were in the past four months, began to surface again. "I...I...I guess I was wrong."

"You stop guessing. Know is better," Somchai was still shouting. "Know that you've been wrong all these months. There isn't any ghost. The only ghost is what you've chosen to create in your mind."

Dong Po nodded. "I'm s-sorry, Uncle Somchai."

"Sorry, my ass," he said gruffly, his voice already dropping back to a conversational tone. "Go and wash up. After you have cleaned up and put on fresh clothes, come with me to eat something. You've got to eat and live again. This is what Suchin would want you to do."

Seeing Dong Po's eyes had narrowed, Somchai looked abashed. "I'm sorry, my boy. I know that even after all these years, you still feel the pain over a careless mention of her name or a familiar tune being played somewhere. She's that special, which is why she cannot be erased away just like that. This is why I have to mention her name again, to remind you that you'll only disappoint her if you carry on like this."

The younger man closed his eyes and after what seemed like a long while, he opened them again and smiled for the first time in many months. "Thank you, Uncle Somchai."

After Dong Po went back into his bedroom to get his things, Somchai, who was about to follow, caught sight of his own reflection in the mirror, stopped and winked at himself. *If I had been in Hollywood, I could have won an Oscar*, he thought smugly.

Having watched the movie, *The Godfather*, some years ago, Somchai had since then been regularly watching re-runs of it on video. As he quite fancied himself in the role of Don Corleone, he felt he had just re-enacted the performance of an affectionate but stern Don Corleone castigating his godson, Johnny Fontane to shake him out of his self-induced depression. Somchai was glad he came to his protégé's home that day because he knew Dong Po would now be all right again.

Sixty-one

*A*s Mao Dong Po hadn't been back in Padang Besar ever since the beginning of the year, he decided to follow his *sifu* who was going to Sadao to visit some friends.

Thus in April 1980, he spent an entire week with his mother in his uncle's house. Age was beginning to show on his mother's face and she complained of body aches. For the first time, Dong Po realized his mother's hair had turned very grey. Though his uncle still appeared sprightly but his hair, like Dong Po's mother, had grayed a lot and his pallid cheeks had taken on a pinched, tired look, making his face looked even more like a dried, wrinkled prune.

The first night, while talking with his mother long after dinner was over, Dong Po suddenly recalled the time he had first brought her for a vacation in Singapore and Kuala Lumpur. Since then he had been too preoccupied with his own affairs that he hadn't taken his mother out of Padang Besar again. He felt momentarily guilty but like most people, was quick to rationalize that he had asked her many times to go visit him in Singapore, Kuala Lumpur, and even in Penang but the old lady had always demurred.

That night he still made an effort to ask: "Would you like to go to Bangkok with me, Mother?"

His mother raised an arched eyebrow. "Have you forgotten *Ching Ming* falls on the day after tomorrow? I'd thought you would want to join me in praying for the soul of your long departed father as you haven't been doing for many years."

"No, I haven't forgotten. Of course, I came home for this purpose and to see you," he lied quickly, and thought: *It was fortunate for me that my sifu had shaken me out of my depression or I would have once again failed my duty as a son to pray for my father's soul.*

"But we can set off for Bangkok after the prayers," he persisted.

"Frankly I prefer to stay home as your uncle needs me to look after him. I feel more comfortable in this house than anywhere out there. Besides, your aunt and cousins are coming to visit."

This time, it was Dong Po who raised a surprised eyebrow. "The relatives we'd left behind in the New Village?"

"Yes, after your uncle had installed a telephone, I'd written to your aunt. Once she got my letter, she'd telephoned me. In this way, we have been keeping in touch with one another. This is the first time they are coming to visit me. It will be nice if you can be around."

And so three days after *Ching Ming*, Dong Po got to see his aunt and cousin.

Like his mother, his aunt had aged very much. Within an hour after their arrival, Dong Po found out that his aunt no longer lived with her eldest son, Dong Hai, the one who had inherited his father's bicycle repairing business.

"After he married the village's butcher's daughter, he sided with his wife to chase me out," grumbled the aunt.

It was her daughter Dong Fong, who had taken in the forlorn mother. Dong Fong had married a tailor who barely made enough to support her, her five children, and her mother. Fortunately for Dong Po's aunt, it was her youngest son, Dong Nan, who gave money to Dong Fong every month, and took care of any other bill, such as those for the old lady's regular medical check-ups and costly medication as she suffered from diabetes. Being a middleman for most of the farmers in their village, Dong Nan traveled a lot to Singapore and was seldom around. He also gave a car to his sister, and it was she who had driven her mother all the way to Padang Besar that day.

For just a few minutes after meeting his aunt and cousin sister, Dong Po felt the tug of nostalgia. He recalled Dong Fong when she was a young girl, and a pang of guilt for having kept his distance from his relatives all these years. But such nostalgic feeling evaporated the moment Dong Fong handed him an old yellowing envelope.

"Ahh, this came for you a long time ago," said Dong Fong gaily.

He saw a Glasgow post-mark, and quickly pushed a finger under the flap to tear the envelope open. It was a letter dated June 3, 1954 from Brother Duffy. The contents told him about Brother Duffy falling ill upon his return to Glasgow, and subsequent hospitalization, which explained his inability to write earlier, and finally, the doctor's diagnosis that he had a cancerous tumor, Dong Po's face turned dark.

If only any of my cousins had made an effort to redirect the letter to me. It's a wonder they still managed to keep it for so many years to finally bring to me, he thought with a mix of anger and frustration. *After all these years, I doubt if Brother Duffy is still around. It's so galling that I couldn't write to him earlier, at least, to let him know how grateful I felt towards him.*

That night, after deciding not to treat his relatives to a grand dinner in a restaurant as he had earlier planned, Dong Po caught the night train departing for Bangkok as he wished to visit the temple where Suchin Suewonglee's ashes were kept.

Sixty-two

*W*as his home on fire? Or was he dreaming it was on fire? Somewhere in his sleep – he knew he was sleeping – he heard the incessant ringing and banging.

Slowly, Mao Dong Po's eyes opened and then his sharp reflexes took over. It hadn't been a dream. Someone was simultaneously ringing his doorbell and hammering at his front door. A quick glance at his watch showed it was already 2:00 a.m. Who could it be so late?

Peering through the peep-hole, he was taken aback by the unexpected sight of his *sifu*.

He quickly unlatched and opened the door for his mentor, mentally noting something was amiss. Though Somchai was as immaculately dressed as ever, unlike the last time he came to Dong Po's apartment, which was already more than a year ago, this visit was ominous. First, it was so late in the night. Second, he couldn't miss the tell-tale dark rings under the older man's eyes. Yes, though Somchai may already be sixty-one years' old, he definitely looked older and very tired. It was like he was under some strain which had finally caught up with him.

Closing the door, Dong Po looked enquiringly at his *sifu*. The Siamese hadn't said anything but just glanced around the elegant living room. Finally, the Siamese said: "I hadn't noticed the furniture the last time I was here. You've good taste, my boy, though they must have cost you plenty."

Dong Po smiled. "I owe it to you, Uncle Somchai, for those jobs in the past. It was Suchin's selection. She told me you were right about buying a property instead of renting, and accordingly, to furnish well since it was our home."

"That's investment, my boy," Somchai nodded approvingly before lowering his bulk onto the comfortable, soft leather sofa. "Even if you decide to sell this apartment later, a prospective buyer will be impressed with it since the furniture give the place an image of class. We must protect ourselves by investing wisely."

Dong Po who had also sat down opposite his *sifu* was about to reply when Somchai held up a hand. "Let me finish, my boy. I have been protecting you all these years by keeping you in the shadows while I took credit for all those jobs done by you. In a way, I'm also protecting myself because I'd sensed the possibility of a day like this where I've no choice but to run to you for safety."

"What has happened?"

"Two attempts had already been made to remove me."

"Who would want to remove you?"

"I'm not sure yet," said the man who had always been so sure. "But I suspect it could be one of my clients who probably thought I knew too much, or it could be the

Americans. One can't trust the Americans, especially those in the cloak-and-dagger business."

"Have you spoken to your childhood friend…I mean your contact guy in the military?" asked Dong Po. "I think he may know something."

"No, right now, I trust no one. Not even my childhood friend," replied Somchai. "But ironically, it was another childhood friend who had helped me, or to be more accurate, I was fortunate to have an ally in a Thai relative of my friend, Chiu Ya Loong. His nephew, a senior police officer, was the one who helped to sneak me out of Thailand."

Dong Po looked at his *sifu* with concern. "So what do you plan to do?"

"I need a place to hide for a while," Somchai said. "As I've said, they don't know about you."

Sixty-three

$\mathscr{I}$t took less than thirty minutes for Mao Dong Po to weave through the city and into the Federal Highway.

Another five minutes ticked by as he meandered his way along the streets of Petaling Jaya until they finally arrived at a Siamese Temple. Earlier that morning, his *sifu* had asked his protégé: "Is there a Siamese temple? Can you bring me there?"

They got out of the car and Somchai walked ahead to go inside the temple where he prayed for a while. Once he was finished, he walked to a quiet garden at the side of the temple. He fished out a cigar for himself, knowing Dong Po carried his own. The two men quietly puffed away for some time. Suddenly, Somchai smiled but the smile never reached his eyes. "Yesterday when you were out, I went to a public phone to speak to the major-general. I've told him I actually had a proxy to carry out all those jobs for which I'd claimed credit."

Dong Po tensed the moment he heard his mentor saying he had made contact with Major-General Wongkot Suttharom. He stared intently at his *sifu* and asked, "And?"

461

Somchai smiled again, a sad smile. As his left hand threw the cigar to the ground on his left, drawing Dong Po's eyes to follow instinctively, his other hand pulled out a silenced pistol which he pointed at the latter. "Well, it has come to this…it's either you or me. He was peeved that I'd turned down jobs in the past few years and even more so when he heard that was because I'd relied all along on you to do my jobs. He said I may live but on one condition, which is, either I remove you or let him have you."

"And have you decided?"

"I know that if I let him have you, then you can never be free of him and those he represents, or for the matter, the Americans. They will make use of you until you're no longer useful, and then they will want to be rid of you because you will by then have known too much."

"Do you really believe he'll allow you to live since you too know as much?"

"I'm in a situation, which you, Chinese, have described as, riding a tiger's back. One has no choice but to continue riding because to get off is to die. Don't ever land in the same situation as me, my boy, and don't forget the letter I've left in your study. Goodbye," Somchai said before turning the silenced Colt.45 pistol to point at his own head. As he pulled the trigger, Somchai's head snapped sideways with the force, spattering his blood and brains, and his burly body fell limply like a rag's doll onto the ground.

Dong Po roared, "NO!"

But it was too late. From where he stood, he felt the stab of anguish in his chest. It was like he was the one who had been shot. Then he went to where his *sifu* lay and knelt down beside him. For just a short while, he knelt there to weep silently. Abruptly he got up and walked away. Now that Somchai had chosen to get off the tiger rather than betraying his protégé, Dong Po knew his *sifu's* sacrifice would all be in vain if he lingered there. Major-General Wongkot must never be allowed to discover the secret that Somchai had given his life to protect.

☆ ☆ ☆ ☆

The major-general, at that moment, was in his office, talking to someone over the telephone. From the grimace on his face, he appeared agitated though he was careful to speak evenly, keeping the anger from his voice. "Yes, sir, I admit my fault but rest assured that I'll get him to hand over his disciple to work for us. After all, he owed me too much to refuse."

Even after hanging up the telephone, Major-General Wongkot was still disturbed as he spoke more curtly than normal with an adjutant who came into his room to request his signature for some documents. Thereafter, he got up from his desk to a side cabinet where he kept a bottle of brandy. Pouring a little into a glass, he sipped it and tried to push away his frustration. *It is so unfair of my boss to blame me over Somchai*, he thought. *As for Somchai, how can he do such a thing to me after what I'd done for him all these years?*

His mind went back, surprisingly not to the day when he shot the customs officer who was about to end Somchai's life as an unfeeling dog-shooter would mercilessly put a bullet into a stray dog. Instead, the major-general was thinking of the day Somchai's mother died. It was about six months after Somchai's father was killed by the rogue customs team. During those terrible months, having lost all they had, both Somchai and his mother had survived on whatever Wongkot, then a second lieutenant had brought them.

Somchai's mother, who was already ill for some time, seemed to have lost her will to live, and died. On the day after 2LT Wongkot had helped seen to her burial, footing the funeral expense and a cheap coffin out of his meager army pay, was about to return to his barrack when Somchai told him, "I owe you a lot, Wongkot. My life is yours to command. I will gladly give it to you any time you wish me to."

He had laughed then as he patted his friend's shoulder, "You'll be more useful to me alive than dead."

Sixty-four

ack in his apartment, Mao Dong Po opened the letter that his late *sifu* had left on his desk in the study room.

His eyes blurred with tears as he read the neat Thai script in his late mentor's handwriting:

My boy, it seems like only yesterday that I took you on as my pupil. How Time flies. As my childhood friend, Chiu Ya Loong, the taikor used to tell me, a Chinese poem laments, "Life is but a dream and soon everything's over and forgotten."

By now, though I am dead and gone but I think, as long as you live, I will still be alive, at least, in your memory since you won't forget me just as you will never forget Suchin Suewonglee. She too will always be with you as the pleasure of your time spent together will live on inside you.

Don't feel bad for me. It was my decision. And I certainly won't want you to go gunning for Wongkot. I owed him too much and this is the only way I can repay him.

As for you, though you'd learned from me the unpleasant skills of removing problems, and subsequently done those jobs for me, it pleased me

*very much at the time when you made the decision
to quit. Only a fool does not know when to stop.
If you had carried on, there will come a day when
your luck will surely run out. I was not wrong in
saying time and again that you're a smart lad.*

*Let me now instead offer you a more
pleasurable assignment.*

*After discovering I may not have much time
left, I have quietly disposed off my assets and
arranged to hide my money in various places. The
first list attached to this letter will show you
where I have hidden my money and also the keys
to the boxes. It will be like a treasure hunt for
you. After you have recovered my hidden wealth,
visit the various orphanages and old folks' homes
which I have identified in my second list, and
each time you visit them, give them only the
amount I have stated in a third list.*

*By not giving away everything at once, but
giving only what is needed at a time, the
recipients won't be too consumed with greed and
I am sure you will find this to be a full-time job.
Actually, helping people is more pleasurable and
meaningful than removing people.*

*Despair not. Live for Suchin Suewonglee. Live
for me.*

Take care, my boy.

SOMCHAI

Dong Po buried his head in his hands and wept. They
were tears of agony and despair, and something more.
He had all along felt the bond between his *sifu* and him

to be similar to the relationship between a father and son. In fact, though he had all these years addressed the Siamese as Uncle Somchai, he actually saw the man as his father. And like a father, Somchai had protected him even till the end. Somchai's suicide was intended to cut him loose from the past.

After that, for a long time, Dong Po slumped on the sofa, feeling absolutely wretched. The thought of going to Bangkok to settle score with Major-General Wongkot Suttharom on his *sifu's* behalf had occurred to him. But like the time after Suchin's death when he had thought of searching out and thereafter hunting down those who had shot her, he dismissed the idea. Like those soldiers, the major-general was taking orders from someone. And Dong Po knew that killing Major-General Wongkot would not bring his *sifu* back to life just as killing those responsible for Suchin's death would not bring her back to life. Besides, he couldn't go against Somchai's expressed wish.

Epilogue

$\mathcal{S}$trangely, I have been finding my new life, traveling from time to time to visit and make donations of money on my late *sifu's* behalf, to the orphanages or old folk's homes which he had named, to be most enjoyable. As I also have plenty of my own money to spare from having made some profitable investments which give me a steady income from dividends, interests, and rentals, I have added a few other institutions as well, such as those which care for animals' welfare.

I remember my *sifu* had once told me, "When I was young, I had a dog for my companion. Actually, he was the pet of my friend, Chiu Ya Loong the Penang *taikor* but when he was forced to leave Klong Ngae with his family, he handed Blackie to my care. Several years later, Blackie died of old age. It was the first time I'd experienced grief. Though I'd avoided having a pet since then, I have always believed that if a man cannot be kind to a helpless animal, he can never be kind to his fellow men."

And when I was not traveling to play the role of a wealthy philanthropist, I lived quite a seemingly dissipated life. I confess to spending a lot of my time in nightclubs to drink and lost myself drifting along with the music and merriment. But I would never allow myself to be coaxed by any dance hostess to the dance-floor to dance even though I had once learned how to dance. I fear the influence of liquor combined with the lighting may lead me to see Boonrwad Wanglee instead of my dancing partner, and that may result in a really tragic consequence for the unfortunate girl.

Since I don't really have much to do when not traveling as a sort of Santa Claus, I have decided that a quality life would be far more desirable than a long, dull one. Towards this end, I am bent on enjoying myself until it was my time to join Suchin Suewonglee and my *sifu*.

This probably explained why a few years ago, I popped into the Nightingale Cabaret and Nightclub in Jalan Ampang. I remember it was on the third night after the Filipinos drove President Ferdinand Marcos into exile on February 26, 1986. A *mamasan* whom I'd known previously as Annie had ushered me to a table ringed by a comfortable sofa.

While I was happily puffing away on a cigar, Annie brought a girl over. To my astonishment, even though the light was quite dim, she reminded me of Suchin. Perhaps it was her shape or the way she smiled at me or it could be the lights playing tricks on my eyes.

"This is Anita..." Annie introduced the girl before someone rudely pulled the *mamasan* away.

"Hi, I'm Anita. May I know whom I have the pleasure of meeting?" asked the strikingly beautiful girl in Mandarin.

Even her voice sounded like Suchin. I heard myself replying, "Mao…Zhuey Mao."

As the girl looked flustered, I tried to explain and was surprised I had spoken in English. "Yes, it's Drunken Cat if that's what you're thinking."

Either Anita was embarrassed from not understanding English or from getting caught in thinking of me as a drunken cat, she laughed to cover her embarrassment. Even her laughter sounded like Suchin's.

I pressed on in English. "It's all right. I'm used to it. My family name's Mao, same as Mao Tse-tung's and my given name is Dong Po due to my father's reverence for a famous scholar who lived during the Song Dynasty. As I'm not cut out to be a poet, I seldom use my given name. Instead, out of a personal weird sense of humor over my fondness of drinking, I added the Zhuey in front and since then the name stuck. Moreover, some years back I watched one of those Shaw Brothers' movies about a beggar-hermit named Zhuey Mao who turned out to be an excellent swordsman. Well, you can say he's my idol."

And then it was my turn to flush with embarrassment because I suddenly realized I had been uncharacteristically loquacious. The girl seemed to know because she smiled at me and tried to make light of the situation, answering in English, "I know that movie, "Come drink with me", right?"

"Yes, you're right," I replied, switching to Mandarin as it occurred to me that she was more at ease in that language. "So, will you come drink with me?"

Like a fish taking to water, she answered in Mandarin by posing a question back at me: "Well, where have you been drinking all the while?"

Before I replied her, I took a long pull of my cigar. And then I told her: "All over, at the Pertama, the Campbell, and anywhere where liquor's to be found."

"But this is the first time you come to the Nightingale?"

"Yes, somehow I had left out this joint until a friend reminded me of its existence. In fact, I'm meeting him here tonight."

"Well, let's hope you will be coming here more often now that you know we exist."

"I think I will."

That was already some three years ago. Since then, I have indeed become a regular at the Nightingale. And each time, I would ask only for Anita's company as I quite liked the thoughtful and intelligent girl who bore some resemblance to my late wife. Though she tried to get me to talk about myself, I have been quite determined not to tell anyone too much, especially to know about my unsavory past, and what I used to do for a living. There were things which ought to be left as they were. After all, even Suchin hadn't been *that* privileged and my late *sifu* had also given up his life to allow me to cut clean from the past.

Moreover, having had met those garrulous types who were bent on telling personal reminiscences to anyone who had no particular desire to listen, I am not keen to become another bore. Although humility wasn't exactly my trait as my *sifu* could also tell you if he was still alive, I also feel tired to talk about the philanthropical work I have been doing on behalf of my late mentor.

Much as I subsequently found Anita – whose real name I later discovered to be May Lee – to be capable of drawing me like a magnet to reveal a little more of myself than I normally would, I was nonetheless careful not to make an ass of myself. I recall one day when my *sifu* had suddenly told me: "There's no fool than an old fool. A man is most vulnerable when he is older and lonely. In such a situation, it's too easy for any elderly man to find pleasure from having a sweet, young thing telling him how clever and interesting he is. Sometimes, an elderly man is also inclined to fancy himself as a sort of guardian angel in wanting to protect the girl he fancies, to shield her from danger, and shower her with gifts and money. And the crazy thing is that the girl often turns out to be more capable of looking after herself. It's the man who's truly vulnerable and to be pitied."

Furthermore, I really no longer have any wish to risk another woman in my life, especially when no one could ever replace my late wife. Though May Lee may in some ways, resembled Suchin, I know she could never ever take her place. Despite having told May Lee a little about Suchin and even brought her to my home now and then to spend some intimate moments together, I was quite firm in refusing to let her comfort me upon learning about the deaths of my mother and uncle.

At the time, she was already elevated from dance hostess to *mamasan* and so had time to accompany me to London had I asked her. But I hadn't. To tell the truth,

I dread getting too close with her or her caring too deeply for me. In an odd way, I do care for her and so wouldn't want her to end up being hurt. Hence, after my return from London, like the Phantom, I have been careful to keep a side of my face hidden.

I reasoned it is best for May Lee because though I am determined to enjoy my life to the fullest but I really have no wish to live too long. Much as I would like to refrain from playing God, as I used to previously, in deciding whether one should live or die, unless I could drink myself to death, I know it's a matter of time that I may decide to end my own life the way my *sifu* had taken that path. I believe it won't be long. After all, the few persons I'd ever known and who truly mattered had already gone, and I know my temperament too well in that I couldn't grow old gracefully like most people. I wouldn't know how to cope with the normal ailments that seem to be part and parcel of growing old. Perhaps it has also to do with my vanity because I wouldn't want to look and smell like an old man. Hence, it is inevitable that I will use my skills once again, this time to remove myself.

Glossary

ajarn   Thai word, meaning teacher or master.

ang moh   Chinese (Hokkien dialect) words literarily meaning "red hair" to refer to white men.

char kway teow   Chinese (Hokkien dialect) words for fried flat noodles.

farang   Thai word, meaning foreign.

jianghu   Chinese (Mandarin) word literarily translated as "rivers and lakes", to denote the underworld.

kor   Chinese (Cantonese dialect) word, meaning elder brother usually used as a suffix after a man's name to denote respect.

lin lau boo   Chinese (Hokkien dialect) words simply meaning "your mother" though it is an implied insult.

Min Yuen   Chinese (Mandarin) words, for the clandestine sympathizers of the communists, or the so-called Mass Movement who lived in the open but secretly supported the terrorists in the jungle with food and information.

Muay Thai	Thai words, for the form of martial art known as the art of eight limbs.
orang putih	Malay words, meaning white men.
pak pao	Thai words, for kites.
sar hor fun	Chinese (Cantonese dialect) words, for fried flat rice noodles served in thick gravy with prawns and pork.
sawadee	Thai word, for greeting someone, e.g. hello.
sinseh	Chinese (Hokkien dialect) word, for traditional herbalist.
Sook Ching	Chinese (Mandarin) phrase, for the screening or purification operations carried out by the Japanese military where undesirables were selected for elimination.
taikor	Chinese (Cantonese dialect) words, meaning big brother, sometimes used to respectfully address a secret society leader.
wai	Thai word, to describe the polite act or gesture of bringing together both hands to greet someone with esteem.
wayang kulit	Malay words, meaning shadow play.
yong tau foo	Chinese (Cantonese dialect) words, for beancurd and vegetables stuffed with fish paste.

The Author

*K*hoo Kheng-Hor is probably Malaysia's most prolific author.

He "hung-up his sword" in 1999 at the age of 43 for semi-retirement from the corporate "battlefield" to live in his mountain sanctuary with his wife, Judy, and "four-legged son", Bandit. But after Judy was called home by the Lord on December 19, 2007, he brought Bandit to live for a while in Penang. As an internationally-acclaimed speaker, he still travels for a few days each month to "suntzunize" his audience at seminars and conferences on Sun Tzu's strategies for contemporary business and management.

The rest of the time, he works on his current novel – his published novels are *Taikor* (nominated for the 2006 International IMPAC Dublin Literary Award), *Mamasan* and *Nanyang* – and reads the Bible as he prepares for that final call from the Lord to go home.

So long as the call is yet to come, he can still be reached by e-mailing him at *sunzi@khookhenghor.com* or visit his website *http://www.khookhenghor.com* where you can enjoy his monthly newsletter for free.

Other exciting novels
by Khoo Kheng-Hor

A historical saga that brings back the past for those who could still remember and for the young who may wish to know how things used to be in the years between 1922 and 1982.

From the beginning in prewar British-ruled Malaya, the story revolves around the life of a boy as he grows to manhood. It traces the migration of his family from South Thailand to Penang after his father passes away, his brief childhood living with his young widowed mother who subsequently remarried, and thereafter his banishment as a youngster by his stepfather to war-torn Shanghai. On his return, he had to find a way to earn a living and thereafter, to survive the bloody days of the Japanese Occupation. Even after the surrender of the Japanese, there was the lawless postwar period, from which he saw opportunities to eventually emerge as a *taikor* (big brother) in Penang's chaotic underworld. Apart from opportunities, the postwar years also saw dangers, like the Emergency period when Communist insurgents tried to destabilize the country's development.

Finally, a nation was born when Malaya became an independent sovereign State. And just as the new nation strived to build a future from its historical legacy, the *taikor* sought to break away from his past involvement in triad activities to build a new life for himself and his family.

ISBN 967-978-878-4

This novel was nominated for the 2006 International IMPAC Dublin Literary Award.